Haley M. Opet

A
BLOODVEILED
DESCENT

The Solwyn Duology
Book One

Published by Velvet Tea Press

ISBN: 979-8-9991769-0-5 (Paperback)

ISBN: 979-8-9991769-1-2 (Ebook)

First Edition, November 2025

Cover Design By: Kelly Guthauser
Editor: Claire Bradshaw
Map Illustration: Carter Norman Phillips

Printed in the United States of America

Content Warning

This book is intended for mature readers (18+). It contains graphic violence, gore, sexual content, and themes of attempted sexual assault that may be distressing to some readers. Reader discretion is advised.

For my husband and children—my joy, my love, my home.
Thank you for allowing me to dream beyond our world.

Western Lands
Nerathar
Northern Mountains
Centaro
Wrenford
Cindermoor
Mokkahli River
Mokkvyrn Forest
Velenshire
Caltheris
Rosewyth
Other Southern Territories
Southern Isles
N
W
E
S

Part One

The Gilded Lie

CHAPTER 1

The executioner arrived with the sunrise, disguised as Evelyne's handmaid and brandishing curtains like a blade. Sunlight spilled into the room, catching dust in its wake and casting golden streaks across the embroidered tapestries and polished mahogany.

Evelyne groaned, flinging an arm over her eyes. "Are you trying to kill me, Seraphine? A slower death would be preferable."

"Trying to wake you, my lady," Seraphine shot back. "The morning's nearly spent, and you've ignored three very polite knocks. I was beginning to think you'd perished in your sleep, only to find you snoring like a grown man."

Evelyne peeled one eye open and smirked. "You exaggerate."

Seraphine crossed her arms, unimpressed. "Do I? I'll drag you out by your toes if you don't rise this instant."

Evelyne sighed and tossed a pillow toward Seraphine, hoping to coax even a hint of a smile, but the handmaid didn't so much as blink.

"My goodness, you're particularly vicious today," Evelyne muttered, pushing herself upright. "At least allow me a moment to adjust to the blinding assault on my senses."

Seraphine exhaled through her nose, shaking her head. "For heaven's sake, look at you. That hair is a tragedy."

Evelyne laughed softly and ruffled it further. "I thought I looked rather ravishing."

Seraphine gave her a flat stare, but the corners of her mouth twitched. "You will be the end of me."

"I certainly hope not," Evelyne teased, reaching for the long silken robe at the foot of her bed.

Seraphine let out a low breath, but the affection in her gaze never wavered. The older woman had been at Evelyne's side for as long as she could remember: part handmaid, part guardian, and part second mother. She was a little plump with age, her once-dark curls silvered, but her hazel eyes remained warm. And her hands were a miracle when it came to taming Evelyne's wild mane.

Unfortunately, last night had undone all of Seraphine's hard work.

Evelyne ran her fingers through her tangled hair, grimacing as they caught in the mess of knots. She had been too exhausted to care after sneaking out for a midnight run through the gardens, collapsing into bed without bothering to untie it. Now, she'd have to face Seraphine's inevitable dismay.

Suppressing a laugh, she swept toward the door, her robe trailing behind her. Whatever lecture awaited, she'd endure it with grace. Life would be unbearably dull without her family's fussing, after all.

Evelyne descended the spiral staircase of Duskwood Manor, her bare feet silent against the burnished floorboards. Daylight filtered through the tall, arched windows, bathing the sitting room below in soft gold. The air smelled of fresh lilacs with a hint of bohea tea, a scent Evelyne never grew tired of.

The delicate notes of a piano drifted through the air as skilled fingers danced over the keys in a melody so fluid, so precise, that there could be no mistake—Aurelia was home.

Evelyne paused mid-step, one hand resting lightly on the banister as she let the music wash over her, a quiet moment of nostalgia before reality pulled her forward once more.

Her older sister had always reveled in the attention her music drew. But Aurelia didn't simply crave admiration for her talent—she thrived on it in every form. She knew how to hold a room, whether through her music, her beauty, or her finely honed charm. And men were utterly helpless in her presence.

Her long, graceful legs, poised figure, and full lips left men spellbound. Golden curls, soft as spun silk, framed a flawless face, her fair skin radiant in the morning glow. But it was her eyes—crystalline blue, like a summer sky—that truly ensnared anyone who dared meet her gaze. Yet for all Aurelia's brilliance, Evelyne could see past the cultivated facade.

There was a time when Aurelia's laughter had filled the air, and she and Evelyne whispered of dreams and secret affections in the quiet of their shared chambers. But now, though Aurelia still wore her allure like a well-fitted gown, something beneath it had dimmed. The fire that once blazed in her eyes had waned, and Evelyne often wondered how much of her sister's joy was real and how much was merely another role she had mastered for the world.

The melody swelled, filling the room with bittersweet notes that mirrored Evelyne's thoughts. Across from the piano, their mother sat on the light blue couch, absorbed in a novel. Lady Celeste Duskwood hardly spoke while reading, always fully focused, but her presence was impossible to ignore. She had a quiet strength that seemed to guide the whole household.

Evelyne smiled softly, letting the music wrap around her like a familiar comfort. But just as she settled into the moment, a loud thud broke the peace, followed by sudden silence.

"Have you forgotten what today is, sister?" Aurelia's voice rang out. She turned on the bench, a single golden curl slipping over her shoulder as she surveyed Evelyne with a critical eye. "How can you still be lounging in your sleep robe? And your hair... Honestly!"

Evelyne sighed dramatically and made her way down the stairs. She crossed the sitting room and pulled Aurelia into a warm embrace, partly to quiet her. Aurelia huffed, but her arms wrapped around Evelyne in return.

"You do realize we've been waiting an entire hour for you, don't you?" Aurelia added, though her voice softened slightly.

"I was tired. And what's wrong with my attire? Surely this luxurious robe and my artfully tousled hair will help me charm a suitor, won't they?" Evelyne smirked.

Aurelia sighed. "Mother, perhaps we should forgo breakfast and summon Seraphine straight away. She's going to need extra time with this one."

Lady Duskwood finally looked up from her book. "Let's have tea first, shall we? No need to overwhelm your sister so early in the day." Her eyes flicked toward Evelyne. "Although, Aurelia isn't entirely wrong. Seraphine will certainly have her work cut out for her."

Evelyne placed a hand over her heart, feigning shock. "So it's a grand scheme, then? The two of you conspiring against me."

"Of course," Aurelia replied. "It's what we are here for."

With a quiet snort, Evelyne waved off the comment and made her way toward the dining room, rubbing her temples, bracing herself for what was coming. The morning had only just begun, and the battle for propriety was already underway.

The dining room was perpetually an impeccable display of wealth and refinement. The oak table stretched across the room. White linen draped its surface, and a golden centerpiece gleamed at its heart. Crystal and fine china were set with meticulous care, reflecting her mother's unyielding demand for perfection.

Evelyne entered the room slowly, her eyes still heavy with sleep. Her mother and Aurelia were already at the breakfast table, moving with practiced rhythm. Celeste kissed her husband's forehead before taking her seat, her posture straight as a blade as she surveyed the neatly set table.

Evelyne stared at her mother, admiring the very image of elegance. Her burgundy gown proclaimed her rank, and every strand of silver-gray hair was neatly tucked beneath a lace cap.

"Mauri, please bring us some tea. The strongest brew you have," Lady Duskwood instructed. The young house servant nodded briskly and slipped into the kitchen.

Evelyne moved toward her usual seat at the table, acutely aware of her mother's assessing gaze brushing over her like a fine-toothed comb before returning to the flawless breakfast spread.

As she passed her younger brother, Evelyne lightly brushed his shoulder, drawing his eyes—golden like hers—from the book he was absorbed in. Though Cillian had reached twenty, Evelyne felt a protective, almost maternal instinct toward him. He had always been different, drawn more to books and quiet study than the loud company of others his age. His sharp mind and dry sense of humor were treasures few ever saw, hidden behind his reserved nature. Their father, Lord Aron, often pushed him toward duties expected of an heir, like hunting, fencing, and politics, but none of it seemed to interest him. And Evelyne admired that about him. He was unshakably himself, never bothered by expectations that might weigh others down, and it only deepened her instinct to look out for him, even when she knew he didn't truly need it.

A faint smile pulled at the corners of Cillian's mouth. His tousled brown hair and slightly rumpled clothes spoke to his disregard for the strict decorum of the Duskwood household, though his kindness usually made it easy to overlook.

"Rough morning?" he murmured.

Evelyne nodded, a trace of a smile curving her lips. "I've yet to have tea. I'm not human without it," she whispered back.

Cillian huffed a soft laugh and returned to his book.

Lady Duskwood's voice cut through the hushed morning chatter. "Evelyne, as you know, the society luncheon is this afternoon."

Evelyne inhaled slowly, bracing herself. "Yes, Mother."

"You are twenty-two now, well past the age of debut, and must represent this family with the grace and dignity expected of a Duskwood," her mother replied, voice tight. "Which means your posture, speech, and every gesture must reflect our standing."

Aurelia leaned forward. "And don't forget the blush pink on your lips. It's subtle, yet inviting. And your smile should be warm but restrained. And your eyes—"

"Aurelia," Evelyne interrupted, her patience thinning. "I believe I can manage, thank you."

Her sister arched a perfectly shaped brow. "I'm only trying to help."

Evelyne leaned back, crossing her arms. "Speaking of appearances, where is Leopold? Still preoccupied with his *important* work?"

Aurelia's smile faltered briefly before she recovered. "Yes, he is. His responsibilities in Rosewyth are vast. You wouldn't understand how demanding his position is."

"Of course," Evelyne responded, her tone honeyed with sarcasm. "What a blessing to have such a devoted husband."

Aurelia's fingers tightened almost imperceptibly on her napkin, though her expression remained neutral.

"That's enough, ladies," Celeste interjected, and the room stilled instantly. "Evelyne, you will ensure your presentation today is without flaw. And Cillian," she added without turning to him, "do not enable your sister's nonsense."

Cillian turned to Evelyne, mischief glinting in his golden eyes. Without a word, he tapped her foot under the table. A minimal gesture, but one that said everything. Evelyne's lips twitched, the tension in her shoulders easing just slightly. As the conversation shifted back to the day's plans, she took comfort in his quiet presence.

Evelyne adjusted her posture, sitting straighter as her mother's critical stare settled on her. She had stepped beyond the age by which women of her standing were expected to be brides. To her mother, this was an oversight, a failure to be rectified. To Evelyne, it was simply her reality. What she could not reconcile was why men were free of such scrutiny, their futures untouched by the ticking clock that bound young women.

Her sister had followed a much different path. Their parents had been cautious with Aurelia's prospects, unwilling to accept anything less than perfection for the family's eldest daughter. That diligence had paid off when Leopold entered the picture. He was handsome and charming. His white-blonde hair was always perfectly kept, and years of successful trade with the southern lands had earned him both wealth and respect. It was easy for Evelyne to see why her sister was so captivated. He was the ideal match, a seamless blend of ambition and power. Their mother had been thrilled when Leopold asked for Aurelia's hand, and even their father had given his approval without hesitation. But Evelyne couldn't help but wonder whether Aurelia truly loved him or had simply fallen in love with the idea of him.

That life was never meant for Evelyne—or at least, it never felt that way. At nineteen, she'd been expected to step into the world of court: attending grand balls, mingling at glittering gatherings, and entertaining the advances of eager suitors. Her late-spring birthday had conveniently delayed her debut by a year, offering a brief reprieve. But just as her time finally came, everything changed.

***

It started one evening in the library. Cillian, a teen at the time, had been reading in a chair by the fire while Evelyne sorted through books at the far end of the room. The atmosphere was peaceful, as it often was when they shared that space, until Cillian's voice broke through the silence. At first, it sounded like faint, nonsensical muttering. Evelyne had laughed, thinking he was teasing her or practicing some dramatic monologue. But when she turned to look at him, her smile faded.

Cillian stood frozen, his gaze locked on the fireplace. His complexion was ashen, and his golden eyes had turned an unsettling shade of black, devoid of any life or awareness. His lips moved quickly, forming words she couldn't understand.

"Cillian?" Evelyne's voice wavered, but he gave no response. His body remained rigid, his focus unbroken. A cold sensation crept over her as she rushed to his side, trying to shake him gently. But he didn't react at all.

Panic hit her. She ran from the room, shouting for her parents.

By the time they returned, they found Cillian collapsed on the floor. He was on his knees, hands grasping at the air like he was struggling against something invisible. Evelyne could only stand in the doorway, trembling, as she watched her brother writhe in agony. When the fit passed, he lay there motionless, his chest rising and falling in shallow breaths. Their mother knelt beside him, her composure cracking for the first time Evelyne could remember.

Healers were summoned immediately, and for weeks afterward, the household was consumed by uncertainty and fear. The hallucinations came and went, each episode more terrifying than the last. But the healers offered no clear explanations and gave only vague assurances that they would likely resolve over time.

One night, Evelyne refused to leave Cillian's side after a particularly harrowing fit. She helped him to bed and pulled a chair close, unable to shake the sound of his anguished screams. Settling into the chair, she began reading aloud, page after page, trying to drown out the memory of his cries with the steady rhythm of her voice.

Sometime in the night, Cillian stirred. She glanced up just in time to see his golden eyes flicker open, locking onto hers for a fleeting moment before darkness pulled him under again.

"No!" he cried out. "Leave me alone. Please..." The last word came out in a whisper, barely audible, before his body stilled and he drifted back into sleep. The sound of his voice struck her like a blow, her chest tightening with helplessness. What kind of torment gripped him so deeply? She wished she could take the pain from him, absorb the fear he carried alone. But that night marked a turning point. From then on, Cillian's nightmares seemed to fade, and Evelyne's entire outlook began to shift.

How could she focus on dances and suitors when her brother's well-being was so precarious? The little excitement she'd once associated with her debut season faded into insignificance. As Cillian gradually regained his strength, Evelyne became increasingly disenchanted with the idea of marriage. Especially when the men she encountered at social gatherings always seemed preoccupied with superficial ambitions, their interests centered only on fortune or appearances. She could no longer feign enthusiasm for their exaggerated stories or insincere flattery. Each interaction left her feeling more distant from the life her parents envisioned for her.

Yet now, here she was, preparing to step back into that world one last time—not for herself, but to appease them. This time, however, it had to end with her finding someone.

CHAPTER 2

When Evelyne returned to her chambers, the bath was ready and the room was filled with the calming scent of lavender oil—no doubt Seraphine's doing. She longed to sink into the warm water, doze off even, but Aurelia's warning still echoed in her thoughts. *"Two hours, Evelyne. If you're not ready, I'll storm in, brush in hand!"* Just imagining her sister lecturing her on the arts of courtship while applying endless rouge made her shudder.

"Seraphine, you are my savior," Evelyne called out as she entered the tub. The water embraced her skin with soothing heat, and she sighed deeply.

"Well, my lady, you might not think so when I lace up your corset," Seraphine teased from the dressing room.

Evelyne chuckled. "I'd still choose you over Aurelia's schemes of matrimony." She leaned back, letting the lavender relax her tense shoulders, though her thoughts were far from calm.

The mere thought of the upcoming luncheon filled her with dread—it would mean enduring the company of Lord Ivan Bavrick of Rosewyth. Though hailing from a land renowned for its enchanting gardens and breathtaking vistas, Bavrick seemed a blight on Rosewyth's beauty, a man whose demeanor and appearance clashed sharply with his homeland's idyllic charm.

Ivan Bavrick was nearing forty, his balding head a patchy canvas of ruddy freckled skin and thinning strands of auburn hair awkwardly combed over in a futile attempt to disguise the inevitable. His perpetually flushed complexion bore the telltale signs of indulgence, whether from his fondness for long days under the sun or a far stronger fondness for liquor. Evelyne suspected the latter, especially given how he always leaned in too close, his breath heavy with the stench of bourbon and garlic.

He was insufferably dull, bloated with self-importance, and spoke in a booming voice that made mundane topics, like estate management, feel like endless lectures. He boasted constantly about his wealth and crop yields, never noticing Evelyne's clear disinterest. And his laugh—loud, grating, and utterly obnoxious—seemed to linger in the air long after he was gone, leaving her nerves thoroughly frayed.

She had perfected the art of avoidance, slipping through crowds and into alcoves at the first glimpse of Bavrick's flushed face. Yet no matter how deftly she evaded him, he always managed to find her, drink in hand, as relentless as a hound on a scent.

Evelyne groaned softly. She could already picture him approaching with those overly enthusiastic eyes searching hers as if daring her to escape.

"Do you think I could pretend to be ill?" Evelyne asked with genuine consideration.

"I wouldn't dare suggest it, my lady," Seraphine replied. "Lady Aurelia would drag you out, nightgown and all."

Evelyne let out a soft laugh. "You're probably right."

After soaking for a while, she reluctantly stepped out of the tub, allowing Seraphine to drape a towel over her shoulders.

"Now," Seraphine said, guiding her toward the vanity, "let's make you a vision no one will forget." Her hands moved swiftly as she pinned Evelyne's brown curls into an elegant style. "If the lords aren't captivated by your hair, they'll be enchanted by your eyes."

Evelyne raised an eyebrow. "My 'plain golden eyes,' as Aurelia calls them?"

"Plain? If the sun had a color, it would look like your eyes. Aurelia only says that because she hasn't got them herself."

"You always know how to make me feel better."

"Flattery is in the job description, my lady."

The gown she chose was a masterpiece. The silk shimmered in soft blue tones, reminiscent of the sky after rain. Silver embroidery traced the neckline and cuffs like frost on winter glass. Modestly puffed sleeves tapered into fitted arms, the tight corset shaping her feminine figure as her skirts gently swayed with each step.

Evelyne sighed as Seraphine pulled the corset strings tighter. "I'll wager I won't manage more than a single tart before this thing has me gasping."

"Nonsense. You'll manage two if you eat standing up," Seraphine quipped.

With a light touch of cosmetics, she completed the look. Evelyne's lashes framed her eyes beautifully, and her cheeks glowed with a faint blush. A soft pink on her lips was the finishing detail.

"There. You'll have everyone craning their necks for a glimpse."

Evelyne twirled in front of the mirror, watching the skirts of her gown ripple. And for a brief moment, her earlier worries melted away.

"Thank you, Seraphine. Truly."

"It's my pleasure."

"If fortune favors me, this gown will distract them from their tiresome prattle," Evelyne murmured with a smile.

Seraphine chuckled. "Miracles do happen."

***

The gardens of the Duskwood estate stretched out like a dream, their opulence a testament to the wealth and status of Caltheris' ruling family. Ancient oaks framed the grounds, their twisted branches heavy with moss and blooming vines. Silken canopies in soft pastels dotted the main lawn, shading tables draped in ivory linens and adorned with ornate porcelain tea sets.

Evelyne halted at the garden's edge, unease settling in. Her dress swayed, catching the sunlight, but her corset pinched tight. Still, she moved with steady refinement, masking her thoughts behind a calm expression.

The society luncheon marked the start of the courting season, where noble families from the south gathered to showcase their eligible sons and daughters. It was as much a show of power as a carefully orchestrated game of alliances. Evelyne couldn't decide which she loathed more—the stifling tradition or the endless parade of suitors.

"Come now, at least try to look like you're having fun," Aurelia said as she slipped to Evelyne's side in a shimmering emerald gown, offering a knowing smile at the ordeal of such courting events.

Evelyne sighed, her gaze drifting over the crowd in search of any excuse to linger at the edges. Near a canopy, she caught sight of Lady Bavrick—striking in a gown of deep sapphire, her silver-streaked auburn hair gleaming with a regal grace her son had inherited in neither looks nor manner. Evelyne's lips curved faintly at the thought, but the amusement faded when she noticed her mother beside Lady Bavrick, deep in conversation. Heartbeat quickening, Evelyne edged closer to Aurelia and shrank back, using her sister's presence as a shield while silently praying their mother's eyes did not find her.

No such luck—Lady Celeste, noticing her daughters at the edge of the garden, offered a graceful wave of her gloved hand, excused herself, and began to glide toward them. *Great.*

"My dears," she said warmly, her keen hazel eyes sweeping over them both. "You look stunning." She took Aurelia's hands first, gently squeezing them, before turning to Evelyne and brushing a hand along her shoulder. "The blue suits you perfectly, Evelyne. Your hair looks lovely pinned up like that."

"Thank you, Mother." Evelyne gave a small dip of her head.

"Now," Celeste continued, "remember to greet every noble family, no matter how tedious it may feel. These events are as much about making connections as they are about appearances. Smile, be pleasant, and for goodness' sake, Evelyne—be polite."

"I'll try my best."

"The luncheon is for your benefit, after all. You never know what opportunities might arise from a kind word or a thoughtful gesture." Their mother's expression softened as she added, "I know this isn't your favorite part of the season, Evelyne, but do try to look entertained."

She sounded exactly like Aurelia, and Evelyne had to fight the urge to roll her eyes. With that, Lady Duskwood patted her hand and gave them both a final, approving nod before gliding back into the crowd.

The crisp notes of laughter and conversation floated through the garden. Evelyne found herself again caught in the endless chatter of debutantes and their mothers, each vying for attention with exaggerated smiles and hollow merriment.

She was about to take refuge by the floral centerpiece when a sudden hush rippled through the crowd. Heads turned, and Evelyne instinctively followed their gaze to the man stepping into the garden.

Alaric Stonebridge.

His rich, sun-kissed brown skin seemed to catch the light, glowing warmly against the deep green of his perfectly tailored waistcoat. His black hair was neatly styled, every strand in place, adding to his cultivated appearance. But his eyes stood out most—light blue with hints of hazel. They were utterly mesmerizing, and looking away was nearly impossible.

Evelyne couldn't help but take notice, as she often did, of how seamlessly he carried both his mother's grace and his father's imposing demeanor. Their families had been closely intertwined for years through friendship, business, and mutual respect. While Alaric's charisma quickly captivated others, Evelyne had long since learned to see past the facade.

His eyes met hers as he approached, and a wry smile appeared. "Lady Evelyne," he greeted her smoothly. "What a delight to see you here. The scenery is much improved by your beauty."

Evelyne raised an eyebrow. "You must practice these lines in front of a mirror, Mr. Stonebridge. How else could they sound so rehearsed?"

His laugh was soft, genuine, and infuriatingly appealing. "And here I thought my charm would win you over."

"Not today, I'm afraid," Evelyne retorted, though she couldn't entirely suppress the smile tugging at the corners of her mouth.

Before Alaric could reply, Aurelia reappeared, looping her arm through Evelyne's. "Oh, Evelyne, why must you talk that way to such a handsome suitor?" She flashed a smile.

Evelyne cast her sister a pointed look. "Perhaps you'd care to take my place, Aurelia? No one has mastered the art of beguiling men so diligently as you."

Alaric chuckled, inclining his head toward Aurelia. "Your sister wounds with words swifter than any sword, yet I wouldn't change a thing about her."

Evelyne folded her arms. "I'm sure you wouldn't. It keeps you on your toes, after all."

There was a momentary pause, and then Evelyne's expression softened just enough to show that, beneath their banter, she valued Alaric's friendship. He returned the look with a faint nod, a sign of mutual understanding, before resuming the playful veneer.

"Well," Alaric said, straightening his waistcoat, "if you'll excuse me, I believe I have an audience to entertain. Ladies, it has been a pleasure." With a wink, he turned and strode toward another corner of the garden.

"You two are impossible." Aurelia tugged Evelyne's arm. "Let's grab some tea before Mother finds us again."

Evelyne drifted toward the refreshment table, releasing a quiet sigh as she noted the thinning crowd. At last, the luncheon seemed to be drawing to its close, and for the first time all day she dared believe she might escape unscathed. The dreaded Lord Bavrick had not appeared—a small mercy in an otherwise tedious affair.

"I'll leave you to it," Aurelia whispered, slipping away.

"What? Why—"

"Lady Evelyne, such a pleasure to see you."

Her stomach dropped, apprehension coiling in her chest. She turned slowly to find Ivan Bavrick far too close, his fixed grin stretched across a face already tinged with wine. Instinct drew her back a step, though he pressed forward, his presence cloying. At his side stood his younger brother, Wesley, auburn-haired and striking enough to remind Evelyne of their elegant mother. At least one Bavrick brother was not unpleasant to look at.

"Lord Bavrick." Evelyne offered a polite curtsey. "I trust you're enjoying the event."

"Oh, immensely," Ivan replied before launching into his favorite subject—the recent triumphs of his estate. His words droned in relentless, mind-numbing detail, while Evelyne fixed a smile in place, nodding at intervals as her thoughts drifted elsewhere.

Her eyes flicked to Wesley, who stood beside his brother with a distinctly disinterested air. He had grown since their last meeting, his boyish features giving way to a strong jawline and a muscular frame that spoke of his time outdoors. Freckles dotted his nose, and there was a spark in his green eyes as they roamed the gathering, more intrigued by the young women flitting about than his brother's lecture. When their eyes met, Wesley's lips formed an easy smile. He interrupted Ivan without hesitation.

"Lady Evelyne, you likely don't remember me. Wesley Bavrick. We met years ago, though I was hardly worth noticing then."

"On the contrary, Lord Wesley, I do remember. You were rather... energetic as a boy."

"And now?" he asked with a playful tilt of his head. "Do I still exude energy, or have I finally reached a state of dignified calm?"

"Dignified? Not yet," Evelyne replied.

"But you've certainly improved."

Wesley grinned. "I'll take that as high praise."

Ivan cleared his throat loudly, clearly annoyed. "As I was saying—"

"Brother," Wesley interrupted again, his voice entirely too jovial. "Forgive me, but I must know, Lady Evelyne, how you've attended these events for so long without becoming dreadfully bored. Is there some secret tonic you take?"

Evelyne laughed softly. "Tonic? Hardly. Though, a healthy sense of humor does wonders for endurance."

"Ah, then I must double my efforts to entertain," Wesley quipped. "Your laughter is worth every ounce of it."

"Just be careful not to strain yourself. I'd hate to be responsible for your exhaustion."

"Oh, don't worry." Wesley leaned slightly closer. "I've always had plenty of stamina."

Evelyne pressed her lips together to stifle her laugh while Ivan bristled beside them. One might hope he would accept the slight and excuse himself, having been so neatly excluded. Yet predictably, he remained rooted at her side.

"Evelyne, a word, if you please." Her mother approached, disapproval gleaming in her eyes.

Evelyne murmured an apology to her companions and allowed herself to be guided toward a quieter corner. Once they were out of earshot, Lady Celeste's expression hardened.

"This is not the time for idle chatter. You are here to form connections, to draw the notice of suitors—not to amuse yourself."

"I was only being kind, Mother," Evelyne replied.

"Dismissing Lord Ivan in favor of bantering with his younger brother is hardly kind. Do you not see how that might be perceived? Lord Ivan is a serious prospect, and this is not a game."

Evelyne drew herself up. "I did not dismiss him. He was quite obviously beside me."

"And yet you offered him no regard whatsoever." Celeste sighed, pressing her fingers to the bridge of her nose. "You must begin to take these matters seriously, Evelyne. Should you fail to do so, I will see to the choices myself. Do I make myself clear?"

Evelyne forced herself to remain composed. "Yes, Mother."

"Good." Celeste's expression softened slightly. "You have so much to offer, Evelyne. Don't squander it."

A mockery—that was all this day had become. Evelyne's patience was spent, her civility frayed to threads. Only a little longer, she reminded herself, and the luncheon would conclude. Yet this was but the first trial; how was she to endure the ball come evening? She unclenched her fists, her gaze following her mother's retreat into the crowd. And just as she thought matters could sink no lower, Lady Callista Evermere came prowling into her path.

The only daughter of a prominent southern lord, and a woman who evoked both admiration and unease within social circles, Callista was in her second season only because she had countless suitors vying for her favor, and she couldn't possibly decide yet. Her raven-black hair was styled in elegant waves that framed a face as sharp as it was beautiful. Her gown, a marvel of lavender silk and glittering gemstones, clung to her figure like starlight, accentuating skin kissed by the sun.

Surrounded by a loyal orbit of fawning girls, Callista tilted her head and flashed a cruel smile. "It's so lovely to see you, Evelyne... though I must say, I'm surprised you're still attending events like this. Surely it's a bit late for you to secure a match?"

The words fell like velvet-edged blades, striking unerringly. Evelyne's jaw tightened as she mastered her composure with a slow breath.

"Why, Callista, surely you know—the rarest vintages take the longest to mature; perhaps one day you'll be more than a pretty bottle with nothing worth pouring."

A ripple of stifled snorts spread through Callista's entourage, their amusement poorly concealed behind fluttering fans.

"Clever," she said, her voice syrupy-sweet. "Do take care, Evelyne. Smart remarks may keep *you* entertained, but won't warm your empty bed at night."

Evelyne's lips curved into a wicked smile as she drank deeply from her tea, swallowing her frustration along with it.

"That seemed spirited," Alaric Stonebridge murmured, biting into a tart as he came to stand beside her. "She has always had a gift for venom. Shall we slip away to the gardens? A walk might serve you well."

Evelyne shook her head. "Thank you, Alaric, but I would prefer a little solitude."

He studied her for a moment before nodding. "As you wish, my lady. But don't let her words linger. She envies anyone she can't overshadow."

With a faint smile of gratitude, Evelyne slipped back into the manor and let the familiar halls guide her to the library's quiet embrace. The scent of aged leather greeted her as she pushed open the heavy oak door. Cillian, sprawled in an oversized chair, looked up from his book.

"Let me guess," he drawled. "An afternoon of flattery and whispers?"

Evelyne exhaled, shutting the door behind her. "Callista Evermere felt the need to remind me of my supposed shortcomings."

"Ah, Callista. Ever the charmer. Why let her rattle you?"

"I try not to," she admitted, sinking into the chair opposite him. "But it's exhausting, pretending to care about their games."

Cillian tilted his head. "Then don't. And if it grows unbearable, we'll run away. A quiet life in the countryside has its appeal."

Evelyne laughed softly. "Tempting. But you'd miss your books."

"True," he conceded, grinning. "Still, I might bear it—if it spared you from Callista."

Evelyne smiled, warmth threading through her weariness. "What would I do without you, Cillian?"

"You'd be forced to actually care what Callista thinks, and we can't have that."

The comfort of his presence, and the stillness of the library around them, wrapped her in ease at last. Before long, exhaustion claimed her, and she drifted into a deep, untroubled sleep.

CHAPTER 3

The quiet sanctuary of the library was shattered as Aurelia flung open the door, her cheeks flushed with exasperation.

"There you are!" she exclaimed, her voice bouncing off the high shelves.

Evelyne stirred, blinking drowsily as she lifted her head from where she'd slumped in the armchair. Her nap, it seemed, had come to an abrupt end.

Aurelia sighed, striding over in an elegant flurry of silk skirts. "Honestly, Evelyne, napping? And you—" She rounded on Cillian, who sat nearby, his eyes slightly unfocused. "Why didn't you wake her? You know how much we have to do before the ball."

Cillian blinked as though dragged back from some faraway thought. "I, uh..." He glanced at Evelyne, his brow furrowing. "She looked peaceful. I didn't want to disturb her."

Evelyne groaned softly. "Whatever has you in such a state?"

"I've been looking everywhere for you," Aurelia said, irritated. "The entire household is in chaos getting ready for tonight, and you're here sleeping like you don't have a care in the world."

Evelyne sat up, brushing her hair back. "Well, I can't exactly care about the chaos if I'm asleep, can I?" She glanced at Cillian, who seemed distracted again, his gaze fixed on nothing. "Cillian?" she asked softly, tilting her head.

His golden eyes refocused, and he offered a faint smile. "Sorry. Just… thinking."

Evelyne frowned slightly, noting how distant he seemed, but she chose not to press him. There were more important matters, *apparently*, given Aurelia's hovering presence.

"Follow me. Now!" Aurelia insisted.

"Okay, okay." Evelyne groaned and followed her sister out of the library.

Inside Evelyne's chambers, Seraphine worked with the careful precision of a sculptor, her fingers deftly arranging Evelyne's hazelnut curls into another intricate updo. A few loose tendrils softened the style, lending Evelyne an almost ethereal charm. She watched in silence while Seraphine's hands brought the vision in the mirror to life.

Seraphine's chosen gown for the evening hung on Evelyne's frame like a second skin, its midnight-blue silk flowing in delicate waves. Tiny diamond embellishments adorned the neckline and hem, catching the glow of the room's candles and sparkling like liquid starlight.

"You'll have the entire room at your feet." Seraphine stepped back with a satisfied nod, scanning Evelyne's reflection as if evaluating a masterpiece.

Before Evelyne could respond, Aurelia bustled in, holding a small jar of shimmering powder, a mischievous grin on her lips. "Don't move," she commanded, dipping a brush into the jar and lightly dusting the glittering powder across Evelyne's collarbone and the swells of her breasts.

"Aurelia!" Evelyne exclaimed.

"What?" Aurelia gave her an exaggerated look of innocence. "You'll thank me later when every man in the room forgets how to speak."

Seraphine smirked while Evelyne rolled her eyes and laughed. "I think you're enjoying this a little too much."

"Of course I am. But you should enjoy it too. You look breathtaking."

The final touches followed: a precise sweep of liner that made Evelyne's eyes seem brighter, almost hypnotic, and a rich berry hue on her lips to add a touch of daring sophistication. With every stroke and adjustment, she felt herself slipping further into the role expected of her tonight. When Seraphine and Aurelia finally stepped back, their work complete, Evelyne couldn't help but take a second, more prolonged glance at her reflection. The woman staring back was radiant, and she even found herself captivated for a moment.

"Well?" Aurelia prompted. "Are you ready to conquer the ballroom?"

Evelyne inhaled deeply. "Ready as I'll ever be."

"Then let's make an entrance," Aurelia declared, linking her arm with Evelyne's.

Seraphine nodded approvingly as they left the chambers, the soft rustle of Evelyne's gown and the click of their shoes echoing through the corridor. The night awaited, and with it, dozens of watchful eyes ready to fall on the vision she had become.

The grand ballroom of Duskwood Manor was a breathtaking display of wealth and magnificence. Crystal chandeliers cascaded from the ceiling like frozen waterfalls, their glow reflecting off the polished marble floor. Above, murals of mythical wolves prowling beneath glistening stars stretched across the vaulted ceilings, adding a touch of magic to the opulent space. Deep red and gold draperies framed the towering windows, casting an air of regal intimacy over the lively gathering.

Music filled the room as women in sweeping gowns of every shade glided about effortlessly, their silks and satins catching the light like rare jewels. The men, dashing in their evening coats, exchanged sly smiles and offered hands, their polished boots tapping in time with the rhythm of the dance. Across the room, clusters of mothers engaged in a silent battle of whispers, carefully orchestrating future unions while their daughters giggled behind fluttering fans.

Evelyne entered on Aurelia's arm. Her sister was stunningly beautiful in a blush-pink gown with golden undertones highlighting her enviable curves. Diamond combs glittered in her curled blonde hair, and her sharp blue eyes twinkled with excitement. She loved this.

Evelyne scanned the crowd in the ballroom, noting ambition and concealed desperation alike. Her observations, however, were cut short by a familiar face gliding through the throng with the confidence of a fox in a henhouse.

Lord Wesley Bavrick. His auburn hair glowed like polished copper, and his perfectly tailored attire did little to hide his flair for dramatic entrances. He wore his grin as if it were armor, a blend of charm and cheek that made him both irritating and entertaining in equal measure.

"Lady Evelyne," he said as he reached her, executing an exaggerated bow that bordered on theatrical. "I could hardly bear the thought of enjoying myself until I secured the evening's most enchanting partner for a dance. May I?"

Evelyne smiled. "If I say no, will you sulk in the corner and ruin the mood for everyone else?"

"Without a doubt," he replied solemnly, though his grin gave him away. He extended his hand, palm up, a silent challenge.

"Well, that simply will not do," Evelyne said, placing her gloved hand in his. "Lead the way, my lord."

Wesley guided her onto the dance floor with a grace that, despite herself, Evelyne found surprising. As the music swelled, they fell into the rhythmic steps of the reel. With a steady hand at her waist and unexpectedly fluid steps, Wesley, she had to admit, wasn't as hopeless as she thought.

"You're quite skilled; I wouldn't have guessed," she said.

"That almost sounded like a compliment, my lady. If you keep that up, you'll lose your title as the sharpest in the room."

She tilted her head. "Oh, I don't mind sparing a morsel of praise now and then. Besides, everyone will know it was your fault if we stumble."

"Cruel but fair," Wesley said. "Though I'm sure I'd be forgiven. A man of my appeal and reputation couldn't possibly be at fault."

Evelyne smiled. "Ah yes, your reputation, charging ahead of you like an overexcited dog. I see you're enjoying the company of this season's fair maidens."

He laughed, the sound rich and genuine, his gaze lingering on hers. "And here I thought you'd bring up my unparalleled generosity."

"I'm sure you are very generous, Lord Wesley," she retorted with a pointed glance. "Particularly when it comes to admiring your dance partners."

"Caught me," he said with feigned remorse, though his grin remained unapologetic. "But can you truly fault me for appreciating beauty where it's due?"

A hint of color warmed Evelyne's cheeks, though she resisted the urge to roll her eyes. "It seems your talent for flattery is greater than I expected."

As they swirled through the final steps of the dance, Evelyne caught sight of Lord Ivan Bavrick lingering near the edge of the ballroom. His hawkish stare made him seem more like a vulture waiting for scraps than a guest at a ball. Evelyne stiffened, inwardly praying that he'd keep his distance.

When the music ended, Wesley released her with a deep bow. "Thank you for indulging me, Lady Evelyne. I trust this won't be our only dance of the evening?"

Before she could summon a retort, he straightened and strode away. Evelyne exhaled sharply, shaking her head as she returned to her sister's side.

"What was that all about?" Aurelia asked teasingly.

"An exercise in patience," Evelyne replied dryly. "And I'd like it noted that I performed admirably." She moved toward the refreshment table, her nerves tingling from the dance.

Before she could gather her thoughts, Alaric Stonebridge appeared at her side. His dark hair was immaculately styled, framing a chiseled jaw and a smile that could disarm even the most guarded heart. Dressed in a fitted evening coat, he looked every inch the charming rogue of the aristocracy.

"Lady Evelyne," he murmured, a teasing note woven into his rich baritone. "Have I mentioned how unfair it is for you to command the room's attention so thoroughly?"

She turned to him and raised a brow. "You might have, but I wasn't listening."

Alaric laughed. "You wound me," he said, pressing a hand to his chest. "But I'm nothing if not persistent."

"And predictable," Evelyne countered smoothly, though her lips quirked upward.

"Ah, but you enjoy it. Admit it." His blue eyes sparkled as he leaned slightly closer.

Before Evelyne could respond, Callista Evermere's crisp voice cut through their exchange. Dressed in a striking crimson gown, she approached with the confidence of someone accustomed to getting what she wanted.

"Alaric," she purred, placing a possessive hand on his arm. "I believe we were to share the next dance?"

Evelyne smiled faintly, masking her irritation. "Don't let me keep you, Mr. Stonebridge. I'm sure Miss Evermere will be a most entertaining partner."

Alaric hesitated, his gaze lingering on Evelyne. "This isn't over," he muttered before allowing Callista to whisk him away.

The evening unfolded in a symphony of music and dancing, with merriment rippling through the ballroom. Evelyne even caught her sister laughing with Alaric, the joy of being part of the courting season again shining through. However, the magic of the ball had faded for Evelyne. The dazzling chandeliers and elegant gowns no longer held their attraction as exhaustion crept in. While she had danced and dutifully met her mother's expectations with forced smiles and polite conversation, all she yearned for now was the quiet solace of her bedchamber. The pins digging into her scalp and the constriction of her gown felt less like beauty and more like a burden she was desperate to shed.

She had endured the expected courtesies, exchanging pleasantries with noble lords and ladies and even partaking in a second dance with Wesley—mainly as a shield against Ivan, who had been watching her with wine-fueled boldness all evening. Each time she felt his gaze linger, she braced herself, knowing another tedious attempt at conversation was imminent. The wine had loosened his restraint, and she knew he'd come close to mustering the courage to approach again.

When Evelyne spotted her mother deep in an animated discussion with a group of matriarchs, she seized the opportunity to slip away, grabbing a flute of champagne on her way out. The night chill greeted her as she stepped into the stillness of the manor's back patio and sat on a cold bench.

Tilting her face to the stars, Evelyne inhaled deeply and closed her eyes, wishing for the freedom of running—her only refuge amid the chaos of life. It had always been her escape, the steady beat of her footsteps silencing every thought until only the hush of exhaustion remained. But tonight, with the ball still alive behind her, she chose solitude instead.

The crash of shattering glass ripped through the stillness, yanking her back to the present. Evelyne twisted toward the sound, her heart jolting as her eyes locked on a silhouette in the dimly lit glass-walled foyer beyond the patio.

Cillian.

He stood among a cascade of broken glass, his hands streaked with blood. His posture was unnervingly still, and his gaze was fixed downward, empty and detached, as red liquid dripped from his fingers to the pool at his feet.

Evelyne gasped and rushed to him. "Cillian!"

He flinched at the sound of her voice, but didn't move. She reached him, her hands flying to his, frantically wrapping the deep gashes with nearby linens. The blood soaked through almost instantly, her fingers slippery as she tried to staunch the flow.

"Cillian," she pleaded. "What happened? Tell me."

His wide eyes met hers, gold flickering in their depths, and for a moment, Evelyne felt like he was a stranger. Terror and confusion flashed across his face as his lips parted as if to speak, but no words came.

Servants arrived in a flurry of motion, bearing bandages and brooms to clean up the shattered glass. Evelyne kept her hand steady on Cillian's shoulder, guiding him carefully inside. He moved in a daze, as if his body was obedient but his mind elsewhere.

Their father entered the room, his composed presence standing out against the commotion. His eyes scanned the scene before locking on Cillian.

"Summon the healers," Lord Aron commanded. "Now."

The servants froze, their eyes darting toward him.

"Not a word to Celeste. Not tonight."

With that, he turned and strode out, leaving no room for argument.

Evelyne stayed by her brother's side, watching as the healers tended to his wounds. Cillian drank a tonic reluctantly, its bitterness evident in his grimace, and soon, his body sagged with exhaustion. Evelyne didn't leave until his breathing deepened into sleep.

No one dared speak of it aloud, but the truth lingered like a storm cloud.

It was happening again.

CHAPTER 4

Evelyne sat rigid at the dining table, absently pushing her eggs around her plate, her appetite nowhere to be found. The morning sun poured through the tall windows, its warmth doing little to thaw the icy tension in the room. Across from her, her mother sipped tea indifferently while her father and sister sat silently.

Cillian's absence loomed over them, but no one spoke of it. The events of the previous night still echoed in Evelyne's mind: the shattering glass, the blood on his hands, and his dazed, haunted expression. The healers had whispered among themselves through the night, but no answers had come.

Finally, her mother broke the silence. "Evelyne," she began, her tone far too casual, "you left the ball early last night. How do you expect to find a husband behaving so... erratically?"

Evelyne's fork clattered against her plate. "Cillian smashed through a glass door last night, Mother. He's ill again, and no one knows why. And this is what you want to talk about?"

Her mother's jaw tightened, but her expression didn't falter. "Relax, dear. Boys his age often go through strange phases. What he needs is rest." She paused. "And what *you* need is to start thinking about your future."

"My *future*?" Evelyne's voice rose, her hands trembling with frustration. "How can you sit there pretending nothing's wrong while your son—"

"That's enough!" her mother hissed. "You will not raise your voice at me. I care about Cillian, but he is being looked after. Meanwhile, you have responsibilities. Lord Ivan Bavrick spoke with me last night, you know." She paused again. "He has asked for your hand in marriage."

Aurelia gasped, her eyes widening as she looked from their mother to Evelyne in disbelief. "Mother... no," she whispered, the words barely audible but laden with shock.

Evelyne's heart sank as nausea churned in her stomach. "Lord Bavrick?" she managed to choke out. "You can't be serious."

"He's a respected man," her mother replied smoothly, setting her teacup down. "Wealthy, influential, and eager to unite our families. You should consider yourself lucky."

"Lucky?" Evelyne's voice broke, her anger spilling over. "He's repulsive! You're trying to sell me off like some—"

"This ends now, Evelyne," her mother interrupted again, her eyes narrowing. "You will not embarrass this family. If you continue this childish behavior, I will have no choice but to take Lord Bavrick's offer more seriously."

Evelyne rose abruptly, the legs of her chair scraping against the polished floor as she pushed it back. Her gaze, full of disbelief, settled upon her father.

"And what are your thoughts on the matter?"

He did not immediately respond. Instead, he continued his meal as though her question were of little consequence before lifting his eyes to meet hers. With a shrug, he said, "I believe it is high time you secured a husband. And if Bavrick is the only gentleman to have sought your hand by the season's end, you would do well to consider his proposal."

Evelyne scoffed. The mere thought of binding herself to that man was unthinkable... laughable, even. But she knew well enough that further protest would be met with the same unyielding stance.

She drew a steady breath, schooling her expression. "Perhaps we might revisit this conversation when both of you have regained your senses." With that, she turned, ready to step away before her temper overtook her.

"Where do you think you're going?" her mother demanded. "I did not excuse you."

"I'm going out," Evelyne snapped, her hands curling into fists at her sides.

"Don't even think about going on one of your reckless runs. A noble lady should not behave in such a manner," her mother warned.

Evelyne laughed and shook her head as she turned away. She left the dining room without another word.

***

The darkness was endless, like a heavy, suffocating void. Cillian stood barefoot on a slick, glassy surface that reflected nothing but shadows. The air was full of whispers, words curling around him like smoke. Then, a sweet, silky voice cut through the haze.

"*My, my...* look at you," it purred, dripping with dangerous seduction. "So strong now. So handsome. And yet... still invisible."

A pale figure emerged from the dark, her icy white hair catching the faintest light, her silver eyes gleaming with an unnatural fire. Her beauty was eerie and irresistible, drawing both admiration and fear as she glided in a slow circle around him. Her cool fingers began grazing his arm. The touch sent a shiver deep into his bones, warning of her power and the danger she embodied.

"They don't see you, do they?" she murmured. "Not truly. A shadow at the edge of their perfect little world. No one believes you could ever be good enough. A lord? *You?* Oh, how they laugh at the thought."

Cillian's fists clenched. "That's not true," he managed, though his voice wavered.

"Isn't it?" she teased, leaning close, her breath warm against his ear. "Your dear sisters, both beautiful. Admired. Loved. While you... What are you, Cillian? A burden? Even they know it. Your father knows it, too."

"Stop," he growled, but doubt gnawed at him.

The world tilted, and suddenly he found himself in the manor's glass-walled foyer, facing the stone patio beyond. The doors loomed tall, glittering faintly in the gloom. Her laughter echoed around him, filling his head.

"Prove them wrong," she said. "Show them how strong you really are. Go on... make them look. Make them see you."

"Leave me alone," he murmured, squeezing his eyes shut. "This isn't real. It's just a dream." He clung to the words like a lifeline.

"Oh?" Her voice curled around him. "Let's test that theory, shall we?"

He moved without thought, like something else controlled his movements. His hands slammed into the glass. The shattering sound was deafening, and shards of glass rained like jagged stars. He stared at his bloodstained hands while the warm crimson flowed freely and pooled at his feet. The sharp metallic scent quickly invaded his senses, yet no pain registered. Only a numb detachment as the blood traced slow, intricate paths down his skin.

"Cillian!"

Evelyne's panicked voice broke through. Dark, inky mist coiled from his thoughts, clinging stubbornly, like it had burrowed too deep to ever truly let go. Then the trance shattered, and reality came crashing back. Evelyne was there, her voice trembling as she called his name, but all Cillian could do was stare at the blood—his blood—pooling beneath him.

***

The morning sun crept into the room as Cillian's eyes fluttered open. His breaths came in short, uneven bursts. The nightmare clung to him, and his mind reeled with the woman's words. He looked down at his bandaged hands, the dull ache a cruel reminder of what had happened. Beside him lay a tray of untouched food and a tonic on the nightstand. He turned away, his throat tightening.

The hallucinations had started a week ago, creeping into his mind with whispers that slithered like venom through his thoughts. He had tried to push them away, desperate not to worry Evelyne or cast a shadow over her season. But last night, they had twisted into something far worse. It felt like something was festering inside him, an infection with teeth. A parasite that writhed beneath his skin, feeding and waiting. Like something not entirely his own... something *demonic*.

He'd caught the way Evelyne watched him in the library yesterday, her eyes full of concern as he struggled to mask his vacant stares. She had seen it. And he knew the truth wouldn't stay hidden from her much longer. Frustration curled hot in his chest. *Why am I such a burden?*

Pain flared through his arms as he slowly pushed himself upright. "It's not real," he muttered. He drew in a shaky breath and whispered it again, desperately this time. "It's not real."

CHAPTER 5

Evelyne ran until Duskwood Manor was a distant memory, her legs carrying her far beyond where reason might have stopped her. The sun was gentle against her flushed skin, but her mind was ablaze with thoughts. Her mother's callous ignorance was unbearable. Even Aurelia had looked baffled at her words. How could she care so little for Cillian's distress, focusing only on matchmaking Evelyne to Ivan Bavrick? The very thought of Bavrick made Evelyne ill. No amount of wealth could make her endure that man's touch.

She inhaled deeply, keeping her pace steady and swift, each breath sharp against the ache growing in her chest. The image of Cillian's strained, terrified face burned in her mind. He must feel so frightened, so utterly alone. But why hadn't he confided in her about the episodes returning? She'd noticed his unease in the library yesterday—how his golden eyes had dulled with fear—but she'd been too caught up in her mother and sister's incessant meddling to act on it. She understood why he stayed silent, though; she always understood him.

Later, she would go to his room, and if words failed, she'd sit with him in quiet solidarity. He needed to know he wasn't alone, and she needed him to know she was there.

The familiar woods eventually gave way to the edges of the Stonebridge estate. She hadn't planned to come this far, but her feet had a mind of their own. Lost in thought, she nearly stumbled over a gnarled branch, but recovered quickly, her breath ragged as she tried to steady herself.

Ahead, Alaric stood on the estate grounds, fencing with his trainer. His lean, muscular frame moved with precision, his dark hair sweaty. She inwardly cursed her luck for ending up here, disheveled and out of breath, but his boyish grin remained firmly in place as he spotted her.

"Lady Evelyne!" he called, excusing himself from the trainer. Concern flickered in his blue eyes as he jogged toward her.

She sighed, brushing a stray lock of hair from her face, and forced a polite smile. "Mr. Stonebridge. I didn't mean to disturb your training. Please, don't let me interrupt. I was running, and... Well, I seem to have gotten carried away."

He stopped a few steps from her, his grin turning roguish. "You're not interrupting at all. Honestly, I was looking for an excuse to stop. My trainer's been trying to kill me with drills all morning." His gaze swept over her. "But it seems I'm not the only one who's been put through their paces today."

Evelyne stiffened, glancing down at her mud-speckled shoes and sweat-dampened clothes. "Are you suggesting I look a mess?"

"Not in the slightest," he replied smoothly, his voice laced with mock sincerity. "You look... determined. Like a warrior fresh from battle. Quite inspiring, really. Though I admit, I've never seen a southern lady dressed in men's riding breeches before."

A reluctant laugh escaped her lips, and she shook her head. "They're my brother's, and you're insufferable."

"But I'm also kind," he quipped, offering her his arm. "Come inside for some water or tea. You've earned it."

She hesitated, acutely aware of her rumpled state. "I wouldn't want to impose—"

"Nonsense," he cut her off. "You'd be doing me a favor. My trainer will have no choice but to let me rest a little longer."

Relenting, Evelyne took his arm, trying to maintain her composure despite her exhaustion. "Fine. But if this is just an excuse to skip your drills, I'm telling your trainer."

Alaric smirked as he guided her toward the house. "You think that scares me? I've survived worse."

***

Evelyne's gaze drifted over the drawing room as she sipped her tea, the warmth grounding her amid her unsettled thoughts. The space was refined yet inviting, with towering bookshelves filled with old tomes and volumes. Near the tall windows stood a harp, its golden strings catching the soft afternoon light as if longing for a touch to awaken its silent melody.

Her attention settled on a framed portrait above the fireplace: Alaric as a boy, standing stiffly between his father and her own. Gaviel Stonebridge smiled proudly while her father's hand rested firmly on young Alaric's shoulder, expressing quiet approval.

Alaric followed her stare. "That was the year your father first invited me to the winter festival," he said faintly. "I remember being terrified of him. He had this way of looking at you like he could hear every thought in your head."

Evelyne huffed a laugh. "He still does. I know that look all too well."

"He's always been fair, even when it wasn't easy." Alaric leaned back, his voice turning thoughtful. "You know, my grandfather once told me the Duskwoods were different from most noble families. He said they lead not just with power, but with purpose. And that their strength comes from how fiercely they support each other, going back generations. That's why our families tied their fortunes together—to be each other's backbone if the world ever turned uncertain."

Evelyne set her cup down, studying him. "And your father? Does he believe that too?"

Alaric's expression softened. "He does. He's always said that wealth and influence mean little without integrity. It's what sets the Stonebridge name apart, even among merchants. My father takes great pride in knowing our success never came at the cost of our principles. Your family recognized that then, and still does, which is why this alliance has lasted for generations."

Evelyne tilted her head, considering. "And you? Do you feel the weight of carrying that legacy and alliance?"

Alaric traced the rim of his cup. "Every day. But I also see it as a privilege. The trust between our families wasn't built overnight. It's my job to protect it... and it certainly helps having you as a friend."

Evelyne smiled, letting his words settle over her. He knew nothing of the chaos from last night, yet his steady presence brought an unexpected comfort.

"I suppose it's reassuring," she murmured, "knowing I'm not the only one trying to navigate expectations. It's nice to be reminded I'm not entirely alone in this."

Alaric studied her for a long moment. "That's the thing about alliances, Evelyne. Whether between families or friends. They remind us that we're never as alone as we think."

She glanced at him. "Comforting, yes... yet even surrounded, loneliness can press upon one's heart more than it should."

"Would you care to share what's on your mind?"

His gaze held such warmth that she nearly relented. But instead, she offered a slight shake of her head, and he understood.

"Well, should you ever wish to, you know where to find me." He winked, drawing a smile from her as she took the final sip of her tea.

An easy stillness settled between them, punctuated only by the delicate chime of porcelain and the faint whisper of the wind against the windowpane. Eventually, Evelyne rose to her feet, brushing her hands over the fabric of her tunic—her brother's, to be exact. "I should return before anyone decides to send a search party. Thank you for the tea... and the perspective."

Alaric inclined his head. "Anytime, my lady."

With a final glance at the portrait above the fireplace, she turned and made her way toward the door.

Alaric rose as well, his brows knitting slightly. "You're not running back, are you?"

She grinned. "It's quicker, and I need to clear my head."

He sighed. "At least let me walk you to the edge of the estate. That way, I can say I tried to be honorable." His flirtatious smile returned, and Evelyne rolled her eyes at the abrupt shift in his demeanor. But she couldn't deny that his relentless habit of making every woman feel noticed was oddly endearing.

"Fair enough," she replied.

The sun was high as they walked down the gravel path. When they reached the estate's edge, Alaric stopped and spoke low. "Try not to cause any scandals on your way back, Lady Evelyne."

"I'll do my best, Mr. Stonebridge."

With that, she took off down the path, her heart lighter than it had been in days.

***

Evelyne hesitated outside Cillian's room, her hand resting lightly on the doorknob. The faint murmur of movement from within reassured her that he was awake, but she couldn't shake the tension in her chest. She took a steadying breath, turned the knob, and stepped inside.

He was propped up against a mound of pillows, his soft brown hair ruffled, a faint shadow of exhaustion lingering in his eyes. Despite his weariness, he managed a small smile when he saw her.

"You look like you could use a nap more than I could," he teased, his voice raspy.

Evelyne sighed dramatically but smiled back, taking the chair by his bedside. "It's been a long day. How are you feeling?"

He shrugged. "Better."

Her heart ached as she saw his effort to hide his pain. His forced smile and trembling hands made his true feelings evident, and her vision blurred as tears welled up. She blinked them back rapidly, clenching her jaw desperately to maintain her composure. Every fiber of her being ached to reach out and embrace him. But she held back, her hands shaking slightly in her lap as she fought against the overwhelming urge.

She took a deep breath and swallowed, her mind racing with questions. What had happened? Why was he suffering? Most importantly, how could she help?

She leaned forward. "Cillian. What happened?"

His mouth opened, a response half formed, but then his jaw clenched and silence won. The hesitation in his eyes was a language Evelyne knew all too well. She didn't push him; she never would.

"It's okay," she reassured him. "When you're ready."

She settled back in her chair. The silence stretched between them, but Evelyne, feeling the need to lighten the mood, let out a quiet laugh.

"You know, if you think you're having a rough time, wait until you hear this... Lord Bavrick has officially requested my hand in marriage."

Cillian blinked at her, then burst into laughter. "Lord Bavrick? Ivan? The one who snores through meetings and has a laugh like a dying donkey?"

"That's the one." She paused. "Mother is considering it."

Cillian's laughter faded, replaced by a worried furrow of his brow. "And what do you think about it?"

She waved dismissively as though the matter were as trivial as spilled tea. "Does it matter what I think?" She sighed. "I guess I'll have to charm my way into every eligible man's heart during these unbearable social gatherings. I'm sure they'll all be lining up to court me soon."

Cillian's eyes lingered on her like he was trying to read between the lines of her humor. "Evelyne, what are you *really* going to do?"

"I don't know," she admitted. "As you see, I am no adept at flirtation or idle games. Likely I shall be left with little more than the donkey for a husband."

Evelyne stood and wandered over to the bookshelf, letting her fingers skim the titles before pulling two at random.

"Here," she said with a grin, dropping one into Cillian's lap. "Let's disappear into a story for a bit. This world's being terribly uncooperative."

Cillian caught the book and smiled as she dragged her chair closer and sat beside him. They read together in silence, broken only by the turning of pages. As the afternoon light faded, Evelyne felt Cillian's hand squeeze hers. He said nothing, but he didn't need to. In that quiet moment, she knew they would face whatever came next together.

A gentle knock sounded on the door and their mother stepped inside. Her rich gown whispered as she moved across the room, her eyes softening as they landed on Cillian. "I see you're awake. How are you feeling, my dear?"

Cillian sat up a little straighter, his demeanor shifting as he attempted to downplay his condition. "Better, Mother. I don't think the healers need to come back. I'm fine."

Celeste gave him a look that brooked no argument. "Nonsense. The healers will return in the morning with additional remedies. I won't take chances with your health, especially now." She adjusted the covers at the foot of his bed before adding, almost as an afterthought, "Particularly at a time like this."

Evelyne's eyebrows lifted at the implication, and she couldn't resist interjecting. "A time like this? You mean courting season, don't you, Mother?"

"One must always consider appearances, Evelyne. You know that as well as I do." Her eyes flickered over Evelyne's attire, the remnants of her earlier run unmistakable. With a quiet sigh, she shook her head.

Evelyne bristled, her protective nature flaring. "Perhaps Cillian should be allowed to make his own choices."

Her mother pressed her lips together tightly but said nothing to refute Evelyne's words. Instead, she straightened and smoothed her skirts. "Your father and I have a meeting with Mr. and Mrs. Stonebridge. Do try to keep yourself occupied in the meantime, Evelyne," she said with a dismissive edge.

Though curiosity sparked at the mention of the Stonebridges, Evelyne resisted the urge to ask. She didn't want to give her mother the satisfaction of knowing she cared. Instead, she returned her focus to Cillian, who gave her a look of quiet gratitude.

Evelyne let out a weary sigh. "I'm going to wash up and scrub away what's left of today's stress and frustration." She paused before adding, "I'm here if you need me."

"I know," he replied.

With a faint smile, she returned her book to the shelf and went to her room, leaving him to rest.

Chapter 6

Tension hung heavy in the library of Stonebridge Manor as Alaric sat rigid, steeling himself for whatever was to come. His father, Gaviel Stonebridge, a rarely rattled man, looked uncharacteristically troubled. The usual strength in his warm-toned features had dulled, his expression clouded with whatever news had drawn them into this uneasy silence.

"It is Velenshire," he admitted with a sigh. "What I must say is hardly cheerful."

Beside him, Vera Stonebridge sat elegantly, her fair complexion contrasting with her husband's. The fire's glow highlighted her sharp cheekbones as she leaned forward, hands resting on the chair's armrests. Alaric had inherited her piercing blue eyes, but his jet-black hair and strong build were unmistakably his father's. Though his mother's expression remained calm, the subtle stiffness in her fingers betrayed the apprehension beneath.

Gaviel glanced at Lord and Lady Duskwood. "As we are all aware, Velenshire has always been... different, but now, the whispers have turned to warnings." He swallowed hard before continuing. "There is something amiss. The forests bordering Velenshire are eerily quiet, and several trade caravans have been discovered forsaken—wagons toppled, cargo scattered, but not a soul to be found."

Lady Duskwood narrowed her eyes. "Where are the merchants?"

Gaviel's face hardened. "We cannot yet say. There have been sightings of a black mist moving through the forest, creeping toward the road to Velenshire. It devours everything in its path. I dispatched a company to investigate. One man failed to return, and no soul can say what became of him."

Silence gripped the room.

"Those who've dared enter Mokkvyrn Forest say they've seen shapes—human figures—slipping between the trees, only to dissolve into shadow," Gaviel added.

"And you believe this is tied to what, exactly?" Lady Celeste asked.

Gaviel shared an understanding look with Vera before addressing the room. "I believe you already suspect the truth, my lady. I think everyone here does." His gaze swept over each person, landing on Alaric momentarily. "Though it has been quiet for centuries, we suspect magic, dark magic, is at the heart of this. Velenshire has always been its final stronghold in the southern lands, and if the balance there has been disturbed..."

"Then we have far greater problems than abandoned caravans," Lord Duskwood finished grimly.

Once more, a weighted quiet pressed between them. Only the Stonebridge and Duskwood families, ancient pillars of Caltheris, carried the knowledge of magic's existence and the witches of Velenshire. Alaric had grown up hearing the story of two queens said to dwell in the frozen wastes of Nerathar, though no human had dared venture that far, nor cared to brave the brutal cold to uncover whether the stories were true. Even when his parents had recently revealed the reality to him, he'd struggled to believe it. After all, if there were any fact behind the old tales, whatever power those queens held had never reached beyond their icy domain.

"If magic is stirring," Celeste said softly, "this knowledge cannot leave this room. Not even my children can know. If the other lords or noble families catch wind of this, they'll fall into a frenzy. Worse, some might act recklessly and draw the attention of creatures we are not prepared to face. This has always been our burden to keep, and Lord and Lady Shaw of Velenshire expect us to do just that."

Lord Duskwood leaned back, his expression grave. "Then we must act quickly and quietly. The borders of Velenshire need to be investigated before this escalates. We cannot risk this becoming a scandal at court."

Vera arched a brow. "And how do you suggest we keep this from spreading? It's courting season—families talk. I trust Alaric to hold his tongue, but what about his future wife? His future family? Will we place this burden on another house? There are plenty of women out there who wouldn't think twice about spilling secrets."

Lord Duskwood glanced briefly at Alaric, then back to the others. "We stabilize the situation near Velenshire before the darkness spreads any further. And... we secure the bond between our families. A union. One that strengthens our loyalty and keeps our secrets protected."

Alaric frowned, puzzled. What was that supposed to mean?

"Our families are among the very few who know the truth about Velenshire's magical history. For generations, it's been a secret passed only to the next heir, and since there's been no need to speak of it openly, things have remained quiet for a long time. But the recent rumors leave us no choice—we must address it." Lord Aron said to Alaric. "Now that you fully understand the gravity of this, and with trade becoming more unstable by the day, we must focus on protecting that knowledge while we gather information and prepare our next steps."

Lord Duskwood turned his gaze upon his father. "An arrangement between my daughter and the heir of your family would secure that secrecy. It would keep the knowledge within our bloodlines and ensure that no outside family, no foreign power, ever learns of what truly lies in Velenshire and beyond the southern territories."

His father held steady, his mother mute with downcast eyes. The truth was plain to them all.

"You are proposing a marriage?" Gaviel asked in confirmation.

"Yes," Aron replied. "Evelyne and Alaric."

Alaric's heart sank. Evelyne, his friend since childhood, was too fierce and independent to suffer being made a pawn. She would despise it, yet the arrangement lay before him, inescapable.

He cleared his throat. "With respect, Lord Duskwood, Evelyne isn't one to accept such decisions lightly. Nor, frankly, am I."

"You misunderstand. This isn't about preference; it's a necessity. Your family carries knowledge that, if mishandled, could unravel Caltheris and the entire southern lands. As your mother pointed out, we cannot risk that secret falling into the wrong hands. A union ensures that risk never becomes a reality." Lord Aron said.

Alaric's thoughts reeled. Evelyne—her laughter, her wit, her strength—she was everything he could ever want, and more beautiful than words could capture. To choose her as his wife would have been the greatest fortune of his life. But this? This *marriage alliance* robbed them of choice, turning something sacred into duty. His gaze swept the room: his father's jaw was set. The decision had already been made, and that was what cut deepest of all.

"Evelyne will hate this," he said quietly.

"That may be," Lady Celeste replied, "but she will understand, in time, the importance of what we ask."

"I don't think she will," Alaric murmured, more to himself than anyone else. His gaze remained lowered for a moment before he slowly lifted it to meet Lord Duskwood's. Then he gave a slight nod.

He would speak to Evelyne, though he had no idea how he would manage to convey this. One thing was sure: neither his life nor hers would ever be the same again.

Lady Duskwood fixed him with an assessing stare. "If you're struggling with this arrangement, Alaric, perhaps the solution is simple: win her heart. If love is what you desire in a wife, give her a reason to love you in return."

"What? You expect me to *woo* her?" Alaric echoed, disbelief plain in his voice. He swallowed hard and turned to his father, hoping for the faintest protest. Gaviel only inclined his head, affirming the necessity of the match.

He couldn't believe it. He'd known his parents were encouraging marriage this year, but he hadn't expected it to come to this. The idea of deceiving Evelyne, disguising obligation as love, left him deeply uneasy. He had hoped for something genuine, something real. *Foolish,* he thought bitterly. *Pathetic,* he corrected himself. He was naive to have ever entertained such notions.

Alaric schooled his features into a tight smile and, with a voice steadier than his heart allowed, declared, "I shall wed Lady Evelyne. It will be my honor."

"Splendid," Celeste said with a clap of her hands. "Then it's decided."

Before she could continue, Lord Duskwood cut in, shifting the conversation to the investigations planned for Velenshire, like Evelyne's marriage had been nothing more than a box to check off his agenda. Alaric remained present in the room but distant in spirit as thoughts clouded his mind. How could he face Evelyne now? The idea of lying to her gnawed at him. His honor demanded that he follow through, but his heart questioned whether the cost was too high.

***

Cillian sank deeper into the steaming bath, his muscles relaxing as the heat consumed him. The sounds of the bustling household faded into a distant hum, leaving him in a rare moment of solitude. The healers, with their endless fussing and tonics, had finally left him alone. It was the first time in days that he could simply *be*.

He closed his eyes, letting the steam caress his face as he inhaled deeply. His thoughts drifted in the quietude of this stolen moment. But as he exhaled, a subtle shift occurred. He opened his eyes to see the steam around him darkening, twisting into wisps of black that snaked through the air like tendrils of smoke. Cillian's brow furrowed, and he sat up straighter, peering through the swirling shadows. He reached his fingers out to touch them. And before he could react, the darkness surged forward, swarming him in a suffocating embrace.

He gasped, his hands clutching the tub's sides as the world dissolved into a void.

When his vision cleared, he was no longer in the familiar confines of his bath. He stood in a surreal, dreamlike landscape, a vast expanse of undulating shadows beneath a sky ablaze with red hues. And there, among the otherworldly scene, stood the white-haired woman.

She was a few paces away, her pale skin luminescent against the somber backdrop. Gone was the unsettling purr of seduction that had unnerved him during their previous encounters. Now, her expression was soft, almost welcoming.

"Cillian," she murmured, her voice a soothing melody that seemed to resonate within him.

He hesitated, his instincts urging him to remain quiet, but her gentle demeanor disarmed him.

"Why are you here?" he asked. "What do you want?"

She tilted her head, her frost-white hair shimmering in the red light. "I'm here for you," she replied. "Whenever you need someone to talk to. Someone who truly understands."

"Understands what?"

"You, of course," she answered with a wide grin. "I see you, Cillian. The real you. Not the boy everyone coddles or the fragile soul they pity. You are far more than they realize."

Her words pierced through the carefully constructed facade he had built around himself. His defenses crumbled as she echoed the doubts and insecurities he had kept hidden for so long.

"You don't know me," he muttered, his voice lacking conviction.

"Don't I?" she replied, stepping closer, her eyes gleaming with something wicked. "Aren't you the heir to Lord Aron Duskwood? The sharp-eyed and clever one who sees what others are too blind or too dull to grasp?" She paused, savoring the moment before her voice dipped lower. "That's what makes you different, Cillian. That's why you intrigue me. And that's exactly why I'm here."

A foreign thought slipped into his mind, one that didn't even feel like his own. *No one has ever truly seen you. Not even Evelyne.* His jaw tensed as he forced the thought away. *No... that's not true.* His sister knew him. She always had. Whatever this woman—this *thing*—was, it was toying with his mind.

He wanted to reject her remarks, to shove them out, but instead he asked, "Why do you care?"

Her smile softened. "Because I see potential in you. Greatness. And because I understand what it feels like to be alone."

He saw through the lie, though a treacherous part of him longed to believe it.

As she turned to leave, she leaned close, her voice a whisper against his ear. "I see you, Cillian. The true you. Don't let them hide you away."

Before he could respond, a blinding flash of red light engulfed everything, and a vivid image of a deep crimson moon seared into his mind. Its eerie glow rippled across the darkened sky, twisting and shifting as though alive.

He awoke with a start, water sloshing over the sides of the tub. His breath came in ragged gasps as he frantically scanned the room. The steam had faded back to its usual pale color, and he shook his head, trying to shake off the lingering hallucination. But the image still pulsed behind his eyes, refusing to fade.

Chapter 7

Seraphine and Aurelia had spent the afternoon meticulously preparing Evelyne for the evening's feast. Their focus was primarily on what she should say, how she should act, and the image she should project. However, Evelyne's thoughts were consumed by a more pressing concern: her mother's threat to marry her off to Lord Bavrick. The prospect filled her with dread, and she was desperate to escape the impending disaster.

Evelyne understood that not all marriages were based on passionate love. Many were arrangements of convenience, alliances formed for political or financial gain. But she had always hoped for something better than the fate that awaited her with Lord Bavrick. He was precisely the sort of gentleman who mistook silence for admiration and wealth for character.

She was to avoid him at all costs during the Stonebridge feast. The annual event was always a grand affair, with a lavish spread of food and drink and a gathering of the most prominent families in the region. Evelyne usually enjoyed the feast, particularly as the seating arrangement allowed her to converse without moving around. She could simply sit, eat, drink, and chat with those around her.

As for tonight, she would still engage in conversation, but her goal would be to catch the eye of any decent gentleman who was *not* Ivan Bavrick. She would smile, flirt, and do whatever it took to attract the attention of anyone who could offer her an escape from her mother's plans. It would be a challenge. Her mother would be keeping a close eye on her, and Lord Bavrick wouldn't be far, ready to stake his claim. But she was determined to navigate the treacherous waters of the feast and emerge victorious, with her future secured on her terms.

The grand hall of the Stonebridge Manor held a splendor Evelyne had always admired but seldom witnessed up close. The vaulted ceilings soared above, their dark oak beams carved with ancient motifs of vines and symbols. Rich tapestries adorned the walls, their embroidered tales depicting battles and alliances, the legacy of the Stonebridge family stitched into every thread. The air was rich with the scent of roasted meats, spiced wine, and fresh greenery, while a pianoforte in the corner added a gentle melody.

Banquet tables stretched the length of the hall, set beneath silver chandeliers that cast a soft, flickering light. Nobles in their finest attire filled the space, their conversations a mix of quiet scheming and lighthearted laughter. Evelyne recognized a few familiar faces but didn't linger, keeping pace with her family as they moved through the crowd.

She wore a deep emerald velvet gown that fit her perfectly. Seraphine had left her long brown hair mostly loose, pinning back one side with a delicate clip to reveal a simple silver earring. She rarely thought of herself as beautiful, but tonight, with so many eyes on her, she allowed herself to feel it. She inhaled deeply, her heart fluttering as she sensed the guests' gazes sweeping over her and her family.

Beside her, Lady Celeste moved with grace in a pale silver gown, a striking contrast to Evelyne's deeper hues, while Aurelia followed closely behind. Although married, Aurelia still attended events to uphold the Duskwood name, a steady symbol of the family's influence. And their father, dressed in black, had a quiet but undeniable presence that commanded respect without a word.

As they made their way through the hall, Evelyne kept her head high, though she couldn't help but wish her brother were there to steady her in the overwhelming crowd. It felt selfish, longing for his company when his mind wasn't ready to endure such gatherings.

Her thoughts slipped back to the brief encounter outside the library earlier that evening. She had nearly collided with Cillian as he'd rushed past, his arms overloaded with a precarious tower of books. He had barely slowed, his steps quick with purpose.

"Just need to keep myself busy tonight," he had murmured, offering a faint, distracted smile.

Evelyne had glanced at the towering stack, arching a brow. "I think all those will keep you busy for weeks."

He'd only nodded before disappearing down the hall toward his room.

Now, as the memory surfaced, she felt a pang of unease. Something about the exchange nagged at her, and she decided she would check on him before retiring for the night.

The sight of Lord Ivan Bavrick by one of the tables jolted her back to the present. His stiff posture and piercing stare set her on edge, just as they always did. Evelyne averted her eyes and let them drift across the room, eager for any distraction.

Her gaze shifted to Callista Evermere. Draped in a shimmering blue gown that accentuated her striking eyes and cascading black curls, Callista was a walking spectacle, and she knew it. The daring neckline left little to the imagination, quickly drawing the interest of the tall man beside her, whose lingering glances made his admiration clear. Annoyance flickered across Callista's face the moment she spotted Evelyne, but it vanished behind a flawless smile. She tossed her hair and laughed, the sound too polished to be real.

Evelyne could read Callista like a well-worn novel—every graceful tilt of her head, every forced laugh, choreographed to command attention. And tonight, her stage was Alaric. Yet it wasn't Callista's performance that unsettled Evelyne now, but the way Alaric seemed to still the instant he noticed her. His eyes found her and held fast, paying no mind to Callista beside him. The intensity of his stare sent a shiver through her, and she tore her gaze away, heat rising up her neck. For reasons she could not name, the weight of it left her suddenly, inexplicably unsteady.

Why was he looking at her like that? And why did her heart trip over itself in answer?

She pushed the thought aside. Tonight was about her family, about maintaining composure and not getting lost in distractions. But even as she forced herself to focus, she couldn't shake the feeling of his stare.

Celeste lightly rested her hands on Evelyne and Aurelia's elbows, her voice smooth as she said, "Now, go enjoy yourselves, but not too much." She gave Evelyne a pointed smile that made it clear she knew exactly how much her daughter despised these gatherings. Without another word, she drifted off to mingle with the other families, their father following behind her.

Evelyne exhaled slowly and turned to her sister. "Shall we get some wine?"

Aurelia, her attention fixed on the pianoforte in the corner, blinked out of her trance. "That sounds delightful."

Two glasses later, Evelyne was more than ready to leave. The conversation around her grew increasingly insufferable, full of petty gripes, romantic speculation, and foolish fawning over Gaviel Stonebridge. One woman brazenly remarked how fortunate Mrs. Stonebridge must be to share his bed, sending a ripple of giggles through the group. Did they actually enjoy these conversations? She turned to make a snide remark to Aurelia—only to realize her sister was gone.

Then, a familiar tune floated through the air, spirited and lively. Evelyne glanced toward the piano and smiled softly at the sight of Aurelia, whose hands danced over the keys with effortless joy. She shook her head, chuckling at her sister's ability to brighten even the dullest room.

"My lady," a voice purred from behind her, shattering the momentary peace she had found in watching her sister. *Oh gods, no.* Evelyne turned to see Ivan Bavrick looming over her, his eyes raking over her figure in a way that made her skin crawl.

"Lord Bavrick," she replied, forcing a polite smile onto her face.

"Please, call me Ivan," he insisted, his breath heavy with the scent of liquor.

Evelyne's stomach churned. "It would be improper, my lord," she said firmly, subtly shifting her body away from him.

Ivan was undeterred. He reached out and captured her hand, his grip uncomfortably tight. "I'd like to meet you in the gardens later," he murmured, leaning in close. "*Alone.*"

Evelyne's composure wavered for a fraction of a second. "I'm feeling quite tired," she began, desperately searching for an escape. He must have meticulously orchestrated this meeting, ensuring that his brother wouldn't interfere this time. She wouldn't be surprised if he had threatened Wesley for spiriting her away during the last ball. In fact, she couldn't even recall noticing Wesley earlier.

"Excuse me, Lord Bavrick," Alaric interjected smoothly, materializing at Evelyne's side. His smile was warm, but his eyes never left hers. "My lady, forgive my delay. We still have that discussion about your book to finish, do we not?"

Evelyne breathed a sigh of relief. "Of course," she said, her voice bright with gratitude as she reached for Alaric's hand. But before she could take it, Ivan raised her captured hand to his lips, leaving a wet, unwelcome kiss on her skin.

"I'll see you later, my lady," he said, his tone laced with a false sweetness that did nothing to mask the threat in his eyes.

As Ivan retreated, Evelyne turned to Alaric. "Thank you for that."

Alaric chuckled. "Think nothing of it. Though I do expect payment for my heroic deeds."

"And what form would this payment take?"

"Well," Alaric said, feigning seriousness, "a conversation about that book would suffice. Though I must confess, I do not know which book we discussed."

Evelyne laughed, the tension finally easing from her shoulders. "You'll have to be more specific next time you swoop in to save a damsel, Mr. Stonebridge," she teased.

"Until then, you're stuck with me improvising."

"Somehow, I think I'll manage."

Alaric peeked over his shoulder at Lord Bavrick, whose displeasure was evident in the scowl across his face. Then, he turned back to Evelyne and smiled.

"Shall we add fuel to the fire, my lady?" He brushed a hand against the small of her back, a subtle and electrifying gesture. "Join me tonight," he whispered. "It might just send the message loud and clear."

His warm touch stole Evelyne's breath for a moment, but mischief quickly lit her smile. Annoying Lord Bavrick while delighting in the regard of a man who valued her was far too delicious to pass by.

From across the table, Callista watched with thinly veiled contempt, her practiced composure doing little to hide her irritation at Evelyne's place beside Alaric. With a dramatic flourish, she leaned forward, show-casing her ample cleavage, and plastered on a smile so sugary it could induce a toothache. Evelyne had to bite back a laugh. She knew then that the night would be very interesting.

Dinner commenced, and as conversation flowed effortlessly between Evelyne, Alaric, and his companions, Callista's agitation grew increasingly evident. Every shared laugh, every whispered exchange between Alaric and Evelyne, seemed to ignite a fresh wave of anger in her.

"Why, Lady Evelyne," Callista drawled, her voice pitched to carry. "You appear remarkably at ease this evening. A rare change, I daresay, from the company you are accustomed to. Which, if memory serves, is… well, almost no one at all—unless the debutantes happen to take pity and draw you in."

Evelyne arched a brow and slowly sipped her wine before responding. "Quite right, Callista. There is something most refreshing in the company of those whose talk has substance. A rare pleasure, I assure you, especially when compared with what one endures among the debutantes."

Callista stiffened slightly. "Indeed. Though I imagine it takes time to fully grasp the intricacies of such company."

Leaning in, Evelyne gave a generous view of her neckline, but with a refinement that made Callista's earlier attempt look clumsy by comparison. "It really isn't difficult to adjust when one has a personality worth attending to, rather than relying on one's neckline to command notice." Her smile sharpened. "I've always had a talent for recognizing subtleties."

Alaric chuckled into his glass, and the others at the table exchanged glances.

"How charming," she retorted. "But do be careful, Evelyne. Men like Lord Bavrick don't take kindly to being toyed with."

"Fortunately, I have no intention of toying with anyone," she replied coolly. "That would imply a level of interest that simply isn't there."

"Well," Alaric interrupted, raising his glass, "I believe we can all agree that tonight's company has been... entertaining. Shall we have more wine?"

Evelyne nodded as she took another sip, catching Callista's look of sour discontent. *Good.*

As the evening wound down and guests began to leave, Alaric offered to escort Evelyne to the entrance hall. The gesture was simple, but she found it comforting.

"Might you come by for tea tomorrow?" Evelyne blurted before fully considering the implications of her actions.

He hesitated, studying her with that same searching look from before. It wasn't intimidating, just deep, as if he were considering the weight of what she offered. The silence that followed prickled at her nerves.

In a rush to explain herself, she added, "It's just... It would be nice to have tea with a friend instead of listening to my mother's endless complaints."

Alaric stepped closer, lowering his head as he gently took her trembling hand in his. His lips brushed softly against her knuckles. "It would be an honor to join you, Evelyne," he said softly.

The way he spoke her name without any formal title sent a peculiar thrill through her. It felt affectionate, almost seductive, and she couldn't suppress the blush that rose to her cheeks.

"Goodnight," he murmured before taking his leave.

Evelyne remained where he had left her, heart pounding. The unexpected invitation, the heat of his touch, and the sincerity in his voice all left her feeling flustered and strange.

CHAPTER 8

The gardens of Duskwood Manor were quiet except for the faint rustle of leaves and the occasional bird call. Cillian welcomed the silence and the warm spring air that brushed his face as he walked.

That woman. Her beauty lingered like a splinter in his mind, impossible to dislodge. Who was she? How had she known his name? Perhaps he was losing his sanity. It wouldn't be the first time someone in his family had.

Cillian tilted his head back, closing his eyes to soak in the sun's warmth. But as quickly as it came, the light vanished, swallowed by thick gray clouds, and a heavy pressure bore down on him. Pain struck, sharp and sudden, blurring his vision as the edges of the garden warped, twisting into darkness. A piercing headache pounded in time with his heartbeat. His legs threatened to buckle. He clutched his head, a raw groan ripping from his throat as the world folded in, collapsing until there was nothing.

His name echoed somewhere in the distance, but all he could do was watch as black mist coiled through his mind and soul, circling like a predator ready to pounce. Just as the dizziness and pain threatened to pull him under, steady hands caught him, grounding him for the briefest moment. He didn't see who it was, only that someone was there as he began to fall. But what burned into his mind before the darkness claimed him was the image of an ancient, sorrowful tree.

***

When he woke, his surroundings were different. The garden's fresh air was replaced by the faint smell of lavender and herbs in his room. A cool cloth touched his forehead, but he quickly swatted it away.

"No, please—I'm fine," he muttered, his voice hoarse.

"My lord, you collapsed—" the healer began, but Cillian's voice grew sharper.

"I said I'm fine. Just leave me alone."

The healer hesitated, concern written plainly on her face, but she obeyed, backing out of the room without another word.

Once alone, Cillian pressed his palms against his eyes and exhaled shakily. "What the hell is happening to me?" he whispered furiously, the words half plea, half curse.

With a frustrated sigh, he flung the sheets aside and strode to his desk. He needed to see it again—the tree, the moon. Grabbing a piece of parchment, he quickly began sketching the vivid images burned into his mind. His hand worked quickly, almost unconsciously, until the lines took shape beneath his fingers.

Cillian stared at the drawings, a mix of awe and dread settling in his chest. He couldn't let this go unanswered. Shoving the papers beneath a nearby book, he stood and headed for the door.

The library. If there were answers to be found, they'd be buried in those old, dusty tomes. For too long, he had relied on healers who treated him like a fragile thing to be coddled. But this didn't feel like an illness anymore. This was something darker, something ancient. As he navigated the halls, his determination solidified. If no one else could uncover the truth, then he would. Whatever this was, it wouldn't steal another year of his life.

Cillian eased open the heavy oak doors of the library, the hinges groaning in quiet protest. He cast a quick glance over his shoulder, checking that the hallway remained empty. Once satisfied he was alone, he stepped inside and shut the doors behind him with care, sealing himself within the library's silent refuge.

Bookshelves stretched toward the ceiling, packed with volumes steeped in generations of knowledge. Cillian moved swiftly, his boots thudding softly over the polished floor. Meanwhile, his thoughts raced with flashes of swirling energy, cryptic images, and the eerie power that had surged through him.

He needed answers, and he needed them now.

His hands moved urgently, pulling books from their shelves with little regard for the organized system. *History of the Southern Territories*, a heavy tome with a worn spine, was tucked under his arm. *Ethereal Bonds: Magic of the Old World*, its cover etched with arcane symbols, followed suit. *Heraldry and Sacred Signs*, a slim volume with a gilded edge, was added to the growing pile. Cillian had often wondered about the strange titles lining the library shelves, but never voiced his curiosity. Now he wished he had.

His heart pounded as he moved deeper into the labyrinth of books. He found a small, secluded table tucked away in a corner and deposited his haphazard collection with a sigh of relief.

The first volume he opened was filled with intricate illustrations of sigils and symbols, but all the images were unfamiliar and only seemed to dance and writhe before his eyes. He let out a frustrated groan, dragging his fingers through his hair. He needed to piece together what had left him so unsteady, but someone would come looking for him soon.

Privacy could only be found in his bedchamber, so he gathered the books into a towering stack that wobbled just beneath his chin, his arms aching under the weight.

As he turned toward his room, he nearly ran straight into Evelyne. The unexpected encounter startled him, but he quickly masked his surprise, trying to appear unfazed despite the teetering pile in his arms.

"Just need to keep myself busy tonight," he mumbled, offering a weak smile as he adjusted his grip on the books.

Evelyne's brow lifted in amusement. "I think all those will keep you busy for weeks," she quipped lightly.

Cillian chuckled nervously, nodding in agreement before hurrying past her toward his room.

"Don't forget to eat," she called after him. He gave a quick wave of acknowledgment, steadying the books in his arms, and didn't risk turning around.

Inside his chamber, Cillian placed the stack of books on his desk with a thud and rubbed his aching arms. The images he'd sketched earlier stared back at him. He took a deep breath, his gaze shifting from the images to the books and back again. The answers were there, somewhere within those pages. And he was determined to find them.

***

By the time his family had returned home from the Stonebridge feast, the hour was late. Yet Cillian remained awake, his attention still captivated by the open books across his desk.

He heard the soft padding of footsteps approach his door, but he didn't need to see to know it was Evelyne. Her footsteps always carried a gentle rhythm that set her apart from the rest of the household. He imagined she was coming to check on him, perhaps to share stories from the feast, to recount the conversations and laughter that had filled the evening. And as much as he yearned for her company, he also craved solitude. He needed to lose himself in his books and unravel the mysteries hidden within their pages.

With a swift motion, he blew out the candle on his desk, plunging his room into darkness. He held his breath as a knock sounded on his door.

"Cillian? Are you up?" Evelyne's voice was barely a whisper.

He remained silent, feigning sleep. After a moment's hesitation, he heard her footsteps retreat, fading into the distance.

Chapter 9

A faint bustle of activity echoed from the hall as the servants began their morning routine. Evelyne stirred, blinking sleep from her eyes as the familiar rhythm of the household signaled the start of the day. Knowing Seraphine would soon barge in, ready to yank the curtains wide and drown the room in daylight, she tossed aside her sheets and reached for her robe before the inevitable intrusion.

Downstairs, Evelyne gave her parents a brief nod before sitting beside Aurelia, who offered a quick smile before returning to the letter in her hand. The slight lift in her mood was telling—an explanation was surely coming.

Mauri, the young kitchen servant, entered the room with a tray laden with hot tea and Danishes. "Good morning, miss," she greeted Evelyne politely as she placed a teacup beside her.

"Thank you," Evelyne replied, grabbing a raspberry Danish and taking a hearty bite.

"You seemed to be enjoying yourself last night with Mr. Stonebridge," her mother remarked with a hint of curiosity.

"Surprisingly, Mother, yes," Evelyne retorted, "I did quite enjoy myself. I'd enjoy any time away from Lord Bavrick's repulsive touch." Her anger toward her mother for even entertaining the idea of a marriage to Lord Bavrick and not immediately rejecting his proposal still simmered beneath the surface.

"Perhaps you shouldn't be so ungrateful, Evelyne," Celeste remarked. "Lord Bavrick is a nice gentleman who has shown interest in you. In fact, he's the *only* man to have requested your hand in marriage."

Evelyne bit her lip furiously. Her mother's insistence on Lord Bavrick was absurd.

"Actually," she added, "I've invited Alaric for tea this morning."

Her mother raised a brow, the faintest glint of approval in her eyes. "Good," she said simply, and the family resumed their breakfast.

It wasn't until several bites in that Evelyne noticed Cillian's seat remained empty. "Where is Cillian?" she asked.

Her parents exchanged glances, but Aurelia responded, "He's probably still resting after his episode yesterday afternoon."

Evelyne stilled. "What episode?"

Aurelia, eyes still fixed on the letter, spoke again. "He dropped in the garden. Thankfully, the guards were swift enough to spare him a cracked skull on the flower bed stones. We really must send them our gratitude."

Evelyne shot up from her chair. "And no one thought to inform me?"

"We didn't want to worry you, especially before the Stonebridge dinner," her father said firmly.

"That is irrelevant and pales compared to Cillian's health," Evelyne said, her voice trembling with anger. "One of you should have said something."

"He's fine, Evelyne," her father insisted.

She was about to storm out of the dining room when Cillian entered, his hair tousled and dark circles showing under his golden eyes. He looked exhausted, but he smiled as he greeted everyone and sat down to eat.

"How are you feeling, Cillian?" their mother asked.

"I'm fine, Mother," Cillian answered calmly. "It was just a headache."

His easy dismissal felt like denial. Like a flimsy cover for what Evelyne feared was the return of the same illness that once plagued him. And as Cillian began eating, she sank back into her seat, guilt creeping in for not noticing his discomfort sooner. She, and seemingly the rest of her family, had been too absorbed in last night's preparations. And when she'd seen him before dinner, he'd appeared fine. A little on edge, perhaps, but nothing that had raised alarm.

Aurelia's chair scraped against the dining room floor as she rose abruptly, her movements filled with theatrical excitement.

"Leopold is coming home!" she exclaimed. "Oh, I simply can't wait to see him. Mother, may I be excused? I must write to him immediately."

Lady Duskwood offered a gentle smile, reaching out to clasp Aurelia's hand. "Of course, my dear," she said warmly. "What wonderful news."

Evelyne resisted the urge to roll her eyes. Aurelia hardly seemed concerned for Cillian—her presence here felt more like a placeholder until Leopold reappeared. Once he did, Evelyne knew she'd cast the rest of them aside without a second thought. *Typical,* she thought. *Self-absorbed as ever.*

Instead of letting her frustration take hold, Evelyne drew a steady breath and shifted her thoughts to the meeting with Alaric. She took a slow sip of tea, intent on grounding herself and clearing her mind.

***

Sunlight streamed through the large bay window of his father's study, an unwelcome glare that matched the thoughts crowding Alaric's mind. He sat stiffly in a high-backed chair, his hands resting on the mahogany desk, fingers idly tracing the wood's grain. Gaviel spoke of dwindling trade and the troubles in Velenshire, but Alaric's mind was elsewhere. He shouldn't have accepted Evelyne's invitation for tea. Hell, he shouldn't have let himself enjoy her company last night as much as he did. Every laugh, every glance, every inch she'd leaned closer during their exchange had left an impression he couldn't shake.

He was such a damned fool. Evelyne didn't know her marriage was already arranged, that her heart had no vote. And even though the plan was clear—make her fall in love without telling her the truth—he hated every second of it, especially knowing he was tricking someone who trusted him.

"Alaric." Gaviel's voice sliced through his thoughts, snapping him back to the present. His father leveled him with a sharp stare. "Are you listening?"

"Yes, sir," Alaric replied, straightening in his chair and bracing himself for the conversation.

Gaviel sighed and leaned forward. "As I was saying, the situation in Velenshire continues to deteriorate. There have been more disappearances near the trade outposts, most along the Mokkahli River, which is now making trade nearly impossible. The fear is spreading, and it's beginning to affect business even here in the south."

Alaric's brow furrowed. "What exactly is going on?"

"The locals speak of shadows clouding their vision, while some claim to see mist-like figures darting through the woods. Most won't even go near the forest anymore." He shook his head. "I can't say for certain what it is, Alaric. But you know the history, and the oaths we've taken."

Of course he knew. How could he forget their last conversation?

"Coal, iron, gemstones... Velenshire's entire economy hinges on them," Gaviel went on. "And if this keeps up, our trade agreements will fall apart."

Alaric nodded, his brow knitting as he considered the gravity of the situation. "What steps are being taken to investigate?"

"Guards have been sent to patrol the area but found nothing unusual. I suspect they're too afraid to dig any deeper. We need someone the people trust. Someone who can ease their fears, get them back to work, and bring me real answers."

"You want me to go," Alaric guessed, his voice flat.

Gaviel's sharp gaze softened slightly. "You have a knack for getting people to trust you, Alaric. This is more than just a trade issue; it's about maintaining our regional influence. The people of Velenshire respect our family and they need to see that we're taking their concerns seriously."

Alaric gave a curt nod, though his thoughts churned.

"Is there a problem?" his father asked.

"No," Alaric said quickly. He squared his shoulders. "I'll go."

"Good. I'll let you know when the time has come, but for now, focus on Lady Duskwood."

Guilt twisted in Alaric's gut. Right—tea with Evelyne. He had a part to play, and distractions weren't an option.

CHAPTER 10

The garden's greenery enclosed Evelyne in its usual embrace, hedges neatly trimmed and flowers adding bursts of color. But today, the space brought her no comfort. She sat at the stone table, absently running her fingers along her teacup's rim. The tea had gone cold, though she had barely noticed.

Her thoughts drifted back to Cillian. To his pale complexion and the dark smudges beneath his eyes. Her parents had kept his collapse from her, because they hadn't wanted to "spoil" her mood before the Stonebridge dinner. Their excuse had been ridiculous, and the lie still stung, but it was seeing him at breakfast that had left her truly unsettled.

The light in him had dimmed, and though it was clear he was pulling away, no one else seemed willing to admit it or offer an explanation. She wanted answers from her parents, from the healers, from Cillian himself. Instead, she sat in silence, tapping her teacup with anxious fingers. Resting her elbows on the table, she pressed her hands to her temples and let out a long breath. She had woken hopeful for a quiet morning with Alaric. Now, she just wanted it behind her.

The crunch of gravel drew her attention, making her sit up straighter and turn toward the garden's entrance. A moment later, Alaric stepped through the ivy-covered archway, his tall frame cutting a striking silhouette against the greenery. He appeared miles away in thought, but upon meeting her gaze, he composed himself and offered a polite smile.

"Good morning, Lady Evelyne."

"Good morning, Mr. Stonebridge," she replied, gesturing to the chair across from her. She noticed a slight hesitation when he reached for it, and caught the brief tap of his fingers against the table before he stopped himself. "You seem distracted," she said, tilting her head slightly. "Is everything all right?"

For a brief moment, Alaric looked surprised, but then he laughed softly, brushing a hand through his dark hair. "You caught me. My mind has been a bit... preoccupied this morning. But I promise I'm here now." He smiled at her, but it didn't quite reach his eyes.

"I see. Well, I suppose we're both a bit distracted today," she admitted, her voice quieter than intended.

Alaric leaned in, his expression gentler with concern. "What's on your mind?"

She opened her mouth to answer but stopped as a sharp cry cut through the garden. Evelyne's head snapped toward the sound, her pulse quickening. For a moment, she thought she'd imagined it. But then it came again, clearer this time, and dread coiled in her gut as she guessed who it might be.

"Cillian," she whispered, rising from her seat.

Alaric stood immediately, his hand resting lightly on her arm as if to steady her. "What's happening?"

"It's my brother," Evelyne said, already moving toward the sound.

Her heart pounded as she hurried through the garden paths, Alaric close behind. When they turned the corner, the sight before made her still.

Cillian was on his knees, his hands tightly clasped around his head as if trying to shield himself from an unbearable noise that only he could perceive. His body shook uncontrollably, each gasp blurring the line between a sob and a breath.

Evelyne was at his side in seconds, kneeling, her hand hovering helplessly above his shoulder as she searched for a way to ease his pain. "Cillian!" she said urgently. "It's me, Evelyne. You're safe. You're all right."

But Cillian seemed oblivious to her presence. His eyes were tightly shut, his lips moving silently as if he were conversing with someone. He began to rock back and forth, digging his fingernails into his face.

"Cillian, stop," Evelyne said softly, trying to hold back tears. But as the blood slid down his cheeks, she could do nothing but watch.

"Get out of my head!" Cillian screamed. Evelyne recoiled at the sound but refused to move away from him.

Alaric knelt on his other side. "Cillian," he said, firmly but smoothly. "Breathe with me. In and out. Focus on my voice."

Evelyne watched as Alaric worked to calm Cillian, his voice gentle, threading through the chaos like a tether. In that moment, she felt an overwhelming surge of gratitude for his steady presence.

After what felt like an eternity, Cillian's ragged breathing eased, and the tightness in his frame began to loosen. Everyone was quiet as he blinked back to awareness. Then, catching Evelyne's gaze, he broke. His sobs rose uncontrollably as he leaned into her, blood marking her once-pristine pink dress.

Evelyne's heart clenched as she held him close, her hands moving gently across his back in a soothing rhythm. Seeing him like this, shaken and bleeding, filled her with a sudden, bone-deep fear.

"Someone get a healer!" she screamed.

Servants rushed forward, their faces etched with worry as they lifted Cillian from Evelyne's arms and carried him away. She watched motionless, her hand lingering in the air where his head had rested.

As Cillian disappeared, Evelyne's eyes fell upon Alaric. "Thank you," she whispered.

Alaric gave a small nod, but his eyes didn't leave the direction Cillian had gone. "He'll be all right," he murmured, finally turning to face her. "He will."

He reached out, his hand resting lightly atop hers. Evelyne glanced at the contact, but unease pressed at her ribs. For all the comfort it meant to offer, they both knew better than to trust in false assurances.

"I'm so sorry." She said, tears streaming down her face. "I'm so sorry you had to witness that. I'm so, so sorry. I saw him struggling, slipping away… and instead of doing everything I could to help him, I turned a blind eye and hoped it was just a phase again." Her voice cracked with guilt and shame. "I smiled and pretended everything was fine. I played the part of the dutiful daughter, focusing on appearances and pleasing my parents…" She trailed off, unable to continue. Then she took a shuddering breath and confessed, "I chose my pride over him. Over my brother. I failed him when he needed me the most." She looked to Alaric. "Do you know what that makes me? A coward. A selfish, spineless coward."

He moved closer. "You're not a coward, Evelyne. You were doing what you thought was right—what you were taught to value. That doesn't make you weak. It makes you human."

She shook her head, anger bubbling to the surface. "Don't justify it. Don't excuse what I did or didn't do. He needed me, and I—" Her words faltered, a sob escaping despite her efforts to contain it.

He squeezed her hands. "And you're here now," he said quietly. "You're here, and that matters. You're trying. That matters."

She allowed herself to meet his gaze fully for the first time, and the empathy she found there tightened her throat. "But what if it's too late? What if I've already failed him?"

"It's never too late to fight for the people we love. Not until the last moment."

"What if I cannot mend what's broken in him?"

He offered a soft, almost wistful smile. "Then let it be our burden to share. You don't have to bear it alone." Alaric wrapped his arms around her, his fingers brushing through her hair with surprising tenderness. "I'm your friend," he whispered. "And I'll be right here—no matter what."

She didn't reply, only leaned closer, letting herself be held, letting the silence say what words couldn't.

When she withdrew from his embrace, she quickly blotted her eyes and pressed her palms to her cheeks, eager to restore her composure. "I must check on him," she said, managing a small smile. "Perhaps we might resume this another day?"

"Of course." Alaric smiled back as he turned to go.

Once he was out of sight, she rushed to Cillian's bedchamber.

The door was cracked open slightly, and as she approached, her parents' hushed voices reached her ears. Evelyne peeked inside and saw Cillian lying still on the bed, his face freshly cleaned but bearing scratches on his temples. A healer had likely given him a potent tonic, leaving him in a deep, necessary sleep.

In the corner of the room, her parents spoke in low tones, their expressions etched with worry. "I don't know what to do anymore, Celeste," her father murmured, frustration threading through his voice. "He can't stay here. It's drawing too much attention, and now these episodes are spilling beyond the walls of this house. Alaric witnessed it today, for heaven's sake."

"And where, exactly, do you suggest we send him, Aron?" her mother shot back. "We can't risk the southern lands, where gossip spreads like wildfire. And I will not have my son sent north!"

The sharpness in her voice startled Evelyne. She hadn't expected such fierce protectiveness, hadn't realized her mother cared so deeply. Were they genuinely considering sending Cillian away?

"I need time to think," her father retorted. "The healers are useless. They've given us no answers and have yet to fix him."

"Perhaps he doesn't need fixing," her mother snapped. "Perhaps he just needs someone to listen to and understand him."

Evelyne's eyes darted back to her brother, his face serene in sleep, unaware of the conversation swirling around him. She prayed he couldn't hear their words; this was not a discussion he should ever have to bear.

"I said I need time. Tomorrow, I'm meeting with the Stonebridge family to handle our other crisis. If Alaric breathes a word of what he saw today, I'll have to explain it to Gaviel."

"Fine," her mother replied.

Evelyne heard their footsteps approaching and quickly slipped away to the safety of her room. Her mind spun with questions. Could she talk to Alaric before the meeting? Urge him to stay quiet? She doubted he would speak out—despite his teasing nature, he was honorable.

She had to get out. Had to run until the wind stung her face and the pounding of her steps chased away the whirlwind in her head. The day had been unbearable and she couldn't sit with her thoughts any longer—she needed an escape, even if only for a little while.

Stripping off her blood-speckled dress, Evelyne let the garment slip to the floor before stepping into a pair of Cillian's old, soft-fitting trousers, then pulled a loose white tunic over her head, its fabric draping easily around her frame. Turning to the mirror, she caught sight of her puffy, reddened eyes. With trembling hands, she swept her hair back and began braiding it, each twist and knot down her back a quiet act of regaining control. By the time the braid was secured, she felt steadier, though the ache in her chest remained.

She paused to take a deep breath before stepping outside. Once the spring air softly brushed her face, she broke into a run without another thought.

CHAPTER 11

Though it tugged at her heart to leave Cillian unchecked, Evelyne knew he needed rest more than anything. So she let him be, resolving to wait until morning, and sent word inviting him for a walk at first light.

The air was cool and carried the scent of coming rain. Evelyne and Cillian walked carefully along the damp path beyond the garden, the manor standing behind them. Somewhere at Stonebridge Manor, their father was deep in his meeting... hopefully focused on trade and alliances, and not Cillian's condition.

Evelyne glanced at her brother. He looked pale but steady, the profound exhaustion from the night before softened in the morning light. She had insisted on this walk, eager to pull him away from the hovering servants and suffocating care. And beneath the open sky, he looked better. More at ease.

Her mother's words lingered in her mind: *"Perhaps he just needs someone to listen to him."* Watching Cillian cautiously, she wondered if her mother had been right. For now, Evelyne let the silence settle between them, setting aside her fears and questions. This moment was for him.

When Cillian finally spoke, it was barely above a whisper. "I'm sorry, Evelyne," he said, his gaze fixed on the dirt path ahead. Every syllable sounded heavy with guilt, leeching the strength from his voice. "For everything. For scaring you. I'm... trying to understand it myself."

Evelyne halted mid-step, turning to face him fully, her expression softening. "You don't need to apologize to me, Cillian. I want to understand. Please, tell me what's happening."

He hesitated, the muscles in his jaw tightening as he glanced toward the horizon.

"I don't think this is an illness," he admitted. "Not the way they say it is." He raked a hand through his hair, the motion frantic, like he was trying to claw the thoughts from his mind. "There's a woman. I keep seeing her. But it's more than that. It feels like something is inside me... waiting. Waiting for me to surrender to it. And I see these images..." He paused, as if thinking. "Strange, symbolic things I can't explain."

The faint quiver in his voice sent a ripple of unease through her, but she forced the fear down. Now wasn't the time for panic; he needed calm. Steeling herself, she asked, "A woman? Like someone in a dream?"

"No," he snapped, his head jerking toward her. "Not dreams. It's different. She's... *it's* there, in my mind. Not just when I sleep, but when I'm awake, too. And the symbols feel like something else—like a signal. Or a warning. Or—" He broke off, dragging his gaze down, hands trembling. "I don't know," he muttered. "I try to block her out, Evelyne. But it's like something's inside me, slowly eating away at my soul."

Evelyne stepped closer, gently resting a hand on his arm. "Cillian, you're not going insane," she said firmly. "I believe you. Whatever this is, we'll figure it out. Together."

He met her gaze, and for a moment, pain gave way to a flicker of hope. "You mean that?" he asked softly.

"Of course I do," she replied without hesitation. "But you have to tell me what you need. What can I do to help?"

He let out a tired breath, his shoulders sagging. "I wish I knew," he murmured. "But I have to keep reading. I have to understand what's happening." His eyes flicked toward the distant sky. "That's why I had those books with me."

"Oh," was all she managed to say. "I'll be here, Cillian. Whenever you need me."

He gave a small nod in thanks and kept walking.

Evelyne watched him closely, noting how the open air had eased something in him. It was clear that isolation and whispered consultations weren't helping; their father's methods had done little but make him feel more confined.

A cool raindrop kissed her cheek, pulling her gaze to the darkening sky, but she let Cillian continue ahead, choosing not to interrupt the calm he'd found. Still, her thoughts stirred. When her father returned, she would speak with him. Cillian didn't need more rest; he needed direction. Something to hold on to. Something that reminded him of who he was.

Though the rain crept in and the cold clung to her, she stayed close, savoring the rare peace of simply being with her brother.

***

Cillian remained in his dimly lit chamber, having told the servants to let his parents know he would dine alone. He wasn't sick, not in the way they thought, but he couldn't handle another night of their wary glances and careful words. He needed to understand it all, but the books he'd taken from the library offered little clarity; only fragmented tales of ancient witches and lost magic that felt exaggerated, even absurd. Yet he couldn't dismiss them entirely. This couldn't be magic; the idea was ridiculous. But it wasn't an illness either—not one that could be treated with tonics or endless examinations. Once, he had believed the healers' theories of possible neurological disorders, but after countless tests and failed treatments, their explanations no longer satisfied him.

Today's walk with Evelyne had offered a rare sense of peace. She hadn't judged or pried, just listened. He hadn't told her everything, not the full extent of the visions or the symbols that haunted him, but speaking even a little of it out loud had lessened the weight on his chest. Still, the visions remained: a gnarled tree and fleeting glimpses of a crimson moon. They felt carved into him, and were impossible to ignore.

Seated at his desk, Cillian began sketching the tree again, just as he had the other night. His hand moved on its own, tracing its twisted form, but his thoughts drifted elsewhere. To the woman in his visions. Draped in black, with snow-pale hair and lips like fresh blood. Her smile walked the line between enchanting and cruel. Beautiful, yes—but there was danger in it. And her voice? That was the real weapon. Each word a trap, soft-spoken and barbed.

He hated that her attention meant anything to him, that her words could reach a part of him he didn't even recognize. He wasn't like the other young men. He stuck to quiet corners, lost in books, watching rather than participating in conversation.

Maybe that was why her attention felt so thrilling.

The last time she'd appeared, he had been outside, though he couldn't remember why. One moment, he was at the breakfast table, and the next, he was crouched in the dirt with Evelyne and Alaric hovering over him. The memory sent a shiver through him. What had they seen? What had he done?

He shook himself free of the thought and opened another book, flipping through pages he had already read twice. His eyes traced the faded text, but his concentration faltered as a knock sounded at his door.

"Come in," he called, hurriedly closing the book and sliding it onto the shelf.

His father entered, the sharp lines of his tailored suit cutting an imposing figure in the small room. Cillian straightened instinctively. His father rarely visited his room.

"I met with Gaviel Stonebridge today. Alaric, thankfully, did not mention your... episode."

The word struck him like a blow. Shame coiled in his chest. Cillian looked down at his desk, unable to meet his father's gaze. "I'm sorry," he muttered.

Brushing past the apology, Aron moved farther in and took a seat at the bed's edge. What startled Cillian wasn't the intrusion, but the unexpected gentleness in his father's expression.

"Evelyne told me she walked with you today. She believes it did you good to get out of the house."

Cillian nodded, unsure how to respond.

After a pause, his father spoke again. "I need to go to Velenshire tomorrow for business. I think it would be beneficial for you to come along."

Cillian wasn't sure about the offer, but his father didn't make gestures like this often. So he didn't overthink the reason behind it—just the tiny hope that his father was making an effort was enough for him to accept.

"Alright," was all he could manage.

His father nodded once, rising to his feet without another word. He left the room as briskly as he had entered, leaving Cillian to sit in the heavy silence that followed.

Cillian turned back to his desk, his gaze settling on the sketch of the tree. Whatever awaited him in Velenshire, he clung to the hope that it might bring him closer to unraveling the mystery of this curse, or whatever force had taken hold of him. Velenshire was renowned for its extravagant library, a trove of ancient tales and records chronicling the continent's history. Perhaps, if he could steal a moment away from his father, he might delve into its shelves and uncover the answers he so desperately sought.

***

The streets of Velenshire pulsed with quiet energy as Cillian stepped beyond the lantern glow and fading hum of night. Slick cobblestones shimmered beneath the dim light, and shadows stretched across buildings of worn stone and dark wood, their peaked roofs jutting like silent sentinels into the star-flecked sky. The crisp air carried the scents of smoke and earth, and the faint sweetness of roasted chestnuts. Yet beneath it all, something hung in the silence. Like the town itself was holding its breath.

Cillian wandered the streets while his father met with Lord Shaw to discuss some vague matter of business, details he was never privy to. Truthfully, he was relieved not to be dragged along. He preferred the freedom to explore on his own. Each turn revealed another quiet corner of Velenshire, its charm unfolding around him.

His attention snagged on a swaying shop sign that read *Relics and Refinements*. Something about it beckoned, like an unseen thread drawing him forward.

As he stepped inside, a bell chimed softly, and warm, jasmine-scented air wrapped around him. Shelves brimming with polished stones and tiny, elaborate figurines made the shop feel like it had barely enough room to breathe.

Behind the counter stood the shopkeeper, her kind smile paired with a crown of brown curls laced with silver that glimmered like moonlight in the glow of the lamps. Her eyes seemed to pierce through Cillian's carefully constructed composure as if she could sense his unease, his questions.

"Evening, young man. What can I help you find?"

Cillian cleared his throat. "Good evening. I'm looking for the library. I was told it's near, but I have lost my way."

The woman's smile widened, revealing slight laugh lines around her mouth. "Ah, you'll find it just a street over. Follow this road until you see the baker's shop, then turn left. You can't miss it."

"Thank you. You've been most helpful."

She chuckled softly. "Go on, now. Don't keep the books waiting."

He left the shop with clear directions but an unsettled sense that the woman knew more than she let on.

The path she described led him to the library, a building that loomed like an ancient guardian in the heart of Velenshire. Its columns rose toward the heavens, their surfaces etched with weathered patterns. The air inside was cooler, laced with the scent of ancient parchment and timeworn bindings. Towering shelves loomed on either side, their sheer height and closeness casting the aisles in quiet shadow. As Cillian followed the elderly librarian, he let his fingers drift across the spines, each one whispering of forgotten knowledge.

When he found himself alone, a hush settled over the space. Then something stirred. It wasn't a sound exactly, but a sensation, like a note held just beyond hearing. It drifted through the silence and curled around his thoughts, coaxing him forward. As if the books themselves were singing, and one voice among them was calling just to him.

His fingers hovered, then closed around a particular volume: *The Concord of Shadows: A Forgotten Rite*. Its cover was cracked and blackened with age, yet it thrummed faintly under his touch. He flipped through the pages, skimming them to grasp what secrets the book might hold, until his eyes fell on an illustration—a tree. Almost the very tree from his visions, except this one breathed with life. His heart plummeted.

Snapping the book shut, he pressed it tightly under his arm, fearing it might vanish, and carried it to the counter. The librarian's eyes lingered on the volume, her lips pressing together briefly before she handed him a cloth bag.

"Treat it well," she said softly. "Some things find you when you're ready."

CHAPTER 12

A few days had passed since Evelyne had urged her father to consider how beneficial it might be for Cillian to spend some time away from the house. To her surprise, he had brought Cillian along to Velenshire. Since their return, Evelyne hadn't interacted much with her brother; he spent most of his time buried in the library or tucked away in his room.

Now, as she stared out of the carriage window, watching the vibrant greenery of fields and trees gradually give way to the bustling cobblestone streets of Caltheris, the sight of the grand market looming closer made thoughts of Cillian drift away. Despite Aurelia's excitement, Evelyne was less than thrilled at the prospect of shopping for the upcoming ball. Her sister's insistence had been overwhelming, and left little room for refusal.

"But you simply must come to help me find a dress for my last ball before returning home," she had pleaded. "And you, too, might find something rather nice! Pleeeease?" She had drawn out the word, a soft, irresistible coaxing. Evelyne had agreed, figuring some fresh air couldn't hurt.

The sun had already begun to dip below the horizon when their carriage rattled to a stop. The streets were alive with merchants calling out to shoppers. As they stepped out, Aurelia immediately linked arms with Evelyne and guided her toward the market, her excitement palpable.

The jewelry shop they entered first was elegant, its wooden shelves lined with velvet trays displaying glimmering treasures under golden lamps. Aurelia's face lit up as she picked up a necklace adorned with intricate emerald drops.

"Evelyne, look at this!" she exclaimed, holding it up to her neck and turning to admire her reflection. "Isn't it exquisite? Imagine how it would catch the light during the ball."

Evelyne smiled. "Yes, it is stunning. Almost distractingly so. Do you want people staring at the necklace or looking at you?"

Aurelia laughed, brushing off her remark. "Don't be ridiculous, sister. Accessories elevate an outfit. Speaking of which, these earrings would be perfect for you!" She held out a pair of sparkling teardrop gems.

"Perfectly unnecessary," Evelyne quipped, inspecting them with feigned interest. "But if I must endure the season, I might as well blind everyone with my dazzling lobes."

Aurelia shook her head with an affectionate grin. "You're hopeless, Evelyne."

"Hopeless but amusing," Evelyne shot back, placing the earrings back on the display.

After some time, Aurelia clasped her hands together decisively. "I think I've seen enough here. There's a dress shop down the street I must visit before we leave. Will you come with me?"

Evelyne paused, then gestured vaguely toward the street. "Actually, I spotted an antique bookstore nearby. I'll meet you at the carriage in an hour—or the dress shop if I get bored of musty old tomes."

Aurelia sighed dramatically. "Fine, but don't lose track of time. I'm not waiting all evening for you to dig through dusty books."

"Noted," Evelyne said with a mock salute, earning an eye roll from Aurelia as she turned to leave.

Evelyne stepped out of the bustling market street and into the hushed serenity of the bookshop. The world seemed to still as she crossed the threshold, the lively clamor of nobles and merchants replaced by the soothing creak of wooden floors and the faint rustle of pages. The air smelled faintly of cedar and parchment, a nostalgic aroma that wrapped around her like an old friend. She moved slowly through the aisles, her gloved fingers brushing over leather-bound spines embossed with faded gold titles.

"Looking for anything in particular?" came a gentle voice.

Evelyne turned to find the shopkeeper watching her. He was an older man, his eyes glinting with the mischief of a thousand untold stories. A wiry gray beard framed his warm, knowing smile.

"Not exactly," she replied, tucking a stray lock of hair behind her ear. "Something for my brother. He's been... unwell."

The man nodded and disappeared behind a wall of books without a word. Evelyne watched, a faint unease prickling at her, but he returned moments later with a small book. Its leather cover was worn, but it was clear it had been cherished.

"This," he said, holding the book out to her, "is for him."

Evelyne's brow furrowed as she studied the weathered volume. Its deep green cover bore intricate gold lettering. The title, *The Lantern's Keeper*, sparked curiosity within her.

"What is it?" she asked.

As the man shifted, she met the unwavering gaze of his gray-blue eyes. "It's a story," he said, pausing just long enough for the meaning to deepen. "And perhaps... a guide for *him*."

"For him?" she repeated, her fingers brushing against the edge of the book as though it might burn her. "How could you possibly know what he—"

"A good bookseller always knows," he interrupted with a wink.

He placed the book in her hands. And though Evelyne still didn't understand, its weight brought a quiet comfort. As her hands closed around it, a strange feeling rose in her chest. Like a hum of recognition, or a sense of connection.

"It feels... right," she murmured, half to herself.

The old man only smiled and whispered, "I knew it would be."

She paid for the book and tucked it into her coat pocket before leaving the shop. Outside, the market buzzed around her, but Evelyne's mind stayed on the book and the strange encounter. Lanterns glowed as nobles drifted between stalls, and she offered polite smiles, eager to reach the carriage and examine her gift. Yet as she walked, the streets suddenly felt unfamiliar. Evelyne paused, realizing she had taken a wrong turn.

The crowd thinned, and the market chatter seemed to fade into an unsettling quiet. Her pulse quickened as she tried to retrace her steps, her hand tightening instinctively around the book in her pocket. Spinning on her heel, she sought to rejoin the busy thoroughfare when a shadow fell across her path.

"Lady Evelyne," came a voice she knew all too well.

Lord Ivan Bavrick approached slowly, a smile on his lips, his steps encroaching on her space.

She offered a curt nod, masking her unease. "Good evening, Lord Bavrick."

"It's a shame we were interrupted the other night," he said, stepping closer. "I was enjoying our conversation."

Evelyne's discomfort grew as his words slurred slightly. The scent of wine on his breath was unmistakable.

"I'm afraid I must get back to my sister," she said lightly, attempting to move past him.

"Oh, come now," he said, blocking her path. "Just a few words. I've been looking forward to seeing you again." He looked down at her hands, clutching her coat. "I've been waiting to be alone with you."

She offered a tight smile, trying to defuse the situation. "Perhaps another time."

She tried to push past him, and his expression darkened. His hand shot out, gripping her wrist tightly.

"You're quite the beauty, Lady Evelyne. But I don't appreciate being made a fool of."

"I don't know what you are talking about." Evelyne tried to shake her wrist from his grip. "Let me go," she demanded, panic rising as he dragged her into a shadowed alley.

He shoved her against the cold brick wall, his body pinning hers in place. "No one's watching," he murmured against her neck.

Bile filled her throat as he brushed his fingers against her cheek. She thrashed against him. His nearness made her skin crawl, and all she wanted was for him to move away.

"Let go, Ivan!" She threw her weight against him, desperate to escape, but instead of freedom, she felt him press in closer.

His repulsive lips grazed her neck, and he let out a groan of pleasure as his foul hands crept beneath her skirts.

She was shouting now. "Stop it! Get your hands off me!"

But the alley walls seemed to swallow her cries. Tears began blurring her vision as he started ripping at her undergarments and touching her. She knew all too well what he was intending, and no matter how much she struggled, she couldn't break free from his unyielding grip. She was going to vomit.

"Stop it!" she tried to scream, her voice now a quiet rasp.

"Hold your tongue," he said through clenched teeth, covering her mouth with a rough palm. "You would do well to show your future husband the deference he is due."

Husband? She would sooner die than wed such a loathsome brute. The very notion of becoming his wife was so revolting it spurred her into action, and she sank her teeth into his hand with all the force she could muster.

He recoiled with a growl, then struck her hard across the cheek.

"A wife ought to know her place," he hissed, seizing her more firmly as he lowered his mouth toward her chest.

Panic flared as his grip locked around her like iron, impossible to escape. And then, as the cruel truth of her helplessness took hold, a faint, broken whimper escaped her lips—a sound heavy with anguish and the beginning of surrender.

He was monstrous. Vile beyond words. A man devoid of decency, or even a shred of humanity. She shut her eyes tightly, steeling herself for the horror she could no longer prevent. But as despair threatened to swallow her whole, a furious voice broke through the darkness like a crack of thunder.

"Let her go!"

Both Evelyne and Ivan froze. Alaric stood at the mouth of the alley, his eyes dark and his posture radiating menace.

Lord Bavrick released Evelyne with a laugh, raising his hands in mock innocence. "Perhaps you should tell this lady to stop being such a tease. She—"

Alaric closed the distance in a flash, his fist colliding with Ivan's jaw. The force sent Ivan staggering backward, nearly collapsing to the ground.

"If I ever see you lay a hand on another woman again," Alaric growled, "I'll kill you."

Ivan mumbled a curse beneath his breath and stumbled out of the alley, one hand pressed to his face.

Though his hands were no longer on her, Evelyne remained frozen. She could only shrink deeper into the wall, her body trembling as she clutched her coat to her chest like a shield.

Alaric approached cautiously and extended a hand. "Evelyne?" he asked softly.

Unable to speak, she practically fell into his arms. His hold was steady, offering the reassurance she desperately needed. Without a word, he led her back to the carriage, his presence grounding her as she struggled to calm herself.

At the carriage, her sister was waiting. Aurelia's usual brightness dimmed the moment she saw Evelyne's tear-streaked face, her expression now marked by concern.

"What happened?" she asked, her voice sharp with worry.

Evelyne opened her mouth, but no sound came. She simply shook her head, unable to force the words past the knot in her throat.

"Evelyne," Aurelia said again, more insistently this time, alarm creeping into her tone. But before she could press further, Alaric met her gaze with a look that said everything without speaking: *not now*.

To Evelyne's surprise, Aurelia actually listened. She sat, lips pressed tight. The silence between them deepened, and Evelyne was grateful; words would have broken her.

As Alaric turned to go, Evelyne reached out with trembling fingers, grazing his sleeve. Her voice barely rose above a whisper. "Stay with me... please."

He hesitated for only a moment before easing down beside her, wrapping her gently in his arms as the carriage rolled toward Duskwood Manor. She needed something—someone—to anchor her, and in that moment, only he offered even the faintest sense of safety. She clung to that, and to him.

CHAPTER 13

As the manor came into sight, a faint sense of calm settled over Evelyne. Alaric assisted her and Aurelia from the carriage and accompanied them toward the steps, his nearness a reminder that the danger had passed. Evelyne's pace slowed, and soon Aurelia moved ahead. Her sister glanced back, a trace of worry in her eyes, but held her tongue. Whatever she perceived was enough. She disappeared through the door, leaving Evelyne and Alaric standing together beneath the gentle glow of the lanterns.

Evelyne turned slowly to face Alaric, and he hesitated before moving closer, as if afraid she might retreat. Something in her gaze must have stirred him, because his blue eyes now carried a sorrowful depth.

"I'm truly sorry for what you have endured, Evelyne," he said sincerely. "He is a wretched excuse for a man, and I swear to you—he will not escape justice."

She regarded him for a moment before taking his hands and lifting them to her lips. Her kiss upon his knuckles conveyed what words could not. When her eyes met his again, a single tear slipped free.

"Thank you," she whispered.

Alaric's expression softened. "Of course, my lady."

"Please stay a bit longer," she murmured, turning toward the manor with her hand resting lightly on his arm. She led him forward, and he followed without resistance.

Inside, Evelyne made for the library and shrugged off her overcoat, carefully laying it over an armchair to keep the book she had brought for Cillian from tumbling to the floor. She eased herself onto the library's familiar leather couch, its worn cushions embracing her as she sank. Her body felt heavy with emotion, and the warmth of the room and the crackling fireplace brought little comfort. Next to her, Alaric settled at the opposite end of the couch, his posture seemingly at ease, though his gaze held a contained intensity.

Moments later, Mauri appeared with steaming refreshments, setting them down gently before retreating. Time blurred. Evelyne wasn't sure if minutes or hours passed as they sat there in silence, and her hands still trembled as she cupped her tea. She hadn't spoken a word since stepping inside, and Alaric, true to his nature, hadn't pushed her.

Evelyne glanced at him, noting the attentiveness in his eyes as they lingered on her.

"If you would prefer solitude, I shall take my leave," he offered softly.

She shook her head. "No. I would much rather you stayed, if it is not an imposition."

"An imposition?" His lips curved faintly. "Never. I would sooner remain, if only to be certain you are truly well."

The tension within Evelyne eased, and her eyes remained upon Alaric longer than propriety allowed. Something tender flickered across his face, and the look was enough to startle her from her thoughts. She cleared her throat.

"Will you remain here tonight? With me?" she asked.

His brows lifted slightly. "If that's what you wish."

"It is."

Alaric stood and began unbuttoning his frock coat. As he kicked off his boots and peeled off the heavier layers, Evelyne turned her gaze aside, a blush creeping up her neck.

"Relax, Ev. I'm not stripping down to my undershorts."

"Oh, hush," she said, her face growing even warmer. "I was just trying to be polite."

"No need for that with me," he said with a roguish grin. "I'm not shy about what I've got."

"My goodness, Alaric, just... go to sleep," she huffed, turning away and tucking her knees to her chest.

His restless movements caught her attention a few moments later when his feet repeatedly brushed against hers as he struggled to find a comfortable position. Feeling exasperated and unusually bold, Evelyne stood and crossed the distance between them. Without a word, she crawled into his arms, her movements slow. Alaric stilled at first, surprised, but quickly adjusted, lifting his arm to make room for her to settle against him. The heat radiating from his body enveloped her, and his steady heartbeat soothed her frayed nerves.

His fingers began to graze lightly along her arm, a rhythmic touch that grounded her. *You're safe*, his actions seemed to say, though he remained silent until she began to drift.

Before she slipped into a peaceful sleep, he whispered, "He will pay for this."

Evelyne placed her hand atop his in quiet acknowledgment, a thank you that needed no words.

***

When she woke the following day, Alaric was gone. The faint impression of where he'd slept remained on the couch, and she wondered if he'd left to avoid her reaction. But as she traced the spot where he had been, a small smile crossed her lips.

Evelyne needed to feel clean again. The memory of Ivan's hands on her, his unwanted touch on her arms, legs, and neck, clung to her like a film she couldn't wash away. A wave of nausea hit the moment she reached the bathing chamber. She barely made it to the basin before vomiting, then slumped onto the cool floor, drained. Curled up there, she waited for the queasiness to subside, her mind replaying fragments of the night she desperately wanted to forget.

She still couldn't fathom how Alaric had found her. Had it been luck? Instinct? A protective intuition that had led him to the market at the right moment? She hadn't asked; the words seemed impossible to form. Yet, beneath the trauma, she was profoundly grateful for his intervention.

Moments later, Seraphine hurried into the chamber—no doubt having heard Evelyne retching. She didn't press her with questions, didn't pry, just began drawing the bath in a comforting silence. Though Evelyne hadn't spoken a word of it, the entire household must have known Alaric had stayed the night in the library with her. Servants always found their ways to notice—and to whisper—but thankfully, none had intruded. After last night, Evelyne couldn't bring herself to care about household gossip or her parents' disapproval. Nothing mattered now but banishing the horror that still clung to her.

Once the bath was prepared, Seraphine left without a word, closing the door softly behind her. Evelyne slipped into the steaming water, sinking lower and lower until the heat surrounded her. She let her head dip beneath the surface, her face fully submerged, shutting out the world and its noise. Silence wrapped around her like a cocoon, offering a momentary escape from the storm in her mind.

She surfaced for air, inhaling deeply before slipping under again. Each time, she held her breath as long as she could, the ache in her chest becoming a temporary distraction from the pain elsewhere. When she finally sat up for good, her breathing was ragged.

She scrubbed her body again and again, her motions mechanical, the soap working into her skin until her hands burned red. Arms, shoulders, legs—each part received the same treatment, as if sheer determination could rid her of Lord Bavrick's touch. Her skin stung, raw and tender, but she didn't stop. Not until exhaustion overtook her, and the water around her was cold. Only then did she lean back against the tub's edge, her head tilted toward the ceiling, a tear sliding down her cheek.

A soft knock interrupted the quiet of the bathing room. Evelyne lifted her head from where it rested, her damp hair clinging to her cheeks and shoulders.

"It's me," Aurelia's gentle voice called from the other side.

"Come in," Evelyne said hoarsely. She didn't care about her state of undress; modesty felt inconsequential after last night.

Aurelia entered, her presence bright as ever. She wore a delicate spring dress of soft green, her golden hair swept into an elegant half-up style, her features adorned with just enough cosmetics to enhance her natural beauty. Evelyne stared momentarily, struck by how her sister always seemed to shine with such radiance.

"Mother asked me to go back to the market today," Aurelia began, fiddling with the bracelet on her wrist. "She wants to pick up more decorations for the ball. I thought I'd look at those earrings you liked. Oh, and I never did get a dress last night, so I figured—"

"Aurelia," Evelyne interrupted. She couldn't bear to sit through idle chatter, not now.

Aurelia stopped mid-sentence, her lips pressing into a thin line.

"Lord Bavrick found me at the market last night," Evelyne began, her voice trembling despite her effort to keep it steady. "He pulled me into a hidden alley, and—"

Her fingers clenched the edge of the tub, knuckles blanching as the memory clawed its way back. "Pinned me against the bricks so I couldn't escape."

Before she could say more, Aurelia crossed the room in an instant, dropping to her knees beside the tub. "And Alaric found you?" she asked, reaching for Evelyne's hands.

"Yes," Evelyne breathed. "He found me—before it got any worse."

The horror in Aurelia's eyes said enough; she didn't need details to understand what had happened.

"I'm so sorry," she whispered, her voice breaking. The words undid Evelyne. Tears welled, then fell in a flood as everything poured out—the fear, the anger, the humiliation. Between trembling breaths and quiet sobs, she told Aurelia everything.

"He's a monster, Evelyne. I'll not allow our parents to see you wed to him. Mother must be told."

"No!" Evelyne said, shaking her head fiercely. "I cannot tell her. I cannot tell anyone."

Aurelia squeezed Evelyne's hands. "You do not have to say a word," she whispered. "I will tell Mother. Men like Ivan must not be allowed to go unchallenged—never again. They ought to be punished, or at the very least prevented from taking innocent wives."

Evelyne stared at her, the phrase *go unchallenged* echoing in her mind. What did Aurelia mean by that? She caught a flicker of pain in her sister's eyes, something deeper than sympathy. A slow, cold understanding crept over her.

"Aurelia... has this happened to you?" she asked.

Aurelia hesitated. Then, she spoke softly.

"Not Leopold. Never him. But years ago, a foul man—one much like Lord Bavrick—took something from me. And you know how society is. Women cannot be seen as *ruined*, not when marriage is their only future."

Evelyne's heart broke at the admission. Her perfect, radiant sister had carried her burden of pain beneath a mask of strength and beauty.

"I'm sorry, Aurelia. I never knew."

Aurelia gave a faint, bittersweet smile. "It's in the past. Perhaps I shall share the story at another time. Besides, I've found happiness now—with Leopold. He makes me feel safe. Loved."

Evelyne nodded, silently vowing to cherish her brother-in-law for being the light Aurelia needed. Sensing her sister didn't want to linger on her own story, she said, "Thank you."

Aurelia stood, retrieving a towel from the nearby rack. She draped it over Evelyne's shoulders, brushing a strand of wet hair from her face.

"That's what sisters are for," she said, giving Evelyne one last reassuring squeeze before leaving.

Chapter 14

Cillian ran his fingers along the wood grain of his desk, the slight motion grounding him as his thoughts swirled. Breakfast had been quieter than usual, and Evelyne's absence hadn't gone unnoticed. *Odd*, he thought, though he'd overheard servants murmuring about Alaric Stonebridge spending the night in the library with her. Servants constantly gossiped, and Cillian had a habit of catching their whispers. His parents hadn't seemed concerned, likely knowing it wasn't romantic. Still, something had happened, and he hoped Evelyne would tell him soon. Even Aurelia, usually full of energy, had been uncharacteristically quiet.

The unease wasn't just in the room but in him, too. There was too much on everyone's mind and far too much on his own. Last night, as he'd pored over the same borrowed book from Velenshire for the third time, another vision had seized his thoughts. It always began with her—the woman who invaded his mind—followed by an image. This time, the vision had brought more than the cursed tree. Wild, unnatural red eyes had pierced the darkness and stared into him until the world snapped back into place.

What did it all mean? The visions felt disjointed, as if they had nothing to do with the strange presence stirring within him. They always came after the white-haired woman faded from sight.

In the book, he found an illustration of a tree strikingly similar to the one in his visions. But the tree on the page was vibrant, its branches full and thriving, like a symbol of resilience. In his mind, it was nothing but a shadow of itself. The exact shape, unmistakable, yet lifeless. Its skeletal branches stretched into a silver haze, reaching for something out of its grasp.

He didn't want to think about the darker parts of the hallucination and the way his thoughts spiraled in its wake. His mind had been a battlefield recently, caught between what he knew to be real and what felt insidiously vivid.

Cillian heard a soft knock at the door, and turned just as Evelyne stepped in. She held something close to her chest, her damp hair curling around her shoulders and clinging to her back. There was a faint crease in her brow, which he recognized as worry, though she seemed determined to mask it.

"I thought of you," she said, stepping closer and extending the object toward him—a small, leather-bound book with a deep green cover. The title caught his eye: *The Lantern's Keeper*.

"Something I found in the market," she added, a shrug accompanying her words as though downplaying its significance. But Cillian saw through her. Evelyne never did anything lightly, especially not for him.

"Thank you." He took the book carefully, letting his fingers graze the cover before flipping it open. It smelled faintly of aged paper and ink, comforting in a way he couldn't explain.

He glanced up to find Evelyne watching him, her expression softer now. Gratitude bloomed in his chest, and for a fleeting moment he wanted to tell her how much it meant. But beneath that gratitude, an unwelcome thought gnawed at him: did she pity him? Did she see him as fragile, broken?

No, he scolded himself. Evelyne wasn't like that.

Those weren't his words anyway. They were *hers.*

The woman.

She had no name, but she haunted his thoughts, the boundary between them blurring with each passing moment.

After Evelyne left, Cillian set her gift on the desk and reopened the book from Velenshire. The familiar pages drew him back in. Rituals of power, forbidden knowledge—it was both fascinating and unnerving.

He had just turned to a passage about rites of blood magic when the room shifted.

And there she was.

Her frost-white hair spilled over her shoulders, a stark contrast against the ink-black cloak she wore, though this time, the garment revealed more—deliberately so. Her collarbones glistened like polished marble, and the fabric dipped scandalously low. She lounged on his bed, watching him with a predatory smile.

"Still chasing the secrets of old magic, are we?" she teased, her voice smooth as silk, wrapping around him like a serpent.

"Leave," he said firmly.

Her laughter was soft, almost mocking, filling the room. She leaned forward. "Why are you so eager to banish me, Cillian? I'm the one who sees you. The *real* you. The part they try so hard to bury."

Her voice dropped to a near whisper, dripping with honeyed malice. "I saw what she gave you. A gesture born of pity, don't you think? They all see you as a burden. And always will."

Her words cut deep, though he fought to dismiss them. He turned back to his book, forcing his attention on the text. Undeterred, she rose and stepped behind him, leaning close until he could feel the warmth of her breath against his ear.

"What's this one about?" she murmured, her finger hovering over the page.

"That's what I'm trying to figure out," he snapped, his frustration spilling over. "Now, leave me alone."

He thought he felt the faintest nip at his ear, a cruel little tease, but when he turned to face her, she was gone.

Again, as if triggered by her absence, a flash of silver seared his mind. The blood moon appeared, glowing red and coiling like a spiral.

Cillian closed the book with trembling hands and glanced at his reflection in the windowpane. The faint scabs at his temples stared back at him, reminders of his past breaking point. He leaned back in his chair, exhaling shakily. Something inside him was stripping away his sanity, eroding who he was. And he had to resist it.

***

Two days had passed since the incident at the market, and Evelyne's restlessness only grew. With the ball fast approaching the next evening, the thought of facing both Alaric and Lord Bavrick without first confronting the turmoil still churning inside her felt unbearable. She had hoped to speak with Alaric after her walk with Cillian, to tell him how much good the fresh air had done her brother. And surely he had been wondering about the episode in the garden—Alaric, no doubt, wanted answers. Yet one subject remained firmly off-limits in her mind: what happened with Lord Bavrick in the alley. She doubted Alaric wished to revisit it any more than she did.

Still, the possibility of Ivan appearing at the ball unsettled her. Questions hung over her like a storm, and though Aurelia had been kind,

Evelyne yearned to speak with someone who had seen the truth with his own eyes.

After lunch, she decided to visit Alaric. Instead of tying her hair into its usual braid and slipping into loose-fitting trousers for a run, she selected a simple off-white spring dress paired with boots, choosing comfort with a bit of elegance. She added a hint of blush and a pale pink stain to her lips to finish the look. It was enough.

The Stonebridge estate was a short carriage ride from the manor, and as she stepped out into the afternoon light, she took in its picturesque beauty. Outside, Mrs. Vera Stonebridge was orchestrating her garden with the precision of a conductor, giving instructions to a nearby servant while occasionally stepping in to assist. She wore a tan sunhat and gloves, her hands occasionally brushing the petals of her flowers as if coaxing them to bloom.

When Vera's eyes met Evelyne's, she smiled warmly and approached. "Lady Evelyne, what a lovely surprise."

"I hope I'm not intruding, Mrs. Stonebridge," Evelyne replied, returning the smile. "I was hoping to speak with Alaric if he's available."

"He is. I'll have Alia let him know you're here." Vera looped her arm through Evelyne's, guiding her toward the house. "Come inside, my dear. There's no sense waiting out here, though I must admit it's a perfect day. A pity about the storm expected tomorrow. I do hope it won't spoil the ball. The air tends to whisper what's coming, if one knows how to listen."

How curious, Evelyne thought. Few could ever foretell the weather, yet there had always been something peculiar about Mrs. Stonebridge. She inclined her head in polite agreement as they crossed the threshold.

Seated on an olive-green bench in the grand foyer, Evelyne found her eyes drawn to the chandelier above. Its beautiful crystals refracted the sunlight, casting fragmented rainbows across the walls. The mesmerizing display distracted her until the sound of footsteps pulled her focus. Alaric approached, but Evelyne's attention momentarily shifted to the young girl beside him. She had delicate features framed by shiny blonde hair tightly coiled into a bun. Her navy cotton dress and apron marked her as a housemaid, and her shy demeanor was evident in the flush that crept across her cheeks when Alaric winked at her.

"Thank you, Alia," he said, his voice warm and teasing. "I can take it from here."

The girl's blush deepened as she hurried away. Evelyne couldn't help but smile to herself. If Alia had worked for the Stonebridge family long, Alaric's charm wouldn't affect her this much.

"She's lovely," Evelyne remarked without thinking.

"She is," Alaric replied, his gaze lingering where the maid had disappeared. "Though she's young and nervous. I like to make her blush." His lopsided grin was equally mischievous and self-assured.

"I can tell," Evelyne said dryly, earning a soft laugh from him.

He turned his attention fully to her, his eyes gleaming. "This is a pleasant surprise," he said, gesturing theatrically toward her. "A very pleasant surprise."

"Don't start," Evelyne chided, swatting his arm.

"Habit," he admitted, rubbing his arm in mock injury. "Come on, let's talk. I was in my study, reviewing painfully dull documents for my father. If you don't mind joining me, I'll tidy them up."

She followed him through the halls to his study, a stark and utilitarian room. Papers were scattered across his desk, and a bookshelf in one corner was sparsely filled with a few well-worn adventure novels. A lone plant perched on the windowsill, its vibrant green standing out against the otherwise drab surroundings.

"Not much for decor, are you?" Evelyne teased, noting his slight discomfort as she scanned the room.

"I don't spend much time here," he admitted, scratching the back of his neck. "I get my work done and leave. I promise I'm more interesting than this room suggests."

She already knew that—they'd known each other since childhood, after all.

"Well, the plant adds some life," she smiled, taking the seat he offered.

As he tidied his desk, Evelyne's eyes fell on his hands. One bore a fresh scab and bruised knuckles.

"Your hand..." she began cautiously. "Is that from the market?"

He paused, glancing at it briefly. "Just a scratch," he said dismissively.

She hesitated, unsure how to broach the topic further, but Alaric shifted the conversation.

"You look better," he observed. "Are you feeling all right?"

"Better, yes, but I'm not sure *all right* is the right word."

"I have not spoken a word of what transpired in the alley," Alaric said evenly. "Though I would not object to seeing the scoundrel receive his due. Still, I thought it best to leave the matter in your hands, so that you might decide how it should be addressed."

Evelyne drew in a trembling breath. "I feel utterly humiliated," she said softly. "There is fear, yes, and anger, but more than that. He touched me in a way no one ought to. He hurt me, not only in body, but in a way I can hardly name. It feels as though he left me hollow... like he claimed something that was never his to take." Her throat tightened as she spoke, and though part of her longed to turn away from Alaric's sorrowful gaze, she didn't. She held her ground, though her eyes dropped to her lap, fixed on her trembling hands. "And I don't know if I can face him anytime soon," she added quietly.

"I know," Alaric murmured after a moment, exhaling heavily as if her pain weighed on him too. "You may count on my presence at the ball tomorrow. And should he have the audacity to attend, I'll ensure he keeps his distance."

"Thank you," Evelyne whispered. "For everything you did for me that night. I don't know what I would've done without you."

Alaric nodded, but she couldn't let it go. The question had lingered in her mind ever since.

"Alaric..." She paused, gathering herself. "How did you know where I was? How did you find me in the market?" She shook her head, her disbelief still fresh.

He exhaled slowly, his hand settling at the back of his neck. "I had no idea you were there," he said, his voice quiet. "It was a feeling I can't quite explain. Something urged me forward, like a tingling at the nape of my neck that refused to leave." His gaze turned distant. "It wasn't reason or chance. It just... felt like instinct. As if something within me pushed me toward that alley. And the moment I turned the corner... I heard you." He shrugged, though doubt flickered in his expression. "Maybe it was a coincidence."

She gave a faint nod, but her mind wrestled with the meaning behind his words. He seemed to sense her unease, and quickly shifted the conversation away, sparing her from having to dwell on it any longer.

When he asked about Cillian, Evelyne felt her chest lighten just a little. While the subject was still heavy, it was easier to talk about her brother. Her worries tumbled forth in a rush of words as emotion surged past the careful guard of her nerves. Alaric listened closely, offering a quiet reassurance that no matter how broken she felt, she wasn't alone in facing it.

"I want to help him," she admitted. "But all he asks is for me to wait until he's ready. He doesn't think it's an illness, but what else could it be? The visions, his actions... None of it makes sense."

Alaric rubbed his chin thoughtfully. "Did he mention anything else?"

"He said he keeps seeing a woman... and symbols. But he doesn't know why. And he said it feels like something is inside him, like it's waiting. But what could cause that? And where would it even come from? I've never heard of anything like this."

Alaric's gaze drifted toward the bookshelf. After a brief pause, he stood and pulled down an old, dust-covered book. "Maybe we can help him figure it out, or at least find someone who can."

He flipped the book open, revealing pages filled with maps and hand-written notes.

"These are trade routes," he explained. "My father insists I study them, though I swear I've memorized every territory by now. Still..." His fingers traced one of the faded lines. "There might be something noted here that can help us understand what's happening. Or a region known for healing..." His voice trailed off as he continued to flip through the book.

Evelyne was taken aback by his willingness to help her brother and could only watch, moved by his kindness.

Alaric glanced her way. "If you want, you can look through the others. There might be something useful. I'm not sure where to begin, but it can't hurt to learn more about the land."

"You would really help me find answers?" she asked softly, her hands trembling at her sides. A sting of tears pressed at her eyes, but she blinked them back before they could fall.

He looked up from his book, like he was startled that she would question such a thing. "Of course, Ev." His gaze locked intensely on hers, and for a moment, she could only see him.

Gods, he was handsome. The vibrant blue of his eyes seemed to glow against his sun-kissed complexion, holding her captive as they bored into her. When he looked back down at the book, a strand of dark hair fell over his brows, adding a touch of softness to his striking features.

What had she done to deserve such a friend?

Her attention shifted downward, tracing the contours of his forearms braced against the desk. The sleeves of his gray button-down were rolled neatly to his elbows, revealing the taut strength hidden beneath his clothes. She swallowed hard, her eyes lingering on how his muscles tensed ever so slightly before daring to look back at him.

He caught her staring. He knew she was taking him in. And he let her. Those brilliant eyes remained fixed on her now, watching as her lips parted slightly, her teeth grazing her bottom lip out of nervous habit.

He noticed that, too, because the moment their eyes met, he slowly closed the book and stepped out from behind the desk. His gaze did not waver as he crossed the room toward her.

Her hands still trembled, but not with fear—with anticipation. She wanted him to come closer. He reached out, his hand wrapping gently around her elbow, the warmth of his touch grounding her even as it set her pulse racing. With the softest tug, he urged her forward. She followed without hesitation, drawn to him like a moth to a flame.

His tone deepened to a husky whisper. "There is nothing I wouldn't do for you, Evelyne. Especially when you look at me like that."

His eyes dipped to her mouth once more, and she drew in a quiet, shaky breath. She'd never heard him speak to her like this before, and the low, intimate rasp of his voice sent a thrill through her.

Her thoughts scattered as his other hand slowly trailed up the back of her neck, settling to cup her head—a touch so tender and full of desire. She wanted him to know she felt the same, so she tilted her head, her eyes fluttering shut. With one arm now wrapped around her lower back, he drew her close, his lips hovering just over her neck. Her heart pounded fiercely, and she wondered if he could feel the rapid rhythm of her pulse. Then, his lips brushed against her skin, featherlight, before trailing soft kisses down her neck. Her breath hitched, and a low moan escaped her lips.

The sound seemed to ignite something within him. In a swift, fluid motion, he turned her, pressing the back of her legs against the edge of his desk. His hand at her neck tightened slightly, anchoring her as she opened her eyes to meet his. His gaze burned with a vivid, electric-blue intensity, leaving her transfixed. He paused for a heartbeat as if giving her the chance to decide. But she didn't need time. Her hands were already threading through his hair, pulling him closer.

And then his mouth was on hers, igniting a spark that swept through them both.

She had no idea what she was doing, but everything felt right. Her center heated as he grazed his tongue against her lips, and she opened her mouth slightly to allow it to sweep in. He groaned against her mouth, and it had her tugging firmly at his waist. He gripped her hips and effortlessly lifted her, setting her down atop his desk, then nudged his waist slightly against her knees, a silent request to part for him. Just as he fit his body between her legs, she pulled his head closer to hers to deepen the kiss.

Her body felt like it had been set free, a rush of liberation flooding her veins. For the first time, it felt like she could breathe. Like every stressful thought melted away, swirling into oblivion as his touch grounded her in the moment. All she wanted was to feel—his hands, his lips, his body. To touch, to kiss, to lose herself entirely in him.

He traced his fingers slowly up her waist, sending a trail of chills along her skin, before pressing one hand firmly against her lower back while the other cupped her breast. On instinct, she pushed her hips into his and arched against the touch.

The kiss was utterly breathtaking, consuming her like the most intoxicating wine. A heartbeat later, he broke it, lips parting from hers with a soft reluctance as they both struggled to catch their breath.

"Evelyne," Alaric began, his voice low, but the solemn sincerity in his eyes made her heart stutter.

His expression was so grave that a chill of doubt ran down her spine. He didn't want this, did he? Panic clawed at her thoughts. Had they crossed a line? What if he didn't feel the same way she did? She was sure he wanted this—she'd felt it, felt him.

But what he said next sent her reeling, so much so that she almost fell off the edge of the desk.

"Marry me," he whispered.

The weight of the words hit her like a bolt of lightning, leaving her wholly stunned. "What?" she breathed, her voice still uneven as she tried to steady herself, her heart racing with shock.

But he didn't falter, gently brushing his fingers against her cheek. "I desire nothing more," he said quietly, "than to make you my wife."

A rush of emotion overwhelmed her: dizziness, joy, disbelief. The thought of a lifetime with him, her closest friend, a good and kind man, felt almost too perfect to be real.

Slowly, she shook her head in amazement. "Why?"

He stepped back slightly, his confidence dimming momentarily as vulnerability crept into his expression. "Because it is you I wish to stand by my side, and to love. This is how I have always wished to feel," he said, swallowing. "To want someone so completely… and to be wanted in return. I would not see this moment end. It is all I ever hoped for."

A genuine smile softened his features, and when Evelyne met his gaze, she saw the truth shining in his eyes.

She pushed off the desk and stood slowly, her heart swelling as she held his stare. "I'd love nothing more than to marry my truest friend."

She smiled and lifted her hands to cradle his face, then leaned in and kissed him softly. She sensed the faintest tension in him at her words, yet whatever doubt lingered quickly faded as he kissed her back.

***

Evelyne hadn't realized how much she'd needed that conversation with Alaric until it happened. She had entered his estate feeling vulnerable, her heart weighed down by worry for Cillian's fragile state and the hovering fear of what Ivan had done to her. But by the time she left, those emotions had transformed into something entirely different: comfort, admiration, and a deep sense of connection.

Engaged.

The word echoed in her mind, almost foreign in its reality. Had this truly happened? It felt like a dream that had unfolded so effortlessly and perfectly that she feared she might wake to find it stolen away. The way Alaric kissed her felt like a dance, as if they knew instinctively where to step, turn, and move together in perfect harmony. So she had said yes—because he was her friend, because his touch felt right, and because, at that moment, she couldn't imagine saying anything else.

He'd asked if he could speak with her father, and she readily agreed, offering him a smile that felt as natural as breathing. *Of course.* In truth, she was relieved that Alaric would be the one to break the news to her parents—far better than her enduring her mother's inevitable shrieks of excitement or the stiff nod of approval from her father.

Tomorrow night at the ball, they would be seen together for the first time as an engaged couple. But the thought did not fill her with fear. Society would talk, and whispers would follow them through the ballroom like a shadow, but she would endure it, because it was *him* she would be tied to. No one else.

And if nothing else, this would undoubtedly keep Ivan Bavrick from so much as looking her way. He was a vile creature, but with Alaric at her side, she could finally put him behind her, a chapter she would never have to revisit. She only hoped he would have the decency to avoid the gathering entirely.

Alaric walked her to the carriage, his fingers lingering on hers just before she stepped inside. "I'll come to your estate later this evening and speak with your father."

Evelyne only nodded, her heart so full she could barely find words. It was a necessary formality, a meeting between men, like a business arrangement in some ways. But she refused to let that notion dim the quiet elation swelling inside her. She didn't care about its propriety. All she cared about was him.

She could hardly contain her smile on the ride home, warmth still tingling along her skin where his lips had touched her. The world outside the carriage seemed brighter and lighter, as if it had been caught up in the magic of this moment. She was completely smitten, like a starry-eyed fool in a romantic tale.

The second she stepped into her chambers, Seraphine took one look at her face, at the flush in her cheeks and the unmistakable glow in her eyes, and she knew.

"You have news," she murmured. "Good news."

Evelyne's throat tightened, her joy spilling over as she took her dearest companion's hands.

"Yes," she whispered, then let out a breathless laugh. "Yes, I do."

Tears shimmered in Seraphine's eyes before she embraced Evelyne, holding her as tightly as a mother might. Evelyne closed her eyes, resting against her, absorbing the quiet, unconditional love in the gesture. It was a moment she had never had with her mother, a moment she had never dared to expect.

She cherished it.

"He's a fine man, dear," Seraphine whispered, brushing back a loose strand of Evelyne's hair. "I am so very happy for you."

And as Evelyne clutched her handmaid's hands, she realized she had never been happier herself.

Chapter 15

"It's done. She said yes to the proposal."

Alaric's voice was calm, even as anger curled around each word like a snake tightening its grip. He was disgusted with himself. Absolutely disgusted.

That kiss had torn him apart. He had never felt anything so consuming. The way her lips molded against his, the way his hands ached to trace every delicate curve of her—he had wanted her in an almost unbearable way. And yet, he fought against it, wrestled with himself even as every fiber of his being urged him to give in.

The moment he'd caught her watching him inside his study, her eyes dark with meaning and her lower lip caught between her teeth, he had felt himself unravel. The look in her eyes had roused something in him beyond reason, and he'd been scarcely aware of moving until he found himself before her. She hadn't drawn back. She wanted him just as much.

But after that world-altering kiss, after he had torn himself away from her intoxicating warmth, she smiled and spoke the words that sent ice through his veins. *I'd like nothing more than to marry my truest friend.*

The moment those words left her lips, his body stiffened as a violent flood of guilt consumed him. *Friend.* That was what she saw him as—her closest, most trusted friend. And yet he had betrayed her in the cruelest way, not by deceit of the heart, but by omission of the truth. Evelyne had no idea this marriage had been arranged. She had no idea their parents had planned this before she had a choice. But he did. And he had merely stood before her and kissed her, letting her believe this was her decision to make.

"Good," his father said, barely looking up from the map he was studying. A glance. That was all he gave. As if his son's marriage, his son's entire future, were nothing more than a task to be noted and dismissed.

Maybe that was the path Alaric needed to take: do as his father had done, silence his heart, and make peace with the life laid out before him. He was to wed a beautiful woman, and that ought to have been enough.

Shouldn't it?

"I will inform Lord Duskwood tonight," Alaric continued. "And we will be seen together for the first time tomorrow."

His father barely acknowledged him. "Alright."

That was it. No words of approval. No words of wisdom. Just another short, indifferent reply before the conversation was over. So Alaric turned on his heel and walked out, his stomach twisting in knots.

This should have felt like a triumph. Instead, it felt like he had already lost something he could never get back.

***

Cillian wiped the sweat from his brow, his fingers trembling as he shook out the pain in his cramped hand. His knuckles ached from gripping the graphite too tightly, pressing into the paper with manic precision. The lead smudged across his palms, dark streaks of obsession staining his skin. Still, he sketched. Again and again.

Tree.

Moon.

Eyes.

The images bled across countless pages, layering over one another in a frenzied haze. His vision blurred as exhaustion clawed at him, but he refused to surrender. He couldn't. Sleep had abandoned him, replaced by an insatiable need to understand. He was chasing a pattern, a meaning that was just beyond his reach, lurking in the fog of his restless mind. The scratching of graphite against parchment was the only sound in his room, rhythmic and urgent.

Earlier, he had read the book Evelyne gave him, which initially seemed like a simple children's fairytale. He hadn't intended to get so caught up in it.

A light to purify the darkness.

A keeper, tasked with balance.

A strength to ward off the shadows.

At first, it read like nonsense, riddled with vague allegories of good and evil. But the more he read, the more the words twisted in his mind. There were no illustrations or symbols to link it to his visions. Only relentless repetition, as though the book itself were trying to force a message into his head. But what?

With a frustrated growl, he slammed the graphite down and yanked the book from Velenshire off the shelf once more. A different kind of story—one not of light and virtue, but of magic. Ancient forces that had once pulsed through these lands. Witches and beings that could bend nature to their will. Could there be truth in the tales? The book's constant pull could not be mere coincidence. Perhaps it was the history he must come to understand before attempting to decipher the riddles.

He resumed his sketch of the withered tree, its bone-like branches etched from memory. It felt more important than the others, lingering in his mind for its eerie resemblance to the Solwyn Tree of Velenshire he'd seen in the book. It was known as a tree full of life and beauty, yet he had no memory of encountering it when he'd been there.

Every time he closed his eyes, she returned. The woman. The beautiful, cruel woman. But, her presence no longer felt unwelcome. He'd grown accustomed to her, even finding solace in the silent moments where she loomed. It was better than being alone in his room, wasting away with thoughts he couldn't control. Tonight, she remained absent. In her place came the blackness, like a beast that had waited long enough. It slipped through the cracks of his mind and struck true. And then, nothing.

****

When he woke, he wasn't in his bed. He wasn't even in his chair. The cold, hard tile of the bathing chamber floor pressed against his cheek, the damp scent of water and stone filling his nostrils. His body ached, and his arms trembled as he pushed himself up. Confusion seized him with unrelenting force as he struggled to understand how he had gotten here.

His hand moved instinctively to his forehead, where a sharp pain flared. His fingers came away slick with blood. A gash. Fresh.

Shit.

The nausea struck suddenly, a wave of sickness rolling through his gut. The room swayed around him, and he barely reached the water bucket before he retched, clutching its rim with white-knuckled desperation. His body convulsed against the emptiness inside him, heaving until nothing remained.

He wiped his mouth with his hand, staring blankly ahead. His mind felt fractured, edges blurred, memories slipping through his fingers like sand.

He had been sketching. And then... nothing. No visions. No whispers. Just an expanse of endless black.

What had happened to him?

His breaths came quick and sharp as he pressed a damp washcloth to his forehead, barely feeling the sting. His reflection in the mirror startled him—dark circles under his eyes, pale skin drawn tight over sharp cheekbones. He hardly recognized himself.

Something wasn't right.

Dragging himself back to his room, he collapsed onto the bed. His body had finally reached its limit, and exhaustion yanked his eyes shut.

This time, sleep did not evade him.

It swallowed him whole.

CHAPTER 16

The steady rhythm of rain against the drawing room's tall windows cast a soothing lull over the space, the glass panes blurring with rivulets of water as Evelyne turned the soft pages of her favorite novel. The storm had come just as Vera Stonebridge had predicted, its arrival ruining any hope of clear skies for the evening's grand ball. Outside, the wind howled through the trees, and inside, the manor was alive with frantic energy.

Her mother had been in a whirlwind since dawn, a flurry of silk and determination as she directed the servants to move the decor and festivities indoors. Though Evelyne hadn't seen her enter the drawing room, she had felt her pass by no fewer than five times in the last ten minutes. The thud of hurried footsteps against polished floors, the clipped commands—

"The wreaths must go near the grand staircase!"

"Why are there no candles in the receiving hall?"

"The violinist should stand near the east wing! No, no—there!"

Evelyne bit her lip to stifle a giggle as her mother's voice faded into the distance, barking another order about the floors still needing mopping. She had never seen her in such a state. The lingering excitement from last night's dinner clung to her like a delicate mist. Alaric had sought her father's blessing for Evelyne's hand in marriage just before the meal, and her mother's elation had been undeniable as she shared the news at the table. For a fleeting moment, Evelyne could have sworn she saw tears welling in her eyes.

Aurelia, overcome with emotion, had pulled Evelyne into an embrace, pressing a soft kiss to her cheek. "Oh, I'm just so happy for you!" she'd whispered thrice before dinner ended.

Her father, always a quiet observer, had seemed relieved. He ate at his usual steady pace, nodding in approval and offering the occasional small smile.

Cillian had gone to his room before the announcement was made. Evelyne tried to see him after dinner, but when he didn't answer her knock, his young red-haired servant appeared, shaking her head with a quiet, guilty look.

"He doesn't want to see anyone, my lady. He's been telling everyone to leave him alone all day."

Evelyne had frowned, finding it odd, and knocked again.

"Cillian, it's me."

Silence lingered before he finally responded.

"Not now."

His voice was different—tense, guarded. So she left him alone.

Now, as the manor bustled around her, filled with the rush of servants, the flicker of candlelight, and the distant notes of a violin being tuned, she tried to focus on her book, using it as a shield against the rising anticipation that coiled inside her. But the house was too alive, too restless, and all too much.

Sighing, she closed the novel and returned to her chambers, where she knew she could find quiet. And indeed, there it was. A peaceful hush, broken only by the steady patter of rain against the window. She curled up by the sill and took a moment to breathe.

Aurelia and Seraphine swept in a few hours later, bringing the scent of fresh roses and lavender.

"It's time!" Aurelia chirped, excitement lacing her words.

Seraphine followed with a half-smile, holding up a gown that shimmered in the dim light.

Evelyne barely had a moment to protest before they ushered her toward the vanity, working with practiced hands to prepare her. Her hair was pinned back on one side, fastened with an ornate pearl clip that glistened like dew. Her gown—a breathtaking rose gold threaded with silver embroidery—hugged her waist, the floral lace sleeves draping delicately over her shoulders. The back dipped into an elegant plunge, revealing just enough to add an air of regality. Dangling pearl earrings, a perfect match to the clip, completed the look.

She was no longer just Evelyne. Tonight, she was a betrothed woman, about to step into a world where she would be seen—truly seen—for the first time on a man's arm.

Her heart fluttered, caught between nervousness and happiness. Tonight, everything would change.

***

Rain hammered relentlessly against the towering windows of Duskwood Manor; the storm outside contrasted starkly with the opulence and warmth within. Guests hurried inside, shaking droplets from their cloaks, while their guards dutifully shielded the ladies' elaborate gowns and carefully pinned curls with umbrellas. The scent of candle wax and fresh roses filled the air, mingling with the crisp breeze that crept through the grand entrance.

The ballroom was alive with a symphony of sounds: the murmur of conversation, the delicate clinking of crystal glasses, the soft strains of a violin weaving a melody through the space.

Embroidered silks shimmered as noble figures glided across the floors, unconcerned by the thunder growling in the distance, their jeweled adornments catching the light.

Evelyne had been waiting for this moment all day, yet now that it was here, she could scarcely believe it was real. Alaric, her dearest friend, the man who had stolen her breath with a kiss, had asked *her* to marry him. The thought left her lightheaded with the enormity of it all.

She moved through the evening, soaking in the attention and accepting congratulations from noble families eager to gain favor with the powerful union of the Duskwoods and Stonebridges.

But Alaric wasn't himself.

He stood beside her, his arm around her waist, but his touch felt distant. His replies were short when the engagement was mentioned, and his smile was too quick to be real. He had looked at her when they first arrived, told her she was beautiful and even kissed her cheek softly before leading her inside. But she couldn't ignore how he emptied glass after glass of champagne, how his jaw stayed tight, and how his eyes kept searching for something just beyond her.

At first, Evelyne ignored it, but as the night wore on, a wave of unease settled over her. The way Alaric avoided her gaze and the growing distance between them tightened a knot in her stomach. Something was wrong.

"Dance with me?" Evelyne asked him with pleading eyes. She expected a smile, a playful quip, something to reassure her, but instead, he only gave a silent, perfunctory nod. Without a word, he took her arm and led her to the dance floor.

Her heart plummeted. He wasn't happy, and the realization hit her like a blow.

"What's wrong?" she asked as they took their first steps, her voice barely above a whisper. She searched his face, praying that he would shake off whatever cloud hung over him and tell her.

"Nothing. Why do you ask?" His tone was calm and careful, but his gaze remained distant.

Evelyne frowned. "Have I done something to upset you?"

That, at least, seemed to pull him back. His eyes softened as they met hers, and before she could process it, his hands cupped her face gently. She hadn't realized how much she needed his warm touch and longed to see his smile again.

"You've done nothing to upset me, Evelyne," he murmured, his lips curling into that smile she loved. "You are perfect."

Relief flooded her, but he twirled her into the next step before she could respond, spinning her into the waltz rhythm. She let him take the lead, allowing herself to surrender to the rhythm of the music. At least Ivan Bavrick was nowhere to be seen. One less problem to deal with. Still, she couldn't help but hope Alaric's punch had left a visible, well-earned bruise—one for everyone to notice.

When the melody slowed, she dared to ask again. "And you? Are you okay?"

He shrugged, casual, unaffected. "Big crowds stress me out."

Evelyne arched a brow. "You?" she scoffed. "Afraid of big crowds?"

He was lying, and they both knew it. Alaric thrived in the spotlight. He loved flirting, charming, and effortlessly commanding attention. This wasn't nerves. This was something else.

She could have pressed him and demanded answers, but not here. Not now. So, she let it go, and they danced. Just the one, and though his movements were precise, they were empty. Even so close, he felt impossibly far away.

And then it was over. The final note of the waltz hovered in the air as Alaric released her. He bowed politely and excused himself, disappearing into the sea of guests.

Evelyne stood there, frozen, her heart pounding against the confines of her corset. She smiled through the congratulations, nodding graciously, accepting well wishes with all the poise expected of her. But her mind was elsewhere.

Where had Alaric gone? And why did it feel like she was already losing him?

It wasn't until she spotted Callista, standing with her usual clique of well-dressed, sharp-tongued friends, that her night took an even stranger turn. Callista smirked as she raised her champagne flute in a feigned salute.

"Lady Evelyne, who would have thought? You engaged to Alaric Stonebridge. What a surprise."

Evelyne lifted her chin, keeping her expression neutral. "Thank you for your congratulations, Callista."

"Oh, don't mistake me," Callista said with a false sweetness. "I'm merely wondering how long this little arrangement will last. Alaric has always been so... selective."

Evelyne narrowed her eyes. She wasn't going to let Callista ruin her night. "Excuse me. I have a fiancé to find."

Callista chuckled. "Already scared him off, have you?"

Evelyne didn't dignify it with a response. Instead, she lifted her chin and walked away, refusing to let the words settle.

She needed to find him. Her eyes flicked across the ballroom, scanning for the familiar dark waves of his hair, the sharp cut of his suit—but he was nowhere to be seen.

Before she could slip away unnoticed, Aurelia's lilting voice interrupted her search. "Oh, Evelyne!" Her sister all but glided toward her, her deep purple gown skimming the floor like liquid silk. Two champagne flutes dangled from her fingers, one of which she promptly thrust into Evelyne's hand. "You both looked absolutely enchanting out there."

Evelyne accepted the glass with a tight smile. "Did we?" She took a sip, letting the bubbles fizz against her lips before adding, "Then perhaps you've seen my enchanting partner? He seems to have vanished."

Aurelia hummed thoughtfully, glancing over her shoulder as if expecting Alaric to materialize from the shadows. "I haven't, I'm afraid. Though I hope he'll save me a dance before the night is through. You know, since I return home tomorrow." She swayed dramatically, lifting her glass in a mock toast to herself. "Oh, I'd love for someone to sweep me across the floor tonight. Will you ask him for me, please?"

Evelyne smothered a laugh, arching a brow. "So you'd like me to hand over my betrothed for the evening? How generous of me."

She downed her champagne in two effortless swallows and handed the empty glass back to Aurelia, who gawked at her.

"What was that?" Aurelia asked, her playful tone shifting to something more perceptive. "Everything all right?"

"I hope so." Evelyne's reply was crisp but uncertain.

Aurelia's voice dropped to a gentle murmur as she leaned in close, whispering into Evelyne's ear, "If it's Ivan you're concerned about, rest assured—Mother will never allow him to set foot in our home again."

"It's not that, but thank you, Aurelia. Truly." Evelyne gave her sister's hand a gentle squeeze in gratitude before turning away, cutting off any chance for further questions, slipping past the gilded double doors and into the quiet beyond.

The manor's hallways were dim, the flickering sconces sending shifting shadows across the cold stone walls. Evelyne's pace quickened, her pulse pounding in time with the rain tapping against the windows. The warmth of the ballroom—the laughter, the music—felt worlds away now. She had let Alaric disappear for too long. If something was wrong, she had to find out.

She rounded a corner, her skirts brushing against the marble, only to stop short. Voices, low and hushed, floated from the room ahead.

She recognized one instantly.

Alaric.

The other sent ice down her spine.

Callista.

Evelyne flattened herself against the wall, scarcely breathing as she turned to look at them.

"It's arranged, isn't it?" Callista's voice was a purr, dripping with amusement. "Does she even know?"

Evelyne's stomach twisted. What was she talking about?

A pause. A heavy exhale.

"No," Alaric said quietly. "She doesn't know."

No. The word echoed in her mind like a tolling bell.

"I knew it," Callista mused. "Tell me, why would you agree to it, Alaric? When you and I have such... history."

The way she lowered her voice and lingered on the word *history* made Evelyne's skin crawl.

Alaric was silent. Too silent.

Then, in a voice raw with something Evelyne couldn't place, he finally answered.

"I didn't want it to be like this," he admitted, his tone strained. "But it's done."

Evelyne gasped quietly.

Done.

A wave of nausea rolled through her as the truth crashed into her with merciless force. Arranged. Their engagement had been arranged. She hadn't been chosen. Not willingly.

And he *knew*.

Evelyne barely registered the rest of their conversation. Her heartbeat roared in her ears. The candlelight flickered wildly in her blurred vision. Her fingers curled against the silk of her gown as if she could anchor herself, as if she wouldn't drown under the weight of this... this lie, this mortifying revelation.

Before she could move or even think, she saw Callista step closer to Alaric. Saw the way her hand trailed along his arm, slow and possessive. Saw the way she tilted her head, her lips dangerously close to his ear.

"You could have had me," she said, her voice sultry, coaxing. "You still could."

And then she kissed him. And he let her.

For a single, excruciating moment, the world spun off its axis. The air in Evelyne's lungs turned to ice, her body frozen in place as reality shattered around her. Something in her snapped. And before she could stop herself, she stepped forward into the candlelight.

Alaric staggered back almost instantly, shoving Callista away, but the damage had been done.

"Evelyne." His voice was panicked and desperate. He looked as though he'd been struck. "It's not—"

Callista placed a hand over her mouth, feigning surprise, but her eyes glinted with satisfaction. She'd known Evelyne would find them and now she was drinking in every second of Evelyne's humiliation.

Alaric pushed off the wall, moving toward her, his expression pleading. "Evelyne, please, let me explain."

She backed up a step, shaking her head. Explain? Explain what? That her engagement was a transaction? That she was a fool? That she had fallen for a man who had never truly chosen her?

Bile burned her throat.

"This…" Her voice trembled with restrained fury. "This was arranged? And you knew?"

His silence was her answer.

"And you told her!" She spat the words like venom, her eyes flicking to Callista.

Callista smirked, the picture of cruelty wrapped in silk. "Pity, really," she mused, inspecting her nails. "Did you actually think he would willingly ask for your hand?"

Alaric turned on Callista, his voice sharp. "Be quiet."

"Oh, don't be cross with me, darling. I didn't force you to lie to her."

Alaric clenched his jaw, then turned back to Evelyne. "Please. This is not what it looks like."

Evelyne let out a cold, hollow laugh, though it tasted of bitterness. "Not what it looks like?" she repeated, her voice shaking. "Then by all means, do tell me, Alaric. What, exactly, is this?"

His mouth opened, then shut. He had nothing.

She swallowed the lump in her throat and straightened, lifting her chin. "Don't." The word was quiet but final. "I don't want to hear it. I don't want to look at you."

She turned away from him, and a quiet gasp broke the silence.

They weren't alone.

Out of the corner of her eye, she spotted a few lingering guests at the far end of the corridor, Wesley Bavrick among them. Callista's friends. Their gazes darted between Alaric and Evelyne, their faces painted with intrigue and amusement.

Evelyne's heart plummeted. The realization struck her like a dagger to the chest. This wasn't just betrayal. This was humiliation.

Alaric took another step. "Evelyne—"

But she didn't let him finish. She turned and fled.

Evelyne couldn't remember how she got to her chambers, but her feet carried her there in a blind, desperate sprint. The moment she slammed the door shut, her shaking hands clawed at every piece of jewelry, ripping off the earrings, the necklace, the dainty rings that now felt like shackles. Each item clattered onto the floor as she moved to the pins in her hair, yanking them free until her curls tumbled in disarray around her face.

Rage, heartbreak, and embarrassment burned beneath her skin, clawing at her throat, demanding release. But she wouldn't cry. Not yet. Not while her blood boiled and her heart thundered with hatred.

The dress had to go. Her fingers fumbled against the intricate buttons and fine embroidery, but she didn't care about the delicate fabric or the craftsmanship. She wanted it off. She needed it off. With a frustrated growl, she shoved the gown down her arms, kicking it away as if it were the thing that had deceived her. Then she reached for the corset, tugging mercilessly at the strings, but her hands were trembling too much—too clumsy, too weak with the weight of what had just happened.

Steady hands appeared at her back, working quickly and efficiently on the loops and ties. Evelyne didn't need to turn around to know it was Seraphine. Her handmaid said nothing, but her presence was grounding. No pity, no questions. Just quiet understanding.

The moment the corset loosened, Evelyne inhaled sharply, her first real breath since she had heard Alaric's voice in the corridor. She stepped out of the discarded garments, now clad in the barest of underclothes. Without hesitation, she pulled on a pair of men's trousers and a large shirt, her fingers moving with renewed purpose as she tied the laces at her wrists and braided her hair back.

"Miss," Seraphine finally said, tone calm but edged with concern. "It's storming out."

Evelyne didn't care. She needed out of this room, out of this house, out of the suffocating deception that threatened to swallow her whole.

She only turned toward the door and said, "I need to run."

Seraphine didn't try to stop her. Instead, she reached for Evelyne's cloak, draping it over her shoulders with a silent nod. Evelyne grasped the fabric, her fingers curling into the wool, then turned and fled into the storm.

Chapter 17

The cold hit her instantly, the wind howling through the trees as rain lashed against her skin. She welcomed the storm's bite, letting the air numb the raw wound of betrayal before it could swallow her whole.

She ran.

The mud sucked at her boots, threatening to pull her down, but she pushed forward, her breath ragged, her legs burning. Her hair whipped against her damp cheeks, strands sticking to her skin as she forced herself to go faster, harder. She needed to outrun the thoughts clawing at her mind, the cruel laughter she imagined spilling from Callista's lips, the echo of Alaric's voice saying, *I didn't want it to be like this.*

Liar.

The word burned through her like fire. She gritted her teeth and sprinted harder, her pulse thundering in her ears.

She had been so naive to believe that one kiss could change everything. To think that the quiet, comforting conversations they had shared meant as much to him as they had to her. That the way he'd held her, the way his lips had lingered against hers, had been anything more than a fleeting moment for him while it had unraveled her entire world.

She could already picture Callista spreading the truth, delighting in the whispers that would soon follow Evelyne wherever she went. *Poor Evelyne, thinking he wanted her. Thinking she was actually chosen.*

Rain soaked through her clothes, and mud splattered her legs and arms, but she didn't stop. She wouldn't go near the woods—not at this hour, not when the darkness there felt far too much like the one threatening to swallow her. Instead, she stayed within the hidden paths of the estate, running until her legs threatened to give out beneath her.

An hour passed before she staggered back toward the manor, her body trembling with exhaustion. She tore off her mud-caked boots at the back entrance and moved on instinct, her steps carrying her to the only place she could think of—the library.

She just needed a moment. A quiet space to breathe. But when she stepped into the room, she stilled.

Cillian sat in the far corner, his back to the window, a book in his hands. But he wasn't reading. He had been, perhaps, but now his gaze was fixed on her. Evelyne's stomach twisted—not with embarrassment, not with shame, but with something far worse.

Fear.

His face was ghostly pale, his skin almost gray in the dim candlelight. His forehead was bandaged just above his eyebrow. And his eyes—his eyes were black as ink.

The book slipped from his fingers, thudding against the table, but he didn't notice. He looked lost. Hollow.

Evelyne's heartbeat, which had been so wild with rage moments ago, now pounded for an entirely different reason.

"Cillian?" Her voice was barely a whisper, but it may as well have been a scream in the stillness of the library.

He didn't answer. Didn't move.

All the anger from the night, the hurt, the ache of it—none of it mattered anymore.

Something was very wrong.

Evelyne stepped forward cautiously, her heart hammering against her ribs. Her drenched clothes clung to her, rainwater dripping from the ends of her hair as she tucked a strand behind her ear with unsteady fingers. She carefully lowered herself into the chair across from him.

"Cillian. Look at me."

He did. But the moment his gaze locked onto hers, she regretted asking. Once warm and full of mischief and life, his eyes were nothing but blackened voids, swallowing all light and humanity. A slow, cruel smile curled his lips, twisting his face into something unrecognizable. He tilted his head, a predator studying his prey.

"Oh, Evelyne," he murmured, voice dripping with mockery. "No need to look so sad."

Horror washed over her like a freezing tide. This was not her brother.

"Always feeling sorry for me," he continued, his smile widening, warping. His voice had shifted, deepened into something unnatural. "Everyone in this family is always pitying poor, sick Cillian."

Then he moved, shoving back his chair as he stood, towering over her. Evelyne flinched, her hands trembling against the tabletop.

"When will you all understand?" he hissed, stepping closer. "I don't need your pity. I don't need your concerned looks, your whispered conversations behind my back. I don't need your fear."

She reached for him; an instinct, a desperate attempt to comfort whatever was left of him. But he recoiled as if burned. In a sudden burst of violence, he smacked her hand away and slammed both fists onto the table. The sound cracked through the room like a gunshot, making her jolt.

"Don't!" he roared.

Evelyne gasped, tears burning at the corners of her eyes. "Cillian, please... What can I do?"

A humorless chuckle left his lips, and he shook his head slowly. "I don't need your help," he spat. "I need to be respected." He turned and began pacing, his fists clenched at his sides, his whole body tense with barely restrained anger. "She's right, you know."

Evelyne's stomach lurched. "She? Who are you talking about?"

"The woman," he murmured, almost to himself. "She sees the truth. You all see me as a burden."

"No, Cillian," Evelyne said quickly, standing now, desperate to reach him, to break whatever trance he was in. "We don't."

But the moment the words left her lips, he whirled on her, his face contorted with something inhuman. His lips curled back, exposing his teeth, and the darkness in his eyes deepened, endless, soulless.

"Liar," he rasped.

Evelyne's breath caught in her throat.

"Maybe..." She swallowed hard, trying to keep her voice steady. "Maybe I should get a healer. You might need rest—"

A book flew across the room before she could finish, slamming into the bookshelf with a resounding crack.

"I NEED NO ONE!" he bellowed.

Then, he stormed out, leaving Evelyne rooted in place and shaking as tears streamed down her face. She had never felt fear like this before—not for herself, but for her brother's soul.

***

Evelyne stirred in her sleep, a chill creeping up her spine. Her brows knit together as she shifted beneath the covers, her body instinctively curling inward against the sudden coolness. Her eyes fluttered open.

Something moved. A whisper of black at the edge of her vision.

The room was dark, but not in the way it should be. Shadows stretched unnaturally, pooling beneath the doorframe. A thin stream of something—was it mist?—seeped from the gap beneath her door, writhing like ink in water.

Pushing back the covers, she sat up, her heart thumping wildly in her chest. She swung her legs over the side of the bed, wincing at the bite of cold against her bare feet. Was she dreaming? The house was utterly silent, yet something about the air felt *wrong*.

She wrapped her robe tightly around herself and moved toward the door. Her fingers trembled as she reached for the handle, hesitating. An unearthly iciness radiated from the wood, crawling into her bones. Slowly, she turned the knob.

The hallway stretched before her, the air heavy with the sense of an unseen presence watching. She inched forward, but hesitated at the staircase. One glance over the edge, and a sudden rush of fear gripped her.

Below, the foyer was veiled in swirling, inky mist. It slithered and pulsed, stretching toward the walls before retracting, shifting as if alive. *What is that?*

Her bare feet were silent as she rushed down the wooden steps, but the mist dissipated when she reached the bottom, as if it had never been there.

She stood frozen, skin prickling, the silence of the house pressing in around her. Had she imagined it? Was she sleepwalking? No... Something had been here. She was sure of it. And whatever it was, she couldn't shake the eerie certainty that it had *taken* something with it.

***

Alaric woke with a pounding head and a hollow ache in his chest. The morning light sliced through the heavy drapes of his chamber, too bright, too unforgiving. He groaned, pressing the heels of his palms into his eyes as if that could push away the burden of the night before. But no amount of pressure could erase the image of Evelyne's face—the devastation in her eyes when she realized the truth.

He hated himself.

The truth of their arranged engagement was never supposed to come out this way. Not like this. Not in front of her. And yet it had unraveled before his very eyes, slipping from his grasp like water through his fingers. When he'd told Evelyne he wanted to marry her, he'd meant it. Every damn word. She was his friend, the first woman who ever truly saw him, and for a fleeting moment, he had believed that what they had—the comfort, the understanding, the intimacy—was real. But now, it was gone. And he had ruined it.

He spent the morning slumped over in silence at the breakfast table, barely able to choke down his tea, his appetite soured by the stinging rebukes of his parents. His mother sighed deeply between sips of tea, her disappointment thick in the air. His father, on the other hand, was not as restrained.

"You humiliated her," Gaviel Stonebridge said coldly, setting down his utensils with a loud clink. "And you humiliated us. Do you have any idea how quickly word has spread? The entire court is talking about it."

Alaric had nothing to say. What could he say? He had done this. He had let this happen. And for what? A moment of weakness? A mistake he couldn't take back?

He should have told Evelyne the truth himself. He should never have let Callista get close to him. He had been a coward, drinking himself into numbness to push back the guilt that had clawed at him all afternoon before the ball. And then Evelyne had asked, *'Have I done something to upset you?'*

He had barely kept himself together. Guilt had torn through him, and the urge to tell her everything had been overwhelming. But he hadn't. Instead, he'd smiled, acted as if nothing was wrong, and played the part of the devoted fiancé—even though he knew she could see right through him.

And then Callista had found him.

He had been vulnerable, drowning in his own self-loathing, and she had seized the opportunity to drive the knife deeper. He barely remembered the conversation, only how his voice had sounded so *lost* when he let the truth about the arrangement slip. And he'd realized his mistake too late. Callista had given him that wicked little smile that meant she had already won, and before he could stop her, she had kissed him.

And then Evelyne had been standing there.

He had felt the moment her heart shattered, had seen it in the way she took a single, staggering step back, her lips parting in silent horror. He'd wanted to chase after her, to drop to his knees and *beg* for forgiveness. But the fury twisting across her face had rooted him in place, like he was trapped between the crushing weight of his shame and the hushed whispers of the onlookers already spreading the scandal.

Coward.

As he sat at the breakfast table, head bowed, he let his father's words wash over him.

"You'll be leaving for Velenshire tonight," Gaviel said sharply. "When you return, you will fix this mess with Lady Duskwood."

Alaric swallowed against the tightness in his throat. He knew what his father meant. He was expected to mend the broken engagement and pretend last night had never happened. But how could he? How could he face Evelyne after what he had done?

He nodded, though it felt like a weight around his neck. His father left without another word while his mother lingered. But after a quiet sigh, she followed, leaving him alone with his misery.

Alaric clenched his fists against the table and exhaled shakily. He had to fix this. He *would* fix this. But deep down, he knew that some wounds never truly healed.

CHAPTER 18

The morning air was crisp, threaded with the scent of wet earth and rain left behind by the night's storm. Puddles shimmered in the early light, and the sky hung low, still heavy with its passing rage. Evelyne stood beside the carriage, her arms wrapped tightly around herself as she watched Aurelia bid farewell to their parents.

Aurelia's husband, Leopold, had finally returned from his business travels, and it was time for her to leave. With everything that had happened the night before, Evelyne was reluctant to see her sister go.

Aurelia turned to her, the warmth in her eyes dimmed by concern. Without a word, she pulled Evelyne into a firm embrace, holding her as if she could shield her from the burden of everything left unspoken. Evelyne sank into her arms, but it did little to calm the turmoil within.

Everyone knew what happened between her and Alaric at the ball. Still, she avoided their curious looks, unwilling to relive it, especially after what had unfolded in the library with Cillian. Her mother had come to her room before she fell asleep, standing quietly in the doorway, waiting. But Evelyne's anger had still burned too hot, disloyalty settling heavily in her chest. She couldn't bear to look at her.

"I can't talk to you right now," she'd said, her voice tight with emotion.

Her mother hadn't argued, hadn't pled. She'd turned and walked away, closing the door softly behind her.

But Aurelia understood. Evelyne saw it in the sadness in her eyes, in the brief hesitation before she finally stepped back. For a moment, it seemed like she didn't want to leave.

Her voice broke through the silence, a whisper against Evelyne's ear. "You're stronger than you think, sister. Don't let them make you feel powerless."

Evelyne's throat tightened. She wanted to hold on to her, to say that all was not well, that she felt as though she stood at the edge of a vast, unknowable abyss. But the words never came. She only managed a nod.

Aurelia pulled back slightly, her hands resting on Evelyne's arms. "I know you, Ev. Whatever it is, don't carry it alone."

The lump in Evelyne's throat grew, but she forced a small smile. "I'll miss you."

Aurelia searched her face for a long moment, before finally stepping into the carriage. As the wheels began to turn, sending the vehicle rolling down the long, muddy path away from the manor, Evelyne remained frozen. The crisp breeze seeped into her skin, but it wasn't the cold morning air that unsettled her.

Something felt wrong.

She turned toward the house, her thoughts tangled, the unease in her chest blooming into a heavier dread, an urgency that clawed at her. It wasn't only Alaric's lie that haunted her now.

Where was Cillian?

He had not been outside to see Aurelia off. He would never miss saying goodbye to family, no matter how ill he had been. The realization sent a sharp pang of fear through her, and she quickened her steps, heading inside.

The house was quieter than usual, a stillness that made her tense. Evelyne's apprehension deepened with each step as she moved through the dim corridors, the echo of her footsteps the only sound in the vast manor.

She hurried to the servants, her voice tense as she asked each one—had they seen her brother? Spoken to him? Heard anything? The answers were all the same: a shake of the head, a quiet "No, my lady." His young red-haired handmaid, always by his side, only stared back with wide, uncertain eyes. No one had seen him since last night.

The storm had been fierce, wind howling through the trees and rain hammering against the manor with relentless force. It would have drowned out the sound of anything: a door opening, footsteps slipping away into the night. Had Cillian left of his own accord, vanishing into the darkness while the tempest raged? *Or*—ice creeping up her spine—had something taken him?

She suddenly remembered the dream—or had it been a dream?—that had plagued her sleep. The inky black mist curling through the hallways, seeping under her door and cooling her skin beneath the warmth of her blankets. Deep in her heart, she felt it had come with purpose. That it had taken something.

Her heart pounded as she forced herself up the stairs and pushed open Cillian's door. The room was eerily silent, and a deep, penetrating cold washed over her when she stepped inside. A suffocating wrongness clung to the walls, the air charged with something unseen but palpable, pressing against her skin like the static before a lightning strike.

Cillian's desk was in disarray, books and papers strewn across the floor as if he'd been frantically searching for something. Loose pages covered every surface—each one filled with his handwriting. Symbols. Drawn over and over again. Some hastily scratched out, others circled in dark, heavy strokes. Evelyne's stomach turned as she picked one up, running her fingers over the grooves where the ink had bitten deep into the page.

She could feel his desperation in every mark—an obsession that must have consumed him. It was as though these symbols had haunted him, demanding to be remembered. Perhaps he'd drawn them endlessly so he wouldn't forget. Or perhaps, by tracing them again and again, he'd hoped to understand what they meant.

Whatever truth Cillian had been chasing, Evelyne feared it had already unraveled him.

She turned and forced herself to move, pushing open the door to his bathing chamber. Everything remained undisturbed: towels neatly folded, his night robe draped over the chair as always. But the familiarity only made her dread grow. Swallowing her panic, she grabbed two books from his desk and hurried downstairs.

In the drawing room, she found her parents, the scent of tea and burning wood lingering in the air. The calm, everyday scene only fueled her frustration.

"He's gone," Evelyne said, her voice slicing through the quiet.

Her mother barely glanced up. "Who?"

"Cillian," she snapped. "No one has seen him since last night."

Her father placed his cup down, his expression firm, while her mother sighed and shook her head. "Evelyne, you're overreacting."

A quick, incredulous laugh burst from her. "Overreacting? He would never leave without telling someone, without saying goodbye to Aurelia! You know that." Her heart thundered in her chest. She took a step forward, gripping the books tighter. "Something is wrong!"

She paused and let out an exasperated breath.

"I saw him last night in the library. He wasn't himself. His eyes weren't gold, Mother. They were black. And he was... He was different. Angry." She swallowed hard, the memory clawing at her mind. "And last night, I swear I saw something, felt something. It was cold and dark. I thought I was dreaming, but—"

Her mother only shook her head again, dismissive, unconcerned. "Have you asked his handmaid?"

"Yes. Sonya does not know where he is."

She looked at her father, but he was silent. *Too* silent. His jaw had tightened, and his eyes flickered with something she couldn't name. He was thinking.

"You know something," she accused.

Her father exhaled sharply but said nothing.

Evelyne stepped closer. "What do you know?"

"Evelyne—" her mother began, but she cut her off, her voice sharp and frantic.

"What do you know?"

A heavy silence fell over the room before her father finally spoke.

"This may be related to Velenshire."

At that, her mother stiffened and turned to gape at her husband. Her lips pressed into a thin line.

Evelyne looked between them. "What is happening in Velenshire?"

"Darkness," her father said firmly.

Her mother inhaled and added, "Dark magic."

Evelyne felt the ground shift beneath her, as though reality had warped instantly. Magic belonged to myths and fairytales—whispers meant for children, not something tangible or real. It couldn't be. A disbelieving laugh nearly escaped her lips at the absurdity of their words, but the weight in their expressions, the unwavering certainty in their eyes, stole the breath from her lungs.

They weren't joking. They weren't mistaken. They *believed* what they were saying, which terrified her more than anything.

Her father continued. "I've been trying to gather information quietly. Trade routes have gone dark. Spies we've sent into the area do not return. And if they do, they can't remember what they saw." He hesitated. "Gaviel Stonebridge is sending Alaric to investigate."

Evelyne flinched at the name, disgust and worry warring within her. She wanted to hate him for what he had done, but the thought of him being sent into something dangerous made her chest tighten.

"Why him?" she demanded.

"If men aren't returning, why send Alaric?"

"Because we need answers, Evelyne. And Alaric has a way of getting them."

Evelyne clenched her jaw, but her thoughts spun back to her brother. To the pages of symbols, to his disappearance.

"I fear dark magic is somehow connected to this," Aron said, turning to Celeste. "To Cillian."

"I'm going to find him," Evelyne said.

"No, you are not," her father snapped. "I will send men out to search."

She turned on him. "I am done being kept blind to the truth. You lied to me—both of you." Her voice trembled with anger as she pointed to her mother. "You will not tell me what I can or cannot do. I will find my brother."

Her father rose and stepped forward, his face grave. "Evelyne, we have no idea what dangers are out there."

"And what are you going to do about your son?" She grabbed a handful of Cillian's sketches, shoving them toward him. "Look at his room! He wasn't sick. He was hiding, struggling! And all this time, you suspected it might be magic, yet you stayed silent and let him believe he was broken."

"I didn't know it was—"

A voice cut through the tension. "My lord."

Their most seasoned and steadfast guard, Marcel, stood at attention, composed but edged with unease. He inclined his head respectfully to her father, then her mother, and finally to Evelyne.

"One of the younger guards noticed the glass foyer doors leading to the stone patio were open this morning," he reported. "At first, he assumed the storm had blown them wide during the night. But after learning Lord Cillian never returned to his chambers, he returned to look closer."

He hesitated, his gaze shifting between them before settling on Lord Duskwood. Evelyne barely breathed as she waited for him to continue.

"There are footprints in the mud," Marcel finally said, his voice low. "Bare footprints leading into the trees."

The words hit like a physical blow.

Barefoot. He was out there alone and barefoot. The storm must have masked his departure, if it had been his choice to leave.

"My lord, there is more. Before the path meets the trees, near the great standing stones, we found... something."

Lord Duskwood narrowed his eyes. "Go on."

Marcel drew in a steady breath. "It's a sigil, carved into the largest stone—seared into its surface as if by some ancient... magic."

For the first time, a brief change crossed Lord Duskwood's face. His command was firm. "Gather the guards. Start searching immediately. Keep the estate under watch, and the moment anyone sees him, report to me."

Evelyne's hands trembled as she clutched the papers and books tighter against her chest, their weight pressing into her ribs. A sigil of ancient magic? How could they possibly know of such a thing? Questions swirled in her mind, but she couldn't afford to linger. She wouldn't.

"Take me," she commanded, striding toward Marcel. "I will see it now."

She ignored her parents' disapproval of her bold defiance. Determined to unravel the mystery, she decided that no more time would be wasted. She would find Cillian, even if it meant venturing into the darkness herself.

PART TWO

MOONBOUND

CHAPTER 19

Evelyne followed Marcel through the drenched clearing in the back of the manor, out past the stone patio. The rain from last night's storm had left the world sodden and the ground soft beneath her boots. Drops of water still clung to the bare branches of the trees ahead, glistening in the late-morning light before falling in slow, deliberate drips. In the distance, a crow called out, its cry stark against the hush that had settled over the woods.

Her father padded beside her, his posture rigid. The barefoot prints found in the mud were barely visible as they headed toward the stone.

Marcel paced quickly through the mud and grass, careful not to splatter any on the lord and young lady behind him. "There," he said as he gestured toward the large stone.

A sigil was carved deep into the rock's face—freshly etched, yet ancient in design. A twisting lattice of interwoven symbols, its lines cut unnaturally smooth, as if scorched into the stone rather than chiseled. Darkened grooves, edged with the faintest shimmer, like dying embers beneath ash. A central rune dominated the pattern, jagged and angular, its shape reminiscent of an eye split down the center or a blade driven into the earth. Even with the daylight spilling over the rock, the markings seemed untouched by the world around them, resisting moisture, resisting decay.

Evelyne felt drawn to them. Her feet carried her forward before she could think better of it. Slowly, she knelt, reaching out. And as her fingertips brushed the stone, the air shifted.

A pulse.

Not a sound; not a movement. It was a feeling. A deep, rhythmic thrum vibrated beneath her touch, slow and steady like a distant heartbeat. The sensation was neither warm nor cold, but wholly different—almost alien. It was as if a presence coiled beneath her skin, creeping tendrils of inky smoke. The pressure climbed her arm, an insidious whisper of something ominous. Then came the chill. The same eerie coldness she had felt the night before and again in Cillian's chambers.

A powerful surge raced through her veins and wrapped around her bones. A soft murmur—more a distant caress than an actual voice—brushed the edges of her mind, a subtle warning not to delve any further.

A sharp gasp escaped her lips, and she jerked her hand away.

In an instant, her father was by her side. "Evelyne, are you all right?"

She turned toward him, her fingers tingling from the phantom pulse beneath her skin. "Did you feel that?" she whispered.

Her father's eyes darkened as he regarded the symbol seared into the rock. He made no move to touch it.

"It's a warning," he stated firmly.

Marcel shifted uneasily. "My lord, this wasn't here yesterday. And there's no evidence of fire, tool, or man capable of carving this so deeply in a single night."

Aron Duskwood exhaled slowly. "A man did not do this."

"Then who? Or what?" Evelyne asked.

Her father ignored the question. "We're returning to the manor. I'll send word to the scholars."

Evelyne's gaze lingered on the sigil, its dark lines stark against the stone. She had never seen anything like it, and she couldn't decide which unnerved her more: its mysterious overnight appearance, or the sensation that it pulsed with life when she touched it.

Swallowing hard, she declared, "I'm going to find Cillian."

Lord Duskwood's jaw tightened, but he did not argue. Instead, he placed a steady hand on her shoulder. "We proceed with caution, Evelyne. We must not blindly follow whatever force left this behind."

Though she said nothing, her intention was clear. She wouldn't wait for the scholars or follow her father's directives—she was determined to uncover the truth alone.

***

Evelyne stood in the quiet gloom of Cillian's room. Every surface was dusted with memories, and her heart pounded as she carefully searched through his scattered books and meticulously drawn sketches. Guilt washed over her as she glanced at his empty bed and the chair where he once sat. She berated herself—she should have been there for him, sitting with him to learn about his fears and experiences instead of indulging in a fleeting engagement with Alaric. Her anger at her own neglect of him stung deeply.

She inhaled deeply, forcing herself to set aside the emotions curling hot in her veins. Regret would not bring him back.

With renewed determination, Evelyne began rifling through his belongings, gathering every page, every scrap of writing that could hold the key to his disappearance. She pulled books from his shelves, recognizing familiar titles from the family library—*History of the Southern Territories, Heraldry and Sacred Signs*—but the more obscure ones caught her attention. She paused as she ran her fingers over an aged tome, its spine cracked, the title barely legible beneath the wear of time.

The Concord of Shadows: A Forgotten Rite.

It wasn't just old; it felt... unnatural. She pressed her palm against the cover, and for the briefest moment, a faint hum vibrated beneath her touch. Not like the dark pulse she had felt when she touched the ancient sigil—no, this was different. It was as if the book wanted to be opened.

Cillian had borrowed this. She was sure of it. He must have taken it from Velenshire's library while visiting their father. It had meant something to him.

Shoving her collected books and notes into a bundle, she turned and left the room.

Back in her chambers, Evelyne shut the door to and slid the lock into place. Exhaustion weighed heavily on her, but she pushed it aside. She had work to do.

She spread Cillian's sketches across her desk, each a puzzle piece that had yet to fit into place. Again and again, she traced the symbols—the gnarled tree, the haunting pair of eyes, the moon. The more she stared at them, the more they seemed to pulse with some hidden urgency, like they were waiting to be understood. At some point, Seraphine knocked and left a tray of tea and lunch by her door, but Evelyne ignored it, too lost in her frantic search for answers.

She opened *The Concord of Shadows,* its brittle pages crackling as she turned them. Dread prickled under her skin as she spotted folded corners marking specific passages. Cillian had been here before her, searching for something in these words.

The first marked page revealed an illustration—a tree, ancient and massive, its branches stretching toward the heavens. Unlike Cillian's dark and lifeless sketches, this one was vibrant, depicting something powerful and alive.

The Solwyn Tree of Velenshire. Evelyne skimmed the text, devouring the words. *A sacred tree. A vessel of power. Witches gathered beneath its boughs to honor its gifts, believing it protected the southern lands. Seers cast visions in its shade. Rituals were performed beneath its roots. It was the source of balance.*

Magic wasn't just whispers of superstition. It was woven into the land, into the bones of Velenshire itself. She folded the page as Cillian had and turned to the next marked section. Her eyes landed on a bold chapter heading: *The Twins of Power.*

Her fingers clenched the book as she read.

Twin witches, Vaelora and Kaya, were born under a rare celestial alignment, which occurs once every thousand years. In the world of witches, twins are an anomaly of immense power. Together, their magic could rival the gods, their bond unbreakable. But such power was both a blessing and a curse. As children, they were inseparable. As they grew older, their hunger for knowledge deepened, pushing them toward the edges of magic's limits. Then, they found it—a forbidden tome detailing the siphoning of magic from living beings.

They drained others of their gifts: shifters, seers, witches. Their power grew as they inherited the powers of other magical beings. When their dark practices were discovered, Velenshire cast them out, banishing them to the northern lands of Nerathar. But the damage had already begun. Fear of their growing magic led the witches to ally with a powerful shifter pack. Together, they forged a sacred rite: a final safeguard against the resurgence of blood magic, the most powerful and dangerous of all.

Evelyne pressed a trembling hand to her forehead. None of this had ever been spoken of at court. Not in the noble circles. Not in any history she had ever read. Witches. Blood magic. Shifter packs. How had this knowledge been buried so deep? Her world had been built on nobility, wealth, and marriage contracts. But now, all of it seemed insignificant.

She closed the book and looked up. Her tea was surely cold by now, and her untouched lunch remained forgotten at her door. She knew she needed to eat, to steady herself, but her mind refused to rest.

Outside, the wind howled against the window panes, rattling them like invisible fingers scraping against the glass. Evelyne exhaled slowly, pressing her palms against the desk, grounding herself. She needed answers—more than scattered pages and stories of ancient magic could give her. Her gaze drifted to the books she had gathered. *Heraldry and Sacred Signs* stood out, its worn exterior promising knowledge of symbols and sigils. But books alone wouldn't be enough. She needed to speak with someone who understood the true history of these lands, someone who could confirm what she had just read.

Velenshire.

The word settled in her mind like a whisper of fate. If there was any place that held the answers she sought, it was there. Deep in her bones, she knew she had only begun to scratch the surface of something far more sinister. And whatever darkness she was chasing had already taken Cillian.

After barely touching her cold lunch, Evelyne pushed the tray aside and stacked the books in a hurried pile. She needed a bag, a portmanteau, a valise, anything to carry them. Her hands trembled as she gathered Cillian's sketches, folding them hastily before tossing them alongside the tomes. She had no time to be careful—every second wasted felt like another step further from finding him.

She turned quickly, eyes scanning her room, her mind racing. Clothes. She needed the right clothes. But how long would she be gone? A few hours? A day? More? She had no idea. The uncertainty gnawed at her, making her movements erratic as she rifled through her drawers, yanking dresses from their hangers and scattering them across the floor. None of them felt right. She couldn't be corseted and tripping over skirts if she needed to move fast.

Just as her frustration began bubbling into panic, a quiet knock sounded at the door before it eased open. Seraphine.

Evelyne exhaled in relief. "Oh, good. I need your help," she blurted, barely pausing to look at her handmaid before returning to the whirlwind of fabric around her. She grabbed a pair of boots and threw them onto the pile before digging through her drawers again.

Seraphine, ever calm, stepped further inside. "Lady Evelyne... what can I help with?"

"I need to find him. I need clothes. Help me pack clothes," Evelyne said hurriedly, her voice fraying at the edges as she threw more garments into the bag. She wasn't thinking—just grabbing. Tunics, pants, boots. Anything that felt remotely useful.

Seraphine's voice remained steady. "Yes, dear, but tell me what is happening first so I can help properly."

Evelyne didn't answer. She couldn't. The words felt like an admission of how lost she was. So she kept moving, shoving more into the bag, refusing to slow down. If she slowed down, she'd think. And if she thought, she'd feel.

"Evelyne." Seraphine's voice was gentle, and a warm hand settled on Evelyne's forearm, stopping her mid-motion. "Please explain."

Evelyne stopped for the first time since she'd entered her brother's room. The pressure in her chest tightened like a vise, and when she finally met Seraphine's gaze, she saw nothing but patience and worry. It nearly undid her.

She swallowed hard and closed her eyes, willing herself to focus.

"I need to find Cillian." She paused. "I'm sure you've heard about his disappearance. I need to find him."

Her words felt heavier than she expected, and her composure suddenly cracked. Fear clawed its way up, suffocating her.

"I wasn't there for him," she admitted, voice breaking. "I *should* have been, and I wasn't."

She dropped her face into her hands, hot tears spilling over her fingers. The weight of it all crashed down, and she let it. She let herself mourn her failure, her regret, her helplessness.

Seraphine's soft hand traced slow, soothing circles against her back. "You *were* there for him. He knew that. But he didn't... No one understood what was happening." She hesitated before adding, "This is not your fault."

Evelyne sniffed, wiped her cheeks, and took a shaky breath. She couldn't afford to cry. She had to act. Lifting her chin, she met Seraphine's gaze again with quiet determination.

"I will find answers, but I need you to help me gather everything I need. I don't know how long I'll be gone, and I need you to keep this from my parents as long as possible."

Seraphine's brows knit in concern, but before she could protest, Evelyne grasped her hand.

"Please." Desperation bled through her voice. "Do this for me."

A moment passed before Seraphine gave a slight nod, and that was all the confirmation Evelyne needed.

Together, they packed with purpose. Seraphine laid out a portmanteau that was sturdy and practical for carriage travel. At the same time, Evelyne retrieved a carpet bag from her wardrobe—compact enough for daily use yet roomy enough to hold her essentials.

She carefully selected two well-made travel dresses designed for ease of movement but still appropriate for her status. A simple evening dress followed in case she needed to maintain appearances. She added a warm cloak lined with wool and a shawl for extra warmth. Gloves, stockings, and undergarments were neatly folded beside them. For footwear, she packed a pair of sturdy leather boots for long walks and one pair of fine shoes, should she need them. And before closing the case, she carefully packed the books, ensuring they were secured among her clothing.

Seraphine tucked a small knife into the folds of her cloak, its discreet weight comforting. Evelyne gathered a water flask, then carefully wrapped dried fruit, nuts, and biscuits in linen, securing them inside the carpet bag. She placed a coin purse beside them, ensuring she had enough funds for unexpected expenses.

But it wasn't enough.

Once they had finished, Evelyne slipped from her chambers, heart pounding as she moved swiftly through the halls. Most of the staff were occupied with evening dinner preparations, and the house was quiet. She reached her father's empty study, glancing over her shoulder before slipping inside.

She didn't hesitate. She knew the fundamentals—how to load the powder and ball, prime the pan, and fire if necessary. Her father had taught her when she was twelve, allowing her to practice for a few years before deeming it improper for a young lady to handle a firearm. She was undoubtedly rusty, but hoped she'd never have to use it.

She pulled open the desk drawer with steady hands, fingers brushing against the polished wood and cold steel of the short-barreled flintlock pistol concealed within. Her father had always kept it in the same spot, safely tucked away for emergencies.

After securing the pistol inside her carpet bag, Evelyne paused, then reached back into the drawer. The weapon would be useless without the proper supplies. She found the small leather pouch her father had always kept nearby, containing powder, lead balls, and spare flint. The faint scent of sulfur and oil clung to the contents. When was the last time it had been used? Was the powder still dry? Would the flint even spark? She didn't know, but she'd sooner take the risk than be left defenseless. Tucking the pouch securely beside the pistol, she fastened her bag shut and exhaled.

She was ready.

CHAPTER 20

Beneath a sky slowly unveiling its first scattering of stars, Evelyne set off into the unknown, the rhythmic clatter of wheels against the road the only sound accompanying her thoughts. Within the confines of her carriage, she finally allowed herself to breathe, her mind easing for the first time in hours as she gazed out the window, watching the darkened countryside slip past.

She was grateful for Seraphine's support and the quiet strength in her farewell. Evelyne had hugged her before slipping into the night, still feeling the warmth of her hands. As she left, she saw Seraphine brush away a silver strand of hair, her eyes glistening with tears. The sight almost made her stop, tempting her to stay—but she couldn't. This was a journey she had to take alone.

She had no idea where it would lead her. The thought scared her, but she had no choice—she would figure it out. No matter how long it took. She refused to let herself imagine the kind of fear Cillian must be feeling—loneliness. Confusion. Whatever had taken him had been tormenting him for months, a darkness cruel enough to twist his mind in ways she couldn't understand. Had he been possessed? Marked by something? She had been skeptical of magic before, but now... now she had no choice but to believe it.

Seated on the driver's bench, Finnegan, a man in his mid-forties, remained as silent as ever. He had served the Duskwood family for years, his questions never extending beyond "Where to?" or "What time shall we be leaving?". His discretion was a gift—one she needed now more than ever. He didn't ask why she was leaving alone, why she had packed as if for war. But she had felt his gaze lingering when she hurried from the manor, luggage in hand, determination in her stride.

She instructed him to take her to the main market of Velenshire, the last place she knew Cillian and their father had visited. And if Cillian had been at the library, then perhaps she would find some clue that could point her in the right direction.

It was a fragile plan, but it was all she had.

An hour later, the carriage rolled to a slow halt. The horses exhaled in soft huffs as Finnegan climbed down, his boots scuffing against the cobblestones as he pulled open the door. Before leaving the carriage, Evelyne reached for her carpet bag, carefully checking that the borrowed book was safely inside.

Velenshire breathed with quiet mystery, its streets alive with an energy that made the hairs on Evelyne's arms stand on end. As she stepped down from the carriage, the city seemed to watch her in silence, its presence felt in the glistening cobblestones, the whisper of distant voices, the flicker of lantern light stretching shadows against the tightly packed buildings.

She took a slow breath, adjusting the folds of her cloak as she surveyed her surroundings. The narrow streets wound through the city like veins, guiding the steady hum of nighttime activity. The air held a strange mix of scents—damp earth, burning wood, and something sweet, like roasted chestnuts—blending with the cool spring evening. It should have felt normal, but it didn't. Something lingered beneath it, something she couldn't name, as if the city were straining to contain its power.

Evelyne kept moving, her boots clicking against the slick stones as she stepped into the heart of the market. The square was busier than she expected at this hour, but it lacked the boisterous clamor of Caltheris' markets. There were no shouting merchants or noisy haggling; instead, the trade moved with a precise, almost ritualistic rhythm.

She passed by wooden stalls draped in thick fabrics, their awnings low as if shielding their wares from wandering eyes. Merchants stood behind their displays with quiet confidence, adjusting trinkets. Glass vials filled with swirling, iridescent liquid caught the glow of dim light, changing colors when tilted. Silver charms etched with unfamiliar runes dangled from wooden racks, their surfaces worn smooth from handling.

Evelyne's fingers twitched at her sides. Magic was woven into this place; subtle, unspoken, but undeniably present.

A sudden gust of wind sent a wooden sign swinging gently on its iron post, catching her attention.

Relics and Refinements.

She slowed, her eyes tracing the elegant, looping script of the shop's name. Something about it made her hesitate. It was nothing special, just another tucked-away storefront among dozens, but she felt a strange pull toward it, like her feet wanted to move before her mind could decide. Instead, she turned to the path ahead, toward the library—where she might finally start making sense of all the unanswered questions. Whatever drew her toward that shop would have to wait. But even as she walked away, the feeling remained, like she had just brushed against something important... Something waiting for her to return.

"Excuse me!" Evelyne called out to a young woman draped in a white cloak, her fingers delicately tracing the silver charms displayed at one of the market stalls.

The woman turned, her brows knitting together in mild confusion as she took in Evelyne's unfamiliar face.

"Could you point me toward the library?"

"Of course, miss," she said, offering a polite nod before gesturing. "It's just one street over, then turn left after the baker's shop." She returned to the charms with a brief smile as if the interruption had never happened.

"Thank you," Evelyne replied, already moving in the direction given.

The library loomed ahead, its towering presence impossible to miss. Evelyne barely had to search for it—the sheer height of the structure made it stand out against the surrounding buildings like an ancient sentinel.

Stepping inside, she instinctively pulled her cloak tighter around her shoulders, clutching her carpet bag as a shiver rippled over her skin. The air inside was cooler than expected, and a quiet hush wrapped around her like a spell. Rows upon rows of towering bookshelves stretched into the dimly lit space, each filled with texts that seemed to whisper their own stories.

At the front desk, an elderly librarian sat hunched over a book, her gnarled fingers slowly tracing the text as if committing every word to memory. Evelyne hesitated before stepping forward, clearing her throat.

The librarian barely lifted her gaze. "Yes?" she murmured.

Evelyne reached into her bag and placed the book on the counter.

That got her attention.

The woman's pale, piercing eyes flicked up, meeting Evelyne's with quiet intensity. Slowly, she straightened, her eyes shifting between Evelyne and the book.

"You are his sister."

Evelyne tried to contain her shock. How could she possibly know that? She must see dozens of books and countless borrowers each day. And yet, she recognized *this* book. And somehow recognized her.

Evelyne opened her mouth, searching for words, but nothing came. The librarian seemed to sense her confusion.

"You have the same eyes."

Evelyne swallowed hard. "Yes." She paused, then asked, "Do you recognize this book?"

The librarian nodded.

"My brother borrowed this from here. I was hoping you could tell me anything you know about it, or anything he said or did while he was here."

Silence stretched between them.

Evelyne exhaled sharply, trying again. "I just... I need to understand why he picked *this* book. Did he say anything about it?" Her words tumbled out too fast, bordering on desperate.

The older woman tapped her fingers against the book's worn cover. "I like to believe the books in this library choose the reader rather than the reader choosing the book."

Evelyne's eyes dropped to the book beneath the woman's hand, an uneasy feeling creeping through her.

The librarian's voice dropped lower, almost conspiratorial. "This book is calling to you, too... isn't it?"

Evelyne stiffened. That was ridiculous. Completely mad. And yet... she couldn't ignore the truth of it. The book felt warm against her skin when she touched it, as though it had been waiting for her all along. She pressed her lips together and shoved the book back into her bag, ignoring how her fingers tingled.

Evelyne exhaled sharply. "I'd like to extend the time on this book, if I may." She wasn't finished with it yet. Not even close.

The librarian gave a slow, sly smile. "Of course, dear. And before you leave, do visit my daughter's shop—Relics and Refinements, just in the market."

That shop. The name alone stirred something unsettling within her, a reminder of the strange, unshakable pull she had felt upon arriving in Velenshire. She needed to leave. Immediately.

Forcing a polite smile, Evelyne murmured her thanks and turned swiftly toward the exit. The library, and everything within it, was starting to make her skin crawl. She wanted to ask more. A lot more. But the entire encounter left her unnerved.

Keeping to the well-lit stretches of the market streets, Evelyne moved swiftly, her bag drawn close. The last thing she wanted was another nighttime encounter like the one with Lord Bavrick. Her focus was clear: reach the main square and return to the carriage.

Yet, before fully registering where her steps had taken her, she stood at the threshold of the shop. The one the librarian had urged her to visit. The one that had pulled at her the moment she arrived. And before she could stop herself, before she could even think, her hand was already on the knob, turning it.

As Evelyne stepped inside, the bell above the door chimed softly, its sound swallowed almost instantly by the warmth of the space. The air carried the scent of jasmine, rich and heady, curling around her like an unseen welcome.

The shop was small but overflowing, every inch crammed with relics, trinkets, and objects that seemed to hum. Wooden shelves lined the room, cluttered with glass vials, intricately carved boxes, and aged tomes. It was crowded, yet everything seemed precisely where it was meant to be.

A woman emerged behind the counter when the bell rang, like she had expected Evelyne. She appeared to be around Evelyne's mother's age, her soft brunette curls laced with silver. She had the kind of beauty that didn't fade with time—gentle yet commanding, with a quiet strength behind her kind expression.

She met Evelyne's stare, assessing without intimidation, fearless without arrogance.

"Welcome," she said smoothly.

Evelyne slowly closed the door behind her, her eyes trailing over the strange and wonderful things that filled the shop.

"I'm glad we've finally met." The woman smiled, her gaze flicking toward the door. "I'm glad we've *all* finally met."

The bell above the entrance chimed. Evelyne turned—and there stood Alaric, stepping into the shop.

***

Alaric had been sent by his father to meet Lord Corvin and Lady Mireya Shaw of Velenshire, tasked with uncovering the true extent of the darkness that had begun swallowing the trade routes. Judging by the grim expressions of the noble couple seated before him, he already knew the news wouldn't be good.

Lord Corvin exhaled slowly, his weathered hands clasped together as he met Alaric's gaze. "We are losing men." His voice was heavy. "Most don't return. They seem to... vanish."

Alaric's brow furrowed. "How do you mean?"

Sitting at her husband's side, Lady Mireya traced the rim of her goblet, her delicate fingers trembling; a flicker of emotion she quickly hid.

"As you know," Lord Corvin began, "we've expanded our trade routes to the eastern lands of Centaro, exchanging meats and spices for coal and fur. The cold is unpredictable in the south, and our people rely on these exchanges to survive the bitter months of late autumn. But the carriages never make it through. We find them abandoned, broken down in the middle of the road, cargo scattered… but no bodies. No signs of struggle. Just… emptiness."

Alaric tightened his jaw. He needed answers, not more warnings.

"Who can I speak to?" He pressed.

"Someone must know more about what's happening."

Lady Mireya rose from her chair, her golden hair cascading over her petite frame, and stepped toward him. She was striking, young and poised, but as she leaned in, her voice fell to a whisper, both playful and edged with warning.

"Find Charise Hallowell, and you will get your answers."

Alaric studied her carefully. "And where, exactly, would I find this Charise?"

Lady Mireya's lips curled into the faintest smirk as her fingers traced the table's edge. Instead of returning to her seat, she leaned back against the table near Alaric, her hands resting on either side to steady herself.

"Go to the market," she murmured. "She will find you."

Alaric exhaled sharply. Cryptic. Great.

Lord Corvin reached for something beside him, unfolding a piece of parchment before handing it to Alaric—a map.

Another map. As if he didn't have enough of those back home.

Lord Corvin must have caught the flicker of frustration in Alaric's face, because his voice took on a graver tone. "This is not a map you've seen before." His expression darkened as he tapped a finger against the aged parchment. "This will help you avoid the shadows."

Alaric narrowed his gaze, unfolding the map entirely. At first glance, it looked no different from any other map of the trade routes—but as his fingers brushed the inked surface, something throbbed beneath his skin, a low pulse of energy that prickled up his arm.

Magic.

He clenched his jaw, tucking the map into his pocket before looking back at the noble couple. "Thank you. I will, uh... do my best to solve this problem."

Lady Mireya tilted her head, watching him with something unreadable in her eyes before she finally smiled. "Do be careful, Alaric," she said, her voice a velvety warning wrapped in amusement. "We'd hate to lose another handsome face from the south."

Lady Mireya was a woman who delighted in her position, draped in the elegance of nobility like a second skin. Lord Corvin, much older than her and seemingly indifferent to her playful flirtations with Alaric, made no effort to curb her boldness. Why would he? He was the one who held the power, the one who could summon her to his bed whenever he pleased.

Yet beneath her teasing smirk was something else—a guarded edge, a glint of unease carefully concealed behind charm and sharp wit. She played the role of the confident lady well, but Alaric suspected it was merely a mask, shielding whatever fears she refused to voice.

He gulped, but forced a chuckle. This was ridiculous. Whispers of vanishing men. Maps that sensed magic. A woman in the market who would "find" him.

And yet... something deep within him whispered that was precisely where he needed to go.

Without hesitation, he set off for the market. As he navigated the bustling streets, a quiet pull—neither forceful nor gentle, but insistent—steered him toward a small shop between the rows of vendors. He stepped inside, and his breath caught in his chest.

Evelyne.

She stood before him, her eyes locking onto his with a fire that burned hotter than any words she could have spoken. Confusion. Hatred. Pain. It seared through him, leaving him hollowed out from the inside.

And he deserved it. Every bit of it.

CHAPTER 21

"Why are you here?" Evelyne spat through clenched teeth. Just looking at Alaric made her skin burn with anger.

Alaric hesitated, his eyes flashing between her and the woman behind the counter. "I... I'm here to see—" He paused, turning to the shopkeeper. "Are you Charise Hallowell?"

At the sound of her name, Evelyne stiffened. Only now did she shift her attention to the shopkeeper, the woman watching them both with an almost amused glint in her eyes.

She smiled. "I am."

Alaric stepped further inside, and Evelyne immediately moved away, carefully keeping as much distance between them as possible. They hadn't spoken since the ball. Not about what had happened or what she'd seen, and she had no intention of starting that conversation now.

"What is this?" Evelyne demanded. "What's going on?"

Charise's smile didn't falter. "I summoned you both here. The pull you felt—that was me." She extended a hand, gesturing toward the back of the shop. It was a silent instruction, a wordless request for them to follow.

Evelyne wanted to walk right back out the door. She should have. But instead, she moved forward, frustration bubbling beneath her skin.

Alaric followed. "So you're able to summon magic?" he asked Charise.

She didn't stop, only parted the heavy curtain leading into the dimly lit back room. "Yes," she answered. The space was small, a single circular table surrounded by wooden chairs at its center. Charise gestured for them both to sit. "Make yourselves comfortable. I promise to answer your questions, but first, let me get you some tea." Without another word, she slipped through the curtain, leaving them alone.

Alaric leaned in slightly. "Did you travel here alone?"

"Yes," Evelyne replied coldly. She had no desire to speak with him.

"Why? What happened?"

Of course—he didn't know. The last thing he likely remembered was tearing her heart apart at the ball.

"Why are you looking for Charise?" she asked.

Alaric exhaled. "My father sent me to meet with Lord and Lady Shaw. They, in turn, sent me here."

He looked at her again; this time, his expression was raw. "Evelyne, please. What happened?"

She released a slow breath. "Cillian disappeared, and no one could find him. So I took it upon myself to get answers."

Instinctively, it seemed, Alaric reached across the table, his hand resting gently over hers. But Evelyne pulled away instantly.

"Please, Alaric. Don't."

Regret and sadness flickered in his eyes, but he remained silent as he pulled his hand away.

When Charise returned, she carried a tea tray and carefully handed them each a teacup. The delicate porcelain was warm against Evelyne's fingers as Charise gently poured the fragrant green tea. A quiet moment settled between them until Charise finally spoke, lightly tapping her fingers against her cup.

"I'm not certain how much you already know, but I'll do my best to answer your questions." She shifted her gaze to Evelyne.

"Your brother came to my shop while he was here. He also spent time in the library—with my mother. And from what I overheard about his disappearance, I'd say my friend was right to bring you both here."

Evelyne's grip on her cup tightened. So many questions swirled inside her; she didn't know where to start. Who was this woman and what *friend* was she referring to? And if magic were truly real... how could she trust her? She glanced down at the tea, suddenly hesitant to take a sip.

Charise caught the look and gave a faint grin. "It's just green tea. Nothing more."

"What are you?" Evelyne blurted, but Charise didn't flinch.

"I'm a witch. As is my mother, and my ancestors before her. My family has lived in Velenshire for generations."

A witch.

The stories Evelyne had once dismissed as childhood myths—they were real. And now, she sat face to face with one.

"And why did you summon us here?" Alaric asked.

"Because you will need each other," Charise replied.

Evelyne scoffed, folding her arms tightly across her chest. "I don't need him." She barely spared Alaric a glance before continuing, "I'm here because I need answers. I need to find my brother, and that's all that matters. Can you help me with that or not?"

Charise exhaled softly, unshaken by Evelyne's stubbornness. "You don't yet understand what lies ahead," she said, eyes flashing toward Alaric. "But you will need him. He knows the paths. He has the knowledge you'll require to find your brother. And in turn, the journey will provide him with the answers he seeks."

Evelyne's head snapped toward him now, suspicion tightening in her chest. "What answers are *you* looking for, exactly?"

Alaric cleared his throat. "My father sent me to investigate the disturbances along the trade routes. There have been reports of... dark figures intercepting them for weeks. And I was forbidden to speak to anyone outside our families and men."

Right. She remembered her father stating Alaric would be sent to Velenshire, though she hadn't thought twice about when.

"Why?" she asked. "Why is magic being kept a secret from everyone?"

"Long ago, the witches of Velenshire struck a pact with a handful of noble families who had stumbled upon our presence—and saw us as a threat," Charise said quietly. "To avoid open conflict, we forged an arrangement. We would remain here, our magic concealed from the wider world, so long as our craft was turned toward shielding humanity from the dangers that prowl beyond. From those who might seek to claim this land—should they ever uncover the power buried beneath it. The covens bound themselves by oath to guard the south from such threats, and in return, we were granted the right to remain hidden, practicing our spells in secret."

"And what of the people living beyond the southern lands?" Evelyne asked.

"Most humans live here," Charise said. "Some reside in the eastern villages of Centaro, and a few dare to settle farther north—but the majority remain in the south. The more humans we keep here, the easier it is to make others believe these lands hold no powerful magic."

This was all too much. And what did she mean by powerful magic? Questions flooded her mind, but time was not a luxury she could afford.

Evelyne released a sharp breath, steadied herself, and reached into her carpet bag, pulling out the worn leather-bound book and setting it firmly on the table. Flipping through its pages, she found the passage she needed and tapped her finger against the title.

"I would love nothing more than to sit here all day unraveling the fabric of my reality," she said dryly. "But I believe I now have a sufficient understanding that my entire upbringing was built on falsehoods, and that I have spent my life surrounded by liars and witches. So…" She tilted her head. "Would you be so kind as to explain what exactly this passage is referring to?"

Charise carefully turned the book toward herself, her eyes scanning the words, lips pressing together as she slowly nodded. "Yes," she murmured. "This is why I brought you here. To tell you the story of Kaya and Vaelora."

Charise started retelling the story Evelyne had only just begun to uncover.

"The twin witches, Kaya and Vaelora, held immense power in Velenshire. Too much power." She traced the rim of her teacup as she spoke. Evelyne felt Alaric's knee bouncing beneath the table—the only sign of his nerves.

"From the moment they could wield magic, the sisters were stronger than any witch before them. Admired, but feared. And power—true, unrestrained power—is dangerous. They reveled in it."

She glanced at Evelyne, weighing how much she wished to hear. "Vaelora, eldest by mere minutes, was the ambitious one. She unearthed a forbidden tome of dark magic and convinced Kaya to join her. Together, they grew stronger than the covens—stronger than any force Velenshire had ever known."

Evelyne's fists curled in her lap. "What happened?"

Charise's expression darkened. "The covens united and banished them. But exile was not the end. They fled north to Nerathar, a land untouched by southern law. There, they conquered—and likely still dwell."

Silence settled over the room like a weighted shroud.

Alaric leaned forward. "You're saying they still *live*?"

Charise's lips pressed into a thin line. "Vaelora is alive, yes."

Alaric tensed. "How? The book states it was over a century ago."

"Because of their magic," Charise explained. "By draining the life and power of others, they made themselves nearly immortal. Their bodies do not wither with age as ours do. At least, that is what the whispers claim. Few venture into Nerathar and return to tell the tale."

Alaric's voice tightened with urgency. "Why exile the witches after working so hard to conceal Velenshire's power? Didn't your ancestors fear they might reveal it to others out of spite? If the secret ever slipped, Velenshire wouldn't remain just another settlement—it would turn into a battleground, a prize for the taking. So why risk it?"

Charise folded her hands in her lap before speaking. "You're right—they could have exposed us all. Had Vaelora or Kaya revealed Velenshire's secret, everything would have been lost. But the covens knew the twins would never permit other wielders to uncover the truth of our land, nor allow outsiders to bind themselves to our balance of power. So they chose patience instead, trusting secrecy to keep us safe. Since the banishment, we've remained hidden. We've done nothing to defy Vaelora or provoke her hand." Charise shrugged slightly. "Perhaps that is why she has not yet claimed Velenshire... or perhaps her designs lie elsewhere. I cannot say. But I can't shake the feeling that she is watching us."

"And Kaya?" Evelyne asked. "You said Vaelora still lives... What happened to her sister?"

"We may not know the manner of her fate, but every witch felt the tremor in the world twenty-five years ago. When a witch falls, we feel the silence they leave behind. Yet this loss was unlike any other. From that moment, our magic began to wither." She exhaled slowly, as if the memory still pressed on her chest.

"Forgive me, but I must understand—how does this connect to my brother?" Evelyne pressed. "Why have you summoned *me* here?"

Charise leaned back in her chair. "Because my great-grandmother was there when the twins were banished. She was the most powerful witch of the Hallowell coven at the time and performed the Great Rite along with the other covens. The final safeguard."

Alaric frowned. "A safeguard against what?"

"Against blood magic."

The words hung heavy in the air.

Alaric swallowed, shaking his head. "But they were already using dark magic. Isn't that why they were banished?"

"Yes," Charise acknowledged. "But there is magic, and then there is blood magic. It is the most powerful and most forbidden of all. Few witches are strong enough to summon it, and even fewer survive its cost. It requires a sacrifice—a great one. And once it is unleashed, it does not stop until it has consumed everything in its path."

She closed the book before her, turning it so they could see the title stamped across the cracked leather cover. *The Concord of Shadows: A Forgotten Rite.*

Evelyne's fingers pressed against her temples as her head began to throb. "And this Rite... It was meant to protect something?"

Charise nodded. "It was a failsafe. If they ever dared to use blood magic, the Rite would awaken a prophecy buried within it. The only prophecy powerful enough to defeat the one who wielded it."

Vaelora. She was the one who wielded blood magic. Was she the woman in Cillian's visions?

"Does blood magic allow someone to enter another's mind?" Evelyne blurted.

Charise's eyes held hers as she nodded. "It is capable of much more than slipping into the mind. This magic can burrow into the body... even bind itself to the soul."

The room seemed to close in around Evelyne. "Do you think she's the one who took my brother—if he suffered this kind of intrusion?"

"I believe she is searching for answers about the prophecy, about what could be her downfall. And I believe the darkness creeping along Velenshire's borders is her warning. A reminder of what she is capable of if we stand in her way."

Evelyne began flipping through the book's pages, searching for the one that had been creased at the top. And then she found it. The Solwyn Tree of Velenshire.

She read the passage aloud, voice barely above a whisper. "*A sacred tree—a vessel of power. Witches gathered beneath its boughs to honor its gifts, believing it protected the southern lands. Seers cast visions in its shade. Rituals were performed beneath its roots. It was the source of balance.*" Her eyes snapped to Charise. "This tree... This is where the Great Rite was performed?"

Charise reached forward, her fingers ghosting over the faded illustration on the page. "Yes," she said softly. "Our ancestors needed a source of balance to conduct the spell. They surrendered nearly all their magic to the ritual... and in return, the tree's life was drained, though not completely." She traced the image one last time, then let her hand fall away. "I wish I'd seen it like this," she murmured. "So alive and full of power. It's hard to imagine the Solwyn Grove once held such magic hidden deep beneath the soil, woven through the roots of Velenshire's ancient heart."

The Solwyn Grove must be where the tree stood—not hidden, but set apart, sacred and removed from the market's din. Evelyne must have walked past it once, never knowing how near she had come.

She tried to make sense of it all. If Vaelora had turned to blood magic, making herself the most powerful witch ever to exist, and if Cillian had somehow become tangled in her web, he was in grave danger. And he had been right all along. He wasn't ill. His mind had been invaded, tainted by Vaelora's blood magic. But to what end? Why seek to control him?

Was it the Solwyn Tree that continued to appear in his visions? And what of the other two symbols: the eyes and the moon? What could they signify? She still had no clear starting point.

Evelyne turned to Charise. "You said a prophecy was awakened when Vaelora turned to blood magic. What does it say? What could possibly have the power to destroy her?"

"We don't know. Not even our ancestors fully understood it. We have spent generations trying to decipher its meaning, but the Rite itself never explicitly stated what the prophecy would be. Only that it was the key to saving our people." Charise reached toward the book. "May I?"

Evelyne paused only a moment before handing it over.

Charise flipped through the worn pages with careful hands, stopping at an aged section filled with symbols and descriptions of ancient rituals. Her eyes traced the inked words before she read aloud: "*When the darkest power is unleashed, a force long tied to the roots of this world shall rise—a key forged in shadow and light, bound by fate to break what has been made. Await the moon bathed in crimson, for it shall mark the beginning or the end.*" She closed the book. "This is all that remains of the prophecy."

Evelyne's fingers curled into the fabric of her skirts. It wasn't enough.

Alaric finally spoke. "Why would she be interested in corrupting Cillian's mind?"

Charise shook her head. "I can't say for certain. Perhaps he uncovered something, or perhaps she sensed a vulnerability in him. Someone she could manipulate to do her searching for her."

Evelyne's head snapped toward her. "My brother is not weak."

"I meant no offense," Charise said gently. "But something was different about him when he visited Velenshire. I sensed it immediately. Like a strong energy surrounded him, but was hidden beneath the surface. I couldn't quite place it, but it made me... curious." She paused briefly. "Later, I learned he had visited the library and spoken with my mother. But more importantly, he found a book that called to him. This book"—she pointed—"about the Forgotten Rite. Combined with the whispers of darkness spreading across the land, that suddenly made sense."

Her expression darkened.

"The magical shift felt across the world nearly twenty-five years ago... That was Vaelora. That was the moment she tapped into blood magic. And now, she must have discovered that the covens performed a ritual capable of limiting her power."

"And your mother—does she possess magic?" Evelyne asked.

"She does," Charise replied, "though it's not as strong as it once was. These days, her duty lies with the library." She folded her hands neatly in her lap. "When the Rite was performed, it weakened the covens. And after Vaelora turned to blood magic, all of our power began to dim. The Hallowell coven has long served as the guardians of Velenshire's great library, preserving what remains of our knowledge. One day, when my mother passes, I will take her place." She glanced around the small shop, where relics and artifacts hummed softly with residual power. "Until then, I will practice small spells and stay here, in this shop."

"So we go north to Nerathar?" Alaric interrupted.

"I believe that's where Cillian may be. But understand this... Vaelora is too powerful. You won't simply retrieve him and walk away. She will see through any deception before you even step on her land."

Evelyne pushed back her chair and stood. "I don't care. I will find my brother and bring him home."

Charise's expression tightened. "Miss, I strongly urge you to stay. To learn more about Vaelora and the prophecy. You may stand a chance if we can uncover what it truly means."

Evelyne lifted her bag, securing the strap over her shoulder. "I cannot waste another moment." She dipped her head respectfully. "Thank you for your kindness, but I must leave. Now."

Alaric rose beside her, nodding in gratitude. "I'm going with her. Thank you for your help."

Just as he turned to leave, Charise caught his wrist, her grip firm, her voice a whisper only he could hear. Whatever she said, his face blanched for the briefest moment. Then, without a word, he followed Evelyne out of the shop and back into the market.

Evelyne strode briskly toward her carriage. She needed to get inside, to breathe, to think. The books tucked away in her luggage held more answers, and she intended to find them.

Footsteps quickened behind her. "Where are you going, Evelyne?" Alaric's voice chased after her as he caught up to her side.

"What do you mean? I'm going to my carriage. I told you—I'm leaving to find Cillian."

"Yes, I understand that. But what about me?"

She froze mid-step. "What about you?" Her words came sharp.

"Did you not hear Charise? We need to do this together."

Evelyne whipped around to face him. "I heard perfectly well. And I'm choosing not to bring you along."

Alaric's hand closed lightly around her wrist, just enough to stop her from storming off. She jerked back, but his grip held firm. "You are not doing this alone, Evelyne. You have no idea what's waiting for you out there. You don't know the land or the people. You wouldn't last a day alone."

"I don't care." Her jaw clenched so tightly it hurt.

Alaric arched a brow. "I mean no offense, but are you at all versed in cartography?"

The insult hit its mark, and for a brief, burning second, she wanted to slap him. "I'll figure it out, Alaric," she hissed. "Now leave me be."

His refusal was instant. "No. You need me, and I need you. And those books in your bag? They hold answers, answers I need just as much as you do. You don't have the luxury of pride right now, Evelyne. You're not going without me." He stepped closer. "Now get your things. You're riding with me."

Evelyne let out a frustrated breath, her fingers curling into fists before she yanked her wrist free. "Fine." She hesitated, her mind warring with itself, before she turned back toward her carriage.

"I'll help you," Alaric replied, though she didn't acknowledge him. Instead, she pushed forward, determined to ignore his presence at her side. Even as she hated every second of this, she knew he was right. Their arranged marriage was a far less pressing concern than what they were about to face, but still, this was not the partnership she wanted.

At the carriage, she lifted her chin and forced herself to speak. "Finnegan, you may return home. I'll be riding with Mr. Stonebridge for the rest of the evening. Please inform my father that I'll be assisting him for the next few days and intend to... make amends with my *betrothed*."

The word sat like poison on her tongue, and she fought not to wince as she said it. Finnegan merely nodded and passed her luggage to Alaric, who took it without a word.

Evelyne inhaled deeply, willing herself to keep her temper in check. Like it or not, this was happening.

CHAPTER 22
THE NIGHT OF THE BALL

The fire in the hearth had burned low, leaving only smoldering embers glowing faintly. At a small table in the library, Cillian sat in the flickering candlelight, its glow casting shadows over the worn pages before him. Outside the library walls, laughter and music filled the ballroom as the court celebrated Evelyne and Alaric's engagement—news his handmaid, Sonya, had shared with him earlier. He was truly happy for his sister and would tell her when the time was right. But for now, he found comfort in the soft patter of rain against the window and the quiet stillness of the library.

The Lantern's Keeper lay open; his fingers traced the words as he read, trying to uncover their meaning.

The Lantern's light must never fade, for in its glow lies the last defense against the encroaching dark. No mere flame, it burns not by oil or wax but by the Keeper's very soul. To be chosen is not to wield power but to become it—to surrender breath, will, and essence to the eternal balance of light and shadow.

Yet the path is perilous. Should the Keeper falter, the Lantern may dim, and in its absence, the darkness will rise unchecked. But to burn too brightly is to be consumed, lost to the very light they sustain. And so, the Keeper walks the edge of fate, neither wholly of this world nor apart from it.

Cillian murmured the words again and again, tasting them on his tongue, trying to feel their significance. He kept asking himself questions he wasn't ready to answer. Could the old stories be more than stories? Could something unnatural have taken root in him? And what if there was a way to purge it? Perhaps the answer lay within these pages, waiting to be uncovered. And if it did... then maybe his suspicions weren't so far-fetched after all. But he kept them to himself, because part of him feared they might be right.

His hand moved independently, circling phrases within the passage. That was when she appeared.

"Hello, Cillian."

The voice slithered into the room like silk, tinged with wicked amusement. He knew it before he even looked up. She stood before him, the woman who had haunted his visions, always beyond his grasp. Tonight, she was here in the flesh, if she was real. Dressed in black satin, the gown clinging to her luscious curves, her lips blood-red against her porcelain skin. Her frost-white hair cascaded over one shoulder, gleaming like a silver moon.

"I felt you were missing me," she smiled, stepping closer, "so I thought I'd pay a visit."

She reached for him, her fingers gliding over the back of his hand, the one that held the quill poised above the book. Her touch was cool, yet it sent a heated prickle up his arm. He met her gaze—eyes once silver, now black, cold, and depthless.

She tilted her head, watching him. He shouldn't have admired her, but he did. Every curve, every perfect, unearthly detail. She noticed, of course. She always did.

"I see you're reading another book." Her voice dipped, sultry and teasing. "What an intelligent man you are. You know, I always admired intelligent men. Perhaps you can teach me about what you've been reading?"

Cillian exhaled through his nose, unwilling to entertain her games tonight. But he did nothing to stop her from moving closer. She was always in his mind anyway. What was the difference now?

"I know you've been thinking about me," she purred, stepping between his legs, her presence pressing into him. "I can feel it when you do. That's why I'm here. For you."

She always said that. *I'm here for you.*

He rubbed his hands over his face, exhaustion seeping into his bones. "Why are you here for me? I don't even know your name."

That made her smile grow. She moved closer still, placing her cold hands against his face, fingers trailing along his jaw. Her breath, warm against his lips, sent an unwanted tremor down his spine.

"Because you are the one I want most, Cillian." Her voice was barely a whisper now, intimate and intoxicating. "If I tell you my name... will you let me stay?"

Curiosity coiled around him. "That's all you want? To stay here with me?"

Her thumb brushed along his cheek, featherlight, coaxing. "Yes, Cillian. That is all I want. To be with you."

His body betrayed him. Heat coiled low in his stomach, a pulse of want he couldn't push down. He swallowed hard, but she saw it, felt it, because she laughed softly.

"I can hear your thoughts." She leaned in, lips nearly brushing his. "I can feel your wants."

Something in him snapped. His hands moved without thought, gripping her hips and pulling her down onto his lap. She gasped, though it was not surprise. It was delight.

"Tell me your name." His voice was low.

"My name is Vaelora."

He whispered it, his voice tinged with something dark and hungry. "*Vaelora.*"

Then her lips met his. And he let himself want it.

His hands slid up her waist, fingers digging into silk and skin as the kiss consumed him. Heat, need, and something unrelenting surged through him. The world narrowed, thoughts slipping away, unraveling, dissolving into her. And then—

A void crept through him, pulling him under. His mind unraveled, slipping through his grasp like water through cupped hands. Too late, he understood.

She was a distraction. The perfect lure to make him lower his guard, allowing the darkness within him to seize control of his mind, body, and soul. He could feel himself slipping, reality unraveling with every breath. It all made sense. The visions hadn't been warnings; they'd been clues. And Vaelora must have known he was close to uncovering the truth.

That was when Evelyne stepped into the library, her face shadowed with worry. A desperate instinct to fight back and rip the parasitic darkness from his mind flared within him. But the moment he resisted, the darkness snapped shut around him, a faint thread of glowing light slipping through the cracks just before everything faded to black.

CHAPTER 23

They had been on the road for an entire day now. The carriage rattled over gravel and broken twigs, the rhythmic creaking of its wheels filling the silence between them. Evelyne had spoken little to Alaric, preferring to bury herself in the books she had packed, her eyes often drifting to the passing landscape beyond the window. The monotony of the journey weighed on her, but she found some comfort in the steady movement of the carriage and the quiet that accompanied it.

Alaric's driver, Reuben, was just as silent, speaking only when necessary. They had stopped twice to stretch their legs and relieve themselves, but nothing more. Their only provisions were dried snacks, enough to keep them going but hardly satisfying. Evelyne's stomach twisted in protest. She needed real food.

Alaric hadn't tried to speak to her, but she felt his glances, saw the way his mouth would part as if to say something, only to shut again. His attention was often drawn to the enchanted map in his hands; a gift from Lord and Lady Shaw of Velenshire. Alaric had told her that the map would reveal dark magic, staining the parchment black whenever it lurked nearby. So far, it remained unchanged. A small mercy.

They followed the trail toward the first trade outpost, situated at the northeastern edge of Velenshire, just before Mokkvyrn Forest. Beyond that stretched Centaro's eastern lands: grasslands, hills, villages, and forests rising toward the snow-capped mountains. Evelyne hoped she had packed wisely.

Alaric had already mapped the best passages for their journey, and since they needed to check on trade along the way, she hadn't argued. Charise was right. Evelyne did need him, whether she liked it or not. It was as if he had memorized the land, barely needing the map, though he still had several open beside him in the carriage.

Evelyne turned another page of *Heraldry and Sacred Signs*, her fingers tightening around the spine. She had searched for any symbol resembling the sigil burned into the stone behind her home, but nothing yet matched. Frustrated, she glanced at Alaric, only to find him frowning at the map.

"Any luck deciphering it?" she asked, breaking the silence. "The map, I mean." She nodded toward the parchment in his hands.

Alaric sighed, tilting the map toward the dimming light. "I understand the terrain well enough, but this…" He ran a hand through his hair. "It doesn't show what lies ahead. But when we approach something… unnatural, the ink darkens. And look here." He pointed to the map.

Evelyne leaned in, her eyes scanning the parchment. Sure enough, a faint shadow had spread at the northeastern edge where the first trade post should be.

"Something is there," she murmured, meeting his eyes.

"We'll know soon enough."

They would reach the outpost within the next half hour. Whatever lay ahead, it was waiting for them.

***

The carriage came to a stop. The last slivers of sunlight had vanished behind the trees, casting the world into early twilight. Outside, the air felt damp, and a cold mist curled around the outpost.

Reuben knocked before pulling the carriage doors open. "We're here, Mr. Stonebridge. Lady Evelyne."

Evelyne reached for his hand and stepped down from the carriage.

The trade outpost stood along the Mokkahli River, its wooden structures rough but sturdy, built for function rather than beauty. Though still many yards away, the river looked black and sluggish, barely moving, as if something unseen had stilled it. Wooden piers jutted into the dark waters, their lanterns flickering weakly, offering little warmth against the deepening shadows.

A strange silence hung over the outpost, unsettling in a place that should be alive with traders and merchants. The few buildings stood close together, some with doors slightly ajar, others shut tight as if trying to keep the night at bay.

And then there was the forest.

Mokkvyrn Forest loomed beyond the outpost, its twisted trees forming a jagged silhouette against the sky. The mist thickened as it clung to the treeline, curling between the branches like spectral fingers. Nothing stirred within the woods. There were no birds singing, no insects buzzing, only silence. It was as if the entire forest held its breath.

Evelyne couldn't shake the unease clawing at her, or ignore the shadow on the map. Something was lurking here. But where?

"Come with me," Alaric said. Evelyne followed without a word, trailing behind him as he led her toward the main trading lodge at the heart of the outpost.

The structure was solid and weathered, built from thick wooden beams with a slanted, moss-covered roof. Its doors hung slightly open, casting a warm glow from the hearth within.

"Go inside and get something to eat," Alaric told her, pausing at the entrance. "I'll be back in an hour. I need to speak with the trade master to better understand what's happening here."

Evelyne hesitated, eyeing him as he reached for the map tucked into his coat. Her stomach growled loudly, and she groaned, deciding food was more important than arguing. "Is the darkness still showing?" she asked.

Alaric glanced at the map. "No. The markings are gone."

Relief trickled through her, and she gave a slight nod before stepping inside.

The lodge was modest, but sturdy. In the center of the main hall, a stone hearth glowed warmly, casting flickers of firelight across the walls. Several long tables stood in neat rows, though most were empty, save for a few weathered traders sitting quietly with bowls. The air smelled of smoke and roasted meat; a welcome scent after a full day of travel.

A woman with graying hair stood behind a makeshift counter, ladling steaming broth into wooden bowls. She wore a plain apron and cast Evelyne a sharp glance before gesturing to an empty seat. "You look half starved. Sit down and I'll get you something."

Evelyne didn't argue. She settled onto a wooden bench as the woman returned, setting a bowl of thick stew before her. The broth was dark and rich with chunks of root vegetables, shredded meat, and crusty bread. It wasn't a grand feast, but it was warm and filling, exactly what she needed. She ate silently, listening to the occasional murmur of voices around her and the crackling fire. Still, she couldn't shake the feeling of being watched.

By the time Alaric returned, Evelyne had finished her meal, her hunger finally satisfied. He dropped into the seat across from her, rolling his shoulders as he set down his gloves and asked for the same stew and bread she had eaten.

"Anything?" she asked, watching as he sipped the broth.

"Nothing unusual," he replied, shaking his head. "The trade master hasn't seen anything strange in the past few days. There were no disturbances, no missing goods, just an unsettling quiet. Trade has been unusually slow, but that's all."

Evelyne frowned. Something still felt off. "That doesn't explain what we saw on the map."

Alaric met her stare. "No, it doesn't."

The fire crackled in the hushed space between them.

"We can stay here for the night," he said finally, setting his spoon down. "The trade master said they have rooms available since it's been so calm here. Reuben chose to stay in the carriage."

Evelyne nodded, sipping from her glass of water as she waited for him to finish eating. She couldn't blame Reuben for preferring the carriage; he was probably used to sleeping outside, and something about the outpost's emptiness made it feel like an abandoned stage waiting for something to happen.

When Alaric finished, they rose and made their way to the sleeping quarters—a narrow hall tucked behind the trading lodge. Thick walls kept out the chill, though the floorboards creaked beneath their steps. The bunkhouse itself was simple, a two-story loft for merchants and travelers, with a rickety staircase leading to low-ceilinged rooms above.

Alaric gestured to the doors ahead. Two rooms, side by side. "Yours is on the left."

Evelyne stepped inside and found a small but tidy space. A sturdy wooden bed with wool blankets stood against one wall, a single window was shuttered tightly against the cold, and a small washbasin with a water pitcher rested nearby.

Alaric took the room next to hers. The exhaustion of travel settled over them both, and after securing their doors for the night, they finally allowed themselves to rest.

At last, Evelyne was alone. The past twenty-four hours had been an endless cycle of travel, tension, and unwelcome company. She needed this. Needed a moment where she didn't have to pretend to be composed. The small room wasn't much, but it was hers—if only for the night.

She sighed as she unfastened her cloak, letting it slip from her shoulders before she reached for the washbasin. The water was cool against her skin, nowhere near the steaming bath she craved, but she didn't care. It would have to do. This journey would be long and grueling. And she had no idea what she was doing. She had no plan or clear path forward, but at least she wasn't alone.

She hated that thought. Alaric was the last person she wanted by her side right now. But as much as she loathed him, she had to admit, begrudgingly, that having someone else with her meant she wasn't completely vulnerable, even if she could never forgive him.

Evelyne changed into her nightgown, letting the soft fabric settle over her skin, and collapsed onto the bed. Exhaustion clawed at her relentlessly, but one thought kept her from surrendering to sleep—the sigil.

She reached for the book of sacred signs and began scanning the pages for something, anything. Weariness dragged at her mind, her vision beginning to dim. And then, at the edge of her awareness, she spotted it. The symbol behind her family's manor.

Her fingers hesitated above the serpentine etchings and angular markings, wary of disturbing the ominous design. She traced the ink lightly, half expecting the page to thrum with the same unnatural energy as the sigil burned into the stone. But nothing stirred.

Still, her pulse hammered in her chest as her focus settled on the title beneath the sigil.

The Sigil of the Lost

The lost must remain lost. Seek them, and the darkness will claim you as well.

This sigil is no mere warning. It is a curse woven from shadow and bound by blood. It cannot be undone or unraveled by fate. To unseal it is to summon the will of its master.

Those who bear this mark are claimed, bound in servitude, their flesh branded with its power. It darkens with their corruption and burns with their defiance. To resist is to suffer.

This is the work of blood magic, wielded by one who does not warn, but takes. What is claimed cannot be returned.

Beware the sigil. It does not herald death but something far worse: eternal enslavement.

Her father was right. It was a warning.

The lost must remain lost.

No. She would find him. She would free him.

With a sharp breath, she snapped the book shut, the sound cutting through the silence. This time, when sleep pulled at her, she let it take her.

***

A cool draft seeped through the room, curling around Alaric's skin like an unwelcome hand. He stirred, shifting beneath the thick wool blankets, but the unnatural chill persisted. A deep exhale left his lips, fogging slightly in the air. That wasn't right. His brow furrowed as he blinked awake, rubbing the sleep from his eyes. His instincts stirred uneasily.

The floor was freezing beneath him, a shock against his feet as he stood. Alaric looked toward the window, expecting to find it open, but it was shut tight. No cracks. No gaps. Where was the cold coming from?

A flicker of golden light caught his attention from the nightstand, and his pulse began to quicken. The map.

Alaric lunged for it, quickly unrolling the parchment and spreading it across the bed. The outpost's location glowed gold, marking where they were. But that wasn't what made his stomach drop. Dark ink bled across the map, spreading like a stain, swallowing the land around them.

Something was here. Something had returned.

His body went rigid as urgency took hold. He yanked on his pants, lacing them up in a rush. Boots followed, pulled on with practiced speed. He grabbed his shirt from the edge of the bed but didn't bother putting it on. There was no time. He had to find Evelyne, *now*.

He stormed out of his room and pounded on her door.

No answer.

"Evelyne," he said frantically.

Then the door creaked open, revealing her standing in the dimness, hair unbound, skin bathed in soft light, the delicate fabric of her nightgown skimming over her toned thighs and barely concealing the swell of her chest.

His breath stilled, warmth creeping along his neck, but the thought slipped past him. He swallowed and snapped his gaze up to meet hers.

"Get dressed," he ordered. "Something isn't right."

They were outside the lodge within minutes, Evelyne struggling to keep pace with Alaric's near-frantic strides. He wasn't sure what he was looking for, only that the map felt alive in his hands, its ink pulsing like a beating heart and spreading deeper into the outpost with every passing second.

The darkness on the map shifted. Alaric's grip tightened as he reached for Evelyne's arm, pulling her close. "I don't know what we're walking into, or who's behind it... but if anything goes wrong, you run."

The fear in her eyes was immediate, but she pressed her bag tighter against her side and nodded.

The night air felt *different*. No sound came from the lodge, not even a stir from the horses. The quiet began to press in. Their footsteps crunched against the gravel as they moved toward the stables, each sound too loud in the heavy silence. Alaric needed to check with Reuben, though he was likely asleep in the carriage.

Stepping carefully, he unlatched the door, mindful not to startle the horses. But as it creaked open, he stopped cold.

Reuben was awake, sitting still and staring. His expression was blank, detached, as if his mind were elsewhere. His head tilted at an almost predatory angle as his dark eyes fixed on Alaric with an unsettling stillness. Then, he blinked. For a brief moment, his irises weren't their usual color; they were black. Not the kind cast by shadows, but deep, unnatural darkness, like something sinister was staring back.

Reuben exhaled, rubbing his face as if shaking off a trance. His features settled back to normal.

"Mr. Stonebridge?" he asked, his voice groggy. "Is everything all right?"

Alaric unrolled the map, his gut tightening as the ink began to recede, drawing back toward the forest. He told himself he was fine, but he wasn't sure he believed it.

"Yes." He cleared his throat. "I just wanted to check in. Did you hear anything tonight? Anything unusual?"

Reuben frowned, rubbing the back of his neck. "No, sir. Nothing. Did something happen?"

Alaric shifted his gaze to Evelyne, who still stood beside him, shivering; whether from the cold or something else, he couldn't tell. At least the unnerving presence that had seeped into his room was gone now, but the thought of it still lingered.

"I want to leave at sunrise," Alaric said steadily. "We eat first. Then we go."

Evelyne stepped closer. "I don't need to eat. If you feel we should leave now, let's go."

Alaric shook his head. "We need our energy. Especially since we still have no idea what we're up against."

By morning, the eerie quiet had lifted, replaced by the mundane clatter of bowls and spoons as they filled their stomachs with grainy oats and weak tea. The meal was nothing special, but it kept them moving. And then, with the first light of dawn stretching over the treetops, they were off into Mokkvyrn Forest.

CHAPTER 24

E velyne drifted into a restless sleep once they were back on the road. Too shaken to relax after the night's events, she'd spent the early hours pacing her room at the outpost. At one point, she had even practiced loading her father's pistol, still tucked away in her carpet bag. It had been years since she'd last fired one, and though she had no plans to use it, she needed to remember how.

Her fingers had moved through the motions mechanically—checking the flint, wrapping lead bullets in cloth patches, wiping dust from the barrel—all while her thoughts spiraled. She thought of the sigil, of Cillian, of the taint of blood magic. Of Vaelora, and the realm of magical creatures that had lurked unseen for generations, veiled just beneath the surface of her reality. She'd been blind to it all. Now, she was chasing ghosts into the darkest forest on the continent.

She stirred, rubbing the sleep from her eyes as she rolled her shoulders, feeling the travel stiffness settle deep in her bones. Even in daylight, Mokkvyrn Forest was smothering. Its canopy of twisted branches wove so thickly overhead that only the faintest light slipped through, casting the forest floor into an unearthly, eternal dusk. Fog drifted through the tangled undergrowth, curling like spectral fingers around the trunks of ancient trees. She should have been afraid. But it was beautiful in a haunting, untamed sort of way.

When she sat up, Alaric's stare was already on her.

Evelyne narrowed her eyes. "Is there something on my face, or do you just enjoy staring?"

Alaric immediately looked away, shifting awkwardly. "No... I—I'm sorry."

Evelyne smirked, leaning back against the seat. "I'm joking, Alaric."

His lips twitched into something like a smile, but neither pressed the moment further. They both knew the weight of the silence between them, the unsaid words, the rift unhealed. But now was not the time. There were far more significant things to worry about, like the inky darkness that had spread across Alaric's map last night.

"Are you well rested?" Alaric asked cautiously, watching her stretch.

"As well as I can be, given the circumstances," she muttered, stifling a yawn. "Though I'd much prefer a proper pillow next time. Or perhaps, I don't know, a certain someone could let me sleep through the night without waking me before dawn?"

He rubbed the back of his neck. "I'm sorry for frightening you. I'm still trying to make sense of this map, and when I woke up, I... I felt something."

"What did you feel?" she asked curiously.

"I don't know. It was like... a chill, but it moved over me. Almost like a cold shadow brushing past. But it felt wrong."

Her breath stilled. She knew that feeling. She had felt it the night Cillian disappeared. "Did you see anything?" she whispered.

"No. Just the ink spreading on the map. But something was there, Evelyne." His voice fell quiet. "Something was watching us."

A shiver ran down her spine, because she had felt it, too. But instead of letting the fear sink in, she reached into her luggage and pulled out a heavy tome.

"I know Vaelora has Cillian," she said, flipping through the pages until she reached the marked passage. "We suspected it, but now I know for certain."

Alaric's eyes flicked over the text.

"This one," she said, pressing her finger to the dark illustration identical to the mark near her family's estate. "This sigil was carved into the rock the night Cillian was taken. My father believed it was a warning, and he was right. But it's more than that; it's a claim. According to the book, it was created through blood magic."

Alaric's shoulders stiffened. "And she's the only witch ever to wield such magic."

Evelyne closed the book, nodding. "At least we're headed in the right direction."

But Alaric's face had gone pale as he glanced at the page again. "Evelyne... did you read the full passage?"

She knew what he was implying. She knew exactly what the message said. "I did. But I'm getting him back, Alaric." There was nothing more to argue.

***

Night had barely fallen when her hunger announced itself with such volume that even Reuben looked over in surprise.

"I'll find something," Alaric muttered, already grabbing his bow. "Rabbit, maybe. I won't risk gunfire out here."

She nodded, pulling the map into her lap while Alaric disappeared into the trees. The fire Reuben had started crackled against the oppressive quiet of the forest. Evelyne took the opportunity to change into something simpler for the evening.

Her fingers curled around the map's edges, checking it every few moments and watching for any sign of the black ink returning. Thankfully, the darkness stayed away.

For now.

When Alaric finally returned, a fresh kill in hand, she refused to watch him skin it. He made quick work of it over the fire, and though the meal was simple, just rabbit and dried berries, it was enough.

"Never thought I'd see the day where Lady Duskwood eats rabbit in the middle of the woods," Alaric teased, spearing a piece of meat with his knife.

Evelyne smirked. She sat on a tree stump, cloak cinched close and boots smeared with mud. "Yes, well, this isn't exactly how I pictured my life as a lady either."

Alaric chuckled and shrugged. "Fair enough. You're handling the bugs better than I thought you would."

Her eyes narrowed. "What bugs?"

He lifted his chin toward her boot.

She followed his gaze and spotted the brown spider crawling up her leg.

She squealed, launching off the stump, swatting at her foot. Alaric burst into laughter, and even Reuben, who had been silent most of the day, let out a faint snort.

"I'm going inside the carriage," Evelyne huffed, clutching her food as she stormed off.

Alaric's laughter followed her the entire way.

She ate in silence, absently chewing as the steady chirping of crickets filled the night beyond the carriage walls. The fire outside crackled softly, casting faint, flickering shadows along the edges of her vision.

Would her father send men after her soon? *Not yet,* she thought. Perhaps in a week, maybe longer. That gave her time to find Cillian before anyone tried to drag her back home.

Her fingers tightened around the tin plate in her lap. Was Cillian okay? Was he afraid? Was he even alive?

Stop it. She clenched her jaw, forcing the thought away. Of course he was alive. He had to be.

A gust of wind rustled the trees outside as she let out a slow breath, trying to ease the anxious weight in her chest. Almost absently, she unfolded Alaric's map, and her stomach dropped.

Black tendrils spread across the parchment, inching steadily toward their glowing location. The map seemed to throb with a sinister energy, and the shadows began to accelerate. Her heartbeat thundered in her ears—and then the forest went silent.

No more crickets. No rustling leaves. Only the fire remained, its crackle suddenly too loud.

Panic tightened her chest as she hurried to fold the map and shove it into her bag. Alaric and Reuben had to be warned. They couldn't stay here.

She grabbed her bag and reached for the door, but the moment her fingers grazed the handle, a shadow fell over the carriage. A smothering darkness, tightening like a noose and carrying with it a cold, breathless dread.

For a second, she saw nothing. Only black mist, curling and twisting through the cracks in the wood, wrapping around her limbs like invisible fingers. Then, just as quickly as it had appeared, it was gone. And Reuben stood before her.

But it wasn't Reuben.

His face was frozen. His features were warped, his eyes black, a wicked smile slicing across his lips.

"Reuben?"

He didn't respond. His skin looked pale and sickly, just as Cillian's had been that night in the library. A warning bell screamed in her mind. She had to move. Had to find Alaric. But she couldn't, because Reuben stood in the carriage doorway, unmoving and unblinking. Fear clawed its way up her throat.

"Alaric!" Her voice cut through the night, but she heard nothing in return. Was he still by the fire? Was he still here?

Reuben's hand closed around her wrist in a flash, unrelenting as iron. Pain lanced up her arm, and she gasped, realizing just how unnatural his strength truly was.

"Reuben, let go!" She twisted and fought, but it was like trying to tear free from shackles.

Then he spoke—but the sound was twisted. No warmth, no familiarity. Just a chilling cruelty that wasn't his.

"Foolish girl," he sneered. "You were warned. Yet here you are, still sniffing around."

His grip turned vicious, grinding down with bone-snapping pressure. He dragged her in close, voice laced with malice. "Consider this mercy my last."

Whatever looked out through Reuben's eyes wasn't human anymore.

Evelyne could barely breathe, panic swallowing her whole. But then, the sound of footsteps rushed toward them.

"Evelyne—" Alaric was close now. But before he could reach her, the trees shuddered. A low, guttural growl ripped through the air just as a massive shadow lurched from the trees.

It was huge. And not just one figure, but... *three*.

Reuben blinked. His eyes snapped back to normal, and the haze lifted. He looked down at Evelyne's wrist, his grip still crushing her bones. Horror spread across his face. He released her instantly, stumbling back.

"I—I'm so sorry, my lady." His voice trembled.

She hardly heard him. Her focus had narrowed to the hulking shapes emerging from the dark. Creatures built to hunt. The snarls grew louder, closer, and her heart thrashed violently against her ribs.

Alaric's urgent voice cut through the moment. "RUN!"

Evelyne pushed ahead, branches snagging at her cloak, hair, and skin. The forest closed in around them, trees pressing from all sides. The ground was rough and uneven, but she couldn't stop.

They were close. Growls split the night, vibrating through her bones. She sprinted harder than she ever had, but the pounding of paws stayed just a breath behind.

"Keep running!" Alaric yelled.

She nearly tripped on a jagged root but caught herself at the last second. A sharp branch sliced across her cheek. Warmth trailed down her skin. But she couldn't slow down. Not as the footsteps became louder—

Her ankle twisted in a hidden ditch. She went down hard, face-first into the mud. A curse had barely left her lips before a massive weight crushed into her back, and hot breath ghosted over the nape of her neck.

The sting of claws raked across her back. She braced for the end, squeezing her eyes shut.

THUMP.

Something struck the back of her head, and the world vanished into blackness.

Chapter 25

"Wake up. Wake up!" Alaric's voice pierced through the haze clouding her mind. "Open your eyes, Ev."

She couldn't move. Couldn't speak. Her head throbbed, each pulse like a hammer against her skull. Even the thought of lifting an eyelid felt impossible.

"Damn it," Alaric swore.

Her world spun violently, like she had been tossed onto one of the festival rides she used to love as a child. Like the carousels at Rosewyth's summer fair, the ones that whirled endlessly in dizzying loops. But this wasn't playful or thrilling. This was nauseating. Her stomach flipped, bile threatening to rise. She squeezed her eyes shut, willing herself to focus.

Breathe. Open your eyes and breathe, a small, steady voice whispered from the depths of her subconscious. *You are alive.*

Fighting against the churning discomfort twisting in her gut, she opened one eyelid. All she could see were blurry shapes and a dull, flickering light. She blinked. Again. And again.

The world slowly steadied.

Alaric sat across from her, his face streaked with dirt and dried blood, his left cheek swollen and bruised. His composure had shattered. His blue eyes, once steady, now flickered with fear as they scanned her.

That was when she felt it. The harsh bite of rope cutting into her wrists; her shoulders stiff and strained, pressing against the rough wooden pole at her back. She was bound. And so was Alaric. To her left, Reuben sat tethered to another pillar.

The realization hit like a slap, sending adrenaline burning through her veins. She twisted her wrists, fighting against the bindings, but the knots held firm. She sucked in a sharp breath, her chest tightening as she took in their surroundings.

They were in a tent. It was dimly lit, the air filled with the scent of something musky and animalistic.

"Where are we?" Evelyne's voice came out hoarse. "What—what were those things chasing us?" She turned to Reuben, but he sat motionless, face pale and eyes empty. He was in shock.

Alaric swallowed hard. "Very large wolves. Deadly."

Evelyne shook her head in disbelief. "Wolves? No... no, that's not right. They were so big—"

"Shh, they're coming back," Alaric whispered frantically. And he was right; she heard something nearing the tent.

But it wasn't wolves that barged inside. It was men. Three of them.

Evelyne's breath trembled as they stepped fully into the torchlight. They were larger than most men, making the tent feel unbearably small. Even the shortest of them, if he could even be called short, stood at least six feet, and all of them were built like warriors carved from stone.

The shortest of the three was blond, with striking green eyes that gleamed like polished emeralds. The shorter cut of his hair set him apart, adding a disciplined edge to his demeanor. And the way he tilted his head while studying her left her unsettled.

He smiled. "Well, look who's finally awake."

Evelyne ignored him. She was too busy taking them all in, noticing the raw, untamed energy coiled beneath their skin and the way they carried themselves like creatures barely restrained. Their clothes, though practical, were unlike anything worn in human society.

The two taller men, their black hair falling just past their shoulders, stood side by side. She wondered momentarily if they were twins, but a closer look revealed the tallest one had more defined features, a few more years etched into his face. Dressed in deep shades of charcoal and forest green, they blended easily into the shadows, perfect for tracking or disappearing into the night. Their dark, heavy tunics covered thick leather-wrapped armor that fit snugly over their muscular frames. Fur-lined mantles draped over their shoulders, keeping out the early spring chill.

The blond wore a sleeveless leather vest, its intricate stitching almost ceremonial. The exposed muscle of his arms was lined with faded scars, each one a story carved into his skin. His dark woolen trousers, reinforced with leather panels at the knees, were most likely built for speed. A bone-handled dagger rested at his hip, secured in a faded but well-kept belt.

Their boots were nothing like the fine-crafted boots of noblemen. Instead, they were hand-stitched, battle-worn leather, wrapped with thick crisscrossing straps. But what caught her eye most were the matching tattoos inked along the sides of their necks, trailing down past their collarbones: dark, intricate symbols that twisted like ancient tribal markings.

Hunters?

She looked to Reuben once more. He hadn't moved, his stare still anchored to the ground as if stunned into stillness. Next, she glanced at Alaric. No fear remained in his expression, only a quiet intensity as he studied their opponents and weighed his chances. Not that he had the freedom to act just yet.

The blond stepped closer, and Evelyne tensed as he crouched before her, his fingers lifting her chin. "Ah, she's a pretty little thing." His lips curved with amusement.

She ripped her face from his grasp, and he chuckled, standing and turning away. Now, his attention was on Reuben.

"What's wrong with this one?" He nodded toward him, his expression shifting from teasing to something colder, but Reuben didn't respond. The blond's eyes narrowed. "Look at me."

For a long moment, nothing. Then, too slowly, Reuben lifted his head and locked eyes with the stranger.

A sharp breath left the man's lips, and he staggered back a step.

"Get the alpha. *Now.*"

The two dark-haired men exchanged a look before disappearing from the tent. Evelyne's heart began to pound. What had he seen?

The blond began pacing around Reuben, circling like a predator. His hand drifted toward his belt. In one fluid motion, he unsheathed his bone-handled dagger and leveled the blade at Reuben's throat.

"You make any sort of move on me, and I'll slit your throat in one swipe."

Evelyne gasped, twisting against her bindings. "Stop!"

Reuben smiled. It was not a look of delight or reassurance. No, it was the same eerie smile she had seen in the carriage.

"Reuben?" she whispered.

He turned his head toward her slowly. When their eyes met, his were black.

"Eyes on me, fucker." The man's voice was cold. Without taking his gaze off Reuben, he raised a hand toward Evelyne and commanded, "Don't speak to it."

"*It?*" Evelyne snapped. "He is not furniture to be pointed at. He is a man. Address him accordingly."

The blond shot her a furious look, but before he could speak, a heavy presence pressed into the tent. The two dark-haired men had returned, yet all focus fell on the figure looming behind them, stepping into the flickering light.

Built like a fortress, he was broader than the others, his short-cropped dark brown hair lending him a look of deliberate severity. His gaze moved with ruthless intent, cataloging the space with the cold skill of a creature used to being at the top of the food chain.

Even in the dim light, Evelyne could see the power in his stance. The steady rise and fall of his chest, the precision of every movement, and the quiet restraint in each breath all spoke of a threat held tightly in check. This was a man who never hesitated, never doubted. He didn't ask for obedience; he expected it.

Then she remembered the blond man's words. *Get the alpha.* There was no doubt now. He wasn't just one of them; he was their alpha.

He seemed young for a leader, though she had no actual frame of reference. Until now, she hadn't even known that men like this existed, whatever they truly were. Yet his mere appearance sent a shiver down her spine, and she instinctively knew that he was the most dangerous person in this tent.

Her eyes drifted lower, taking in the clothing and armor of a warrior who commanded respect and fear. He wore a sleeveless tunic reinforced with stitched leather panels across his chest and shoulders. But unlike the others, his armor wasn't just practical; it was marked with intricate, battle-worn etchings, as if symbols had been burned into the leather.

A heavy jet-black wolf pelt draped over his shoulders, fastened by a metal clasp shaped like a snarling wolf's head. A clear symbol of power. Leather bracers wrapped his forearms, and a thick, worn belt secured a large bone-hilted dagger. It was similar to the blond's, but looked far more deadly on him.

Her gaze floated to his dark, fitted trousers, reinforced with stitched padding along the knees and thighs. They looked made for running. A fleeting thought passed through her mind: how effortless it must feel to move in something like that. She'd have chosen them in a heartbeat over the weight of her usual gowns, or even her brother's stiff riding trousers.

Ridiculous, she scolded herself. *Now is not the time.*

It wasn't just his clothing that set him apart. Evelyne noticed the matching ink etched along one side of his neck, which she now assumed was a mark of their kind. But unlike the rest, his markings didn't stop there. A second tattoo wound down the opposite side of his neck, its ritualistic patterns snaking over his shoulder, along his arm, and down to his wrist. Even with the leather bracer concealing most of his forearm, she could still make out the ancient design.

"Which one?" the alpha commanded.

"Him," the blond replied, pointing directly at Reuben.

The alpha's stare shifted, assessing Reuben, then turned to Evelyne and Alaric. "And these two?"

Evelyne lifted her chin, refusing to let her fear show, even as terror twisted in her gut and sent tremors through her core.

"Haven't seen anything yet."

The alpha ran his hand along his jaw, coarse stubble rasping beneath his fingers. The silence that followed was unbearable. Evelyne's nerves frayed until tremors shivered through her.

At last, his hand dropped to his dagger, his posture straightening with resolve. "Slit his throat and burn him outside." The alpha turned toward the tent's exit.

"Pardon me?" The words ripped out of her before she could stop them. Her breath came in panicked bursts. *No, no, no*—this wasn't happening. "You... you can't kill him!" Her voice shook. "He did nothing wrong!"

The alpha turned to her slowly, his head tilting, as if he were entertained by her boldness. But no words came. Instead, he simply lifted a hand and the others sprang into motion.

"What did he do?" Alaric demanded. "He's innocent!"

"It's not what he did," the alpha replied. "It's what he is."

Evelyne barely had time to register the words before she caught the gleam of metal—the blond man's dagger, glinting in the light as it hovered dangerously close to Reuben's throat. Her pulse roared in her ears.

"No! STOP!" Evelyne struggled against the ropes binding her wrists, digging her heels into the ground as she twisted and writhed.

Reuben remained calm as his empty eyes drifted to the tent's roof. Like he had already accepted his fate. Why wasn't he fighting back?

"Please, don't do this!" she sobbed.

"Reuben!" Alaric yelled.

Reuben's black eyes flashed toward the blond at the sound of his name. Fury twisted his features as he heaved against the ropes, so fiercely that the pillar bracing him began to splinter. Where had that strength come from?

"Now!" the alpha demanded.

In less than a heartbeat, Evelyne saw the blond's dagger flash—and in one clean stroke, it cut across Reuben's throat. Blood spilled to the ground as his head slumped.

"You wretched monsters," Evelyne spat, rage tremoring through her limbs as her glare locked on the alpha with blistering intensity. "And you! You're the worst of them all. Nothing more than a soulless beast playing at being a man."

Alaric's stare stayed locked on Reuben's lifeless body.

The men didn't hesitate. There was no remorse, no second thoughts. They dragged him outside, and moments later, the flickering glow of flames swallowed what remained.

Murdered. Burned. Erased.

***

Alaric was stunned, unable to move or speak. He could only watch as the three strangers dragged Reuben's body from the tent and burned it. Evelyne shook uncontrollably against the pole across from him, and he couldn't even attempt to comfort her.

Reuben had been his family's carriage driver since he was a young teen. He had always been quiet, but kind and respectful. Alaric had never felt as helpless as he did at that moment, having already spent the last three hours, while Evelyne was unconscious, trying to escape from the rope.

"Why?" she said now, voice cracking. "Why would he just order them to kill him? What are they?"

Alaric barely registered her words. He was trapped in his thoughts, his mind spinning in a void of disbelief. How long had it been since they'd dragged Reuben's body away? Since the fire had swallowed him whole? Minutes? Hours? He couldn't tell anymore.

"Alaric!" Evelyne yelled, yanking him back to reality. "Look at me."

His head snapped toward her, eyes finally focusing.

Her stare burned into him. "What. Are. They?"

Alaric cleared his dry throat. "They're shifters," he said quietly. "They can shift... from man to wolf." He blinked hard, struggling to believe it himself. But he had seen the wolves shift into their human forms, and it was a terrifying, hideous sight. He was glad that Evelyne hadn't been awake to witness it, but she would see soon enough. "We need to get the hell out of here."

"Shifters?" She shook her head. "How could that be possible? Did you... see it?"

He couldn't fault her for struggling to understand. Even after months of knowing, he was still trying to wrap his head around magic himself.

"Yes. They hauled us here, and then I watched them turn. One after another." He grimaced, haunted by the memory of those monstrous creatures towering over him with their blood-red eyes, their hot breath searing his skin. Their saliva-slicked fangs hovering over Evelyne's body, ready to strike.

These weren't the gentle wolves of fables. No, these were ten-foot-tall beasts born to hunt and kill.

Alaric shook his head. "I never want to witness something that hor-rific again." Yet seeing Reuben killed before his very eyes was, without question, the most haunting moment of his life.

The blond ripped open the tent flap. "You're being moved to separate tents. Say your goodbyes."

"What do you mean?" Alaric's eyes darted back to Evelyne.

She appeared composed—shoulders squared, chin lifted just so. But he saw past it, past the mask meant to hide fear or fragility. And damn if he didn't respect her all the more for it.

"I mean exactly what I said. Were you dropped on your head as a child, or do you have a natural talent for being slow?"

Frustration flared hot in Alaric's chest. His fists clenched behind the pole, bound and useless. But before he could snap back, Evelyne cut in smoothly, "And why, may I ask, are we being separated?"

The blond shrugged. "Because the alpha said so, and we don't question him."

Evelyne let out a slow, thoughtful hum. "Sounds like he's got you by the balls."

Alaric let out a startled cough, caught off guard by her audacity. The blond's expression darkened, and his lips pressed into a hard line, but she wasn't done yet.

"Let me guess." Evelyne tilted her head. "He barks, you fetch?"

Alaric's eyes widened as the man took a step closer to her.

"Careful, human," he hissed.

Evelyne arched a brow. "Or what? Will you summon your alpha? Or maybe you'll—"

A sharp crack echoed through the air, a sound so chilling it could only be that of bone breaking. Before Evelyne's wide eyes, the figure of a man was no more. In its place stood a massive wolf, its fur a stark mix of white and gray, its teeth bared in a menacing snarl.

Evelyne's face paled as she met the beast's crimson eyes. Its front paw dug into the dirt, the picture of imminent violence.

Panic seized Alaric. It was going to kill her. Those behemoth jaws could tear out her throat in an instant.

"Holden!" The urgent cry pierced through the air. "Holden, no!"

A young woman with golden hair burst through the tent's entrance. Cautiously, she approached the wolf—Holden, she had called him—and slowly raised her hand to touch his head.

"You cannot hurt her," she said firmly. "We were ordered *not* to hurt them."

Holden's ears flicked toward her voice, his deathly gaze snapping away from Evelyne. A low growl rumbled deep in his throat, his hesitation palpable. For a moment, it seemed as if he might ignore the command altogether. But after what felt like an eternity, the great wolf let out a huffing breath, his body shuddering with restrained aggression.

Another sickening shift sounded. Muscles twisted, bones cracked back into place, and fur receded as the grotesque form melted back into that of a man.

A naked man.

Alaric's eyes flicked down briefly to see the discarded remains of Holden's clothing strewn haphazardly near Evelyne's feet. Holden, however, seemed utterly unbothered by his state of undress. A slow, wicked grin spread across his face as he casually bent down, scooping up his clothes without a shred of shame. Alaric wasn't sure what was more disturbing: the fact that this man had nearly ripped Evelyne apart, or that he was now standing there, stark naked, acting like nothing had happened.

Alaric looked to the blonde woman, who stood with quiet composure, her gaze fixed stubbornly on the ground as if annoyed, refusing to acknowledge Holden's bare form. And Evelyne—poor Evelyne. She was frozen, her mouth agape, her expression caught between shock, horror, and complete disgust.

The woman waited until Holden silently walked out of the tent. Before leaving, she looked over her shoulder at Alaric and said, "I'll have someone else show you your tents."

Two muscular, dark-skinned men entered, ignoring Alaric and Evelyne. A dagger flashed, and their ropes fell away just as strong hands seized them. Alaric was dragged left, Evelyne right.

"Evelyne!" Alaric cried out as they were pulled away from each other, but she didn't look back.

CHAPTER 26

A week had passed in captivity. Though the air had begun to warm, Evelyne wore the same travel-worn dress, its fabric stiff with dust and sweat. Her bindings had been removed, but she knew without doubt she was still their prisoner. At least four men stood guard outside her tent at all times, their presence a constant reminder that escape was impossible.

And then there was him. The *alpha*.

She hated his daily visits, the cold, silent routine that had become her new reality. He never spoke, just watched her with that hard, unreadable stare. Every time, he would step in, grip her chin, and tilt her face up until their eyes met. With unsettling intensity, he would search her gaze, looking for the same dark corruption that had consumed Reuben.

The first time he approached her, she flinched and fought against his grip, but it was useless. He was too strong. When she spat at him as he turned away, his body stiffened, like he was weighing whether to return the favor. For a second, she thought he might. Instead, he clenched his jaw and shook his head, as if deciding she wasn't worth the trouble.

They had taken her weapons while rummaging through her bag like she was nothing more than a prized possession to be stripped of its worth. But they had left her two things: the book she'd gifted to Cillian and Alaric's folded-up map. Everything else was still in the carriage, left stranded in the woods somewhere.

She hadn't seen Alaric since they were separated, but she had pestered the guards relentlessly, demanding to know if he was alive. Their short, clipped responses were always the same—*Yes*. And she had no choice but to believe them, because the thought of him dead made her stomach churn.

The only kindness she received came from Heidara, the young blonde woman who had stopped Holden from killing her. Heidara visited daily, gentle and calm, bringing her water, broth, meat, and bread.

Evelyne listened to the pack beyond her tent, absorbing every word as they spoke of hunting, protecting their women, and feeding their children. At least they looked after their own. But not humans. Not Reuben. They had slaughtered him and burned him. And their alpha—the one who looked at her like an annoyance, like she was beneath him—had ordered it without hesitation.

She had only spat at him, but wanted to do worse if given the chance.

At least Heidara had brought her a washbasin this morning, allowing her to scrub the filth from her skin and rinse the tangles from her hair. Evelyne had even asked, perhaps foolishly, if there were spare clothes she could wear.

Heidara nodded. "I'll see what I can find for you... and your friend."

The words bolstered her. They meant Alaric was alive. But was he suffering? Was he being tortured? She never received any answers.

Each day Evelyne remained confined within her makeshift prison. She passed the hours pacing in anxious circles, her every step accompanied by the dreadful symphony beyond the tent's walls. The gruesome grind of shifting bones, followed by low, feral growls, served as a grim reminder of the beasts that roamed freely outside. But she hadn't seen another wolf up close since Holden. Since that nightmare.

She'd wet herself that night, and Holden had known. That smirk he'd given her before picking up his clothes hadn't just been arrogance—it had been satisfaction. He relished the fear he had instilled in her, the power he held over her. And she hated him almost as much as she hated their alpha.

Never again. She would get answers today. She would make Heidara talk. Or, if it came down to it, she would force the alpha himself to speak. She still didn't know his name, and she didn't care to ask.

The tent flap rustled as Heidara stepped inside, the early afternoon light highlighting the long, thick golden hair tightly plaited down her back. A few loose strands framed her sharp yet delicate features. She carried a folded bundle of clothes in her arms, the fabric frayed but clean, smelling faintly of firewood and something Evelyne couldn't quite place; wild, like the forest itself.

"I brought you something to wear." Heidara placed the bundle beside Evelyne's cot, revealing a simple, long tunic of dark green linen cinched at the waist with a braided leather cord. The sleeves were fitted but flexible. Beneath it was a woolen skirt, charcoal gray, with slits at the sides. "I figured you'd want something more practical than that dress," she added, nodding toward Evelyne's tattered, travel-worn gown. "And cleaner."

Evelyne stared at Heidara. She wore a fitted dark brown tunic with a sleeveless leather bodice layered over it. Her woolen skirt also split at the sides and fell just past her knees. Thick leather wraps wound around her forearms and calves, the latter tucked into hand-stitched, fur-lined boots that laced up to her knees. A bone pendant rested against her collarbone. She may have lacked the towering build of the men, but Heidara's presence was no less commanding. There was a hardened grace to her, the kind shaped by survival.

She set strips of cloth and a small bowl of warm, herbal wax on the ground beside Evelyne's cot.

"What's that?" Evelyne asked, eyeing it with curiosity.

"Heated tree resin. It's a type of wax—for your legs. If you wish."

Heavens—the court ladies would be positively scandalized by her neglected legs.

Heidara continued, shrugging slightly. "Not all the women in our pack use it. Some prefer an obsidian blade; others don't bother at all. But since I'm not allowed to give you a weapon... Well, I figured this was better than nothing."

It was a simple yet thoughtful gesture, and Evelyne found herself softening toward her captor in a way she hadn't expected. "Thank you," she said.

"Get changed." Heidara pushed a stray strand of hair from her face. "Kaldrek will be here soon. And if you plan to talk your way out of this, don't. Just stay quiet around him. He's the one who decides whether you and your friend get to leave."

Kaldrek?

"Who is—"

But Heidara was already gone.

Evelyne dressed quickly. She ran her fingers through her tangled, now-dry hair, trying to smooth it down, but her mind was elsewhere. Who the hell was this man—this shifter, or whatever he was—coming to see her?

She didn't have time to dwell on it. Instead, she focused on figuring out the damn skirt. The slits on the sides left more of her legs exposed than she was used to, and the unfamiliarity made her hesitate. But she had to admit the clothes were a vast improvement over the suffocating corset and heavy gown.

The tunic fit comfortably, allowing her to move without restriction, and the skirt, though unsettlingly revealing, felt light and was perfect for quick movement. The boots, however, were another matter entirely. The leather laces were frustrating, a tangled puzzle she fumbled through until she managed to tie them, probably incorrectly.

With a quiet sigh, Evelyne finally sat back on the cot, her hands resting on her lap, her heartbeat steadying. Now, all she could do was wait for Kaldrek and a chance to convince him to let her go.

She sat quietly for about fifteen minutes, struggling to keep her patience. But when she couldn't sit still any longer, she got up and began pacing the tent again. Her fingers grazed her brother's book, and she pulled it from her bag, flipping to a passage to read.

And so it is told, when the darkness rises unchecked, slithering into the heart of the land, the Lantern shall stir from its slumber. A beacon of light standing alone against the endless void. But light cannot solely banish the creeping shadow. To burn away the corruption, to unmake that which was forged in darkness, the Lantern must be bound—its flame entrusted to a soul strong enough to bear its fire, to wield its cleansing light.

Heavy footsteps neared the tent. Evelyne quickly snapped the book shut. Stuffing it back into her bag, she barely had time to react before the tent flap opened. And of course, it was him again—the alpha.

"You," she said, her expression sour.

One dark brow lifted, a flicker of interest breaking through on his otherwise cold, unreadable face. "Me." His dark brown eyes swept over her, noting her freshly cleaned skin and the pack's clothing now draped over her frame.

"I was expecting someone else," Evelyne muttered, folding her arms. She already knew the routine: he would lift her chin, examine her eyes, then leave without a word. "Let's just get this over with." She rolled her eyes and strode toward him.

The corner of his mouth twitched, almost a scoff, before his hand reached for her chin.

"What is so amusing?" she asked.

His calloused fingers firmly tilted her head, but his eyes narrowed in silent curiosity this time. "Who exactly were you expecting?" he asked.

"Oh my word, he actually speaks! And here I was beginning to think your only skill was looming in silence like a particularly moody statue."

He didn't so much as flinch, merely held her gaze. She fluttered her lashes in exaggerated innocence, just to be insufferable.

"Still gold. Still normal. No dark possession. Looks like I'm in the clear, and you may see yourself out now."

"You've heard me speak before," he replied, voice low.

"Ah, yes. How could I forget? That one memorable moment when you sent Holden and your matching pair of gloom-drenched bodyguards to do your dirty work."

His expression darkened, and his grip remained firm as he continued his thorough, frustratingly silent examination. Evelyne yanked against his hold, but he didn't let go.

"Are you hoping to find something wrong with me?" she hissed. "A reason to kill me too?"

He finally released her chin, but didn't step back. "I did what I could to keep my pack safe."

Evelyne's hands curled into fists. "Well? Did I pass your test? If so, can you please leave?"

She just wanted him gone so she could charm her way past this *Kaldrek* and finally get out. She was tired of being treated like a prisoner, examined day after day. She wasn't infected or corrupted, but if they didn't let her out of this tent soon, she might start acting insane.

He didn't answer. Instead, his dark eyes flashed with something like curiosity or predatory instinct, before he seized her wrist and yanked her forward. Before she could even protest, he leaned in dangerously close, and—

Gods above, was he *sniffing* her? Like a damn dog?

Disgust propelled her hand before thought could catch up, and it slapped across his face.

The impact stung her palm more than it seemed to affect him. His body stilled. His hands fell to his sides as he turned away, jaw tightening with such force she half expected fangs to burst through his skin. She had gone too far, and she knew it.

She took a step back, her heart hammering in her chest as she forced words out. "Don't ever come that close to me again."

For a heartbeat, she thought he might tear her limb from limb. But then his shoulders dropped, as if something in her eyes caught him off guard. "You are free to leave, Evelyne," he said, steady as stone.

It was the first time a stranger had spoken her name without the burden of her title, and somehow, it felt achingly personal.

She stiffened in surprise. "I thought that decision was up to—"

"Your friend," he interrupted, crossing his arms. "Who is he to you?"

Why was he asking her that? "He's..." Evelyne hesitated, confused. "My betrothed."

The alpha's mouth curved slightly—not quite a smirk, but something close to it. "Cute."

For once, her wit abandoned her. Not that it made a difference, since Holden pushed into the tent seconds later, Alaric following close behind.

Her chest tightened at the sight. He looked tired, but alive. His bruises had faded to faint traces, and though she had never seen him this unkempt, the rough stubble along his jaw somehow suited him. Most importantly, he was here. Standing. Whole.

"Kaldrek, he's clear," Holden said, his green eyes flashing to Evelyne.

She snapped her head toward the alpha, her voice caught between a question and a realization. "You're Kaldrek."

Of course.

"That's me," he said smoothly. "Try not to look too impressed."

She sighed in frustration before rushing to Alaric, wrapping her arms around him. Yes, she was still angry and likely would never see him the same way again, but he was still her friend. And she still cared.

"Tonight is the moon ritual," Holden interrupted. "You can stay another night, but come dawn, the Ironwolf pack will be gone. You'll be on your own."

Ironwolf. The name sounded powerful, a pack she would never want to fight against. Evelyne couldn't help but wonder why Holden was issuing commands while his alpha was present. Perhaps he held the position of beta or second-in-command. She couldn't picture Kaldrek, this arrogant brute, allowing others to make decisions.

"Moon ritual?" Alaric asked. He had changed into new clothes as well—sturdy leathers that looked similar to Holden's, though noticeably less battle-worn.

"It's a full moon tonight. Our time to shift as one, to run with the alpha and elders. A way to display our strength and unity as a pack." Holden's mouth spread into a wide grin as he added, "And, of course, a good excuse to drink, dance, and enjoy the company of our women." He threw Evelyne a wink.

She resisted the urge to roll her eyes. The last thing she wanted was to spend another night stuck here, but slipping away into the dark? That would be as good as signing her death warrant.

"Why should we believe you'll let us stay another night unharmed?" Alaric asked.

Holden scoffed. "We've had plenty of chances to gut you, human. Didn't take them, did we?"

The alpha gave a simple nod. "You already have a tent, and the pack leaves at first light. There's no reason to send you off when nightfall is only hours away. The choice is yours."

Oh, now they had a choice? Evelyne folded her arms and lifted her chin. "And what if we decide to kill you now that we're not at your mercy?"

Kaldrek huffed a short laugh, shaking his head before turning and stepping out of the tent without a word.

Evelyne's jaw tightened. She could have smacked him for brushing her off so quickly.

Holden stared at her, mouth slightly open. "He's not someone you want to cross. Push him the wrong way, and you won't live to regret it." Despite the words, amusement flickered in his eyes. With that same smug arrogance, he added, "You wouldn't even leave a scratch on us."

Evelyne's face burned with a mix of frustration and embarrassment. But he was right. There was no way she or Alaric could actually hurt the shifters. They'd both be dead before they even had a chance to try.

Holden turned to leave, but paused at the tent's entrance. "Oh, and I'd cover those pretty eyes of yours tonight, little viper," he mused. "You're about to see a lot more men shift, and you know where our clothes end up." He smiled wickedly before leaving them alone.

Evelyne let out a long breath and looked over at Alaric. "Are you okay?"

He sank onto her cot and slowly shook his head. She knew it wasn't from pain, but from disbelief. Everything that had unfolded over the past week, and what had happened to Reuben, was simply too much to process.

"I'm fine," he murmured, but she didn't miss the deep sorrow in his eyes. "Did they hurt you?"

She sat beside him. "They didn't lay a hand on me—aside from Kaldrek, of course, with his daily ritual of searching my eyes."

Silence stretched between them. And then, as if something inside him finally cracked, Alaric spoke, everything spilling from his lips in a rush.

"I'm so sorry, Evelyne. For everything. For keeping the truth from you, for kissing Callista, for humiliating you." Tears welled in his eyes as he reached for her hand. She didn't pull away, though part of her wanted to. "Please know my feelings for you were real. *Are* real. I never meant to hurt you. And I'm so sorry I couldn't keep us safe."

She sighed, her heart aching at his sincerity. "There was nothing you could have done to stop us from being hunted down by a pack of wolves." Her voice softened as she shook her head. "And I know you didn't mean to hurt me. I wish none of this had ever happened. And I want to forgive you for lying to me... I really do."

But she couldn't. Not yet.

"You're still my friend," she continued. "And I understand you were put in an impossible position. But friends don't keep secrets like that, Alaric. Not ones that toy with someone's deepest emotions."

She had meant every word. That day in his study, when he kissed her, she'd trusted him completely—felt as if she could give him every piece of herself. But now, something was fractured. And she wasn't sure it could ever be made whole again.

Alaric lowered his head, shoulders sagging. "I'm sorry," he repeated.

She nodded and let out a long exhale before changing the subject. "I haven't seen anything on the map since the night we were captured. I've checked it every time I've been alone."

Alaric's head snapped up. "They didn't take it from you?"

"No. I don't think they even thought about opening it. They only took my weapons, and they better return them to me."

She reached for her bag, pulled the map free, and unfolded it. No black. Thank the heavens.

Alaric frowned. "What do you think happened to Reuben?"

Evelyne had been waiting for this moment. To say the words out loud, and finally speak the thing that had been clawing at her mind for days.

"You saw his eyes. He wasn't himself. It was like he wasn't even there." She held the edge of the map like an anchor before forcing the words out. "That night in the carriage... he cornered me. Grabbed me." She turned to Alaric, voice trembling. "He was so strong. I thought he'd snap my wrist."

Alaric stiffened. "He hurt you?"

"I'm fine," she said quickly. "Honestly, with everything that happened after, I almost forgot about it. But when he talked to me, it wasn't *him*. It was something else. Something hateful." She glanced back down at the map before passing to Alaric. "Here. It's yours."

"Thanks, but you keep it for now. It seems to give you comfort."

She nodded and tucked it back into her bag. "I think the pack is hunting the darkness. Maybe they know more about Vaelora than we do, but I need to know more." She sighed softly. "And as much as I want to leave, I think staying tonight might be our best chance at finding answers."

Alaric slowly nodded. He understood what they had to do. "Then I guess I'd better get ready," he said with a playful wink.

Evelyne huffed a laugh. "Good. We're going to need your Stonebridge charm."

He turned to leave, then glanced back over his shoulder. "That's quite the look on you, Ev. Not at all what I'm used to... but I can't say I mind."

CHAPTER 27

Evelyne sat cross-legged on the cot, watching Heidara move gracefully around the tent, gathering clothes and accessories as if she'd done this a hundred times before. The young woman looked wild and untamed, yet elegant, like she belonged to the night itself. She was already dressed for the ritual, her golden-blonde hair woven into a beautiful braided headband that circled the crown of her head. A thin leather strap rested just above her brows, fastened with a small silver emblem shaped like a wolf's head.

Evelyne had never seen a woman dressed like this. Heidara's cropped leather top clung to her form, leaving her toned stomach bare, and her slit skirt revealed strong, muscled legs that moved with confidence. A thick belt sat at her waist, lined with small sheathed daggers.

"You're staring," Heidara teased as she caught Evelyne's wide-eyed gaze.

"I've just never seen a woman dress like... this. At least, not in front of men."

Heidara chuckled, tightening the last strap of her belt. "You southern women cover yourselves up too much." She motioned to Evelyne's tunic and slit skirt. "That's already an improvement, but the boots ruin it." She knelt and placed a pair of simple leather sandals in front of her. "Here. These will suit the night better."

Evelyne hesitated, then sighed and unlaced her boots. The sandals were lighter, and though she wasn't sure how practical they'd be in a forest, she had to admit they were comfortable.

"Better." Heidara nodded approvingly. "But your hair needs work."

Evelyne instinctively reached up, brushing her fingers through her long hair. "What's wrong with it?"

"Nothing," Heidara said, already moving behind her. "But if you're going to attend a moon ritual, you should at least look the part."

She worked quickly, weaving Evelyne's hair into a similar braided headband, her fingers surprisingly gentle as they twisted and threaded through the strands. Evelyne sat still, listening to the rhythmic sound of Heidara's movements.

"There." Heidara stepped back, nodding in satisfaction before tying a matching strap across Evelyne's forehead. "Now you look less like an outsider."

She held up a small, cracked hand mirror, and Evelyne smiled at her reflection. The braids framed her face beautifully, and the leather band, while simple, made her look... different. Stronger.

She looked to Heidara, who stood with arms crossed, a mischievous glint in her striking green eyes. "You're stunning," Evelyne admitted, eyeing the soft freckles dusting Heidara's nose. "You don't even need the effort."

Heidara laughed, adjusting her daggers. "Flattery will get you everywhere. Now, come. The pack is waiting."

She extended her hand, but Evelyne paused. Instead of taking it, she asked, "Why are you so kind to me?"

Heidara's brow furrowed. "Is there a reason I shouldn't be?"

"It's just hard to tell if your pack plans to kill me or not. And I already feel like Holden is waiting for the first excuse to try."

At that, Heidara stepped closer and took Evelyne's hand anyway, squeezing it lightly. "Holden is insufferable," she admitted. "He's powerful, irritatingly protective, and incapable of minding his own business when it comes to me, but beneath all that, he has a good heart. He's also fiercely loyal to Kaldrek, like we all are. So if Kaldrek has decided you won't be harmed, Holden has no choice but to obey."

"Are you and Holden… together?"

"Oh, gods, no." Heidara cringed. "Gross. He's my brother."

Evelyne's jaw nearly hit the ground. Holden—the same man who had shifted into a monster before her very eyes, who had looked moments away from ripping out her throat—was Heidara's brother?

But then she remembered how Heidara had stepped into the tent that night and stopped him with a single touch. She looked at Heidara again, and suddenly, it was apparent. The golden hair, the striking green eyes. It was a wonder she hadn't pieced it together sooner.

"Hard to believe, I know. He's an ass, and everyone likes me better."

Evelyne huffed a laugh. "How old are you?"

"Nineteen. But Holden still treats me like a child, even though he's only three years older." She rolled her eyes, then shrugged. "I suppose it's not the worst thing in the world, having someone watching out for you. Though I'd prefer someone a little more handsome. And not, you know, related to me."

Evelyne found herself smiling. Aside from her sister, she had never really had close girlfriends before, but this felt easy. Nice.

"Don't worry," Heidara went on. "Holden won't give you any trouble. Honestly, even the smallest hint of interest from you, and he'll probably spend the whole night trying to prove himself."

Evelyne scowled. "Not in this lifetime."

Heidara laughed. "Unless, of course, you and—what was your handsome friend's name again?" She tapped a finger to her chin, pretending to think.

"Alaric."

"Right. Unless you and Alaric are already... acquainted in that fashion?" There was a teasing lilt to her voice, and her eyes were full of curiosity.

Evelyne sighed. "It's complicated."

Heidara hummed in response, then tugged her out into the night.

CHAPTER 28

T he night sky sprawled endlessly above, the full moon's silver glow
peeking through the towering trees of Mokkvyrn Forest. A blazing pyre stood at the center, flames of gold crackling into the dark, their
light dancing over the crowd of shifters.

Evelyne stood in quiet awe, taking in the scene before her. The entire
pack had assembled—men, women, children, even the elders—all gathered in honor of the full moon. They perched upon tree stumps and large
stones or crouched upon the earth like they were one with the land. The
scent of burning firewood blended with the crisp spring breeze, carrying
the sounds of the pack: laughter, hushed conversations, and the steady
rhythm of drums.

Regardless of age, the men were bare-chested, their muscular forms
painted in swirling patterns as women traced delicate, ancient symbols
upon their broad shoulders and sculpted torsos.

Evelyne had never witnessed such a seamless blend of beauty and
strength. The women were just as striking, some wearing the same
leather headbands as she and Heidara, while others wove their long hair
into thick braids, strands threaded with tiny wildflowers. Their cropped
leather tops left their stomachs bare, and their slit skirts swayed fluidly
with each graceful movement.

The drum beats grew louder, echoing like the very heartbeat of the
forest. Men and women moved in hypnotic patterns around the fire,

their bodies swaying, stepping, and twisting with fluidity. It was nothing like the stiff, choreographed ballroom dances Evelyne had been taught as a child. This was something entirely different. This was primal, unrestrained, and alive. Like a celebration of connection and life itself.

Her eyes drifted to a young couple, their hands on each other's waists, hips rolling in time with the beat. The movement was intimate, sultry even, and Evelyne's face warmed watching them. But as the drums changed rhythm, the pair parted, smoothly transitioning to new partners as if nothing had changed.

Before she could process it, a deep voice rumbled behind her.

"Dancing is a way we express ourselves here."

Evelyne jolted, whipping around to find Kaldrek behind her, his towering frame looming over her.

Her breath caught at the sight of him up close. His dark brown hair was tousled, and his deep, earth-toned eyes gleamed like polished mahogany in the unsteady light of the flames. His bare chest was a solid wall of muscle, marked with the pack's sacred ink. A massive wolf stretched along one side of his neck, its fierce form naturally woven into twisting tribal patterns that coiled down his shoulder and wrapped along his arm like living shadows.

She had to tilt her chin upward to meet his eyes. He was so damn tall.

He lifted a drinking horn to his lips, taking a slow gulp of the amber liquid inside. Evelyne watched the muscles in his throat move, his skin gleaming with a faint sheen of sweat from the fire's heat.

He grinned as he lowered the horn. "Glad to see you haven't tried to kill us yet."

She swallowed, momentarily caught off guard. Was he... joking with her?

Turning her focus back to the fire, she watched the shifters moving in rhythm around it. "I've never seen a gathering like this before."

He only held out the horn toward her, offering what remained. She hesitated. This was hardly the sort of thing one did at a proper soirée. But really, what harm could it do?

"Just stay out of the way when we shift." His voice dipped lower, carrying a quiet warning. "Or else you won't even make it to morning."

Evelyne gaped as he turned and walked away.

She looked down at the drink and took a small sniff. It was definitely not wine or champagne like in Caltheris. No, this smelled strong, like it could strip paint off walls. She took a tentative sip and instantly choked on the bitterness, her face grimacing.

Alaric's laugh rumbled nearby. "Not a fan of their ale?"

She turned to see him slowly approaching, his bronzed skin glowing in the firelight. He had shed his tunic, matching the other men in the pack. She had never seen him like this before—bare-chested, at ease. And though she tried not to stare, she found her eyes drawn to him.

She remembered the last time his hands had been on her. The way he'd pressed against her, the heat of his mouth on hers—

A flush crept up her cheeks, and she quickly pushed the memory aside, letting the sting of his betrayal take its place.

"Well, it's certainly not wine," she muttered.

Alaric's grin grew as he tipped his head back, taking a long, easy sip from his horn, the picture of carefree indulgence. "Come on," he said, nudging her. "Let's try to enjoy the night."

Before she could protest, he gently took her wrist and led her toward a circle of shifters sitting in the grass, drinking and talking.

Her stomach relaxed when she spotted Heidara already seated, her bright green eyes twinkling with delight. The two black-haired men

Evelyne recognized from the night of her capture were seated beside her. Between them was a striking woman with cascading fire-red hair. She couldn't help but notice their unwavering focus on the young beauty. Both men stared at her as if the rest of the world had faded into nothing.

Directly across from Heidara sat Holden. Evelyne's body went rigid, but before she could resist, Alaric leaned in and whispered, "You said we needed answers. We need to play the part."

"Come, sit with us!" Heidara called out excitedly.

Alaric led Evelyne forward, and she lowered herself onto the grass. Holden's gaze still lingered, but she refused to give him the satisfaction of seeing her falter. He was enjoying her discomfort. She knew it.

Instead of looking away, she turned to face him, meeting his stare head-on and arching a brow in challenge. How many had backed down from that cold, predatory look? She wouldn't be one of them. She was done being afraid.

Holden smiled wickedly. "Do you like what you see, little viper?"

Evelyne tilted her head. "Should I? And why do you call me that?"

He laughed before taking a long drink. "Because I like a woman with a bite."

"And I like a man who knows when he's about to get bitten," she shot back.

Holden's eyes glinted with intrigue. "Perhaps I'll see just how sharp your teeth are out there." He nodded toward the fire, where dancers moved in pulsing, instinctive rhythm, their bodies tangled and lost to the beat.

Her stomach sank. She couldn't move like that. Couldn't let someone touch her that way, not with so much feeling, not with so many eyes on her. But she wouldn't let her nerves show, no matter what she felt.

"Or perhaps you'll show me what you're capable of first," she countered. "Since I like the view so much."

Holden's tongue flicked across his lower lip as he leaned in, close enough that she could feel the heat of him. "Careful," he murmured. "Don't tempt me."

Then he pulled away, walking off to refill his drink, leaving Evelyne to release a slow, trembling breath.

She turned her focus back to Heidara just as the young woman grabbed Alaric's arm and beamed. "Come dance with me!"

Evelyne laughed as Alaric was hauled to his feet, the expression on his face somewhere between amused and panicked. Heidara wasted no time leading him toward the fire, where the beat of the drums deepened, the energy of the dance wild. To Evelyne's surprise, Alaric caught on quickly. Soon, his hands found Heidara's waist. Not in the intimate, seductive way she'd seen before, but fluid and comfortable. His laughter was real, the kind she hadn't heard from him in a long time.

Holden returned, dropping onto the ground beside her and handing her another horn of ale. "You're fun," he admitted. "But not as convincing of a flirt as you think. What is it you really want?"

Her fingers tightened around the drink. He was sharper than she'd given him credit for. She took a long sip, forcing herself not to gag at its strength, and then turned to face him fully.

"Why are you hunting those who've been... corrupted?" she asked, all traces of humor gone.

Holden exhaled, considering her for a long moment before answering. "Because we're trying to protect our pack. The magic is spreading through the eastern lands like a disease. Every day, it gets closer." He took another drink before continuing. "And our alpha... He can feel when it's close. We can't afford to lose any more of our pack to it."

A lump formed in Evelyne's throat. They'd lost people, just like she had. Reuben. Cillian. But Cillian was still alive, and she would not lose hope.

"What happens to them?" she asked quietly. "To the ones who go dark?"

Holden's expression hardened. "At first, they resist. A few hold out longer than you'd think. But it always wins. First the mind goes, then the body. After that... the person they were is lost."

Lost. The very thing the sigil had foretold. A chill passed over Evelyne. "Lost how?"

"They become something unrecognizable," he said darkly. "Blood-fed things—swifter, stronger, and utterly mindless. There are nights when four of us are barely enough to bring one down." A beat passed. "Your friend Reuben... He was changing. We had to act before the rot rooted deeper, or leapt to one of us."

"That can't be right," she whispered, her thoughts racing.

"My brother—"

She stopped short, but the damage was already done.

Holden's eyes sharpened. "What about your brother?"

She swallowed hard. "He was taken over a week ago, and now we are trying to find him."

"Are we talking taken—or infected? Because if it's the same darkness that claimed Reuben..." He shook his head. "Don't hold on to hope."

Evelyne bit her tongue, unwilling to let this man's harsh realism shake her belief in Cillian. A wave of dizziness washed over her, but she pushed to her feet regardless. She needed to leave *now*, before the doubt sank in.

Holden leaned back, smirking. "I'd take it easy on that ale. You don't have the tolerance for northeastern spirits."

"Thanks for the warning," she tossed over her shoulder before slipping into the night.

Evelyne's thoughts coiled in a dizzying haze of ale and revelation. Kaldrek could sense the darkness and hunted those touched by it to protect his pack. If she or Alaric had shown the slightest sign of taint, he wouldn't have hesitated to kill them. That alone should have sobered her, but the warmth in her veins made her restless, lighter. All she wanted was to let go, to be swept into the dark and wild pulse of the evening.

She stepped toward the fire, following the drums, until she saw him.

Kaldrek moved in sync with a striking woman, her long black hair cascading down her back, her warm-toned skin illuminated by the flames. She moved like the night was hers, and those barely-there leathers hugged curves carved by temptation itself. Evelyne couldn't help but admire her... and resent just how effortlessly she drew so many eyes.

Her gaze lingered on Kaldrek's large hands gripping the woman's waist, his fingers pressing firmly as they swayed. Then he leaned in, his head dipping toward her neck. The gesture was unmistakably intimate, and Evelyne felt a slow heat bloom across her skin as she watched him.

She told herself to look away, to stop staring at the way he wrapped himself around the woman with such possessive mastery. But she didn't. Couldn't. She only stood there, watching... wanting. And for one reckless heartbeat, she wished someone would hold her like that.

Without warning, Kaldrek's dark gaze snapped to hers.

Shit.

She remained frozen, caught, trapped like prey beneath the hunter's stare. But he didn't stop moving, didn't pull away from the woman, just watched her watching *him*.

Mortified, Evelyne spun around and walked back to her tent, cursing herself the whole way. Inside, she yanked out the map, eyes locking onto the glowing parchment, grounding herself in something real.

The map was clear. No danger in sight. She exhaled, tension easing from her shoulders. Tomorrow, they'd be on their own again. She needed that. Time to think. Time to plan. But she still had to get her weapons back. Perhaps Heidara would lend her some clothes and supplies, but it didn't change the fact that she felt dangerously exposed without a way to protect herself.

A gravel-rough voice cut through the silence behind her. "What is that?"

Evelyne spun, clutching the map to her chest. Kaldrek stood in the tent, his tall frame blocking the entire entrance. His dark eyes flicked down to the parchment in her hands.

She forced a casual shrug. "Just a map. Planning our next route."

His stare pinned her in place. "That's not a normal map. Open it."

Her fingers tightened around the parchment. *Demanding bastard.* "I think not," she said flatly. "You've taken enough from me this past week. My weapons, my pride. You don't get this, too. Now, kindly leave."

He took a step closer and quickly ripped the map from her hands.

Evelyne gaped at him. "I beg your pardon?" She lunged to snatch it back, but he merely lifted one muscled arm, blocking her effortlessly. "Give me that."

He unfolded the map, his expression hardening as he took in its strange, glowing markings. "Tell me what this is, and maybe I'll consider it."

Oh, he was an expert in irritation.

"Do you habitually steal things that aren't yours, or is it just me you enjoy tormenting?"

His jaw ticked, but he didn't answer. This was going nowhere. If she didn't give him something, he'd never let it go.

"It shows us when the darkness is near," she admitted, irritation lacing her voice. "It's our only warning. And since you can sense it yourself, you do not need this."

Faster than he could react, she snatched the map from his hands, stepping back before he could grab it again. His fists clenched at his sides, but he made no move to take it. Instead, he studied her with those unreadable brown eyes and asked, "Who told you I could sense the dark magic?"

"Holden."

A low chuckle rumbled from his chest. "Of course. He can't keep his mouth shut around pretty women."

Heat bloomed across her cheeks. Traitorous warmth. Had he just complimented her? She shoved the thought aside. *Focus.* He was an arrogant, controlling brute, and she wasn't about to let him distract her.

"Why are you even here?" she snapped. "Shouldn't you be entertaining your companion?"

He smirked. "You seemed rather taken with me and my companion." His tone carried a clear challenge.

Evelyne scoffed. "Don't flatter yourself."

"I saw you watching." He took a slow step closer, his presence filling the space. "Just let me know if you'd like a turn."

Her body went rigid. Willing away the heat rising to her face, she forced her voice into something steady. "I want my weapons back."

Kaldrek studied her for a beat before nodding. "I'll have Heidara leave them outside your tent before we're gone."

"Why not now?"

His smile deepened with amusement. "Because I don't know if I can trust you, *Evelyne*." He dragged her name out just enough to make her shiver.

Her resolve faltered, exhaustion settling deep in her bones. She had been too guarded, too careful with her words. But why? He already knew what lurked in the shadows. They all did. So what was the point in holding back?

"She has my brother," Evelyne confessed. "Alaric and I need to find him, and I need whatever I can get to make it to Nerathar." She let out a slow breath, her voice quieter now. "If you're hunting the shadows, you already know who I'm talking about."

His eyes darkened with something dangerous.

"You're going to Vaelora?"

"Yes," she whispered.

"You'll die before you even reach her," he said, his tone grave. "Or worse, she'll take your soul before you even realize it's gone."

"I know it seems impossible. Foolish, even. But I have to find him."

For the first time since she'd met him, his expression wasn't mocking or unreadable—it was grim. Cold.

"Well," he said after a long silence, "you should enjoy the rest of the moon ritual. It'll likely be the last you'll ever experience." Before she could form a sharp retort, he turned toward the tent entrance. "We shift in two hours," he said over his shoulder. "Stay out of our way."

Without another glance, he stepped back into the moonlight, leaving Evelyne alone. But she refused to dwell on his words. If Alaric and everyone else could enjoy the night, so could she.

With newfound determination, she stepped out of her tent, grabbed a horn of ale, and headed for the fire. The steady beat of drums echoed through the night, and before she could second-guess herself, Alaric darted to her, grinning, his bare chest streaked with painted swirls like the other men.

"I have no idea what I'm doing," she admitted, leaning close to his ear to be heard over the music.

He just laughed and spun her into the firelight. "Then let me teach you."

She downed the rest of her drink in one go, the warmth of the ale flooding through her, emboldening her. Her body loosened, her laughter light as she swayed with him, trying to follow his lead. The tension between them melted away, and she allowed herself to enjoy the moment.

New hands settled at her waist, guiding her in time with the music, and when she glanced back, she was startled to find Holden behind her.

"Just listen and let your hips move freely," he said, flawlessly adjusting his movements to match hers.

The music thrummed through her veins, and time slipped away in a blur of moments—perhaps minutes, perhaps hours. It was the first time in weeks that she had truly felt free. The weight of her mission, her fear, her grief—it all dissolved, lost to the pulse of the drums and the warmth of eastern ale.

She felt it before she saw it, a heaviness settling over her skin. Turning her head, she found Kaldrek across the fire, his eyes locked on hers. He wasn't just looking. He was *studying*. And judging by the intensity of his stare, he'd been watching far longer than she realized.

When their eyes met, he didn't look away. Instead, he lifted his ale and drank with agonizing slowness, his gaze fixed on hers until a strange flutter stirred in her chest. Then, without a word, he turned and disappeared into the night.

"Fun, isn't it?" Holden grinned, completely unaware of the shift in her mood.

She nodded, though her mind was no longer entirely in the moment.

Heidara and Alaric joined them, both flushed with exhilaration. "We're shifting soon," Heidara warned. "The elders will gather first and perform the ritual. Lots of chanting, but once it's done, the pack will shift as one and take off." She paused to glance between Evelyne and Alaric. "If you're in the way, move. You do not want to get caught between us."

Alaric touched Evelyne's arm. "Come on. Let's head back."

But she didn't want to leave. She wanted to see this. To witness the raw power of the shift. Still, she knew they had to prepare for the morning.

She reluctantly tore her eyes from the fire and followed him, casting one last glance over her shoulder. Whatever happened tonight, she felt it would be burned into her memory forever.

CHAPTER 29

"Are we awful people?" Evelyne asked softly, sinking onto her cot with a sigh.

Alaric glanced over as he sat beside her. "Why would you say that?"

She stared at the floor. "Because we just spent the night laughing with the people who killed Reuben."

The name landed between them like a blow. Alaric's expression shifted, the lightness of the evening fading into something far more solemn.

"Evelyne… he wasn't Reuben anymore. Or at least, he wouldn't have been in a few months, maybe weeks, according to what Heidara told me."

Frustration flared in her chest. "But they didn't even give him a chance, Alaric. How can I hold on to any hope of saving Cillian if what they say is true? Do *you* think he's already lost?"

"I don't know. But I think we have to keep looking for him." Alaric's eyes met hers. "You said he fought this before, right? If the darkness took him once and he resisted, maybe… maybe he's different."

She told herself it was true. She *needed* it to be. Cillian wasn't loud or fearless, but his strength had always run deeper than hers. If anyone had a chance to fight this—it was him.

She forced a slow breath through her nose, steadying herself. "Did you learn anything new?"

Alaric swallowed hard and nodded. "I did, but I'm not sure you'll want to hear it."

"Tell me, Alaric. We need to know what we're up against."

Alaric ran a hand over the back of his neck and exhaled slowly. "The magic doesn't just control the mind. It consumes the body and soul. The darkness within evolves, changing them over time."

She remembered Holden mentioning something similar, but she needed a deeper explanation. After a long pause, he finally continued.

"Once blood magic fully consumes a soul, the person that remains is no longer human. They become something else. Something deadly. Like a creature of the night." Hesitation had crept into his voice, as if the final truth was too dark to name.

"What is it you aren't saying?" Evelyne asked.

"They feed, Evelyne."

She stiffened. "Feed?"

"They can drain every last drop of blood from their victims." Alaric leaned in, lowering his voice. "They're killers—so powerful that even the pack has lost people trying to take them down. And that darkness on the map? I'm starting to think it's them. Heidara said they're shifters, but not wolves. They shift into shadows. Not metaphorical ones... Real ones. Living, black, liquid shadows." A flicker of dread flashed across his face. "If we cross paths with one, we won't be fast enough to escape."

Her stomach knotted as the truth settled over her.

Monsters walked among them, and her brother might already be one of them.

"Evelyne, we can't ever lose that map. It's the only warning we have."

She spun toward her bag, yanking the map out and unfolding it with trembling hands. The surface still remained clear. She blew out a long breath before folding the parchment.

Chants began to rise in a haunting crescendo outside her tent, the deep voices weaving into the night like a call to something ancient. Evelyne and Alaric rushed to the entrance, peering through the opening just as the shifting ritual began.

A ring of elders stood with arms outstretched to the full moon, their chants thick with power, pulsing like a heartbeat through the clearing. All around them, men and women knelt in unity, heads lowered in sacred submission. And at the center of it all, Kaldrek knelt alone, still beneath the moon's gaze.

Then he rose, squaring his shoulders as he struck a fist to his chest—once, then again. The deep, echoing thuds rang out like a signal, calling the pack to attention.

The wolves answered as one, fists pounding against their chests in perfect unison. The sound reverberated through the clearing like a steady, thunderous drumbeat.

A violent crack sounded, jolting Evelyne to her core. She flinched as the sickening snap of bone and the wet rip of shifting flesh filled the air. Kaldrek's body convulsed, limbs twisting at unnatural angles as coarse fur erupted through tearing skin. He grew, stretched, and reshaped, until the man vanished, and in his place stood a wolf.

An enormous wolf. A creature unlike anything she had ever seen. He towered over the others, his sheer size making even Holden's form seem small. His flawless coat caught the moonlight, gleaming with an icy brilliance. He looked white as frost, like a phantom of winter come to life.

But his eyes weren't the blood-hungry red she'd seen on Holden that first night. No—Kaldrek's were black as a void, rimmed in a glint of cold, merciless silver.

One after another, the elders transformed, their bodies twisting with the brutal music of cracking bones and tearing flesh as they became something inhuman. The others followed, their pain a symphony of breaking bodies and snarling beasts. Evelyne and Alaric winced, covering their ears against the unbearable noise.

And yet, the display of power was mesmerizing.

Wolves now stood where warriors once knelt, their fur ranging from dark as ink to pale as smoke, from earthy brown to steely gray. They were all enormous, far larger than any ordinary wolf could ever be, and each bore the telltale red glow of shifter eyes.

But none stood as large as Kaldrek. None carried the same eerie black gaze.

A feral growl rumbled from the pack, rising in volume as more joined, like a sound of primal anticipation. The very ground seemed to vibrate beneath Evelyne's feet.

Then, Kaldrek ran.

His massive paws struck the earth, and he launched into the night in one fluid motion, followed by the elders and the pack. They streaked into the darkness, moving so fast their monstrous forms blurred, silent save for the whisper of wind through the trees. It was both breathtaking and utterly horrifying.

"Holy shit," Alaric murmured beside her.

Evelyne stood speechless. Magic like this was never meant to exist. But it did. And she was standing in the heart of it.

***

Alaric retreated to his tent nearly an hour after the pack had shifted and disappeared into the forest. By morning, they would be on their own again, and Evelyne still awaited her weapons. Kaldrek had said Heidara would leave them outside her tent once they returned, but when that would be, she had no idea. Would they even come back to say goodbye?

Or would they simply take their things and disappear, leaving her and Alaric behind as if they had never been here?

Holden had warned her that by dawn, the pack would be gone. No more food. No more shelter. It would be just the two of them, alone on this journey north—on foot.

A sharp pang of guilt coiled in her stomach as Reuben's face flashed in her mind. She had spent the night drinking and dancing with the very people who had killed him, who once held her captive. What was she thinking, letting her guard down? She pressed her palms to her eyes, trying to silence the regret. But Reuben was gone, and no amount of mourning would change that. She had to focus on the living, on Cillian, on reaching Nerathar before time ran out.

Evelyne changed into the nightclothes Heidara had given her. The fitted wool leggings kept her warm against the late-night chill, but she chose a loose white cropped top, relishing her freedom. Running a hand through her hair, she exhaled slowly, exhaustion settling deep in her limbs.

Tomorrow, they would set out, and everything would change again.

CHAPTER 30

A faint vibration hummed through the tent. It felt subtle, as if it were a warning meant to rouse her from sleep. With the wolf pack gone, the camp felt hollow, like an abandoned village on the brink of being claimed by the dark.

Evelyne felt it again, stronger this time, and bolted upright, the last traces of sleep vanishing in an instant. Drawn by the vibration, she shifted her gaze to her bag, where a soft light pulsed from within.

The map.

Her hands trembled as she tore open the bag and yanked out the parchment. Her breath caught at the sight of inky blackness bleeding across the camp's outline.

Something was here.

A sudden chill rushed through the tent, extinguishing the lantern beside her. In the moonlight spilling through the flap, Evelyne saw her breath.

She bolted.

Tugging on her boots, she scrambled outside, her breath coming in quick, panicked gasps. The full moon bathed the camp in silver light, but it wasn't enough to see through the shifting black mist curling around the tents. It writhed with a life of its own, moving in ways that defied nature.

"Alaric!"

Evelyne's shout was swallowed by the eerie silence.

"Alaric!"

Which tent was his? *Shit*, she didn't know—

She froze at what she saw near the edge of the trees.

Two tall, preternatural figures shifted from shadow to solid form, and between them, pinned against a tree, was Alaric.

The first creature, built like a man, had its clawed fingers wrapped around Alaric's throat. Its gray skin was stretched too tightly over its bones, black veins pulsing beneath the surface like ink spreading through paper. Its mouth, an unholy grin of jagged, needle-sharp teeth, was smeared with blood. Alaric's blood.

The second creature hovered beside it, clutching Alaric's arm in a deathly grip. Its lips pressed against his skin, siphoning the blood from his veins. Alaric's head hung forward, lifelessly still.

No! No, no, no—

Before Evelyne could cry out, a bone-rattling snarl rolled through the forest, halting the creatures mid-feed.

A massive blur of white shot past her, slamming into the demon gripping Alaric's throat. The force sent it crashing against a tree with a sickening crack. The white wolf positioned himself between her and the creatures, a barrier of muscle and power. She could only stare at the rise and fall of his shoulders, each breath a quiet vow to protect.

Kaldrek.

Every muscle in his body was wound tight, like a bowstring ready to snap. A feral gleam lit his dark eyes as they locked onto the creatures, and Evelyne felt a cold ripple of fear. He sank into a low crouch and bared his fangs, a beast on the brink of bloodshed.

Yet despite the brutal image, something eased within her. He was back.

Another figure exploded from the trees—a gray-and-white wolf landing at Kaldrek's side. Evelyne recognized him instantly. Holden. The two stood shoulder to shoulder, ready to tear their enemies apart.

But where was the rest of the pack?

Alaric lay slumped against the tree, barely conscious, his breath shallow. He was alive, but one of the creatures still clung to him. The other stood still, like they were both biding their time. Or planning their next move.

A sick churn gripped Evelyne's stomach as their soulless eyes tracked the space between the wolves.

No, not the wolves. *Her.*

Realization struck like ice in her veins. She was the prey. And when twin smiles stretched across their merciless faces, she knew they could see the terror blooming behind her eyes.

Before Kaldrek or Holden could lunge, they shifted into streaks of darkness, slipping past the wolves like a phantom wind. Evelyne watched as Alaric's body crumpled to the ground like a broken puppet, but before she could scream, cold, strong hands seized her arms, wrenching her backward. She thrashed, kicking wildly, but their grips remained locked.

She screamed until her throat burned, but they didn't stop moving. They dragged her deeper into the forest, their reeking scent a choking mix of decay and metal.

They moved so fast that the world blurred. Evelyne doubted even Kaldrek or Holden could match their speed. Suddenly, a clawed hand jerked her head sideways, baring her throat. A gust of rancid breath swept over her skin, and she instantly knew. It was going to feed.

A surge of white slammed into the creature pinning her, the impact so fierce it knocked her backward into the dirt. Evelyne's vision spun as she caught sight of Holden lunging at the second figure, his jaws locking around its gray-skinned throat. But it didn't go down—it was too strong.

With inhuman speed, it ripped Holden off, its clawed hand grasping his scruff and hurling him across the clearing. Holden crashed against a tree, the clash so violent it shook the ground. A quick, painful whimper escaped him before his body fell.

Horror clawed at the edges of Evelyne's mind, but she shoved it aside. She needed to move.

Panting, she crawled, dirt and twigs scraping against her palms. When she reached Alaric, she cradled him close, relief crashing through her as she felt the faint rise and fall of his chest. He was alive.

And still, the fight hadn't stopped.

The creatures were too fast, moving in flickers of shadow, ducking, dodging, striking. Kaldrek lunged, his white fur streaked with blood that wasn't his own, his jaws snapping just inches from his opponent's throat. He was vicious and terrifying and undoubtedly the strongest in the pack, but she wasn't sure he could bring the creature down alone.

They were outmatched. But as hope began to slip away, the heavy thud of approaching steps and rustling leaves cut through the night. Suddenly, they were no longer alone.

The trees trembled as the entire Ironwolf pack returned.

Dozens of fierce wolves burst into the clearing, their growls rumbling like an oncoming storm, their eyes blazing red with fury. Instantly, the creatures vanished. Their forms morphed from flesh to shadow before dissolving into the darkness. The only trace of their presence was the blood staining the ground.

Evelyne's attention was fixed on Alaric. He was too still, and his normally tanned skin was unnervingly pale. Blood continued to seep from the bites on his forearm and neck. With frantic hands, she ripped the hem of her shirt, tearing the fabric into strips.

"Damn it—" She gritted her teeth as she pressed the fabric against the wounds. But it wasn't enough.

It wasn't until she caught movement from the corner of her eye that she realized the others were shifting back. Bodies, some naked, some cloaked in robes, emerged from the carnage. Holden was down but alive, and Heidara was already kneeling beside him, draping a cloth over his lower half.

When their eyes met, she rushed toward Evelyne without hesitation. "Are you all right?"

"I'm fine, but please help him." Her chest ached as she looked down at Alaric's still body. "Please."

Heidara's warm hand landed on Evelyne's shoulder. "Lorena is coming. She's our best healer."

"Thank you, Heidara."

Lowering her brow to Alaric's, Evelyne let the tears fall.

***

Within minutes, Alaric was wrapped in white bandages and healing herbs, but Evelyne remained at his side in the tent.

Please wake up. Please. Please.

She knew she should try to sleep—by dawn, they'd be on their own. On foot, wounded, and without the protection of the pack. But how could she sleep after what she had just witnessed? Alaric had been bitten, fed on, nearly drained of blood.

A sharp gust of air whipped through the tent as Kaldrek pushed inside. He was still bare from the waist up, his chest smeared with dirt and dried blood. His jaw was clenched so tight it looked like it might snap, and his dark brown eyes flicked between her and Alaric.

"Did they hurt you?" Kaldrek's voice was stern, clipped, like he barely had the patience to ask.

"No, I'll be okay. But—" Evelyne's fingers curled into the blankets as she stared at Alaric's pale body. "What were those... *things*? They were horrible."

"We call them the Noskari. They are the spawn of her bloodcraft, mindless thralls tethered to her darkness."

Her thralls? A chill ran through Evelyne. "Vaelora's?"

He nodded. "They're stronger and faster than we are. We were lucky the others showed up when they did."

As much as she feared admitting it, he was right. Kaldrek had held his ground, but his strength had been waning. If the pack hadn't arrived, she'd be dead.

"So they can invade the mind, devour the body, and kill without remorse—if that's what they choose?" she asked, more to hear it spoken aloud than to be told.

Kaldrek hesitated. "Yes. And there's a very high chance your friend here is now one of them."

Evelyne shot to her feet. "No, he is not."

Kaldrek's expression darkened. "You don't know that."

"And neither do you. They were only feeding on him. I saw it. Nothing passed between them. No shadow, no mental intrusion."

Kaldrek laughed. "You have no idea what the Noskari are capable of. It happens faster than a breath. No one has ever seen the magic spread. It's instant. And since they didn't get to drain him completely, who's to say one of them didn't slip inside your friend before vanishing?" He stepped closer. "We need to move him. Now."

"Don't you even *think* about killing him, Kaldrek," Evelyne snapped.

"He is a potential threat to my pack. I'll do what is necessary."

"You will not touch him." Her hands trembled as she clenched them into fists.

Kaldrek took a slow step forward, and whispered low, "We'll see." And then he walked out.

She was done with his arrogance. Frustration boiling over, Evelyne tore through the tent flap and into the biting night air, unwilling to let him walk away unchallenged. "You haven't even given him a chance to wake up yet, you coward!"

Kaldrek whirled on her. "That's not how you speak to an alpha," he growled, baring his teeth. "I'd watch your tongue."

Evelyne stepped closer, tilting her chin up defiantly. "You are not *my* alpha. You are an *animal,* and I am a southern lady. You will not touch him, or so help me, I will slit your throat while you sleep."

His lips curled into a dangerous smirk. "Watch yourself," he warned, leaning in just enough for his breath to graze her skin. "You keep testing me, and you'll be on my radar, just like your lover."

"He's not my—" She stopped, refusing to take the bait. "You are a wretched excuse for a man."

He laughed low, but Evelyne didn't wait for his reply. She turned on her heel and stalked back to Alaric's tent, fists still clenched at her sides. She didn't care if he shifted and tore her apart right now. He *deserved* to be spoken to like that. What an entitled brute.

*****

"Here." Someone nudged Evelyne's shoulder. Morning light streamed into the tent as she blinked awake, still heavy with exhaustion. She had fallen asleep beside Alaric's cot, keeping watch over him through the night. Rubbing her eyes, she looked up at Heidara, who stood over her, holding her carpet bag along with a larger leather travel pack.

"Get up," Heidara urged, nudging her again. "We're leaving in a few minutes."

Evelyne's mind jolted back to reality, and the night's events slammed into her like a tidal wave. She shot up, eyes darting to the cot beside her.

It was empty.

Panic flared in her chest. "Where is he?"

"He's fine," Heidara said quickly, her voice gentler this time. "We moved him onto a travois."

Evelyne narrowed her eyes in confusion.

"It's a wooden sled we use to carry the injured or extra supplies," Heidara explained. "Anyway, he's awake, and..." She paused briefly. "He seems like himself."

Evelyne released a shaky breath, relief washing over her like a cool breeze. Thank heavens Kaldrek hadn't killed him in the night—not that she would have put it past him. She was still furious.

Heidara lifted the leather bag in her hands. "I packed your pistol and dagger inside. The rest of your things are in here. You can throw it over your back when we leave."

Evelyne frowned, still piecing it together. "We? As in, all of us?"

"Yes," Heidara sighed, rolling her eyes. "Kaldrek didn't take kindly to being challenged in front of the entire Ironwolf pack. He nearly lost it—but Holden got him to simmer down just long enough for me to convince him not to leave you both behind. We're heading north as well, so leaving you would be pointless."

"And Kaldrek is fine with this now? Even after I—"

"*Oh*, he's definitely not fine with it." Heidara smiled slightly. "I'd suggest keeping your distance for a while, unless you have a death wish. I also managed to talk him out of killing Alaric, which seemed to piss him off even more. Especially after I told him you were right."

Evelyne offered a small, sincere smile. "Thank you, Heidara. Truly. I'm still trying to wrap my head around the fact that you'd go to such lengths for people you barely know." Though she was grateful, the words felt strange to say. Could she trust Heidara? Could she trust any of them when their alpha was still deciding whether to kill her friend in his sleep?

Heidara must have read the doubt shadowing her face, because she quickly reassured her, "Lorena says his wounds aren't showing any signs of infection. And we have strict orders to check on him every few hours, just in case... Well, you know."

Evelyne nodded. "Remind me to thank her later. And Holden? How is he?"

Heidara huffed, shaking her head. "Back to being an overprotective ass. He hit his head, but he'll live. Unfortunately."

A small laugh slipped from Evelyne's lips, and the tension eased slightly. Heidara rummaged in her pack and pulled out a cropped leather vest and a slit skirt, tossing them to Evelyne.

"Change into these. The sun will be brutal today, and we won't be making many stops."

Evelyne held up the clothing. "You don't shift to travel?"

"Normally, we do," Heidara admitted, "but given the circumstances, we're walking until we can find horses for you and Alaric. He says there's a trading outpost east of here with stables."

Naturally, Alaric was familiar with these lands as well. Evelyne whispered a silent prayer of gratitude to Charise Hallowell for guiding him to join her.

"Why is the pack heading north?" she asked.

"Kaldrek has his reasons, but I don't think it's my place to share them. That said, after last night's attack, getting the hell out of the forest seems like a smart move."

Evelyne nodded, choosing not to push further. "Thank you. Again."

This time, she stepped forward and pulled Heidara into a hug. The shifter stiffened, caught off guard, but after a moment, she returned the embrace. And Evelyne realized, perhaps for the first time, that this was what the start of a real friendship felt like.

Chapter 31

Heidara hadn't been exaggerating about the heat. Evelyne was grateful she had woven her hair into a long braid. At least it kept the sticky sweat from clinging to the back of her neck. The warmth still made the leather stifling, the material sticking uncomfortably to her skin. Yet, she had to admit, she didn't miss the dresses, or the corsets.

Still, wearing a cropped leather vest that bared her stomach in front of others left her feeling exposed. Not that anyone seemed to notice, except for Alaric. The moment she approached the wooden sled to check on him, he bolted upright, his tired eyes widening slightly.

A familiar, flirty smirk curled his lips. "*Lady Evelyne,*" he drawled, his voice still hoarse from exhaustion. "You do wear leathers well."

Her cheeks flushed slightly, and for a second, she had the urge to smack that smirk right off his face. But what struck her most was the absence of the usual fluttering warmth his voice used to stir in her. There was no racing pulse, no stolen breath, just the easy familiarity of friendship. And maybe that was all they should be now. Just friends. Whether he felt the same, she wasn't sure.

The afternoon sun blazed mercilessly as they continued their trek, and Evelyne felt the burn of it across her forehead. Despite the canopy of trees, their path remained oddly exposed to the brutal sunlight. One of the elders must have noticed her struggle, because she tossed a thin cloth over her head—a small mercy in the unforgiving heat.

She walked near the center of the pack, flanked by the elders. Kaldrek led the front, with Holden trailing close behind him. The woman beside her met Evelyne's glance with a smile and a quiet explanation. The alpha and beta—Holden, as Evelyne now recognized—guided the front, while the pack's elders and vulnerable remained safely nestled in the center. The strongest warriors and scouts took the rear, guarding the pack from behind.

Their structure and fierce loyalty to one another awakened something in Evelyne. A sense of respect, perhaps. And this, she'd come to learn, wasn't the only pack in the eastern lands. There were dozens more, though most had gone into hiding or fallen under Vaelora's control.

Curiosity burned within her, an eagerness to know more about the wolves and their world. But exhaustion pressed down on her shoulders, reminding her she'd need her strength to keep going. She silently thanked the fact that she'd been an active runner back home—she would have collapsed by now if she'd spent her days lounging in parlors and sipping tea like many women of her standing.

She found herself thinking of Caltheris, of her father and Seraphine. Was he still looking for Cillian? Was he looking for her? And how was Seraphine taking her absence? She would have given anything for her handmaid's calming presence.

A painful twist in her stomach pulled her back to the present—hunger. How were they still walking? She couldn't remember anyone stopping to eat or even to relieve themselves. Heidara had warned her they wouldn't take many breaks, but she hadn't expected this relentless pace. If they didn't stop soon, she would drop on the forest floor.

Heidara jogged up from the back of the pack, falling into step beside Evelyne with ease. "How are you holding up?" she asked.

Evelyne eyed her suspiciously. Not a single sign of exhaustion. Just a little sweat glistening on her sun-kissed skin. Meanwhile, Evelyne was pretty sure she looked like she had been dragged through hell and back.

"I'm still standing," she panted, pushing a stray strand of hair from her face.

Heidara smiled. "Impressive."

"Barely," Evelyne muttered under her breath.

Heidara chuckled. "Well, we'll be stopping soon to rest. Alaric thinks we'll reach the outpost by tomorrow."

Evelyne nearly collapsed from relief. Fatigue was manageable. Hunger and a full bladder, however, were not so easily dismissed.

"I have to admit, I'm surprised you lasted this long," Heidara said, giving her a teasing glance. "No offense, but I figured a southern lady wouldn't have the stamina." She had a glint in her eyes, no doubt remembering Evelyne's words to Kaldrek the night before. *I am a southern lady.*

Evelyne scoffed. "I'm surprising myself, too."

As they walked, Evelyne glanced over her shoulder, her eyes landing on the two dark-haired males near the rear of the pack. They moved in perfect step, eyes sharp as they scanned the trees, but it wasn't them who caught her attention. It was the striking red-haired woman gliding between them, her presence so radiant it felt like the sun bowed to her. Evelyne remembered how both men had watched her as if she were their entire world.

Heidara noticed her staring.

"That's Nathan and Ty. They're brothers."

"They look like twins," Evelyne said.

"They do, but Nathan's two years older."

Evelyne raised an eyebrow. "And the woman they're watching like she hung the stars?"

Heidara chuckled. "Ah, Reyna. That's their mate."

Evelyne turned fully to face her. "Mate?"

Heidara's smile widened. "Wolves find mates. Sometimes, we even have two." She sighed dramatically, pressing a hand to her chest. "Can you imagine? Two gorgeous men devoted entirely to you?"

Evelyne nearly tripped over a tree root. "I—I don't think that's something I've ever... considered."

"Oh, come on. You mean to tell me you wouldn't enjoy having two devastatingly handsome men worship you every night?" Heidara grinned.

A blush rose to Evelyne's face. No lady at court would ever speak with such boldness. There, people spoke in careful whispers, never this openly. But Heidara said it so casually, like it was nothing unusual. Evelyne opened her mouth to respond, but laughter spilled out instead. And before she knew it, the two of them were laughing so hard that even Kaldrek turned around to glance at them.

"She could have chosen just one, you know," Heidara continued, shaking her head. "But I guess she couldn't decide. And honestly? I don't blame her."

Evelyne wiped a tear from the corner of her eye, still giggling. "And you? Do you have a mate?"

"Not yet. The elders say you'll just know when it happens," Heidara said, her voice taking on a dreamy, almost wistful tone. "They say the scent hits you like a bullet to the chest, so strong it can stun you. And that the bond is so powerful, mates can communicate mind to mind. Of course, we can all speak with our alpha that way. It's how he commands us in wolf form, and only alphas can reach other alphas. But mates—they can hear each other, no matter the distance."

The idea of something so powerful and irresistible binding two people together felt strange, yet undeniably intriguing. "That sounds intense."

"It is," Heidara said, her green eyes shimmering with excitement. "But until then? I'm going to have my fun." She winked.

Evelyne shook her head and smiled. She didn't doubt it for a second.

***

The pack had only stopped for an hour, just enough time to eat, drink, and stretch sore limbs before pressing on. Evelyne's legs screamed in protest, every step an aching reminder that she was not built for this kind of travel. But she pushed forward, refusing to let anyone, least of all *him*, see her struggle.

Kaldrek called out just before dusk that they were nearing camp, and she had no idea how he knew. There were no markers, no visible trails, just endless trees and tangled undergrowth. But he led them with unwavering certainty, like he'd memorized every inch of this wild terrain since childhood.

The moment they halted, the pack sprang into motion like a well-oiled machine, each member slipping into their role without hesitation or instruction. Some unrolled tarps and stacked logs, assembling makeshift shelters, while others gathered stones, arranging them into the familiar shape of a fire pit. A few disappeared into the trees, returning moments later with thick branches to serve as tent supports. They moved efficiently, like they'd done this a thousand times before.

Evelyne stood in the middle of it all, aimlessly shifting her weight and watching. She wanted to help, but where would she even begin? Alaric was already moving through the camp, much more adept at fitting into this world than she was. He wasn't struggling, wasn't wandering around feeling lost. And maybe that stung a little.

Kaldrek's voice cut through the noise. "Will someone help Lady Defiance pitch her tent, please?"

Every muscle in her body went rigid. He was talking about *her*. A few heads turned, and some younger pack members snickered at his remark. Her jaw clenched so tight she thought her teeth might crack. She knew exactly what he was doing. He wanted to embarrass her, remind her she didn't belong. But if he thought that would break her, he was dead wrong.

Lady Defiance. She could practically hear the smirk in his voice. If that was how he saw her, then she'd make sure to live up to it. Squaring her shoulders, she met his eyes with a steady stare, a silent promise that this wasn't finished.

A few minutes later, Alaric, Holden, and two other wolves appeared, carrying what she assumed were the materials for her tent. Holden grinned, of course, ever eager to run his mouth.

"You sure you two want separate tents?" he mused, tilting his head between her and Alaric. "Seems like a waste when you could keep each other warm."

"I'd rather sleep alone," Evelyne shot back. To her relief, Alaric didn't seem offended. He only nodded, understanding exactly why she felt that way.

They worked quickly; before long, her tent was up, and the fire was roaring. The pack settled into small groups, huddled close to the heat of the flames as the night deepened. Families sat together, parents pulling their children onto their laps. Friends passed around food and drink, their quiet conversations blending with the crackle of burning wood.

Evelyne sat among familiar faces, the low hum of conversation filling the space around her. Holden lounged beside Heidara, smiling at something she said, while Alaric sat close, his strength returning, though fatigue still lingered in his features. Across from her, perched on a flat stone, Kaldrek methodically sharpened his dagger.

He hadn't spoken to her all day. Not since the little jab he'd made at her. Not even a glance in her direction. And that only made her more aware of him.

She found herself stealing glances, drawn in despite herself. The firelight bathed his skin in a warm glow, accentuating the tattoos that traced down both sides of his neck, winding over one shoulder before spiraling down his arm to his wrist. His broad frame, thick with muscle and littered with scars, remained still save for the steady pull of his dagger against the sharpening stone.

As if sensing her gaze, he looked up and met her eyes.

Evelyne quickly turned away, but it was too late. He'd already caught her staring. And she couldn't stop the warmth from rising in her cheeks.

Holden leaned back on his elbows, a cocky grin tugging at his lips as he launched into one of his infamous tales, hands sweeping through the air for dramatic effect.

"So there I was," he began, "thinking I was about to have the best night of my life at age seventeen."

A few chuckles rippled through the group.

"Her name was Isla. And gods, was she was gorgeous. A wild beauty wasted on a scoundrel such as myself." He paused, winking at Heidara, who rolled her eyes. "But I figured, with my charm, I had a chance."

Evelyne smirked, taking a sip of her drink. "Oh, I'm sure she was positively swooning."

Holden shot her a playfully wounded expression. "You doubt my skills, little viper?"

"I highly doubt you have any."

Laughter rang out, but Holden pressed on. "We were visiting one of the outposts near the northern border, and I met Isla at the tavern. She had this dark, wavy hair and the sharpest tongue I've ever encountered—like you, actually," he added, with a pointed glance at Evelyne. "She tells me to meet her outside the healer's hut after sundown. So, obviously, I go and wait in the shadows like some mysterious brooding warrior." He paused for dramatic effect. "Except... she never shows."

The group listened in silence, clearly entertained by every word.

"I think, 'Alright, maybe she's shy,' so I follow her scent. And guess where it leads?" Holden let the tension build, then threw his arms out. "Straight into the middle of a patrol camp. And not just any patrol camp, but her father's patrol camp."

"Damn," Alaric muttered, shaking his head.

Holden nodded. "That's right. Her father, the highest-ranking wolf in the outpost, turns around, sees me standing there like a lost pup, and immediately assumes I'm there to challenge him."

Kaldrek let out a short, unimpressed snort.

"I don't even get a chance to explain before the bastard shifts and barrels straight at me! I barely manage to shift before I'm running for my life, dodging trees, trying not to get my throat ripped out, and all the while, Isla is standing on a damn rock, laughing her ass off."

Evelyne sputtered mid-sip, coughing as Heidara and Alaric burst into laughter.

"The worst part?" Holden continued. "When I finally escaped and returned to the pack, Kaldrek was waiting. And do you know what my dearest friend said to me?"

Kaldrek didn't even look up as he muttered, "'You're an idiot.'"

"No sympathy. No concern for my wellbeing. Just... *You're an idiot.*"

Evelyne grinned. "Well, he wasn't wrong."

"I regret nothing." Holden shrugged. "She sought me out the next night anyway."

"Gross," Heidara mumbled.

This time, Evelyne let herself laugh, truly laugh, and savor the rare ease of the moment—the warmth of shared laughter, the brief illusion of normalcy. But it didn't last. Because when she glanced at Kaldrek, he was watching her.

Her stomach fluttered beneath the intensity of his stare, but she didn't have time to analyze it, because Holden said something that made the air turn to ice.

"You gave us quite a scare last night." He smirked, eyes flicking to Evelyne. "Got a little too close to death, didn't you? Makes me wonder what the Noskari would've done with a pretty little thing like you." He leaned in slightly, his tone dropping to a dark, taunting murmur. "I bet they'd have drawn it out, slow and sweet. Savoring every bite of your body."

Evelyne flinched as the words landed, yanking the memory of Ivan's unwelcome touch from where she'd forced it to stay hidden. The fire's warmth vanished instantly, replaced by a cold dread curling through her veins. Evelyne's heart plummeted as her mind flashed to rough hands gripping her waist, fingers clawing at the fabric of her skirts, vile breath whispering against her ear.

The memory seized her, like a ruthless tide threatening to drag her under. The laughter around her faded into a dull hum, her vision narrowing as the blood drained from her face.

A familiar hand covered hers. Alaric. His touch was gentle but grounded her back into the present.

"It's a good thing our mighty wolf pack swooped in to save you," Holden laughed, and Heidara rolled her eyes, oblivious to the sudden change in Evelyne's expression.

But not Kaldrek. He was watching her closely, his gaze intense—like he'd picked up on something she hadn't meant to reveal. Before he could speak, she swallowed hard and masked her expression with a calm look. She wasn't going to talk about it. Not now, not ever.

Instead, she lifted her chin. "I want to learn how to fight." She paused. "To defend myself."

Holden immediately perked up. "I'll teach you."

"Or you can join us," Heidara added eagerly. "Kaldrek trains us early each morning."

Evelyne turned to him, waiting, but he did not look pleased. His grip tightened on his dagger, and for a second, she thought he might flat-out refuse.

"I'd like to learn as well," Alaric added.

Kaldrek's eyes flicked between them. After a long beat of silence, he sighed. "I won't stop the lesson for you, so do your best to keep up." His words were laced with doubt, a challenge coiled beneath them.

Evelyne let a slow smile creep onto her lips. "Oh, I will."

CHAPTER 32

Evelyne woke just before dawn, the sky still deep blue with the first light creeping through the trees. And of course, he was already up.

Kaldrek stood alone in the clearing, wearing training leathers that were loose enough for fluid movement yet fitted enough to reveal the strength and discipline that defined him. The morning mist drifting through the trees seemed to hesitate near him, curling at the edges as if uncertain of his presence. Every motion he made was controlled: a jab, a duck, a sharp kick. He moved with the power and precision of a force of nature, strong, focused, and entirely composed.

She should be getting changed and preparing for whatever awaited her in this training session, but she couldn't look away.

He bounced lightly on the balls of his feet, shaking out the tension in his fingers before striking again, faster this time, more brutal. She had no idea how long she stood there watching, but when Heidara appeared beside her, grinning like she'd caught her in a scandal, Evelyne nearly jumped out of her skin.

"Enjoying the view?" Heidara teased, her emerald eyes alight with mischief.

"I was just... trying to get an idea of what I'm getting myself into this morning."

"Yes, *of course*. But it's perfectly normal to admire our alpha, too." Heidara winked before slipping into Evelyne's tent.

Evelyne scowled after her, but couldn't help feeling grateful when Heidara hand-picked a set of training leathers and boots for her. Without a word, Heidara stepped behind her and began weaving her hair into a braided crown, tucking it neatly to keep every strand out of her face.

When Evelyne stepped out of the tent and into the clearing, she could feel Kaldrek's gaze burning into her. The training leathers hugged her figure more closely than anything she was used to, and for a moment, she considered turning back, adjusting the vest, and covering more skin. But then she noticed how he looked at her—not with ridicule or judgment, but with something that made her feel seen. Admired.

She stood taller, lifted her chin, and let him look.

The morning started with a warm-up, which, to Evelyne, felt like a full-on battle. The so-called "basic stances" left her legs aching within minutes, and the constant crouching and squatting made her thighs burn.

Alaric stood near the front, paired with Ty, moving like this was second nature to him. Meanwhile, Heidara patiently corrected Evelyne's every misstep.

"Now stand with your dominant foot slightly behind your lead foot," Kaldrek instructed as he paced between the trainees.

"Feet shoulder-width apart, knees bent. Balance is everything."

She adjusted—again.

"Keep your hands up by your face, palms inward, elbows close to protect your ribs," he continued. "Drop them, and you're asking for a broken nose." As if on cue, he barked at a scout who had dropped their hands, "Do not drop your guard, dammit!"

"Does he always stomp around barking orders like a rabid dog?" Evelyne whispered to Heidara.

She stifled a giggle. "Yes. And don't ever let him hear you say that."

They moved into punching drills. Kaldrek quickly demonstrated each strike, making Evelyne want to punch him just for existing. His movements were perfect and powerful. She really tried to focus, but he was built like a warlord, which was incredibly distracting.

"The jab needs to be quick," Kaldrek continued, shifting into position. "This is your setup punch, meant to keep distance and create openings. Keep your elbow tucked, extend fast, then snap back to guard."

Evelyne's attention snagged on the way his muscles coiled and flexed with each movement. How was someone that big still that fast?

A sharp elbow jabbed into her ribs, pulling her from her daze, and she turned to find Heidara smirking.

"What?" Evelyne whispered.

"You're staring."

Her cheeks heated, and Kaldrek's voice cut through the training field before she could defend herself.

"Can you hear me back there, or are you too busy daydreaming?"

Every pair of eyes turned to her. She wanted to crawl under a rock and die. Instead, she cleared her throat, forcing herself to meet his piercing stare.

"Loud and clear, *Alpha*."

His expression darkened slightly at the title. Good. Let him think she was mocking him.

"Then show me."

She turned to Heidara, desperate. "Can you—?"

Heidara, bless her, broke the motion down step by step, walking Evelyne through the jab until she got it right.

They repeated the punches over fifty times, and her shoulders throbbed. She was getting sloppy, her arms slower than before—

WHACK.

A sudden burst of pain shot through her nose.

"Shit!" Heidara gasped. "Evelyne, I'm so sorry!"

Evelyne staggered back, her hands flying to her face. Warm blood was already dripping onto her fingers.

She groaned. "Well, that's embarrassing."

Alaric rushed over, his blue eyes filled with concern, but Kaldrek? He stood with his arms crossed, looking pissed.

"This is exactly why you don't drop your guard."

Evelyne glared at him through the pain. "Bastard," she muttered under her breath before walking away.

***

The day's journey was grueling. Her swollen and tender nose throbbed beneath the bandage, and the heat only worsened things. Sweat clung to her skin, soaking into the cloth and making her feel uncomfortable—and, frankly, a little foolish.

Lorena had bandaged her nose quickly that morning, offering a gentle reminder to rest and drink plenty of water. Rest, of course, was a luxury Evelyne couldn't afford, not while traveling with a pack of wolves that barely slowed down. Still, she appreciated the healer's concern.

As if things couldn't get more irritating, Kaldrek had been waiting for her when she left Lorena's tent. He'd been standing just a few paces away, arms crossed, eyes fixed on her with that unreadable intensity. She wasn't sure if he actually cared that she was hurt. It had looked like he might say something, but she'd turned her back before he could. Probably not the most brilliant move to turn away from an alpha, but she didn't care. After all, she was *defiant*.

Alaric walked beside her now, his stride strong and posture steady. If not for the faint scars on his neck and forearm, no one would guess how close he'd come to dying. And she wasn't the only one who noticed. More than once, she caught Holden watching him, eyes narrowed, like he was waiting for Alaric to sprout fangs and prove he wasn't entirely human anymore.

And then there was Reyna, radiant under the afternoon sun, her beauty impossible to ignore. But it wasn't her glow that made Evelyne's stomach turn—it was the two small, precise bite marks on her throat.

Had a Noskari attacked her?

Heidara noticed her staring and casually explained, "They're claiming marks. It's considered the most intimate part of mating. When the female allows her mate to mark her."

"Or, in Reyna's case, mates," Evelyne muttered.

Heidara grinned. "Exactly. A declaration to the world that she belongs to no one else."

The whole idea sounded wild. Still, she supposed it was better than the mark of a Noskari's bite.

"And what about the males? Do they get 'marked' too?"

"I guess they can," Heidara said with a shrug. "But it's more common for females. Honestly, I think the males just like showing off their possessiveness." She laughed softly.

Alaric had been right; they reached the next outpost by nightfall. But the real problem was figuring out how to get the horses. They couldn't just stroll in and ask for them without drawing attention. And using her gold would leave a trail just as dangerous.

"We've gotten this far," Evelyne said to Alaric. "We can't risk it."

Kaldrek had already devised a plan: wait for the outpost to fall into a slumber, then send in his quickest scouts to steal the horses. Which meant they had to wait.

At one point, as the others wandered off for privacy or quiet conversation, she found herself alone with the alpha.

"My nose is fine—thanks for asking," she said with a bite of sarcasm.

Kaldrek didn't so much as blink. "If you'd followed my instructions properly, it wouldn't have happened."

Evelyne narrowed her eyes. "You think I'm defiant, but did you ever stop to consider that maybe you're just stubborn and insufferable?"

Irritation flickered across his face. "I'm their alpha. There's no room for softness."

"Well, that's just sad," she shot back. "You can be strong and still have basic human decency."

He smirked slightly. "You need to toughen up, *Lady* Evelyne."

"Yes, well, that's exactly why I asked to be trained," she countered. "Though you didn't seem particularly eager to help. Maybe I'll take Holden up on his offer. He seemed more than happy to give me one-on-one training."

Kaldrek barked out a sharp laugh, shaking his head. "Oh, I'm sure Holden's intentions have nothing to do with fighting."

Feeling daring, she hummed. "Maybe I wouldn't mind learning his intentions."

His smile faltered. Just slightly, but she saw it.

"Be my guest."

An awkward silence stretched between them before Kaldrek spoke again, his voice quieter this time.

"Who was the man that touched you?"

The words were like ice water down her spine, and she hated how easily he had read her last night.

"That is none of your concern."

He grabbed her chin, forcing her to look at him. His touch was firm, but not rough. "It *is* my concern. We kill men for things like that."

His voice was deadly and resolute, a quiet promise in every word. And she had no reason to doubt him. Kaldrek struck her as the kind of man who would hunt down anyone guilty of such a crime and make them suffer. Slowly.

Evelyne swatted his hand aside. "Alaric found me. He saved me from—" Her voice faltered. "He saved me. That's all you need to know."

Kaldrek's eyes darkened. His entire body tensed, muscles coiled like he was about to snap.

And strangely, it made her feel safe.

He exhaled, ready to walk away, but before he did, she blurted out, "Do you like being alpha?"

His brows lifted slightly, as if he were surprised by the question. "I didn't have a choice," he admitted. "When our previous alpha—my father—died, the mark chose me."

She frowned. "So whether you enjoy it or not doesn't matter?"

"No," he said. "I must protect my pack. That's all that matters."

"So you don't enjoy the killing and bossing people around?"

He grinned. "I never said that."

And damn him, because that wicked smile sent a rush of cruel excitement through her. For once, she could only blink, completely speechless.

Before disappearing into the trees, he tossed over his shoulder, "Take that bandage off. You look ridiculous."

***

The trading outpost was nothing more than a skeleton of what Evelyne assumed it had once been. A few wooden structures stood in silence, their roofs sagging under the weight of neglect. Lanterns flickered dimly outside a single tavern, the only sign of life amid the decay. The market stalls were abandoned, and the scent of damp wood and stale ale lingered in the air. A scattering of old wagons sat unused near the treeline, overtaken by creeping vines.

Trade had severely diminished. People had vanished into the forests, into the unknown, and what remained of this place felt like a forgotten relic of a time before the darkness came creeping in.

Beyond the outpost, the stables stood at the edge of the clearing, tucked against the thick treeline like an afterthought. The structure was small but well-maintained, with only a few stalls. Most of the horses had already been sold or taken elsewhere. Probably because fewer mouths to feed meant a better chance at survival. Still, two remained: strong, sleek, black-coated creatures, their ears twitching in the moonlight as they dozed in their stalls.

Kaldrek sent his quickest. Nathan, Ty, and younger scout Drakin moved like ghosts through the night, their forms slipping between shadow and torchlight. They wasted no time creeping past the slumbering guards, weaving through the dark corners of the outpost with an ease that spoke of years of practice. Kaldrek, of course, went as well. He wouldn't send his scouts without their leader. Holden had been ordered to stay behind and guard the pack—a duty he clearly didn't take lightly. His clenched fists said all he needed to.

When they returned, Evelyne barely had a moment to react before Kaldrek's firm hands gripped her waist and effortlessly lifted her onto the horse's saddle.

"I hope you know how to ride," he muttered, fastening leather bags against the saddle straps.

Before she could retort, he reached for the hem of his shirt and peeled it off. Then his hands went to his belt. Evelyne's stomach dropped.

"What are you doing?" she whispered, eyes wide with horror.

Kaldrek's lips curved into a wicked smirk. He was clearly enjoying her discomfort. But before he could respond, she noticed the others around them—Holden, Heidara, Nathan, Ty—all shedding their clothes down to their undergarments, swiftly packing them into bags secured to the saddles and the wooden sleds that some of the pack would pull along.

Realization hit her like a bolt of lightning.

The pack was going to shift.

"This is the craziest thing I've ever seen," she muttered, torn between fascination and sheer disbelief.

Kaldrek finished securing his belongings, his eyes flicking up to meet hers. "Get ready to ride," he warned. "The shift will be loud."

And then, the night filled with the visceral sounds of transformation. Bones snapped, bodies twisted, and before Evelyne could even process it, the horses reared, hooves kicking up dirt. They took off into the night, chasing the wolves that ran like shadows beneath the moon.

They rode until exhaustion weighed heavy, stopping only when Kaldrek deemed it safe. No camp this time. Just sleep and food. Just enough time to keep themselves from falling apart before moving on.

Dawn came cruel and relentless. Evelyne's body ached, her muscles stiff from riding, but there was no time to dwell on discomfort. They trained. Again.

And this time, she kept her damn hands up.

CHAPTER 33

He could see, hear, and feel, but the thoughts swirling in his mind, the words slipping from his lips, were not entirely his own. He sat upon the cold black stone of the dais, positioned beside her... His queen, his woman. She was breathtaking, draped in dark silks, a crown of black obsidian and gleaming gems resting atop her silken white hair.

He spent most of his time watching her, studying how she moved, the effortless command she held over the room. One by one, demon warriors entered to report on the state of the land: disruptions, victories, the successful acquisition of new Noskari. They were grotesque, twisted things—leathery gray skin stretched tight over their muscular frames, with pulsing black veins writhing beneath the surface. Their soulless black eyes remained fixed on one figure alone: Vaelora.

Her name ignited something within him, a warmth coursing through his veins despite the cold pallor of his skin. Outwardly, he was unchanged, his complexion pale, his body chilled, but inside, he burned for her. His eyes had darkened like hers, like the Noskari, and he embraced it. Welcomed it. He was no longer who he had been. He was something more. Something powerful. And with every word she spoke, every glance she bestowed upon him, she tightened the chains around his soul, binding him to her in ways he no longer resisted.

She did not see a boy when she looked at him. No, she saw a man, and he was hers.

It was more than control. More than devotion. It was possession. She commanded not just his body but his very mind, shaping his thoughts, twisting his desires with nothing more than a look, a touch, a whisper.

And he did not fight it.

He would give himself over completely, drowning in the intoxicating pull of her presence, if only to remain in this existence forever. But were those truly his wants? Or was something still buried deep within him, something that resisted, however faintly?

"My queen," a voice rasped, cutting through the haze in his mind.

One of her Noskari stood before them, his darkened eyes locked onto Vaelora. She tilted her head slowly.

"Yes...?"

"I've received word that the girl has been seen beyond the southern territories."

He avoided naming her, but there was a deliberate meaning behind his words, a silent warning that Cillian was not meant to know who she was. *What girl?* Cillian thought distantly, the question flitting through his mind before slipping away like smoke.

"Where?" Vaelora hissed.

The Noskari flinched as tendrils of inky black mist curled from her fingertips, coiling and writhing like living things. "Mokkvyrn Forest," he answered quickly. "She's traveling with a wolf pack."

Vaelora's eyes flashed with something darker, something lethal. "Which pack?"

"The Ironwolf, Your Grace."

"And she was left alive?" Vaelora spat.

The Noskari bared his teeth in a low snarl, black veins pulsing with frustration. "Our scouts in the area reported that the pack arrived too soon. They were outnumbered before the task could be finished."

Vaelora let out a slow, dramatic sigh. "I can't open another portal to retrieve her," she said. "I drew too deeply on my magic when I pulled my... *lover* through." Her eyes slid to Cillian, a purr in her tone.

He stiffened. She'd opened a portal? All he recalled was the warmth of her kiss and a glimmer of golden light flickering through his mind before darkness had claimed everything.

The witch queen exhaled again, and a wicked smile curved her lips. "Perhaps," she said, almost lazily, "it's time we send another message."

Cillian stayed quiet, watching. Listening. Because there was no room for questions here. Vaelora allowed none. And still, something in him twisted.

Who was this girl the queen wanted dead so badly? And why did something deep in his hollowed soul stir at the mention of her?

***

The vast clearing spread before them, the eastern reaches of Centaro opening wide after their long escape from Mokkvyrn Forest. For nearly a week they had crossed the quiet expanse of the Sunmere Stretch, and Alaric relished its stillness after the forest's tangled depths. The Stretch was a bridge between wilderness and the world beyond—and with its end in sight, civilization lay ahead.

Centaro felt like an entirely different world from the one they had left behind. Soon, they would arrive in Cindermoor, where settlements and people awaited. But for now, it was just them, the pack and the endless open land rolling in golden waves beneath the sky, broken only by the occasional treeline on the horizon.

Throughout the journey, Alaric had watched Evelyne change completely. She was relentless with waking at dawn, training until her muscles shook, and mounting her horse with unwavering determination. He knew the search for her brother drove her forward, pushing her past exhaustion, but there was something else, too.

She was growing into her strength, and for the first time, it seemed like she was learning to love it. She took the training seriously. Fiercely. And though she had suffered a few bruises and a busted nose from her early missteps, she had improved. Alaric had also become sharper and faster—learning the nuances of hunting and surviving in the wild. He had always loved the outdoors, but now he saw the world beyond what had been allowed in the south.

Could he ever go back to that life? To a world of wealth and privilege, of polished floors and gilded cages? The thought felt more foreign with each passing day. Not that it mattered. He doubted he'd even survive long enough to have that choice.

Thankfully, they hadn't encountered any Noskari since the night of his attack. He tried not to think about it, about the pressure of their hands pinning him down, their razor-sharp teeth sinking into his skin. Instead, he focused on the present.

Today, Kaldrek was running them through dagger maneuvers, and Evelyne was... struggling. Badly.

Alaric hid a chuckle as he watched her drop the dagger for what had to be the fifth time. Unlike him, Heidara didn't laugh. She never did. The blonde warrior was as skilled as any man in the pack, powerful, but with a softness in her smile that could make Alaric forget his own name. He'd caught himself staring into those emerald eyes more than once, and each time, she met his gaze without flinching, unshaken. And then she'd smile.

Once, Holden had noticed and, true to form, growled his disapproval. The warning hadn't been subtle, and Alaric understood it well enough.

No matter how often he tried to dismiss it, guilt crept in every time he found himself admiring someone else, even if the idea of marrying Evelyne was something he'd let go of. Still, no passing distraction could keep him from noticing how Kaldrek had been treating Evelyne lately.

The alpha had always been hard on her, on both of them, really, but this was something else. It wasn't just about dominance or proving a point. There was something sharper in his training with Evelyne, something relentless. He wasn't just trying to make her stronger. He was trying to break something in her. Or maybe... to bring something out.

And today, he wasn't holding back.

Kaldrek switched up the partners, pairing Evelyne with Nathan after noticing Heidara was too easy on her. Nathan was one of the pack's most seasoned scouts, and the difference was brutal. His strikes were fast and fluid, his blade movements controlled and deadly. However, Evelyne was still too stiff and slow in her counters. She was getting better at holding her stance, but her footwork was predictable, and her parries were reactive instead of instinctive. Every block sent her reeling back slightly, every deflection off-balance.

And Kaldrek saw.

"Is Lady Defiance struggling to keep up today?"

His voice cut through the clash of steel, loud enough for everyone to hear. A few of the trainees chuckled, but Evelyne froze. Alaric saw the moment she blocked out the noise, the laughter, Nathan, and the rest of the pack. Now, it was just her and Kaldrek.

She locked onto him, golden eyes blazing, her grip tightening around the dagger. She was furious. But anger made people sloppy, and Evelyne was still learning.

She lunged too early. The blade missed by an inch. Nathan shifted effortlessly, catching her movement and knocking the dagger from her hand in one smooth motion. It hit the dirt with a dull thud.

Kaldrek sighed.

"Again."

Without a word, she picked it up. Again. And again.

But Kaldrek didn't watch her like an alpha sizing up a trainee. No—it was different, like a man staring at something he didn't quite understand, but couldn't look away from.

Evelyne was embarrassed. Anyone could see that. Still, she never quit. And Kaldrek's gaze never left her.

Alaric couldn't help but wonder exactly what was building between them and how long it would be before it boiled over.

CHAPTER 34

No matter how often Evelyne ran through the maneuvers, her footwork was still too slow; her blade work was sloppy. Frustration clawed at her insides as she dropped the blade again during the morning training. Maybe it was the restless sleep—or perhaps it was him. Kaldrek had been incredibly insufferable lately, but last night? Last night had unraveled her, confused her.

They'd all been gathered around the fire, eating whatever game the pack had hunted down and cooked over the flames. Evelyne was getting used to the meals now, lean meat, rich with protein, strengthening her in ways she hadn't expected. She could feel the difference in her body, in the toned muscles and the endurance she was building.

Aside from the rain-soaked nights that left her shivering in whatever makeshift shelter Kaldrek deemed safe for the pack, she had to admit she didn't hate it out here. Alaric seemed to be enjoying himself, too, adapting with ridiculous ease. He made friends faster than anyone she'd ever known; if anything, this wild life suited him.

She had just popped the last bite of food into her mouth, barely enough time to chew, when Kaldrek dropped into the open space beside her without warning.

"For a betrothed couple, you and Alaric don't seem very intimate," he said bluntly, tearing into his meat with lazy precision.

Evelyne nearly choked on her last bite. Of all the things he could've said, that was the last she expected.

She raised her brows, but forced herself to chew, to swallow. Answering him with her mouth full would be unladylike, and she refused to give him the satisfaction of flustering her.

"How exactly is my relationship with Alaric any of your business?"

Kaldrek only shrugged smugly. "Everything that happens within my pack is my business."

Of course he'd say something so self-important. The arrogance was unbearable. But still, she couldn't shake the feeling that his interest in this subject wasn't just about leadership.

She should have left it at that, should have walked away and ignored him. Instead, she kept talking.

"Alaric and I... care for each other," she admitted. "But we're just friends. And will only ever be just friends."

Kaldrek hummed, expectant. And damn him—she gave him more.

"There was a moment between us. Just one stupid and impulsive moment. And somehow, it ended in an engagement. I know that sounds absurd." She paused, swallowing. "Then I found out it was arranged. And he knew. He knew the whole time... and never said a word." Her voice stayed even, but the hurt slipped through anyway.

"I see." His voice had dipped lower, a shade rougher. Was that the answer he wanted to hear?

"Is this the kind of information that keeps you up at night, Alpha?" she drawled, dragging out the word to irritate him.

A muscle in his jaw ticked, and she swore the corner of his mouth lifted. "I just find it interesting that your betrothed spends half his time sneaking glances at Heidara when he already has a beautiful fiancée."

The compliment should have made her blush, but it didn't, because he was right. Alaric did look at Heidara. *A lot.* And for some reason, that realization didn't make Evelyne jealous. It made her happy. Hopeful, even. Maybe he could move on, and she wouldn't be holding him back.

She shrugged. "Heidara's gorgeous. I catch myself looking at her, too."

Kaldrek chuckled.

"Does it bother you when he looks at her?" she asked. "Do you have feelings for her?" The thought made her a little jealous.

His smile grew, and she immediately regretted asking.

"Heidara? No. She's like a sister to me." That was oddly comforting. Then he said, "But it would bother me if his glances upset you."

"Why?" Evelyne didn't see why her feelings mattered to him.

"I honestly don't know. Especially since that attitude of yours is irritating as hell."

She laughed. "Yeah, well, you deserve it."

He was still smiling. She could tell his guard was down, and she wasn't about to waste it.

"Why go north?" she asked. "You know my reasons, but I don't know yours."

His smile vanished, expression hardening. After a pause, he answered. "Because she has taken too many of my loved ones and continues to corrupt our lands." He spoke softly, but with an edge. "We need to band together and get revenge, or else we will all die."

Vaelora. Evelyne's mind raced. Who had she taken from him? A lover? A sibling? Then she remembered their first real conversation—when she'd asked if he liked being alpha.

The words slipped out before she could stop them. "She killed your father?"

His eyes flashed with fury, the kind that burned deep and never truly faded. But she didn't flinch; his rage wasn't directed at her.

"And my mother," he added quietly.

The pain hung between them, thick and unspoken. His loss, his grief, was something he carried with ruthless control. She saw it now, in the sharp line of his jaw, in the tension winding through him like a wound that had never healed.

Evelyne swallowed down the urge to press further. He didn't want to talk about this.

Instead, she exhaled softly, reached out, and placed her hand gently atop his. "I'm sorry."

Kaldrek dipped his head, sorrow shadowing his features. She missed his smile, the teasing, the banter, that infuriating spark in his eyes that always made her chest tighten. She had to shift the mood and bring back the part of him that made everything feel lighter.

So, she did the only thing that came to mind.

She turned slightly and gave him a slow, knowing smile. Then she let her eyes move over him—staring at his chest, pausing there, then drifting lower, all the way to his boots, before lazily making their way back up.

Kaldrek lifted a brow, and she knew she had his attention. She let the silence stretch between them, making sure he felt the heat of her stare.

"Evelyne?" His eyes darkened.

"So tell me, Kaldrek... who keeps you warm at night? Do you have a mate?" Evelyne's voice was smooth with false confidence. Inside, she was shaking. She'd never pushed this far before.

For just a second, his body stiffened, like she'd caught him off guard. His lips parted slightly, surprise flickering across his face before something settled in his gaze. Good. He would play along—

Oh.

He leaned forward, folding his muscled forearms on the rock between them, eyes locked onto hers like a wolf sizing up prey. "Does that question keep you up at night, *Lady*?" His voice was pure sin, laced with something dangerous. "Wondering which one of these beautiful women shares my bed?"

She should have had a quick response ready. A laugh, a scoff, anything. But her mouth went dry, and she could only stare at him like a fool.

He grinned.

"No," he murmured, his eyes drifting to her lips, then back up again. "You'd know if someone warmed my bed at night. The whole damn forest would hear her screaming my name while I pleasured her."

She swallowed, her teeth sinking into her bottom lip on instinct. His eyes tracked the motion, and he let out a slow breath. He knew exactly what he was doing to her. And she hated that her body betrayed her—pulsing with want, flushed with heat. Not from anger. Not from shame. From *him*.

Kaldrek stood abruptly and rolled his shoulders.

"Goodnight, Evelyne."

He winked and walked away, leaving her flushed, speechless, and burning with frustration.

***

She wondered if Kaldrek felt even a fraction as off-balance as she did during their morning training, but if he did, he didn't show it. He was all fire and focus, and he didn't hold back for a second.

What started as a routine session quickly shifted. After a few warm-ups, he moved straight into takedowns, pairing her with Heidara. Meanwhile, he demonstrated each move with Holden, and Evelyne couldn't help but notice how Kaldrek exhaled after every slam with long, controlled breaths, like he was forcing something out of himself with each impact. Rage. Frustration. Something deeper.

Holden, to his credit, didn't flinch. He just kept getting back up, again and again, only to be slammed into the ground with staggering force. It was a rhythm that felt practiced, like this wasn't the first time the alpha and beta had used each other to burn through whatever darkness weighed them down.

Kaldrek's strength was something else entirely. Watching him throw Holden around like he weighed nothing made it clear why the alpha mark had chosen him. His power was unmatched. And still, Holden grinned every time he hit the dirt, brushing himself off and asking, "That's it?" before stepping back into position.

Heidara, thankfully, was much gentler with Evelyne, guiding her through each move with patience. But then Kaldrek switched to blade work, and everything went to hell.

He'd paired her with Nathan, whose skill with a blade left her thoroughly embarrassed in front of everyone. Nathan was following orders, sure, but Kaldrek? He was pushing her hard. Too hard. Maybe she'd crossed a line last night. Perhaps this was his version of punishment.

Whatever it was, he made sure every mistake she made rang loud and clear across the clearing. Every misstep, every falter, called out for everyone to hear. But she wouldn't break. Instead, she pushed through the rest of training, ignoring the burn in her muscles and the agitation simmering beneath the surface.

When the rain came, she slipped behind her tent, soaked, sore, and far from finished. She still had something to prove, and needed to do it alone.

Rain poured in relentless sheets, drenching Evelyne to the bone and turning the ground beneath her into a slick mud pit. She barely noticed. Kaldrek had told the pack they would set out in an hour, giving her enough time to practice somewhere away from watchful eyes.

She tightened her grip on the dagger and planted her feet, trying to steady herself. Each movement was controlled and focused until it came time to defend. *Thrust, slash. Thrust, slash.* Her strikes were solid, but her defense kept falling apart. Over and over, she tried to redirect an invisible blow, but her grip slipped, and her balance gave out. In a real fight, she'd already be bleeding.

Her next sidestep sent her boots sliding in the mud. "Shit," she hissed, swiping wet strands of hair from her face.

"You need to start slow. Control first, then speed."

She didn't need to turn to see who stood behind her.

"Are you here to humiliate me more? Haven't you done enough of that today?"

There was a slight pause. Then footsteps approached, stopping behind her. She didn't move.

Kaldrek's hands, rough and strong, rested over hers, adjusting her wrist with surprising gentleness. He nudged her foot with his boot, fixing her stance. Then he stepped in close, his chest lightly touching her back, his warmth cutting through the cool, damp air. She clung to her breathing, though the nervous heat rising in her belly threatened to give her away.

His voice was low against her ear. "You want to hold the dagger like you're shaking hands with it. Keep the blade angled outward for control." He guided her arm forward. "Extend. Drive the tip straight toward your target. Keep your wrist firm."

Then his hand was on her thigh, the contact of his palm striking through her soaked leathers. She inhaled sharply, and he didn't miss it.

"Feet apart. Stay light. Watch me."

He stepped forward to demonstrate. Rain slid down his face and followed the line of his jaw. His arms tensed with each movement, every precise step keeping her eyes locked on him.

"Now you."

For a moment, she forgot why they were even here. Why was he helping her now after being such an ass earlier? Was it guilt or something else? She didn't ask, mostly because she didn't want it to stop. So she reset her stance and mirrored his movements, pushing herself to focus. Again and again, until the burn in her muscles drowned out everything else.

When they stopped to catch their breath, she asked, "Did I do something to upset you last night?"

He stilled, his mouth opening then closing again.

"You always do something to frustrate me," he said at last, a faint smirk tugging at his lips.

"I mean it, Kaldrek. You seemed... particularly annoyed this morning. Why?"

A muscle in his jaw twitched. "You didn't do anything."

"Really? So you just enjoy making a spectacle out of me?"

His laugh was soft, edged with something close to bitterness. "I push you to see what you're capable of. Not to humiliate you."

Evelyne stepped forward, closing the space between them. "That's it?" Her tone sharpened. "You expect me to believe today was just some *test*?"

He didn't answer, exhaling through his teeth as she approached.

"No," she said firmly. "Not good enough. Tell me the real reason. Why did you come at me like that? What are you trying to prove?"

His voice cut through the rain. "That you need work."

She stared at him, unflinching, so he kept going.

"No one's pushing you. You're pampered. Alaric watches you like you'll fall apart if the wind shifts. And Heidara?" He scoffed. "She's too soft to say it, but she knows. Deep down, she knows you won't survive when it matters."

Each word landed like a blow. A cold reminder of just how unprepared he thought she was. And still, as Evelyne looked at him, one question kept circulating: why did he care? Kaldrek had treated her and Alaric like burdens since this journey began. If he thought she was useless, why not let her fail? Why did it seem to bother him so much?

How generous of him to let them both tag along on this grand mission north. But now she saw what he really thought of her: that she was weak, useless, and nothing more than dead weight. He was being a prick, but she didn't believe for a second that was the real issue. Something else was eating at him, and she wasn't about to back down.

Not a chance.

She took another step forward, lifted her chin, and met his eyes. "So you think I'm too fragile to care for myself?"

His face twisted with aggravation. "No. I never said you were fragile. I think you're more than capable of surviving. But I also think you're too pampered."

"That's not really why you're on edge, though, is it?" Her voice dipped, laced with quiet certainty. She moved in again, close enough to catch the faintest shift in his breathing. "Tell me what truly set you off, Kaldrek."

The air between them changed, and his gaze flicked over her face like a predator assessing its prey.

"You love pressing, don't you?" His voice lowered too, rough and edged with warning.

Evelyne didn't waver. She held her ground, heart hammering. "Maybe I just don't like being lied to."

He shook his head slowly as a wicked smile played at his mouth. "You want to know why I'm on edge?"

He moved before she could react, one hand slipping to the back of her neck, tilting her chin upward. The other found her lower back, drawing her in until there was no space between them.

A quiet gasp left her lips as his mouth lingered near her ear, his breath warm against her skin.

"Because you drive me mad, Evelyne." His breath shuddered as his grip on her tightened. "Everything about you gets under my skin, and I don't know why." His eyes dropped to her mouth as his thumb brushed her bottom lip. "Especially this defiant mouth."

Her pulse slammed in response, each beat a war drum between them.

"I caught the shift in your scent last night. It seems my little comment got you all worked up." As if reliving it, he closed his eyes and let a satisfied growl rise in his chest.

He could *smell* it—her arousal.

"And that sweet scent of yours kept me up. All. Damn. Night."

Her knees nearly buckled when his lips ghosted over her throat, the barest touch, a tease meant to unravel her. And it did.

A quiet, breathy moan slipped past her lips, so soft, so fleeting, she barely registered it. But he did—and groaned, taking in another slow breath, savoring her scent. Then his voice lowered further, rough and heavy with hunger.

"*Fuck.* I can't even think when you smell like that."

He dragged his tongue along the curve of her throat, unhurried and possessive, claiming her without restraint. Evelyne dug her fingers into the leather at his shoulders as her resolve slipped with every passing second, and the heavy ache in her abdomen deepened.

She should stop this and step away. But all she could think about was how damn good his touch felt. How effortlessly he broke down her defenses. And how badly she wanted more. If he didn't kiss her soon, she might drop to her knees and beg for it.

Kaldrek growled softly against her skin, pressing tormentingly slow kisses along her jaw, each one igniting another spark of heat inside her. Her patience snapped, and she grabbed the collar of his leather vest, pulling him in. She needed more.

He let out an amused huff and clicked his tongue. "It seems I drive you just as mad. Is this what you want, Evelyne?"

Her breath came faster, her chest rising with each unsteady inhale. "I..." Gods, what *did* she want? "I want—"

She never got the chance to finish. Instantly, he went rigid, his head snapping to the side. Every muscle in his body coiled tight like he was sensing something unseen.

Her pulse pounded in her ears. "What is it?" she panted. All desire and heat faded.

He turned to her, and her breath caught when she saw his eyes. They were no longer brown but pure black, and a threatening snarl pulled at his lips.

"We have visitors."

CHAPTER 35

It all happened in a blur. Kaldrek and his strongest packmates shifted, their bodies rippling and reshaping into towering wolves. The transformation was swift and deadly.

He had told her to stay back, to keep hidden. But Evelyne couldn't obey. She had to see for herself. What kind of visitors would drive the Ironwolf pack to reveal their most dangerous forms?

A charged tension filled the clearing, making her pulse race. Moving carefully, Evelyne slipped behind the nearest tent, keeping low in the shadows as the pack assembled into a wall of snarling wolves.

The energy shifted.

Three men stepped out from the treeline, calm and unhurried. Every movement radiated quiet confidence. They didn't flinch or pause as they walked straight toward Kaldrek and his fiercest warriors, who met them with bared teeth and lethal intent.

They didn't show a hint of fear. If anything, they looked bored. Then one of them laughed, deep and easy, as if the whole scene were some joke. The sound made Evelyne stiffen. That wasn't normal. Any sane man would hesitate under the weight of so many unblinking crimson eyes locked onto them, and would at least recognize the raw power standing between them and death.

But these men? They looked entertained.

The tallest of the three, a man with long golden hair, tilted his head and gave a playful grin. His shoulders were loose, hands tucked casually into his coat pockets. He didn't look like someone facing danger. He looked like someone who knew he had no reason to be afraid.

A snarl cut through the air, low and menacing, as Holden began to circle them. His massive wolf form moved with a quiet, predatory focus. Claws scraped the earth. Each breath was a warning.

Still, the men didn't flinch.

Evelyne nervously played with her fingers, fear tangling with curiosity. Who the hell were they, and why had they strolled into a pack of wolves like they were stepping into a tavern? She was supposed to stay hidden and wait, but her mind was already made up.

A few more steps. That was all she needed. Pressing herself against the tent's fabric, she crept forward, barely daring to breathe. She wanted only a brief look, enough to see their faces and hear what they had to say. She paused. Was speech even possible in their wolf form?

Before she could dwell on the thought, the blond shifted slightly, his head turning as if he sensed her. His smirk curled into something darker—cruel, and curious enough to jolt her.

She had made a mistake.

Kaldrek's dark eyes locked onto hers, his lips pulling back in a silent snarl as fury radiated from him. She had disobeyed him, and he was livid, but it didn't matter. The damage was done. She'd already been seen.

"Well, well," the man in the center drawled. "Who is *that*?"

A surge of fear climbed up her throat, threatening to choke her. But she forced herself to stand tall, lifting her chin to mask the nerves thrumming beneath her skin. The man's striking hazel eyes gleamed as he studied her.

"I've never seen this beauty before." He stepped closer and inhaled deeply. "And she's... human." He paused and turned to look at Kaldrek. "But with a hint of the alpha's scent. How interesting." His voice was a purr, smooth and dripping with intrigue.

Evelyne's cheeks burned as she wondered if he was a wolf too. How else could he scent her? Damn wolves and their heightened senses. Now the whole pack would know that Kaldrek had been... Well, she wasn't exactly sure what he'd been about to do, but it had come dangerously close to a kiss. Could they scent that, too?

In a flash, the Ironwolf pack shifted back into human form, the women quickly stepping in to drape cloaks over them. The two men standing beside the blond stranger said nothing, their faces unreadable, but Evelyne barely noticed them. Her attention was locked on the blond, who was still staring at her, his eyes following the way her damp leathers clung to her curves. She met his gaze head-on, refusing to look away. If he was trying to make her squirm, he'd have to do better than that.

His grin curled into something wicked as he turned to Kaldrek. "Come on, now. At least tell me her name before I start begging."

He was clearly enjoying himself, but Kaldrek wasn't laughing. Not even close. His black eyes burned with barely restrained fury that she could only guess came right before blood was spilled. Whatever patience he had left was hanging by a thread.

"She's—" Kaldrek started, voice taut, but Evelyne stepped forward, cutting him off without hesitation.

"I'm Evelyne," she said, voice smooth and cool. "And yes, I'm human. However, I find it difficult to understand why I apparently smell like the alpha. Maybe the rain makes everyone smell like wet dogs." She folded her arms across her chest, masking the slight tremble in her fingers, and arched a brow at the stranger. "And *you* are?"

Her words seethed with intent, testing like a viper ready to strike. She might've been nervous, but she'd be damned if she let either of them see it.

The man's eyes lit up, not with surprise, but with something darker, like her boldness was a gift he hadn't expected but was more than willing to unwrap. "*Evelyne*," he repeated, dragging out the word like it tasted good. "Lovely."

Kaldrek snapped. "My tent. Now."

The blond looked at him, clearly unfazed, and Kaldrek's voice dropped lower.

"Obren."

So that was his name.

The smug gleam in Obren's eyes didn't dim, but he inclined his head slightly, finally tearing his gaze away from Evelyne. Whatever business they had to discuss was significant enough that Kaldrek would let these men walk freely into his camp. They wouldn't have made it this far if they posed an actual threat.

Evelyne said nothing, watching as Kaldrek led them away. Obren was the last to turn, his eyes resting on her for a moment longer before he followed.

***

The rain continued past midday, its steady rhythm drumming against the tents and pooling in muddy patches across the camp. The world outside was soaked and gray, but inside her tent, Evelyne felt oddly detached from it all. She had expected the pack to be traveling by now, but Kaldrek, Obren, and the other two men were still in his tent, locked in whatever conversation had stalled their plans.

Heidara had explained earlier that the men were from the Glaciermaw pack, a shifter group that usually kept to the north, just beyond the mountain range. According to her, they weren't exactly well-liked by her people, which probably explained why Kaldrek and several of his men had shifted the moment they arrived.

The camp had grown restless, people lingering outside their tents, waiting. But Evelyne had stopped waiting. She knelt beside the washbasin and let the cool water rinse away the grime of the day. Mud and sweat ran from her skin, along with the warmth that still lingered from the touch of Kaldrek's mouth on her neck.

She pressed her lips together, scrubbing her arms as if she could wash the memory away. But she didn't want to. Not really. She hadn't hated it. If anything, it had been the most intimate, electrifying moment of her life, and he hadn't even kissed her.

He had grabbed her like something inside him had finally snapped. Like the war he fought within himself had spilled over. The thought of his mouth on her jaw, his breath at her ear, sent warmth curling low in her belly, and she shifted, thighs pressing together.

His tongue against her throat.

His hands gripping her waist.

His thumb brushing her bottom lip.

She could still feel every moment, like her body had memorized him.

What *was* it that she wanted? Did she truly want him, or was this just another reckless moment? Another impulsive decision waiting to go wrong?

And then there were the words he'd murmured. *You drive me mad.*

Had he meant them? Because he had looked and acted like a man barely holding himself together. Like whatever he felt had been locked away for too long, and only sheer will was keeping it contained.

Evelyne took a sharp breath and dragged the damp cloth over her neck one final time before tossing it aside. It did nothing to cool the fire smoldering beneath her skin.

She pulled a brush through her hair and left it to dry in loose waves before settling onto her cot with Cillian's book. Her fingers traced the worn cover before she opened it and scanned the familiar pages. She was getting closer to unraveling the prophecy. She could feel it. This book wasn't just the ramblings of an old scholar or some forgotten fairytale. It was a clue, a puzzle waiting to be solved. And somehow, it had ended up in her hands—the hands of someone who had seen the darkness for herself, who had already watched it take someone she cared about.

No. Cillian wasn't lost. Not yet. He had to still be in there.

The words blurred slightly as she stared at them. *A keeper of light to smother the darkness.* But who, or what, held this light? Was it light at all, or something hidden beneath the surface? What did it all mean?

At least the symbols were beginning to make sense, piece by piece. The tree, she now recognized, was the Solwyn Tree—the sacred place where the Great Rite was performed back in Velenshire. The eyes had taken longer to figure out. She had pieced that together in the stillness of night, lying on her cot and going over every detail of Cillian's sketches. She knew those eyes. Predatory. Horrifying. The eyes of a wolf that brought death.

But the moon—she still couldn't make sense of that part. Maybe it was connected to the celestial event Kaya and Vaelora had been born under. It seemed possible. Still, why had Cillian been seeing these symbols at all? Evelyne frowned at the page and turned to the next as if the truth might finally rise from the paper and speak for itself.

A distant voice cut through her thoughts, and she shut the book.

Kaldrek had gathered the pack.

Evelyne dressed quickly, pulling on a set of dry leathers before stepping into the muted light of late afternoon. The rain had settled into a light mist, and heavy clouds loomed overhead. At the center of the clearing, Kaldrek stood tall. Beside him, Obren lingered with his two men, looking far too satisfied for a moment so tense. Evelyne folded her arms and turned her attention to the pack gathering around them, all eyes fixed on their alpha.

At last, he spoke.

"We've received word from the Glaciermaw pack that the northern mountain ranges outside of Nerathar have been overrun by a Noskari army," Kaldrek announced. His expression was calm, though his words stirred through the wolves around him. Murmurs rippled through the Ironwolf pack, and hushed gasps slipped between them.

Evelyne's heart pounded. An army? She didn't fully grasp the implications, but an army of Noskari could only mean one thing: death.

"Half of the Glaciermaw pack has been murdered or corrupted by Vaelora's Noskari. The survivors have abandoned their homeland and are seeking allies."

A sick feeling settled in Evelyne's stomach. Half the pack was gone. Families torn apart, children and mates either lost or twisted into something monstrous. And yet, despite the devastating news, the Ironwolf pack remained composed. Why weren't they panicking?

Her eyes landed on Kaldrek. He looked calm and steady, like someone they could all count on. She wondered if he was why the pack stayed strong, holding together like iron. How could anyone be afraid when their alpha looked like that?

Beside her, Alaric's frame was tense, and she knew him well enough to sense the fear hidden underneath.What chance did their home have if Vaelora could destroy a northern pack?

"And you trust his word, Alpha?" one of the elders asked, distaste evident in his tone.

Kaldrek gave a firm nod in response just as Obren stepped forward. His arrogant smirk from before was now replaced by a far more serious expression.

"We all know there's been... history between my pack and the Ironwolf members," Obren said. "But I swear to you, this is not a lie. Now is the time to put aside our past. If we don't fight back together, we'll all be slaughtered separately."

Silence fell over the camp.

"How?" One of the Ironwolf warriors stepped forward, gaze locked on Kaldrek. "How do we defeat an army of Noskari?"

Kaldrek's shoulders tensed, but his face remained impassive. When he spoke, it was with lethal certainty.

"We train. We find other shifters. And we fight." His eyes swept across the pack. "The worst thing we can do is hide. Because if we don't stop them, they will eventually come for us. And then what? What happens to our families? To our pups?"

A shudder ran through Evelyne. The pups. The children of their packs. Would they be drained of blood to fuel Vaelora's growing army? Or worse—would they become Noskari? The idea made bile rise in her throat.

"I say we rip the fuckers to pieces," Holden growled.

A surge of fierce agreement erupted through the pack, their voices rising in battle-hungry approval. Even Obren and the two men flanking him, likely his second and third in command, smiled at the sound. But Evelyne couldn't share in their bloodthirsty excitement. All she could think about were the wolves Glaciermaw had lost—the ones twisted by corruption, the ones who had become the monsters they were now being called to fight.

Why had Vaelora targeted Cillian, a southern boy without connection to the wolves, the mountain packs, or anything linked to the Noskari? None of it added up.

"Good," Kaldrek said, his voice cutting through the rising energy in the crowd. "Sounds like my pack agrees." He turned to Obren. "We move at first light. If we push hard, we'll reach Cindermoor in three or four days. Stay alert."

Evelyne barely registered the rest. *Cindermoor.* The name sparked recognition. Alaric had told her it was the first settlement beyond the wilds. After weeks of travel, she would finally set foot in civilization again. And despite everything—the danger, the loss—a tiny flicker of excitement stirred inside her.

She would finally see normalcy again, something that felt long lost. If such a thing even existed anymore.

Part Three

The Bearer of Light

CHAPTER 36

Several days had passed since the Glaciermaw pack joined their journey. Obren hadn't stopped watching Evelyne, his hazel eyes lingering on her far too long, far too often. And every time, Kaldrek noticed. But he never said a word.

Since that heated moment at camp, he'd kept his distance. During training, he was focused, precise, the perfect alpha, but his gaze never met hers for more than a passing second. He spoke to others. He gave commands. Yet somehow, he moved around her like she no longer existed.

What had she done this time?

Evelyne wondered if defying his order to stay out of sight had been the breaking point. He should've known that she never thoroughly listened. And honestly, what did it matter? Obren would have seen her eventually. For heaven's sake, he and his pack were traveling with them. It wasn't as if her presence that morning had changed anything.

Still, she was growing weary of attempting to decipher Kaldrek's moods. One moment, he was present, his touch lingering just long enough to leave her breathless and burning. The next, he looked at her like she was a problem he didn't have time to solve. Maybe it was for the best that they hadn't kissed. She could only imagine how much worse things would be if they had.

The rain had finally passed, giving way to warm, golden days. The light soaked into her skin, deepening its tone with a soft, sun-kissed glow. She found comfort in the warmth and the quiet peace it brought. If she was honest with herself, she also didn't mind how it brought out the strength and beauty in the men around her.

If she had counted right, her birthday was just two days away. The thought nearly made her laugh. Twenty-three and still unmarried. Courtship and finding a suitable husband felt absurd now. The life she was once meant to live had become a distant memory, buried beneath the harsh weight of survival. None of that mattered anymore.

What mattered was reaching Cillian.

Each day that passed pulled the knot in her chest tighter. Every night, she whispered the same quiet plea: *Please, whatever god is watching him, keep him safe. Keep him whole.*

She had to find him. And soon.

Her father's men still hadn't caught up, though she doubted they could keep pace with a wolf pack and horses moving at full speed.

According to Alaric, they were about a day from reaching Cindermoor. They'd likely stay a night or two, take time to rest, eat proper food, and recover. Holden had also mentioned another moon ritual was approaching. Had it been that long since the last one?

"The ones in Cindermoor are even better," he had said. "Way more intense and exhilarating. Unlike the ones deep in the forest, the ritual is held just outside the city, so no humans are caught in the frenzy of the shift. And when we run, we make for the treelines."

They continued their journey across the vast expanse of the Sunmere Stretch, riding until the sun dipped low on the horizon, casting the sky in warm amber tones. When night settled in, they made camp, and Evelyne slipped into her familiar rhythm: eating, washing away the day's dust, and poring over Cillian's book by firelight.

Then there was the map.

She studied it repeatedly, tracing their route and checking that their path remained clear. Alaric hadn't asked for it since he'd told her to keep it. He had a strange knack for remembering the land, and he seemed to trust that she'd speak up if anything felt wrong or if darkness crept too close. It had become a quiet ritual she repeated each night after the pack settled, the scouts took their posts, and the camp fell into silence. Only when her thoughts finally slowed would she let herself rest, just for a few hours.

Afterward, she would rise, train, and continue the journey.

Cindermoor was waiting.

***

As they crested the final hill, Cindermoor came into view, nestled between the sweeping plains of the Sunmere Stretch and the thick belt of trees that bordered the town like a protective frame. The scent of fresh earth mingled with woodsmoke, carried on a warm evening breeze that stirred faint echoes of conversation and the distant clatter of a busy marketplace.

Alaric sat up straighter in his saddle, rolling his shoulders as the familiar shape of civilization unfolded before them. Cindermoor didn't have the luxury of the southern noble estates—no shiny marble, tall spires, or perfect courtyards. Yet it pulsed with something more meaningful. It breathed with life, with a sense of home.

The streets were wide and well-worn, shaped by the passage of countless carts and travelers. People moved through them with ease. Merchants called out their prices, children darted between stalls with sticky fingers and mischievous smiles, and laughter rose above the din like birdsong at dusk. Timber-framed homes and lodges lined the streets, their thatched roofs sloping gently, windows glowing in the fading light. Smoke curled from chimneys, carrying the scent of roasting meat, fresh bread, and spiced cider, making Alaric's stomach stir.

The stables sat near the town's center, filled with sturdy horses bred for long travel. Nearby, blacksmiths worked their forges, the ring of hammer on metal echoing through the streets. But the taverns were what made Cindermoor truly unforgettable. They stood large and inviting, their windows glowing with golden light that spilled onto the cobbled streets as evening lanterns flickered to life. Music drifted from within, a lively mix of fiddle, drum, and voices raised in song. And the people, with their open joy and easy laughter, brought comfort that made the town feel like somewhere one could truly belong.

As the Ironwolf and Glaciermaw packs rode into town, a ripple of recognition passed through the crowd. Smiles broke out, hands lifted in greeting, and a few eager souls stepped forward to clasp arms with the shifters, as though welcoming home old friends rather than fearsome warriors.

"Damn, I almost forgot how much I liked this place," Holden muttered beside him, already eyeing the nearest tavern with clear intent.

Alaric let out a slow breath, taking it all in—the simple yet enduring charm of a town that thrived not through wealth or politics, but through community bonds.

After weeks of exhaustion, tension, and battle-hardened silence, Cindermoor felt like an exhale.

An older woman stepped out from one of the stone-fronted shops, brushing flour onto a well-worn apron. Her silver-streaked hair was tied in a neat bun, and her sharp eyes swept over the group with a flicker of familiarity. Before Alaric could fully register what was happening, she walked straight up to Kaldrek and wrapped him in a firm embrace.

Alaric blinked.

The Ironwolf alpha—the man who so often seemed incapable of affection—stood frozen, arms rigid as though the very idea of softness stunned him. But then, in a breath, the tension seemed to ease from his shoulders, and a genuine smile spread across his face.

Heidara was the next to rush forward, her excitement unrestrained as she wrapped her arms around the woman's middle like a child greeting a long-lost relative. Alaric wondered if they were family, or something just shy of it.

The woman pulled back, cupping Heidara's face between her flour-dusted hands before flicking her gaze toward Kaldrek. "You're far too thin," she huffed. "And I don't even want to know how much sleep you've lost."

Kaldrek let out a quiet, rare laugh. "And yet, I live."

"Barely," she shot back.

One by one, the older woman greeted each pack member as if welcoming long-lost kin. It was clear now that this town was more than just a stop along the way. It was home to many of them.

"Come, then," she said, dusting off her apron. "We have plenty of rooms between my husband's tavern and the lodges. If more are needed, I'll speak with the other families. You'll all be taken care of."

She turned, leading them through the streets and toward the tavern beside her bakery. At the entrance to the tavern, a stout man with broad shoulders and a white beard leaned against the door frame, his arms crossed.

"Took you long enough," he called out, a reluctant smile tugging at his lips.

The older woman rolled her eyes. "Don't be rude, Garek."

"I ain't rude, Eda. I'm stating facts," he said, pushing off the frame and clapping Kaldrek on the shoulder, then nodding toward the others. "Good to see you lot in one piece."

Turning toward the tavern full of patrons, he lifted his voice.

"Clear out! We've got packs needing a proper meal and a place to sit!"

A typical tavern owner might have been met with groans or complaints, but here, the response was immediate and eager. People rose from their seats, drinks and meals barely touched, offering bows or friendly waves before filing out with a surprising amount of cheer. This wasn't a begrudging favor. This town welcomed wolves as its own.

The pack members stepped inside, filling the space until the tables could hold no more. Some took seats at the bar, and others found corners to settle into. Plenty remained outside, mingling with the townspeople.

Alaric sat near the hearth, settling beside Evelyne, Heidara, and Holden. He had just started to unwind when Obren slid into the remaining chair beside Evelyne. Heidara exhaled a dramatic sigh, rolling her eyes as if she had expected this nonsense. On the other hand, Holden stiffened, his fingers tapping idly against the table as if he were restraining himself from saying something... impolite.

Evelyne seemed to catch their reactions, too. There was still history between these packs; whatever uneasy alliance had been formed, it hadn't wiped the past clean. Obren, naturally, appeared completely unbothered. He leaned an elbow on the table, his posture relaxed and his eyes locked on Evelyne.

"You've managed to remain remarkably untouched." He smiled. "Impressive, considering the company you keep."

"Is that your way of calling me delicate, or are you just bragging about your pack's superior resilience?"

"A little of both, if I'm being honest," Obren said smoothly.

"How generous," she replied, her voice cool.

"I give where I can."

Alaric watched, paying close attention. He recognized the game for what it was: the charm, the banter, the easy pull into conversation. He'd used the same tactics himself, back during the courting season. It meant Obren might actually be interested in Evelyne, or he was deliberately trying to provoke someone. And if Alaric had to guess, it wasn't Evelyne he was aiming for. It was Kaldrek.

The Ironwolf alpha had been keeping his distance from Evelyne. No lingering looks. No quiet moments. He hadn't spoken to her in days. Alaric had wanted to ask her about it more than once, but she seemed withdrawn and didn't want to talk. So he hadn't pushed, especially now when things between them had finally started to feel normal again.

Instead, he watched and waited. Evelyne would talk when she was ready. He was almost certain Obren had picked up on Kaldrek's deliberate silence and the distance he kept from her. The difference was that Alaric suspected Evelyne hadn't realized it was intentional.

At first, he'd wondered if Kaldrek simply didn't like her. But when Obren pointed out the alpha's scent on her and Heidara quietly confirmed it was true, everything shifted into focus. Kaldrek wasn't avoiding her out of indifference. He was trying to hide his feelings. And now, seeing how easily Obren slipped into flirtation, Alaric understood why Kaldrek might want to keep those feelings buried.

Obren leaned closer, voice dropping just enough to make his intent clear. "You know, Lady Evelyne, for a woman raised among nobility, you handle yourself far better than I expected."

Evelyne smirked. "And you, for a man raised among wolves, talk far more than I expected."

Holden choked on his drink.

Obren let out a booming laugh, tapping his fist against the table. "I do believe I like you."

Evelyne tilted her head, smiling sweetly. "How tragic for me."

Alaric laughed, but his gaze flicked to Kaldrek, deep in conversation with Garek near the bar. The alpha's face gave nothing away, but his fingers were clenched too tightly around his drink.

The tavern soon filled with chatter, laughter rising from a nearby table, the scent of fresh ale lingering in the warm air. Obren lounged beside Evelyne, a cocky grin plastered across his face as he volleyed playful jabs her way. To Alaric's quiet amusement, she gave them right back. He had expected eye rolls, maybe a dry remark or complete disinterest. But instead, Evelyne was sharp, engaged, and unfazed by Obren's charm. It was like she saw right through him, and Alaric couldn't help but admire that.

Obren poured a shot of something strong and slid it her way, waiting. Alaric thought she might pause or play it safe, but Evelyne didn't. She grabbed the glass and knocked it back like water. It had to have burned going down, but she didn't flinch. Instead, she set the glass down, tilted her head, and gave Obren a smirk.

"Alright, Glaciermaw. Why is the room tense whenever someone mentions your pack?"

The table fell silent for a beat.

Then, Obren exhaled a quiet laugh. "Straight to the point. I like that."

He leaned in, elbows resting on the table, his eyes trailing over her with a playful glint and a focus that felt far too intimate to be casual.

"It's simple, really." He traced the edge of his cup, glanced at Kaldrek by the bar, then looked back at Evelyne. "I love competition. I live for it. And Kaldrek?" He grinned wider. "Well, I always knew one day we'd both be alphas. It only made sense to challenge him whenever I could."

"Ah," Evelyne said, nodding slowly, "so you weren't a menace. You were just testing your future opponent?"

Obren chuckled, swirling his ale. "Something like that."

"Hmm. And did you win?"

"Depends on who you ask."

"Oh, please." Heidara rolled her eyes, cutting through the tension with disdain. "The truth is, the Glaciermaw pack is full of hotheaded assholes who can't stand to admit there's a stronger pack among these lands."

Holden smiled and lifted his drink in salute to his sister's words. Obren, to his credit, didn't bristle. Instead, he slouched further in his chair, releasing a long, exaggerated sigh.

"She's just upset I never took her to bed."

Holden moved before the words even fully landed. His fist slammed against the table, and a thunderous crack sounded over the low hum of the tavern. Evelyne jerked slightly at the sudden noise, as did several others.

The room shifted. Conversations quieted. Across the tavern, Kaldrek turned toward them. His eyes were dark, and his relaxed demeanor from earlier was gone. He wasn't just watching, but assessing like a wolf sensing a threat.

Obren lifted both hands in surrender, completely unbothered. "Calm yourself, Holden. I'm joking."

Holden didn't look convinced. His lips curled into a quiet snarl, his hands clenched into fists, but he sank back into his chair after a long breath.

Alaric, sensing the need for a distraction, lifted his tankard and grinned. "Please, let's not start tearing into each other just yet. I'd like to finish my ale and a hot meal before getting mauled by two enraged wolves mid-shift."

The words did the trick. Evelyne turned to him, laughing loudly, nodding as she raised her cup. "Agreed. Cheers."

The others followed suit, the heavy moment melting away as their glasses clinked together in a quiet toast.

Heidara was the first to steer the conversation back toward something meaningful. She leaned back, glancing toward Eda and Garek, then at Evelyne.

"This town has always been home to the surrounding packs—or, at least, to what's left of them." Her voice was softer now, more thoughtful. "The people here have provided us with food, shelter, and kindness for generations, so long as we protect them in return. We aren't bound by blood, but it might as well be family."

Alaric couldn't take his eyes off Heidara. She looked stunning even after a long day of travel beneath the spring sun. The warm lantern light made her skin glow, and the flicker of the flames danced in her emerald eyes. A few strands of golden hair had slipped loose from her braid, but instead of looking messy, she looked—

Beautiful.

Tearing his eyes away wasn't easy. It took Holden clearing his throat—a quiet sound, but unmistakably a warning—for Alaric to blink and finally look away. He let out a slow breath and reached for his drink. Holden didn't need to say a word. They both knew it. Alaric had been staring too long.

Obren leaned back and stretched, moving with the ease of pure confidence. He picked up his ale and stood. "Alright, beautiful," he said to Evelyne, that maddening grin still plastered on his face. "Time I found myself a place to sleep for the night."

He leaned in, mouth close to her ear, but did not attempt to keep his voice down—ensuring every wolf at the table, and likely beyond, could hear him.

"You're welcome to join me if the alpha isn't keeping you warm enough." He winked, entirely too pleased with himself.

The tension at the table shifted as steady bootsteps sounded behind them. Alaric didn't need to turn to know Kaldrek was approaching. And judging by the charged energy rolling off him, he had heard every word.

The alpha stopped at the table's edge, and Alaric could feel the intensity of his stare. But Evelyne, damn her, didn't so much as waver. Instead, she gave a smile that was sweet on the surface but sharp underneath and purred, "I'll be sure to consider your offer."

Obren's eyes gleamed with satisfaction as he slowly turned to Kaldrek. It wasn't subtle. It was a challenge. And Kaldrek? He looked like he might rip Obren's throat out.

Obren lifted his tankard in casual acknowledgment before strolling out of the tavern, completely unfazed. Evelyne didn't spare Kaldrek a single glance. Instead, she reached for her ale, tipped it back, and finished it in one swift motion. Kaldrek finally sat down, his movements calm on the surface, but Alaric saw the tightness in his shoulders and the tension running through every line of his body.

"Take it easy on that ale," Kaldrek said firmly. "Or you won't even be able to walk out of here."

Evelyne lowered her glass, licking the last drop of ale from her lips. "Oh, hush. I've only had one."

She turned to Heidara, and the two shared a mischievous, knowing smile. Alaric couldn't help but love the bond between them, love that Evelyne had finally found someone she could truly trust. He supposed he could call Heidara a friend, too. She was the one who had patched him up every day after his capture, the one who'd checked on him—twice a day—after the Noskari attack. She was kind. Too kind. And gods, he needed to get his mind off her.

The ale clearly made him reckless. Holden remained at the table, and he would likely tear Alaric apart if he even thought about looking at his sister the wrong way. So Alaric wisely dropped his gaze to his plate, took a bite of his meal, and said casually, "Eh, let her drink up. After all, it's her birthday tomorrow."

He shot Evelyne a wink just as Heidara gasped and spun toward her, eyes narrowing in mock accusation. "You didn't tell me that!"

Evelyne shrugged. "It's just another day."

"How old?" Holden asked.

"Twenty-three," she said, her voice quieter now, almost like she was reluctant to admit it. Maybe the others missed it, but Alaric didn't. Back home, twenty-three was considered old for a noblewoman without a husband, though she was still technically engaged to him. He wasn't even sure where they stood anymore. Sooner or later, he knew he'd have to ask.

"Oh! I must take you, and you," Heidara said, pointing at Alaric, "on a tour through town tomorrow. I'll show you all the best shops!"

Evelyne smiled slightly. "I'd like that."

"So would I," Alaric added.

Heidara practically vibrated with excitement, clapping her hands together. Then, as if something even better had just occurred to her, she let out a delighted squeal. "And it's a full moon tomorrow! This is going to be so much fun."

Kaldrek raised his drink in an easy salute. "Well, in that case," he said, "drink up, Lady."

Alaric caught it. The way his eyes lingered on Evelyne's just a little longer than necessary. Like he was thinking something he wouldn't say aloud. And Evelyne didn't look away.

CHAPTER 37

Evelyne stirred in the softest bed she'd felt in weeks. For a blissful moment, she didn't move. Eyes half-lidded, she let herself melt into the warmth of the mattress, breathing in the clean scent of fresh linens and listening to the faint hum of life drifting in from beyond the lodge. She had missed this—the comfort of a real bed; the illusion of safety, not just from solid walls, but from the two wolf packs now standing guard over Cindermoor.

She exhaled and stretched beneath the covers, only to regret it instantly. A dull throb bloomed behind her eyes, and memories from the night before came rushing back: Heidara laughing as she half dragged her back to their room, arms looped tightly around Evelyne's shoulders, both of them stumbling and breathless. *Yeah. Kaldrek was right.* She should not have drunk that much.

Still, at least she'd slept. Better than she had in weeks. She blinked toward the empty bed beside hers, already made, the hint of soap hanging faintly in the room. Heidara was long up, no doubt washed and ready. Meanwhile, Evelyne had slept in. No training today. A birthday gift from Kaldrek? She scoffed at the thought, but she wasn't about to complain.

The sun outside was already bright and warm, promising another beautiful day. For the first time in what felt like ages, Evelyne felt a flicker of excitement. She and Heidara were going to explore the town with Alaric. No trekking through the wilds, no sore muscles or grueling routines. Just wandering the streets, sharing laughter, and maybe, if she was lucky, feeling a little bit normal again.

That thought alone was enough to get her moving. She undressed and stepped toward the small copper tub in the corner. A *real* bath. No icy streams or rushed washes at camp, but a proper soak with warm water and soap that carried the soft scents of vanilla and lavender. Sinking into the tub, she exhaled sharply, letting the heat soothe the remnants of last night's indulgence.

By the time she was finished, Heidara had returned, balancing a wooden tray in her arms. And on that tray—

Evelyne's eyes widened.

"Tea!"

She nearly yanked it from Heidara's hands, grinning as she curled her fingers around the warm cup.

"You act like I brought you gold," Heidara laughed, setting down the rest of the tray.

"This *is* gold," Evelyne murmured, inhaling the rich, spiced aroma, savoring the heat against her palms. "Gods, I missed this."

"Well, then, consider it a birthday present." Heidara plopped onto the bed beside her. "Now, drink while I do your hair."

Evelyne obliged, sipping slowly while Heidara worked her fingers through her damp hair, twisting and braiding it with practiced ease. Once she had finished, Evelyne slipped into a leather skirt with a high slit, a cropped vest, and sandals suited for the warm weather and the moon ritual that awaited them later. She paused at the small, fogged mirror near the washbasin, catching her reflection. She looked different. Sun-kissed and sharper. Stronger. Like someone who had endured and lived through things most couldn't imagine.

Cindermoor's streets buzzed with life, filled with the calls of vendors, the murmur of conversation, the rhythmic clang of a blacksmith's hammer; the scent of fresh bread, spiced cider, and hints of lavender and sage from nearby apothecaries. The town struck a balance between rugged and refined, shaped by trade and quiet resilience. Tanners, tailors, herbalists, scribes, and leatherworkers lined the streets, along with traders from across the eastern lands.

And Heidara was determined to see it all.

Evelyne was dragged from shop to shop and led through winding streets as Heidara eagerly pointed out the best bakeries, the finest silk vendors, and the liveliest market stalls. To her surprise, Evelyne didn't mind. She had expected to feel out of place, like a foreigner in a town built for wolves. But instead, she found herself drawn in.

She ran her fingers over delicate perfume bottles, admired a silver hairpin shaped like a crescent moon, and smirked as Heidara haggled with a fruit vendor like her life depended on it. For a fleeting moment, it almost felt like... normalcy.

As Evelyne set down a wooden pendant etched with swirling runes, Alaric suddenly stepped in front of her, something held gently in his hand. A flower. Its petals were pale blue, delicate yet resilient, catching the sunlight in a way that almost made it glow.

Evelyne blinked. "What's this?"

"A birthday gift," he said with a shrug.

She paused, then took the flower, rolling the stem between her fingers. "Thank you, Alaric."

"Careful. You're not about to get all sentimental on me, are you?" he said with a smirk, watching as she brought it to her nose and breathed in its soft, fresh scent.

She gave a low chuckle, but beneath it, something warm settled in her chest. Despite everything, they still had this—this friendship. And for that, she was grateful.

They followed Heidara's lead for two hours, ducking into shops filled with delicate fabrics, passing outdoor cafes where townsfolk sipped tea, and weaving through the market stalls whose vendors welcomed them as though they belonged. But eventually, Heidara pulled up short.

"I need to check in with someone," she said, flashing an apologetic smile. "I'll catch up with you both later, okay?"

And then it was just Evelyne and Alaric. At first, they walked in easy silence, the sounds of the town filling the space between them. But after a few quiet minutes, Alaric cleared his throat, and Evelyne knew precisely where this was headed.

"So," he said, glancing her way, "our betrothal."

Evelyne slowed a little, tilting her head. "Ah. That."

"That," he echoed.

She let out a breath, then met his eyes. "We should probably end it officially, shouldn't we?"

Alaric nodded. "Yeah. I think we should."

There was no sadness in her voice and no hesitation in his. It felt... right.

"I do want you to know something," he said, his voice softer now. "I'm still here for you, Ev. I always will be. And I am truly sorry."

Her smile was small but sincere. "I know. And for what it's worth, I'm glad you're here."

They slipped into silence again for a moment until Alaric nudged her with a grin and lifted a brow.

"So... are you ever going to tell me what's happening with you and Kaldrek?"

Evelyne tensed, her smile fading as a frown tugged at her lips. Honestly? She had no idea how to answer that.

"I…" she began, but the words slipped away as her eyes caught on something. Tucked between two taller stone buildings was a shop with a faded sign, its windows framed by flickering lanterns and bundles of dried herbs. It held a feeling of age, something timeless and quietly mysterious. It reminded her faintly of Charise's shop back in Velenshire, like a place that felt touched by something beyond the ordinary. Evelyne was already moving toward it before Alaric could ask what had caught her attention.

Inside, the air was even warmer and carried the scent of cinnamon. There was something about the space that felt strangely alive. Like Relics and Refinements, it was cluttered, but in a way that felt intentional. Charms of bone and glass hung from the wooden beams, gently swaying despite the still air.

At the center of the room sat a large circular table covered in scattered tarot cards, stones carved with runes, and an assortment of candles that had long since burned down to their wicks. A low-burning flame flickered beneath a small iron cauldron, releasing wisps of scented smoke that curled toward the ceiling. It felt like a place of secrets.

Behind the worn wooden counter stood a woman, younger than Evelyne had expected. Her dark curls were loosely pinned back, a few wayward strands softly outlining her striking features. Her rich brown skin glowed softly in the dim light, and her deep brown eyes studied them with delight.

She smiled. "Welcome," she said softly. "I wondered when you'd walk through my door."

Evelyne stiffened. "You… expected us?"

The woman inclined her head slightly as though weighing her words. "I heard whispers of two humans traveling with the Ironwolf pack. So, in a way, I expected you."

She stepped forward, her fingers lightly grazing the tabletop, moving a few scattered tarot cards aside as she studied Evelyne. For a brief moment, Evelyne had the strangest feeling that this woman could already see something about her that she did not yet know herself.

Without warning, the woman gasped.

Alaric's hand went straight to the dagger at his belt. "What?"

The woman's eyes flashed to Evelyne. "What do you have on you?"

Evelyne blinked. "I beg your pardon?"

"I can feel it." Her expression changed, and her fingers twitched like she was reaching for something just out of sight. "You're carrying something. Something that doesn't want to be found."

Evelyne glanced at Alaric, and he was the first to speak. "How... What are you?"

"A witch, of course. Did my shop not give it away?" She raised both eyebrows, seeming genuinely surprised they hadn't figured it out.

"There are witches outside of Velenshire?" Evelyne asked, her voice edged with disbelief.

The woman laughed lightly. "Oh, dear. Witches exist all over these lands. We are not confined to one place." She motioned around the shop with a small smile. "My name is Selene. I'm part of the Cinder Coven, one of the founding families of this town." She nodded toward Evelyne's bag. "Open it."

Evelyne hesitated, then slowly unfastened the clasp and reached inside. Her fingers brushed something familiar, and she pulled it free. The book. *The Lantern's Keeper.*

The moment it touched the counter, Selene's expression shifted. There was a flicker of shock, maybe even recognition. Her voice dropped to a whisper.

"Where did you get a Hallowell book?"

What? Evelyne's pulse quickened. She opened the book with trembling fingers, turning to the final page. And there it was, written in elegant, slanted script: the author's signature.

Vespera Hallowell.

Was this woman an ancestor of Charise Hallowell? Could she be the great-grandmother Charise had mentioned, the one who had performed the Great Rite? If that were true, then everything was connected. But how had this book, this piece of history, ended up in Evelyne's hands?

She recalled that night in Caltheris when she and Aurelia had gone shopping for the ball. The night Lord Bavrick—

No. She forced that thought away and focused instead on the old bookseller. He had chosen the book himself, placing it in her hands and saying it would be helpful for her brother. Evelyne had thought it strange then, how confident the man had been that it was the perfect gift. But now, she wondered if there had been more to him than he let on. Could the bookseller have been a witch? Or whatever they called men who practiced magic. Could men even be witches?

She drew in a sharp breath. "An older gentleman gave me this book. He owned a bookshop in Caltheris, in the southern lands."

Needing to steady herself, she walked over to the circular table at the center of the room and sank into a chair. Her thoughts felt murky and tangled. Thankfully, Selene and Alaric followed.

"I told him I was looking for a gift for my brother, Cillian. I only mentioned that he was unwell, but it felt like he already knew. As if he understood exactly what I needed and who my brother was, even though

I had never met him before." Her fingers traced the worn cover of the book. "And then he gave me this."

Selene leaned in, eyes sharp. "What did he say? About the book?"

Evelyne shook her head, trying to remember the man's exact words. "He said it was a story. And a guide—for my brother."

A guide.

The word echoed in her thoughts as she tried to understand it. A Hallowell witch had written the book. Maybe even the same one who had performed the Great Rite a century ago. It was a story, but she had never stopped to see it as something more. A key. A map. A prophecy hidden in plain sight, threaded through its pages. Had Cillian discovered that before he vanished?

"I never understood why this book ended up with me," Evelyne murmured, the words tumbling over one another. "At first, I thought it was just an odd tale, something to lift Cillian's spirits. But maybe he saw something in it that I didn't." She looked between Alaric and Selene. "When the man gave it to me, I felt something. A kind of hum. Like the book was... content to be with me."

Selene's eyes widened, as if a missing piece had just fallen into place. A small smile touched her lips. She spoke softly, almost to herself. "You met a seer."

"A what?" Alaric asked, turning toward her with full attention.

Selene leaned forward, resting her arms on the table. "A seer," she said again, her voice steadier now. "They're incredibly rare, so rare I wasn't sure any still existed on this side of the continent. Maybe it's because witches can't sense their magic. But their gift allows them to glimpse the past... and what might lie ahead."

Alaric's brow furrowed. "Like an oracle?"

Selene nodded. "In a way, yes. Some receive their visions through dreams, others through touch. A few can only see fragments, while the most gifted can glimpse events unfolding far away as if distance means nothing to them. Some seers even possess rarer abilities, like sensing changes in the land itself or seeing how nature will respond to what's coming. Their sight is powerful, but it's not without weight. Knowing the future doesn't always mean it can be changed."

Evelyne swallowed, the memory of the bookseller flashing in her mind. He had looked at her with a knowing gleam, like he recognized her and had always known their paths would cross. "So you're saying this man knew I would come to him?"

"Not just that." Selene paused. "He knew you needed this book long before you entered his shop." Her eyes dropped to the weathered cover resting between them. "I don't know the reason why. But whatever it is, don't let this book out of your hands." She placed a gentle hand over Evelyne's. "Listen to the seer's words. Trust what was given to you."

Evelyne's brows knit together. "But he said it was meant to guide Cillian. Not me."

Selene leaned back slightly, thoughtful. "Maybe it was, at first. Maybe it served its purpose for your brother. And now, it's with you. Waiting for you to uncover what comes next."

Of course; Cillian might have already figured it out. He always had been the sharp one. Meanwhile, she'd been holding on to this book for weeks and still hadn't unlocked its meaning. Frustration rose in her chest, but she pushed it down. Now wasn't the time to dwell on what she hadn't done.

"We should go." Evelyne glanced at Alaric, her tone leaving little room for debate. He nodded once in agreement. She turned back to Selene, her voice softer. "Thank you. I'm sorry if we took up too much of your time."

Selene offered a warm smile. "You're always welcome here. If you want to talk more, you know where to find me." As Evelyne and Alaric stepped toward the door, she called after them, "Enjoy the ritual tonight."

CHAPTER 38

As they stepped out of Selene's shop, Alaric caught the way Evelyne's fingers drifted along the worn edges of *The Lantern's Keeper*, her eyes distant and unfocused. The strain of their conversation still clung to her, quiet but heavy, like something she hadn't quite shaken off. He knew she needed time to sort through it all—but there was something he needed to take care of first.

He cleared his throat. "Ev."

She blinked and turned to him. "Hmm?"

He raked a hand through his hair. "I need to check something. The trading post, just outside town." He tapped his temple with two fingers. "I haven't been there before, but know the routes well enough to navigate it."

"You think something's wrong with trade up here too?"

"Probably." Alaric exhaled. "If the southern trade routes are shifting, it wouldn't be surprising if things are off here too. Everything's already a mess, and I have no idea how we're supposed to fix it." His jaw tightened. "But there are still people back home who have no idea what's coming. If something's wrong, I must try to set it right at least."

Evelyne studied his face. He sighed.

"Can I walk you back to the lodge? I don't like the idea of leaving you alone."

She waved him off. "Please. Don't worry about me. Do what you need to do. Go get your answers." A flicker of a smirk touched her lips. "Although, let's be honest—you got plenty today."

Alaric let out a quiet laugh, shaking his head. "Not enough. I'll regret it if I don't check in at the outpost before we move on. I think one of my father's men is stationed there for the season."

Evelyne hugged the book to her chest and glanced toward the market street. "I'll be fine. I was planning to see more of the market anyway."

"I won't be gone long," he promised.

"Go, Alaric," she replied gently.

And with that, he left.

***

Derran Ashby was one of the youngest men to serve under Alaric's father's trade group, just a year younger than Alaric. But unlike many in their circle, Derran preferred the outskirts of society to the polished halls of nobility. Alaric couldn't blame him. Navigating Caltheris' rigid hierarchy must have been difficult without a family name to offer protection, but Derran likely never had to endure arranged courtships or the constant pressure of noble expectations. Seeing him stationed out here in the eastern lands of Centaro wasn't a surprise. If anything, he looked like he belonged in Cindermoor.

The pair had never been particularly close, but their paths had crossed often during Alaric's travels to nearby outposts. Derran had always struck him as sharp, someone with a dry sense of humor and the rare ability to know exactly when to speak and when to stay silent.

He greeted Alaric with a firm handshake. "Didn't expect to see you here."

Alaric clasped his hand. "Thought I'd stop by, make sure things are running smoothly." His voice lowered slightly. "I'd like to keep my presence quiet, if you don't mind."

Derran nodded once—a man who knew how to keep things discreet. Alaric did not doubt that both his father and Lord Duskwood had expected he'd pass through this trading post eventually. But what unsettled him was the silence—why hadn't there been word of Lord Duskwood tracking them? Surely, by now, he had men searching for Evelyne.

"No delays?" Alaric asked.

Derran scratched his jaw, eyes narrowing in thought. "A few things here and there, but nothing out of the ordinary. One shipment from the Southern Isles came in a day late, and there have been some reports of missing cargo, but nothing serious."

Alaric gave a slow nod. That was still far better than the unrest near Mokkvyrn Forest. And the fact that goods from the Southern Isles were arriving was promising. If the delay happened further north near the northeastern stretch, the south and the seas would likely still be untouched by the Noskari.

His gaze drifted, landing on a worker a few feet away. Alaric wasn't familiar with most of the men stationed at this outpost besides Derran and a few of his father's trusted men, yet this one stood out. Something about him held Alaric's attention.

He was tall and broad-shouldered, carrying himself with an unsettling stillness. His dark tunic looked far too heavy for the day's warmth, the sleeves pushed up just enough to expose tanned forearms. Even Alaric was sweating beneath the sun, his linen shirt clinging to his back, but the man appeared untouched by the heat. As the stranger shifted to lift a crate, something caught Alaric's eye. A scar. Not just any scar, but a deep mark burned into his skin, raised like it had been branded. Its shape struck a chord of recognition. It was disturbingly familiar.

"Something wrong?"

Derran's voice pulled him back. Alaric masked his unease. "Is he new?" He tilted his head toward the man.

"Yeah. Arrived yesterday. Quiet type. Doesn't leave that spot much."

Something gnawed at the back of Alaric's mind, an instinct he couldn't shake urging him to look closer. Without hesitation, he crossed the distance to the worker. The man seemed to sense his approach and turned, offering a faint smile.

Alaric extended a hand. "Alaric Stonebridge."

The man took it, his grip unexpectedly strong, far stronger than it should have been. Alaric withdrew his hand a moment later, a frown forming as a quiet tension stirred beneath his thoughts. Strangely, the man didn't give his name.

Forcing an easy smile, Alaric tried again. "They've got you on unloading duty? That's no fun in this heat."

"I'm fine." The response was clipped and dismissive. The man turned back toward the gravel road, staring into the distance as if the conversation had ended. Quiet type, indeed.

Alaric glanced toward Derran with a look that said, *Alright then*. Derran merely shrugged, clearly just as aware of the awkwardness.

"I'll be in town until tomorrow," Alaric told Derran before leaving. "You know where to find me if there's anything worth reporting."

Derran gave him a nod. "Good seeing you, Alaric."

But Alaric's mind wasn't on the farewell. It was still on the scar.

***

Evelyne stood before the mirror in the quiet room she shared with Heidara, studying the face that stared back at her. It no longer belonged to the girl who had once stumbled into the forest, aching, uncertain, and afraid. That girl was gone. In her place stood someone stronger, steadier. A woman shaped by survival. A warrior in her own right.

The slit skirt she wore shifted with each step, soft leather brushing one thigh while the longer panel draped low on the other side, offering a teasing glimpse of newly sun-kissed skin. This time, Evelyne didn't shy away from the cropped leathers. The dark brown top hugged her frame, wrapping neatly around her ribs and ending just above her navel. It highlighted the strength she'd earned, the faint lines of her stomach visible beneath the candlelight. For once, she reveled in the sight.

"You look perfect," Heidara said, stepping up behind her.

Evelyne turned, lips parting slightly as she caught sight of her. Heidara had outdone herself. Dark lashes framed her green eyes, the smoky kohl expertly blended at the edges, making them appear almost otherworldly. A soft touch of rouge warmed her cheekbones, and her lips, painted a deep red, stood in striking contrast against her skin. She looked fierce. Beautiful.

Heidara grinned at her reaction, then stepped closer, raising something over Evelyne's head before gently settling it in place. "For you," she said softly.

A crown made of flowers.

The delicate white blossoms wove together, resting just above the small braids Heidara had threaded through Evelyne's hair, the rest cascading down her back in loose, effortless curls.

Evelyne swallowed past the unexpected tightness in her throat. "When did you—?"

"When I left you and Alaric in the market," Heidara admitted with a smirk, adjusting the crown slightly. "I wanted to find something special. A proper gift for the birthday girl." She stepped back to admire her work. "Oh, wait—just a touch of color on your lips." Heidara leaned in, then let out a satisfied hum. "There. Now you look like the goddess of the moon herself."

A light, unrestrained laugh slipped from Evelyne's lips. She couldn't remember the last time she had felt so entirely herself. Not the noble-woman paraded in silk and lace, forced to plaster on a smile and endure dull exchanges. No... tonight, she felt free. And perhaps, like a woman who might catch the eye of an alpha.

Heidara must have noticed the glint of mischief in her expression, because she raised a brow and grinned. "Oh, you are turning heads tonight." Leaning in with a teasing whisper, she added, "Maybe even a certain brooding, insufferable one."

Evelyne rolled her eyes, but couldn't fight the warmth that spread through her.

"Come on." Heidara tugged her hand. "The moon is high, and the ritual is about to begin."

Evelyne exhaled, her heart thrumming with anticipation. She had spent weeks fighting to survive. Tonight, she would celebrate.

***

Evelyne had nearly forgotten how striking the men looked on ritual nights. Their bare chests and broad torsos were adorned with swirling paint, and their leather or loose-fitting pants hung low on their hips. The usual intensity in their expressions had softened into easy smiles, their tousled hair catching the firelight. It was beautiful—intoxicating, even.

And if Heidara hadn't been tugging her forward, Evelyne might have been content to linger at the edge, simply watching it all unfold.

A bright smile lit up Heidara's face, glowing beneath the full moon's light. Her golden hair fell loose around her shoulders, held back only by a leather band across her forehead with a small iron emblem at its center. Her darkened lashes and scarlet-colored lips added to the natural confidence she always seemed to carry. Evelyne couldn't understand how someone like her hadn't yet found a lover or mate.

"Come on!" Heidara urged, tugging at their linked arms with barely restrained excitement. "For once, Evelyne, just relax. Let go. Enjoy your night. Just one night."

Evelyne exhaled and smiled. "Alright."

As they moved through the crowd, past the women painting the warriors' chests and the steady pulse of drums, Evelyne's attention briefly landed on the Glaciermaw pack. They were still here, which meant she'd likely cross paths with Obren again. Not that she minded. Their banter had become something she looked forward to, though it never failed to put Kaldrek on edge.

Ahead, three men turned. Three sets of eyes flicked in her direction, but only one made her heart catch. Kaldrek. His gaze locked onto her the moment he saw her, and everything around them seemed to fall away. The noise, the firelight, and the crowd all blurred as his dark brown eyes fixed on her alone.

Heat prickled along her skin as he looked at her, his eyes dragging slowly down the length of her body before rising, just as slow, to meet her stare again. There was nothing subtle about it. His gaze was scorching, and something inside her coiled and pulled taut beneath it. She didn't know what thoughts ran through his head, but holy hell, she could feel them.

Every part of her said this was a bad idea. And none of her cared.

Holden let out a low whistle. "Little viper, you look like something I might take a bite of tonight."

Evelyne rolled her eyes, and Heidara groaned. "Holden, that's disgusting. Don't say things like that to her."

Alaric chuckled beside them, shaking his head.

"You both look beautiful."

"Well, obviously," Heidara quipped, flipping her hair over her shoulder with exaggerated confidence.

Evelyne snorted, grateful for the lightness of the moment. But her eyes had already returned to Kaldrek, who was still watching her the same way he had days ago when his mouth had been on her jaw and throat. Damn him, she still wanted more.

"Happy birthday, Evelyne." His voice was deep, and the sound rolled through her like embers catching fire.

"Thank you, Kaldrek."

"Shit," Holden cut in, "I forgot it was your birthday. Happy birthday!" Without warning, he threw his arms around her, lifting her clear off the ground in a crushing embrace.

Evelyne let out a startled laugh, breathless from the strength of it. And... was that a laugh from Kaldrek?

The thought barely had time to register before Holden set her back down, throwing an arm around her shoulders and announcing, "Let's drink!" With that, he strode off toward the barrels of ale, leaving Evelyne standing there, still reeling.

The night was a blur of dancing, laughter, and the warm burn of ale. It was precisely the kind of distraction Evelyne needed. The steady pulse of music thrummed in her chest, and the firelight flickered off the shifting bodies around her, casting shadows against the trees.

Alaric hadn't strayed from the fire for over an hour, dancing with anyone who joined him, but mostly with Heidara. Evelyne didn't miss how he watched her, a mix of interest and curiosity in his eyes. She recognized it all too well. She'd worn the same look herself, though her stolen glances had always been for Kaldrek.

She had to get a grip on whatever this was between them. Maybe it was nothing. Maybe she was imagining it all. But every time he so much as looked at her or spoke her name, her body reacted before her mind could catch up. It was infuriating. Unwanted. Dangerous. She couldn't keep wondering if he thought about her the way she thought about him—about her hands on his skin, his voice in her ear, the quiet ache that never seemed to fade. She shoved the thought aside, burying it deep. She wouldn't do this to herself.

He finally settled beside her on a large rock, silent as he watched the pack celebrate. The heat of his presence was impossible to ignore, the space between them feeling smaller than it was.

"You look... very nice tonight," he said, his voice rougher than usual.

She turned, her lips twitching as she studied him. "Is the alpha actually giving me a compliment?" She batted her lashes dramatically, then let out a soft chuckle. "Thank you."

A muscle in his jaw flexed before he breathed out and shook his head.

She tilted hers. "Are you done ignoring me now?"

His brows pulled together. "I wasn't ignoring you—"

"Oh, you absolutely were," she cut in. "Days, Kaldrek. You avoided me for days. Which is odd, considering the last time we were alone, you seemed a heartbeat away from kissing me."

His lips parted slightly before he closed them again as if debating his next move. He lifted a brow, the teasing glint in his eye unmistakable. "Who said I was going to kiss you?"

Her stomach tensed, and a flush crept up her neck. But she wouldn't back down. "I think you wanted to do a lot more than just that. Don't even deny it."

He exhaled a low breath, then leaned back on his hands, shoulders rolling as he smirked. "I'm not denying it."

She had expected a clever remark or a casual deflection, but his response caught her off guard. So he had wanted to kiss her that day. She hadn't imagined it.

The firelight cast sharp lines across his face, making his expression more intense, harder to read. And just like that, the playful teasing between them no longer felt like harmless fun. He was watching her closely now, like he was waiting for something.

And she was tired of waiting.

"Then why pull away?" she asked, her voice softer this time, edged with uncertainty. "Why the sudden distance?"

His smirk faded. "Because he scented me on you."

She frowned. "Who—"

"Obren." The name left his mouth like a curse. "And I knew that if he saw I had any interest in you, he'd use you against me. Maybe even hurt you." His teeth bared slightly, barely contained fury rippling off him. "I wasn't going to take that risk."

Her pulse quickened. "Hurt me?" She searched his face. "If he's that dangerous, why are we traveling with his pack?"

"Because we don't have a choice." His voice was tight. "And because he can sense I don't have a mate. Which means any unmated female is free game."

She scoffed. "I'm not some prize to be won."

"Tell that to him." His eyes flickered toward the fire, where Obren stood, laughing with his men. "Or have you not noticed how much he wants you?"

The heat in his tone wasn't just anger. It was something else. Jealousy.

Evelyne smiled. "At least he's easier to read. Someone who isn't afraid to show emotions or go after what he wants."

The air between them changed instantly. Kaldrek's eyes darkened, his entire body tensing before he suddenly leaned in—so close she felt his breath against her ear.

"Did my mouth on your neck not give my emotions away?" His voice dipped, sending a shiver down her spine. "Did my tongue not tell you how much I wanted you that day? Or do you need to feel it again to be sure?"

Her body burned at the words, the memory of his lips on her skin unraveling in her mind. Oh, no. He was not going to do this to her again. Not when he had spent days ignoring her, only to come back swinging with seduction and smirks.

"I prefer someone who can actually tell me how he feels." Her voice was sharp, cutting through the thick tension. "And not just physically."

His smirk vanished, his jaw locking tight.

"Why is it so hard for you to let me in?" Evelyne pressed. "Why can't you just say what you want?"

They stared at each other, neither blinking, silence stretching thick between them. She thought he was about to shut her out again, raising that stone wall between them, the one he rarely let fall. But this time, he didn't. Instead, his shoulders eased, tension slipping from his frame as the sharp edge in his eyes finally softened.

"I don't let people in easily," he said, and the honesty of his words hit her harder than she was ready for. "I'm afraid that if I let myself care for anyone else, I'll lose them too." His hand curled into a fist at his side. "It's already hard enough with Holden and Heidara. I wake up wondering what I'd do if something happened to them."

She stayed quiet, sensing the significance of whatever he would say next.

"It happened a few years ago." He swallowed, his throat bobbing. "I now understand that I can sense when the Noskari are near, but I ignored it the first time it happened. I felt something, but I brushed it aside and went back to sleep." His fingers dragged through his hair. "By the time I ran outside, I heard screaming from a voice I knew all too well."

Evelyne's chest tightened.

"My mother."

He didn't look at her, but she reached for his hand, running her thumb lightly over his knuckles.

"I was too late," he continued. "Because I went back to sleep. I could've reached them sooner, but I didn't. And when I finally arrived, the Noskari were already standing over my mother's body. My father was lying beside her, still breathing, but just enough to say goodbye."

Her throat burned, her fingers tightening around his.

"That's when I realized my ability," he said bitterly. "I screamed loud enough to wake the entire pack, but by the time they reached me, the Noskari were already gone. And then..." He gestured to the tattoo swirling down his arm. "This claimed me."

She frowned. "Claimed you?"

"The alpha mark chooses the next strongest member in the pack when an alpha dies. Not by birthright, but by strength and loyalty. And I was chosen." He paused, jaw clenched, before going on. "A few weeks after they died, I learned something worse. The Noskari don't just feed and kill, but can transfer a piece of themselves to a host, if they choose. Like a parasite that anchors to one's soul. And once it's inside, it takes root and grows. Sometimes quickly, sometimes slowly, depending on how strong the host is, and whether they fight it. But once infected..." His eyes flicked to hers. "Well, you know what happens."

Evelyne's stomach twisted at the thought, but beneath the horror was a deep ache for him, for everything he had endured. "It wasn't your fault, Kaldrek," she said softly.

He let out a slow breath, his gaze locked on hers, like he was trying to find truth in her words. Then he cleared his throat and shook his head, his expression flickering before settling into something guarded again.

"I didn't mean to push you away," he said quietly. "Or make you feel like you weren't wanted. I just—"

"I understand," she cut in gently. "You already have people to protect. Holden and Heidara... They're your family."

He nodded. "They've both been through more than most. But that's not my story to tell."

A beat passed before he pulled his hand away from hers, and a small smile tugged at his lips, an attempt to shift the mood.

"I got you something," he murmured. Her brows lifted in surprise as he reached beside him and pulled out a small, leather-bound book. "For your birthday," he added.

She stared at it for a moment, touched. "You..." she whispered, accepting the gift, fingertips brushing over the worn cover. "You didn't have to."

Kaldrek shrugged. "I wasn't sure what kind of stories you liked, but folklore about witches and handsome wolves seemed like a safe bet."

Warmth bloomed in her chest, and she chuckled. "I love it." She paused, then smirked. "Didn't know you noticed that I liked to read."

"I notice everything about you," he said without hesitation.

Her breath caught, and she ducked her head, a flush rising to her cheeks. He really could be gentle when he let his guard down. And maybe those days of silence had been his way of protecting her. If that was true, she could forgive him for it.

"Thank you," she said softly. "For the book, and for being honest with me."

She leaned in, pressing a kiss to his cheek. When she pulled back, his eyes were wide, lingering on her lips with a hunger that made her pulse stutter. But before either of them could speak, a familiar voice cut through the moment, and she felt Kaldrek go tense beside her.

"Evelyne, love, I have been searching for your beautiful face all night," Obren drawled, looking her over with a widening grin. "And damn, was it worth the wait."

She fought the urge to roll her eyes.

"My, my," Obren continued, his voice smooth as ever, eyes dragging over her with open admiration. "You look far too stunning to be sitting on a rock. Dance with me."

Evelyne parted her lips to decline, already bracing for the smug persistence that would follow, but Kaldrek spoke first.

"You should go," he said flatly. "Enjoy yourself."

She blinked. *What?*

Her gaze snapped to him, searching his face, but his expression gave nothing away. Cold. Detached. Just moments ago, he had looked at her like she was the only thing that mattered, and now he was handing her off like she meant nothing.

Anger bubbled up fast. She was done playing along if this was still his way of protecting her from Obren. She wouldn't pretend her feelings didn't exist just because he was too afraid to name his own.

She turned to Obren and smiled sweetly. "I'd love to."

Obren's grin widened, triumphant and dangerous all at once.

As Evelyne let him lead her into the crowd, she could already feel Kaldrek's stare searing into her spine. She refused to glance back.

CHAPTER 39

The drums pounded, deep and primal, a rhythm that seeped into Evelyne's bones, her pulse, and every sway and roll of her body. The air was rich with smoke and laughter, with the electric hum of bodies moving in tandem beneath the moon's glow. And at the center of it all was Obren, his hands firm on her hips, his grip possessive as they moved together.

He was as bold and flirtatious as ever, but Evelyne wasn't fooled. This wasn't about charm anymore. It was a performance, one meant to needle Kaldrek. And if Kaldrek wanted to sit back and stew in silence, fine. Let him.

She wasn't about to hold back.

Evelyne surrendered to the rhythm, letting the music move her. She tipped her head back, eyes closed, the beat pulsing through every line of her body. A smile touched her lips as she arched into each step, her hips finding an easy rhythm with Obren's practiced touch.

Still, she felt it. That burning stare from across the fire.

She didn't need to look to know Kaldrek was watching. His anger clung to her like smoke, jealousy simmering beneath the surface.

He'd once told her she drove him mad.

Let him unravel if he wasn't willing to claim what he so clearly wanted.

Obren's hands skimmed over the bare skin of her stomach, teasing and lingering, but before she could even process the contact, the fire seemed to burn hotter, the air suddenly charged with something dark.

A low, lethal voice cut through the sound of the drums.

"That's enough."

Evelyne turned. Kaldrek stood nearby, his posture rigid, muscles drawn tight as a bowstring. His eyes burned with something fierce and unspoken.

Obren, of course, didn't budge. He only smiled and kept his hands firm on Evelyne's hips, gripping a little harder. "Can I help you?" he asked, his tone all mockery.

Kaldrek didn't answer, not at first. He just stared, the fire casting sharp shadows across his face.

"We're in the middle of something," Obren added, his voice low, taunting. "You'll have to wait your turn."

Evelyne swore she heard a low growl deep in Kaldrek's throat. Then he stepped forward.

"I said that's *enough*."

Obren's grin sharpened. "Does it bother you when I touch her like this? She doesn't seem to mind. Do you, love?"

She didn't speak. Couldn't. Her eyes flicked between them, two alphas locked in a silent war. Somehow, she was the battlefield.

Kaldrek looked at her, just for a heartbeat, before locking eyes with Obren again.

"She's mine."

The words hit like a blade. Not a declaration, but a warning. A challenge. Something inside her clenched so hard she didn't know if it was want or shock that stole her breath.

Obren's fingers shifted against her waist, the spark in his eyes dimming just slightly. He might have been bold, but he wasn't foolish.

Not when Kaldrek was like this.

"Fine, fine," Obren finally relented, raising his hands as he stepped back. "Didn't realize the birthday girl came with a leash." His grin was all teeth, but he backed off, melting into the crowd.

Evelyne barely noticed. Her attention was locked on Kaldrek.

Mine.

The word rippled through her, awakening something buried and primal. His gaze devoured her, and she felt its pull in the quickening of her breath, the tremble beneath her ribs, the thrum of her heartbeat echoing in her chest.

"Come here." His voice was low, his finger curling in quiet command.

She didn't even hesitate. Her body moved before her mind could catch up, drawn to him as if by gravity.

Kaldrek's eyes dropped to her mouth, and she bit her lip without thinking. A flicker of dark satisfaction passed over his face, like he knew exactly what he was doing to her.

Then he moved quickly—turning her in a single breath. Her back met his bare chest, his hands settling firmly at her waist like they belonged there. Their bodies found a rhythm, moving together with seamless precision as if they had always known how to do this, how to fit.

Every sway of her hips against his, every slow grind in return, sent sparks racing up her spine. She didn't care who saw. Not the pack, not the crowd, not even the gods above. Tonight, she was his, and she wanted everyone to know it.

His grip tightened at her waist, fingers pressing into her skin like he was barely restraining something wild. Then he lowered his head, lips grazing the shell of her ear as his breath stirred against her skin. "Did you hear me, Evelyne?" His voice came out rough. "You're mine. And if another male touches you tonight, I'll tear his throat out."

A tremble rolled through her as a shaky breath escaped. She knew she should be furious, should push him away and remind him she wasn't something to be claimed. But all she could think was *yes*. Yes, she wanted him to say it again. Yes, she wanted his hands everywhere. Yes, she wanted him.

So she gave herself to him. And gods, did he take it.

***

She didn't want his hands to leave her, but the pack would be shifting soon. With one last lingering glance over her shoulder, Evelyne slipped away with Alaric, the quiet weight of Kaldrek's claim still clinging to her skin. They walked silently toward the lodge, the night air buzzing with leftover energy. Evelyne clutched her new book to her chest, barely registering the path ahead, her thoughts tangled in the memory of Kaldrek's touch, the sound of his voice, and how he had looked at her like she was already his.

By the time she reached her room, her body was still humming. She drew herself a hot bath, sinking into the warmth as she scrubbed the remnants of the night from her skin, but no amount of water could wash away the way he made her feel. The way she still ached for his touch.

She must've dozed off, because she jolted upright when a knock came at her door, eyes blinking groggily.

Alaric?

"Just a second," she called, stepping out of the tub and grabbing the thin robe draped nearby. Water dripped from her legs onto the wooden floor as she padded to the door, pulling it open just enough to peer outside.

But it wasn't Alaric.

"Kaldrek."

He stood tall. His dark eyes traveled over her intensely, and suddenly, she became hyperaware of how the damp fabric clung to her body.

"I should be shifting right now," he said thickly.

"Then what are you doing here?" she whispered, heart hammering.

"I needed to see you first." He stepped closer, filling the doorway, his heat swallowing the space between them.

Her pulse fluttered. "Is something wrong?"

"Yes." His breath ghosted against her lips. Her stomach flipped, and he went on before she could press further. "You're in my head. Every second of the goddamn day. Your body, your mouth..." His hands lifted, framing her face, thumbs brushing against her cheekbones. "You consume me," he said, each word low and full of need.

Her breath fanned against his lips. "Then I suggest you act on it."

A flicker of a smirk touched his mouth. Then he closed the distance and kissed her.

It was fierce and unrelenting, as if he'd held back for too long. And she didn't pause, not for a second. Pure lust flooded through her as he claimed her mouth. His tongue swept in hungrily, desperate to taste every inch of her. She melted into him, meeting his movements with equal intensity, her fingers digging into his bare chest.

He groaned against her mouth, gripping the back of her head with one hand, his fingers threading through her hair as if anchoring himself to her. His other hand grasped the curve of her backside, pulling her flush against him. She arched into him, the hard lines of his body making her gasp as he walked them backward, shutting the door behind him with a decisive click.

His mouth dragged along her jaw, down her throat, his tongue flicking over the rapid pulse there. "I need more of you," he rasped against her skin. "But I want to hear you say it. Tell me what you want."

There was no hesitation. She already knew.

"You," she breathed. "Only you, Kaldrek. Nothing else could ever compare."

His lips curved against her throat. "Only me?" he asked, voice dark and edged with desire.

"Yes.".

"Good," he growled. "Because no one touches what's mine. And you, Evelyne... You are mine."

Then his mouth was on hers again, and with effortless strength, he lifted her, hands firm on her waist. Instinctively, she wrapped her legs around him, holding tight as he pressed her back against the wall.

He pulled back just enough to let his mouth glide down the curve of her throat, his tongue tracing fire in its wake before he bit down lightly. She moaned, the slight pressure sending a jolt of pleasure straight to her core.

A wicked chuckle rumbled in his chest. "I can't wait to hear the sounds you make for me."

Yes. Please. The words screamed in her mind, but all she managed was a strangled whimper. She tugged at his hair, pulling his mouth back to hers, desperate to taste him again. This time, he kissed her slower, like he wanted to savor every moment. Like he was mapping her, memorizing her.

She pressed her hips into his, seeking more. He hissed against her lips, his grip tightening. "Not so defiant now, are we?"

Of course he would tease her at a time like this. But damn it, he was right. There wasn't a single defiant bone left in her body—she was his. Completely.

He carried her to the bed, his warmth searing through her robe's thin, damp fabric. But even as her body burned for him, a thought surfaced through the haze.

"What about the shift?"

He laid her down gently, his body settling over hers, and murmured, "They can't shift without their alpha." He brushed his lips along her collarbone, his fingers tracing the edge of her robe, teasing. "They can wait."

A shiver rolled through her as he eased the fabric from her shoulders, his mouth trailing in its wake, pressing kisses against the newly exposed skin. Heat spilled from his breath, his touch awakening every nerve in her body.

"Tell me if you want me to stop," he said against her skin.

She exhaled, fingers tangling in his hair. "Don't stop."

His gaze snapped to hers. "Do you want me to touch you?"

"*Please*," she whispered, desperate now. Every inch of her throbbed with want, her skin feverish beneath his hands.

His fingers drifted lower, finding the laces of her robe. He pulled, untangling them so painfully slowly that she thought she might combust. His palm slid up the center of her stomach, parting the fabric as he went, revealing her inch by inch.

He stilled.

His eyes devoured her, tracing every curve, every shadow and hollow of her body before he exhaled, "Look at you." He shook his head in awe, his voice hushed with reverence. "So fucking beautiful."

A soft moan escaped her as he dipped his head, his mouth closing over one breast while his hand cupped the other. The sensation surged through her in a wave of pleasure, heat pooling between her legs as she arched into his touch. He groaned against her skin, teasing her breast before finding her lips again in a kiss steeped in hunger.

She needed to touch him, but as her fingers fumbled with the ties of his pants, he caught her wrists, halting her movements. A quiet click of his tongue followed.

"Not yet, my lady," he rasped. A frustrated whimper left her, but then his mouth brushed her ear. "I've been dying to touch you," he admitted, and before she could form a response, his hand drifted lower, tracing gentle circles down her stomach.

She gasped as his fingers found her, pressing precisely where she craved him most. The sensation was exquisite and tortuous. Instinctively, she rocked into his touch, drawing an approving growl from him.

When she bit back a moan, he gently pried her hand away from her mouth. "I want to hear you."

Her head tilted back as his touch grew firmer, his thumb rolling against that perfect, sensitive spot. He kissed his way down her stomach, his teeth grazing lightly against her skin.

And then he pressed into her, a single finger sliding in with aching tenderness.

Her body clenched around him, another moan ripping free as she lifted her hips, begging him for more. She felt him smile against her skin, and just as she adjusted to the stretch, he added another finger, pushing deeper.

Her entire world tilted.

Her fingers dug into his shoulders, her body shuddering as he worked her, coaxing her higher with every precise stroke. His touch, his kiss—he was unraveling her piece by piece, stripping her bare in every possible way.

She was already teetering on the edge, gasping, trembling, and gods save her, she never wanted him to stop.

"I love the scent of you." He kissed her mouth again like he knew she was close. As his fingers worked deeper, his thumb discovered that sensitive place once more, a perfect pressure that tipped her into release.

A sharp, breathless moan tore from her lips, swallowed by his mouth as pleasure crashed through her. He didn't stop, didn't relent, guiding her through every wave, his fingers stroking until she trembled beneath him, completely spent.

He kissed her deeply, over and over, until her breathing slowed, and the shudders that wracked her body faded into a lingering hum of pleasure. But his eyes weren't just laced with desire; it was something deeper, something that made her stomach tighten and her fingers twitch with the need to touch him again.

So she did.

Her hand found him through his pants, fingers tracing the rigid length beneath the leather. A sharp hiss escaped him, his body jerking into her palm as he clenched his jaw.

"Evelyne," he groaned, his voice strained, wrecked.

She wanted to see him undone. To make him feel every ounce of what he'd just stirred in her. But, *damn it*, he had to return to his pack.

Her eyes widened. "Oh gods, I'm so sorry. You need to go!"

Reality came crashing back. The ritual. The wolves. They were waiting for him. She bolted upright, facing him in a panic. He, on the other hand, looked maddeningly unbothered. His dark brown eyes were calm... and a little *too* amused.

"You have to go!" she insisted, flustered.

"I know," he said with a lazy smile, yet made no move to leave. Instead, he leaned in and pressed a kiss to her shoulder. "I'd much rather stay."

She let out a breathless laugh and shook her head. "You're impossible."

His smirk widened. Too confident, too handsome. It made her want to smack the grin off his face.

"Do you make a practice of this?" she asked, voice light and teasing. "Keep your pack waiting while you"—she waved a hand vaguely between them, cheeks flushing—"seduce someone?"

His brows lifted. "Do you really want the answer to that?"

Her stomach twisted. Of course he'd been with other women—he was an alpha, a powerful one. It was only natural.

"No," he laughed softly. "I've never made them wait before." He cupped her face. "But they will for you."

Her heart fluttered as he kissed her again, deeper this time, his fingers tangling in her hair like he never wanted to let go.

Heavens above. He was going to ruin her.

When he pulled back, his tone softened. "And if you're wondering how many women there have been... the number is far less than whatever wild story you're imagining."

She narrowed her eyes. "How would you know what I'm thinking?"

His smirk returned. "Because I know you. Now sleep," he whispered, brushing her hair back. "I'll find you in the morning."

She offered no argument, sleep tugging hard at her. Within minutes she drifted off, his touch still a ghost upon her skin.

CHAPTER 40

Alaric couldn't sleep.

Hours had passed since the ritual, since the firelight had burned low and the last echoes of laughter had faded into silence. The lodge was quiet now, save for the occasional creak of settling wood, but his mind refused to rest.

He turned onto his side with a frustrated exhale, dragging a hand down his face. He could still feel the curve of Heidara's waist beneath his palms, see the way her green eyes sparkled when she laughed, utterly unaware of how easily she'd disarmed him. The memory clung to him, vivid and maddening. He wanted her badly, and that want was beginning to feel less like desire and more like need. That was the problem.

But she wasn't the only thing haunting his thoughts. Even now, lying alone in the dark with the scent of smoke and damp earth clinging to the air, his mind kept circling back to the man at the trading post. The unsettling strength in his grip. The way he stood slightly apart from the others, eyes fixed on the road like he was expecting something. And that raised scar burned into the skin in a shape Alaric couldn't shake. He was sure he'd seen it before. Somewhere.

Then it hit him.

He sat up so quickly his vision swam. That scar. It wasn't just a burn. It was a sigil. The Sigil of the Lost. A mark forged through blood magic, etched with purpose.

Dread crept in, slow and merciless, settling into his bones.

Something was wrong. Deeply, undeniably wrong. Who had that man been waiting for? Were there others nearby?

The answer came swiftly, as a familiar unnatural cold seeped into the room and crept beneath his skin. The same chill he'd felt when the Noskari dragged him from his tent and bled him dry. The same cold that had filled the air the night shadows twisted Reuben's mind.

They were here.

His pulse pounded against his ribs as he shoved on his boots and tore out of his room, urgency fueling his every movement. He needed to find Evelyne and the others.

He was at Evelyne's door within minutes, pounding hard enough to rattle the hinges.

"Alaric?" Her voice was groggy, heavy with sleep as she opened the door, rubbing at her eyes, her robe pulled loosely around her.

He pushed inside without hesitation, his gaze scanning the room. "Did Heidara ever come back?"

Evelyne's expression sharpened instantly. "No, I... I don't think so."

She didn't wait for more explanation. She rushed across the room, grabbing her clothes. Alaric turned without needing to be asked, giving her a moment to dress as he grabbed the map from her bag.

"*Shit, shit, shit.*" His voice was tight as he watched the ink bleed across the parchment, dark tendrils unfurling far beyond their location.

The Noskari weren't just here. They were surrounded.

Then the screaming started. Bloodcurdling screaming.

Alaric grabbed Evelyne's wrist and pulled her into the hall. "We have to go. Now."

The streets were chaos. Townspeople ran, some dragging loved ones behind them, others frozen in terror. Alaric barely had time to register the grotesque figures tearing through the market square, some flickering between shadows, others fully formed, their gray skin stretched taut over pulsing black veins, their mouths smeared red with fresh blood.

The Noskari were feeding.

Bodies lay strewn across the ground, drained and lifeless, their skin pale and waxy under the moonlight. Blood pooled in the dirt. The air was thick with the coppery scent of death.

"Where are the packs?" Evelyne whispered, her voice laced with terror.

Alaric didn't answer. He grabbed her arm and pulled her into the shadows, pressing her back against the cool stone of the alley wall. The distant snarls and pounding of paws against the earth told him what he needed to know—the packs were coming.

But were they enough to fight off dozens of Noskari flooding the market square? Alaric guessed fifty, maybe sixty. Too many.

The wolves struck first, a blur of fur and teeth crashing into the Noskari. Alaric had seen them fight before, but never like this. The creatures didn't just fight back; they overpowered the pack. Fast. Brutal. It took two, sometimes three wolves to bring one down.

Beside him, Evelyne trembled, but only for a second. Then she inhaled sharply, reached into her bag, and pulled out a dagger... and her father's pistol. Her fingers fumbled over the weapon, trembling, struggling with the next steps.

"Let me," Alaric said, taking it from her, trying to sound steady despite the pounding in his chest.

"I can shoot, I just—" She swallowed, eyes wide. "I can't remember how to—"

"I've got it." He dropped low and got to work. Muscle memory kicked in. He flipped open the frizzen, poured the powder, loaded the ball and wadding, and slammed the ramrod down the barrel. His hands moved fast, but not fast enough.

He was priming the pan when movement caught his eye. A shadow peeled from the alley wall, and the Noskari lunged straight for Evelyne.

Alaric's heart stopped.

She didn't.

Her dagger met the creature's stomach, the blade sinking deep, but it barely recoiled. It staggered and smiled, a grin slick with blood and menace. It was toying with her.

Alaric's grip on the pistol tightened. He rushed to finish.

Evelyne pulled the dagger free and struck again, this time to the throat. Still nothing. It raised a clawed hand toward her—

The shot cracked through the alley.

The Noskari's head snapped back in an explosion of blood and bone. It crumpled at her feet.

Evelyne stood over the body, panting, streaked with red. "Is it dead?"

Alaric didn't wait to answer. "Move."

She grabbed her dagger and ran close behind him as they darted through chaos. Around them, wolves fought with everything they had, but they were losing ground. Fast.

A massive blur of white cut through the mayhem and barreled right into a Noskari pinned by two wolves. The creature had no chance to react before Kaldrek's powerful jaws closed around its throat.

His wolf form was all muscle and feral dominance as he dragged the Noskari to the ground. With a savage shake, he ripped its throat clean out, then tore its head from its shoulders in one brutal motion.

Blood sprayed across the dirt as he lifted his head, his muzzle slick with crimson. Even amid the turmoil, his dark, focused eyes found Evelyne, but shadows closed in before he could reach her, devouring the light.

***

The mist swallowed them whole. One second, Evelyne stood near Kaldrek's massive wolf form, Alaric at her side, and the next, darkness consumed everything.

A frigid, grotesque cold wrapped around her, seeping deep into her bones. Suddenly, hands, far too strong and far too many, clamped down on her arms and yanked her backward. She screamed, twisting and kicking, but there was no ground beneath her, no sense of direction or gravity.

Then, there was light.

She staggered as the shadows released her, boots scraping against blood-slicked cobblestones. The air was thick with smoke and something far worse—a stench of rot and decay that turned her stomach. Ahead, two Noskari stood, gripping a man by the arms with their black-veined hands. His head hung low, chest rising and falling in shallow, ragged breaths. He looked gaunt, beaten, stripped down to nothing but his undergarments.

Then she saw his abdomen, and nausea rolled through her. A fresh burn marked his skin, intricate lines woven into a twisted pattern. The edges were still raw, the flesh angry and red, making it difficult to discern the full symbol. But her heart pounded as recognition struck.

The sigil.

This wasn't just an attack or a random act of killing. It was a message, a warning, and it was meant for her. For ignoring Vaelora's first warning. And the second. Now, the price had been paid in blood.

The Noskari holding her sneered, one of them giving her a rough shove forward. Her knees nearly buckled as she stumbled closer, her eyes locked on the sigil, on the way the burned flesh still wept, the way the man's shallow breaths barely stirred his ribs.

Who was he, and why were they doing this to him?

The second Noskari grinned, yanking back the man's hair so his head snapped upright. Evelyne flinched as his face came into view. He was bruised and covered in blood, his eyes dull and distant. But his face was so familiar it struck her like a blade to the chest.

"No," she whispered, horror twisting inside her, as a strangled sob escaped her lips. "Father?"

His head lifted slowly, weakly. His eyes, heavy with sorrow, locked onto hers.

They had beaten him, broken him, all because of her.

Evelyne's chest heaved, her body shaking violently. "Please—please, let him go," she sobbed, her voice raw and desperate.

A Noskari clicked its tongue in mock pity and moved closer, its ice-cold fingers curling under her chin, forcing her to meet its black, soulless gaze. Kaldrek growled nearby, a deep, guttural sound that sent a chill down her spine. She didn't need to look to know he was ready to tear through them. She could feel it in every fiber of her being. But she was pinned in their grasp. And there were too many. If he attacked now, they'd rip him apart before he ever reached her.

The Noskari curled its lip, blood staining its fangs. "Foolish little girl," it hissed, voice slithering over her skin like oil. "She warned you to turn back, and yet..." It tilted its head, mock curiosity flashing in those hollow black depths. "You surround yourself with friends."

It turned, arms outstretched, gesturing to the carnage. To the wolves and humans closing in. To all the warm, pulsing blood.

"Plenty for us to feast on."

Bile burned in her throat. This was her fault.

She tore her gaze away, looking back to the man on his knees, to the one who had raised and protected her. To her father. His body sagged between his captors, barely upright. But his eyes were filled not with pain or fear, but with love. And guilt.

"Don't do this," she pleaded once more, though deep down, she knew it was futile. Her mind raced. Why was her father here? Was he traveling alone? How long had he been in pain? He looked so weak and broken.

Time seemed to freeze around her, trapping her in an endless moment. She barely registered the warm trickle of blood sliding down her arm as a Noskari dragged a razor-sharp black fingernail across her skin, slicing it open. The sting was distant, insignificant compared to the horror unfolding before her. It was going to feed on her, but she couldn't bring herself to fight or even look away. Its strength held her captive, but it didn't matter, because all she could see was her father.

"I was looking for him too, Evelyne," he rasped. "Don't give up on him. I... I know he's still in there."

The Noskari snapped its head toward him, snarling. "Silence."

Her father hadn't come to drag her back. He had been searching for Cillian, just like her. And he trusted her to find him, believed in her. Pride and anguish swelled inside her, tangling into something unbearable.

The Noskari turned back to her. "This is your final warning." A cruel smile twisted its face as it leaned in close, whispering the words against her cheek. "Let the lost stay lost."

"No." The plea left her lips before she could stop it, but she knew, even before she spoke, that they were past mercy.

The creature moved.

Too fast.

Her stomach dropped, ice flooding her veins. "NO!" she shrieked, thrashing against the iron grip of the Noskari holding her back. She watched helplessly as the other Noskari knelt before her father.

His lips parted. "Stay brave, Evelyne. I've always been so proud of—"

There was a brutal thrust, and the Noskari's arm punched through his chest with a sickening crack.

Flesh ripped. Bone splintered. A wet, gruesome sound filled the air, followed by the slow, gurgling choke of a man gasping his final breath. Then—blood. It spilled in thick, pulsing waves, slick and dark, seeping into the earth as if the ground itself were drinking him dry.

Evelyne's broken screams erupted through the night as the Noskari wrenched its clawed hand free. Clenched within its grasp was her father's glistening heart.

His body spasmed. Once. Twice. Then crumpled like a puppet with its strings cut.

Lifeless. Gone.

For a moment, the world stood still. No sound. No breath. Just the horrific sight of that still-beating organ, slick with blood, pulsing weakly before the grip around it tightened. Thick droplets splattered onto the soaked earth, mingling with the ruin of so many before him.

Then everything erupted.

Kaldrek lunged, a savage rush of muscle and fury, his fangs sinking deep into the Noskari's throat. Blood gushed in thick, steaming ribbons, but the creature didn't fall. It snarled and wrenched free, hurling him to the ground with a brutal force that cracked bone and left the earth trembling.

Pain ignored, he rolled to his feet with a guttural growl and launched himself at the creature again. And again. And again.

There was nothing measured in his attack—only despair and blind rage. The Noskari grinned through it all, its twisted mouth stretching in amusement as if it relished the torment.

But Kaldrek didn't stop.

He was the only one who could face such a monster alone.

The wolves descended, a violent wave of fur and snapping jaws, tearing into the chaos with savage purpose. Evelyne saw Alaric fighting his way to her, blade slicing through anything that came too close, reloading the pistol with every precious second he could steal.

And then, suddenly, the Noskari began to vanish. Their forms unraveled into black mist, twisting and curling away into the night like smoke fleeing the light.

The battle was over.

Silence fell. Evelyne crawled forward, knees sinking into the blood-soaked dirt. She barely felt it as her shaking fingers brushed the burned sigil seared into her father's abdomen.

"I'm sorry." Her voice cracked. "I'm so sorry." She rocked back and forth, her forehead pressing against his cooling skin. "I love you. I'm so sorry."

She didn't know how long she sat there, whispering apologies into the cold night. Time had lost all meaning. The world had shrunk to nothing but her father's lifeless body and the hollow ache inside her chest.

She might have stayed there forever if not for the warmth that suddenly enveloped her. Strong, steady arms wrapped around her, pulling her in. She lifted her gaze and realized everyone had shifted back. Kaldrek's grip tightened as he lifted her effortlessly, pressing her against his chest. She didn't fight it. She couldn't. And the moment his fingers tangled in her hair, his lips brushing a soft, lingering kiss against her forehead, the dam inside her shattered. She broke completely in his arms.

"We can't leave him," Evelyne sobbed into Kaldrek's chest, her voice breaking. "We can't—"

"I know," he muttered, his arms tightening around her. "Shh. I know." His voice was gentle, a lifeline in the frenzy. "We'll move him, Evelyne. I promise."

Kaldrek turned to the gathered warriors, his voice carrying through the night.

"Burn the Noskari. We will bury our loved ones."

It had been the best night of her life, and the worst. A revel beneath the full moon, her birthday marked by festivity, Kaldrek's confession, and the closeness they had finally allowed themselves. For one brief moment, everything had felt real, whole, and right. Then came the ruin. The blood. And her father's heart being torn from his chest.

A wave of nausea surged through her.

"Put me down," she demanded, and Kaldrek obeyed.

The moment her feet touched the ground, she doubled over, her stomach wrenching violently. The world blurred as bile and grief plunged through her in heaving waves. But he stayed kneeling beside her, rubbing slow, soft circles on her back. Heidara was there as well, wordlessly pulling her hair back as Evelyne emptied every last drop of ale and food onto the grass.

When it was over, she sagged, breath unsteady, staring at nothing.

"Let's get you cleaned up, alright?" Heidara said quietly.

There was no one like her. A true friend. And Kaldrek, whatever he was to her—she didn't have a name for it yet—she was grateful he was here. But at this moment, all she wanted was to disappear.

"I'm going to pick you up now." Kaldrek's voice was calm, but firm. His arms slipped beneath her, lifting her carefully against his chest. He carried her past the lodges, but didn't take her to her room. He took her to his.

Heidara followed without question; either she understood or didn't care where Kaldrek took Evelyne, as long as she wasn't left alone. Inside, she busied herself, drawing a hot bath while Evelyne stood motionless and numb. She felt almost nothing—only the sticky weight of blood clinging to her skin. Not her own. Theirs. The Noskari's... and her father's.

"I'll take it from here, Heidara."

Her friend gave a slight nod and left without a word. Evelyne knew she should thank her, but she had nothing left to give.

"Are you hurt?" Kaldrek asked, his voice edged with concern.

Aside from the shallow gash on her forearm where the Noskari had cut her, she was physically unscathed. But she could only imagine how she looked: bloodied, shaken, barely holding herself together. She couldn't find her voice, so she simply shook her head.

Kaldrek nodded toward her boots. "May I?"

She could undress herself, but she couldn't be alone right now. And he'd already seen her bare and vulnerable. So she nodded.

Carefully, he helped her out of her boots and then her bloodied clothes. She stepped into the bath, sinking into the steaming water, letting it scald away the night's filth. Kaldrek stayed, kneeling by her side, his touch impossibly gentle as he washed the blood from her hair and face.

He gathered bandages from the small closet and wrapped the cut on her arm. When he was done, he didn't move. He stayed where he was, his gaze fixed not on her body but on her eyes.

"This is my fault," she whispered as guilt and sorrow clawed back in. "All of this."

"Don't say that." Kaldrek reached out, tilting her chin so their eyes met. "Look at me."

She did.

"None of this was your fault. None of it. Vaelora did this. Do you hear me?"

His words were a tether, something solid in the storm. He leaned in and kissed her forehead, and she breathed again.

"Come on," he said softly. "Let's get to bed. We'll have the burials tomorrow. I'll make sure of it."

She didn't argue. She needed his steadiness. But what now? Her thoughts drifted to her mother, to Aurelia, to Seraphine. Oh, how she missed her handmaid, her *friend*. Missed her quiet comfort and the way she held her when everything felt too heavy. But tonight, Evelyne could let herself lean on Kaldrek, and for that, she was truly grateful.

CHAPTER 41

The morning after the attack was cloaked in oppressive silence. The scent of charred wood filled the air, along with remnants of the horrors that had unfolded just hours before. Smoke still clung to the ruins, curling in the early light like ghosts of the fallen. Cindermoor had suffered, and yet, its people stood.

Alaric felt sick. His stomach twisted as he watched them gather, moving with solemn purpose. Every face was drawn. There was grief, but within it, something else. A quiet determination, a shared understanding that this was not the end. That vengeance would come.

The burial pyres had long since turned to ash, their flames having consumed the monstrous remains of the slain Noskari. Now, they needed to bury their own. It was time to lay to rest those who had fought, those who had not deserved the end they met.

Among them was Lord Aron Duskwood.

Alaric's hands curled into fists as he stood at the crowd's edge. He could still hear it—Evelyne's scream, desperate and piercing as she crumbled beneath the weight of her loss. He could still see the blood on the earth, the look in Lord Duskwood's eyes before one of Vaelora's monsters sliced through his chest. It had been hell, and he had been powerless to stop it.

A group of elders stood over the freshly dug graves, their voices rising in a rhythmic chant. The words were foreign to him, but the sound was something he felt in his bones. It was ancient and sacred, and even the earth beneath him seemed to sag with sorrow, as though mourning beside him.

Evelyne stood at the forefront, silent and pale. Kaldrek was beside her, his presence calm and his gaze distant. But Alaric could see the fire in him.

The alpha looked feral. His jaw was tight, his shoulders rigid. The man who had been so gentle with Evelyne, who had carried her through the night like she was the only thing holding him to this world, now radiated something primal and violent. The grief in his eyes had festered into something sharper, deadlier. If anyone so much as breathed wrong, Alaric feared they'd meet the brunt of his fury.

The Noskari had done this. They had taken Kaldrek's people, his family, and his home. Now, there would be blood.

Alaric let out a slow breath and forced himself to look away. Heidara stood nearby, her face marked with streaks of dried tears. She had made it. Most of the pack had. But not all. Too many lives had been lost, wolves from both Ironwolf and Glaciermaw. Their ranks were thinner now, their strength pushed to the edge. Yet there was no turning back.

They still had to save Cillian.

But how the hell were they supposed to fight these demons again? How could they reach him in time? They couldn't afford another surprise attack, another massacre. They had to move, and they had to do so carefully. The eastern lands stretched vast before them, and the path to Nerathar was long and treacherous. Vaelora's numbers were unknown, and she would be waiting.

Alaric needed to speak with Kaldrek. And Obren.

When the burials had ended and the mourners began to scatter, he found himself in the center of a tense meeting. Kaldrek sat at the head, his fingers drumming impatiently against the wooden table. Holden, Ty, Nathan, and Obren were there, along with three warriors from Glaciermaw.

Alaric took his seat and exhaled. "We need a route. The fastest one."

Obren nodded. "There's still a lot of land between us and the mountains. The terrain will slow us if we don't plan carefully."

"Then we plan," Kaldrek said, his voice edged with annoyance. "We move north by nightfall."

"We need to be smart," Nathan added. "We cannot risk being caught off guard again. We should assume Vaelora has sent more of them."

"She has," Kaldrek growled, eyes flashing. "And I don't intend to let anyone live if they stand in our way."

A heavy silence followed. They all knew what was at stake. They all knew what had to be done. The road to Nerathar would be long. And it would be bloody.

The dim light of Garek's tavern flickered over the worn wooden table. The tension among them was almost tangible, the weight of the previous night pressing on every set of shoulders hunched around the map Alaric had spread before them. Holden and Obren were back at it, their voices sharp, cutting through the thick silence of the room.

"We take the western pass," Holden argued. "The terrain's rougher, but there's more coverage. We stay hidden that way."

Obren shook his head. "That's foolish. The Noskari attacked us once. Do you think they won't have their eyes on the same pass? They know we'll head north. We need open ground, not an ambush waiting to happen."

"Open ground means exposure," Nathan cut in. "We can't afford to be seen."

Alaric listened quietly for a while, letting the argument loop around itself. Then he cleared his throat and finally spoke.

"The Noskari attack at night," he said. The bickering stopped, and all eyes turned toward him. He placed a firm hand on the edge of his map, the only one he had left. "If we keep moving during the day, we can avoid them best. But that also means we need safe places to camp before nightfall. Wolves can push through exhaustion, but horses can't. We have to plan for that."

Obren folded his arms, studying the map.

"So what are you suggesting?"

"There are hills, high grasses, and scattered forests throughout the eastern lands," Kaldrek added, eyes narrowing over the parchment. "We could use the land to our advantage. Keep to the forests when we can. Move fast when we need to."

Alaric nodded. "It's a start. But there's something else." He hesitated, then traced a path along the map with his fingertip. "I once found an abandoned trade route on a map back home. It doesn't appear on this one, but I remember it. If it still exists in some form, even overgrown, it could be our best chance at reaching the mountains undetected."

"There's no such path," Obren said flatly.

Alaric met his stare. "Not on this map. But I swear it was on another one. Maybe it's been lost to time, but if there's even a chance it still exists, we must find it."

"So we're supposed to chase after some path we're not even sure is real? That's ridiculous," Obren said, shaking his head.

Kaldrek scratched the stubble on his chin as he thought about it. To Alaric's surprise, he said, "It's worth a try, Obren. We're out of options."

The others exchanged uneasy glances, but didn't argue. Reaching the northeastern mountains would take at least three to four weeks, which was a problem for another day. For now, they needed a path and a plan.

The door burst open with a force that rattled the walls.

Evelyne stormed in, breathless, her face lined with exhaustion. Her eyes burned with something fierce. She clutched a book to her chest, her fingers digging into the worn leather cover as if it were the only thing tethering her to the ground. She didn't so much as glance at the others seated at the table, didn't acknowledge their meeting or the startled silence that followed her entrance. Instead, she pushed between Kaldrek and Alaric, slamming the book onto the map sprawled across the table.

"Evelyne?" Kaldrek asked with a look of confusion.

"There's a way to defeat her," she declared, voice trembling with urgency. "And it's the only way."

Alaric stiffened. He had never seen her so wild-eyed and desperate.

"There's a prophecy," she continued, turning to Alaric as if willing him to understand. "There is something out there that can stop her."

Kaldrek's brow furrowed. "What are you talking about?"

Evelyne exhaled sharply, her fingers working furiously to flip through the pages. "The witch in the marketplace recognized this book. *The Lantern's Keeper*. Selene knew what it was the second I pulled it from my bag. It's more than just a book. It's a guide, or a key. And the man who gave it to me back in Caltheris—he was a seer. That can't be a coincidence. He must have given it to me for a reason." She looked between Alaric and Kaldrek, gaze pleading. "I know this sounds insane, but please just listen to me."

She took a breath, steadying herself before continuing.

"We cannot take on the Noskari after what we witnessed last night. And we don't know how many more Vaelora has in the north. But we can't just walk into this blind. We need a way to stop her. And maybe—maybe this book, this artifact, is the answer." She hesitated, then pressed on. "A Hallowell witch wrote it. Perhaps the same one who performed the ritual a hundred years ago."

"What ritual?" Kaldrek asked, and Alaric realized he had no idea what she meant.

The others fell silent, the tension in the room thickening as Evelyne quickly explained everything she and Alaric had uncovered. By the time she finished, Kaldrek's expression had darkened, his hands curling into tight fists.

"You didn't think to tell me about this?"

Evelyne snapped her gaze to him, her patience worn thin, her voice cutting. "You never asked. And you never seemed to care about our mission, so I didn't think it was worth telling you." She sighed and flipped through the book, eyes scanning the words. "I thought this was just a storybook. But then Selene told us a Hallowell witch wrote it, and that got me thinking." She paused as if realizing something. "The seer in Caltheris told me Cillian should use this as a guide. And if he was truly a seer, then…"

Her hands trembled as she turned the pages. She skimmed her fingers over a passage as she read it aloud:

"When the night devours the land, and the stars fall silent, a Lantern shall be kindled in the hands of the Keeper. A soul bound to a lineage unseen, carried by blood long shrouded from fate's reach. The darkness will beckon, weaving shadows into chains, but the light will rise—pure, unyielding.

"By a shift, it will stir, and the rightful heir shall burn away the veil. In the Keeper's grasp, the Lantern will reveal what was lost and what must be

found. When the hour is near and the crimson moon calls, cries of agony shall echo, but the light will rise to cleanse them all.

"A soul bound to a lineage unseen. *A soul*. A rightful heir," she mumbled to herself. "It's Cillian." Her breath shuddered as she lifted her gaze. "Cillian's soul. Why else would Vaelora put so much effort into targeting him? She knows. She knows he is the subject of the prophecy. *Oh, gods*."

She pushed away from the table and began pacing.

"This book was meant for him. It was guiding him to figure out that he is the key." Though her face had gone pale, she kept moving, clearly trying to piece it all together. "This is why she's been corrupting him, brainwashing him."

Alaric's whole body tensed as realization and truth clawed its way in. He swallowed hard. "And the sigil, the warnings. She's trying to stop us from uncovering this."

Evelyne nodded. "I think she's been trying to keep us from reaching him, so he never learns the truth. Or maybe she's trying to control him to stop the prophecy from coming true. I... I'm not sure."

Her words lingered, heavy with a fear that neither Alaric nor Kaldrek dared voice. But beneath that fear, something else stirred—hope.

If Cillian was the key, if he truly was the light, then there was still a chance.

"Sit with us, please," Kaldrek said, his hand finding the small of Evelyne's back, the touch both protective and intimate. Alaric noticed it, and couldn't help but wonder if something more had passed between them. His eyes followed the slow drag of Kaldrek's fingers along Evelyne's spine, and a sudden protective instinct rose in him. He clenched his jaw, trying to tamp it down.

Kaldrek must have sensed it, because he turned, meeting Alaric's stare with a look that held a silent warning. A challenge. As if to say, *Don't.*

That touch was a claim, an unspoken declaration, and Alaric hated it. But he bit his tongue, forcing a tight smile just as Garek arrived, setting down food and drinks, breaking the tension that thickened the air.

***

They departed at dawn the next day, the golden light spilling across Cindermoor like a quiet farewell. The packs gathered silently, exchanging soft goodbyes with the townsfolk, their voices heavy with grief. Eda and Garek lingered the longest, embracing the wolves like their own kin, and in many ways, they were. They had guided them, protected them. The thought made Evelyne's chest ache. Her father was gone, murdered before her eyes. And her mother, Aurelia, Cillian—they didn't even know. Still, she had to leave her father behind, buried in unfamiliar soil among the graves of so many others lost to the same nightmare.

She might be the one who had to tell her family. She wasn't even sure she would survive the journey home. But she had to try. She needed to find Cillian and do everything she could to understand what was happening. Somehow, he was the key; she could feel it. How it all connected still escaped her, but there was no turning back now. All she could do was keep going and hold on to the hope that he was still alive.

Kaldrek had given her space. More than that, he must have ordered the entire pack to leave her alone, because no one dared mention her father. Alaric had spoken to her, though, and she hadn't minded. He had been close with her father and had witnessed his brutal death as she had. And in some dark, morbid way, she was grateful for his presence.

She felt numb, incapable of processing the storm of emotions within her. Even thoughts of Kaldrek and what had happened between them felt distant. She longed to touch him, to kiss him, but the idea of feeling happiness or pleasure at a time like this seemed wrong. He understood, though. Vaelora had stolen his parents, just as she had stolen Evelyne's father. They were bound together by loss.

The first week of travel passed in near silence. Everyone moved quickly, following Alaric's lead toward the abandoned trade route he swore he had seen on an old map. A supposed trade route, anyway.

No one in either pack had heard of it before, and Evelyne couldn't shake her doubts. But they had no other choice. They had to take the risk if they wanted to avoid the Noskari.

They traveled by day, moving through the eastern lands, the alphas of both Glaciermaw and Ironwolf scouting ahead for shelter. Each night, they found whatever cover they could. Sometimes, luck was on their side, and they came across fallen trees that curved over them like sheltering caves. On other nights, they had to rely on tall grasses and the shadows of hills and rocks. There were always scouts keeping watch, always weapons within reach. No tents, no fires. Only the cold, hard ground beneath them.

Kaldrek never failed to check on her, and his presence was a constant reassurance. More often than not, he lay beside her, his warmth seeping into her bones. She felt safe with him, comforted. But she also knew Alaric watched him whenever he came near, his protective instincts evident. She hadn't told him how far things had gone between her and Kaldrek. And maybe it shouldn't matter. But back home, in the world of polished ballrooms and whispered judgments, a woman who gave herself to a man before marriage was branded. There was no undoing it now. She had crossed a line and knew exactly what they would call her.

Ruined.

Unfit to marry.

She didn't regret it. Not for a moment. That night had meant something. It had been real, and it had changed everything. Kaldrek felt it too; she saw it in how he moved around her now, protective and always watching. The pack had noticed as well. Even if they weren't mates, they could still smell him on her, a silent claim no one dared to question. Not even Obren.

He kept his distance, whether out of respect or because the horrors of Cindermoor had shaken something in him. Maybe chasing her no longer felt worth the effort. But through it all, Heidara remained by her side.

With each passing day, as they drew closer to Nerathar, the grief and guilt that had weighed Evelyne down began to shift. Sorrow hardened into rage, and heartache turned to resolve. She was no longer a noble lady from the south, no longer a delicate thing meant for ballrooms and courtly whispers.

She was not the girl she'd once been. She was stronger now—a warrior in her own right. And she would fight for her father, for her brother, until her very last breath. No matter how dangerous this path became, she would not give up.

CHAPTER 42

The second week of travel brought them closer to their destination. The air grew colder. Each mile forward felt heavier, the unknown pressing in on all sides. The rolling hills flattened into long stretches of dry grass, the occasional cluster of trees breaking the monotony of the landscape.

Alaric rode in front, scanning the horizon. Kaldrek stayed in his human form, sharing the saddle with Evelyne so he could talk with Alaric as they neared their destination. She leaned into him, comforted by his steady presence. The journey had been long, but she felt more at ease with him behind her.

Alaric had been waiting for some sign, something undeniable to prove they were headed in the right direction. While the rest of the pack questioned whether the path even existed, he held on to a quiet conviction, insisting he could feel it was still out there and urging them to trust him. Evelyne chose to believe him. Kaldrek hadn't argued; it was their only real option. All she could do now was hope Alaric would find what he'd been searching for.

At last, he did. A small, nearly forgotten village was nestled in the valley below.

"That's it," Alaric said, pulling his horse to a stop and gesturing toward the distant settlement. "That's the village of Wrenford."

Evelyne followed his gaze. The village was nothing like Cindermoor. It was smaller and quieter, its streets empty save for a few wisps of smoke curling from chimneys. It looked abandoned in some parts and barely hanging on in others.

"A trade route must have once run through here," Alaric continued, turning in the saddle to face Kaldrek. "It was supposed to connect the eastern villages to Nerathar before it was abandoned. If we're seeing Wrenford now, then we're close."

Kaldrek nodded, his expression unreadable. "Then we keep moving. No stops. We can't risk being seen."

They rode on, leaving the village behind. The ground sloped downward, the terrain shifting subtly as they followed Alaric's path. Eventually, they reached an area where the land broke apart into jagged stones scattered haphazardly around a narrow stream. Some of the rocks were massive, standing like ancient sentinels, their surfaces worn smooth by time and water.

Alaric dismounted first, moving toward the largest of the stones. He traced his fingers over the surface, eyes narrowing in thought. "This is it," he murmured. "The trade route ran through here. If I'm right, the entrance should be..." He scanned the ground, then pointed toward a small opening where the stones clustered together.

Kaldrek moved forward, sniffing the air.

"You think it's underground?"

Alaric nodded. "It makes sense. If this route was forgotten, it was either swallowed by the land or hidden on purpose." He knelt near the opening, brushing aside dirt and debris until a deeper passage was revealed. "This was once an entryway."

Obren stepped forward, now in human form, his cloak draped around him as he peered into the darkness. "How far down do you think it stretches?"

"Deep enough to keep us hidden," Evelyne said, a hint of hope rising through the cloud of doubt. "But what about the horses?"

One by one, the pack began shoving the loose rocks aside, revealing a large, gaping hole in the earth. The entrance yawned wide and dark, a hidden passage swallowed by time, but as Evelyne peered inside, reality settled over her. There was no way the horses would fit.

Kaldrek stepped forward, slipping into the tunnel's shadowed mouth. He disappeared for a moment, surveying the space, before emerging again.

"We'll have to leave the horses," he said. "We can pull you both on sleds while we travel or move on foot if necessary."

"Won't that slow us down?" Evelyne asked, though she already knew there was no alternative.

But Alaric only smiled. "This route cuts straight under the mountain ridge into Nerathar. We won't have to deal with the rough terrain above. This path was hidden for a reason—because it trims our journey by days, weeks even."

Evelyne's breath caught. "What?"

Alaric's grin widened. "I told you. I memorized the maps. I figured this little secret would be more fun to reveal at the right moment."

And there it was: that telltale wink, the playful arrogance he wielded so easily when he felt particularly pleased with himself. She let out a breathless laugh and wrapped her arms around him in a brief, grateful hug.

"Well, don't celebrate just yet," he teased. "I have no idea what awaits us in that tunnel. You might end up cursing my name before this is over."

His voice was light, but he wasn't wrong. The tunnel stretched before them, dark and full of unseen dangers. But a sense of relief settled over Evelyne for the first time since leaving Cindermoor.

Alaric had been right. They had found their path.

***

At least they didn't have to worry about the weather down here. It was cold, damp, and eerily silent, but there was no rain or wind. The deeper they went, the further the temperature dropped, a creeping chill that settled in Evelyne's bones. Luckily, they had prepared well for the journey. Packs were stocked with dried meat, fruit, nuts, and dense loaves of bread, ensuring they had enough sustenance for the weeks ahead. In their shifter forms, the wolves required far less food than the humans, but even they carried provisions, knowing that hunting would be impossible in the darkness of the tunnels.

Water would have been a concern, but to their relief, a small underground stream ran along parts of the tunnel, its crystal-clear waters trickling over smooth stone. Holden had tested it first, sniffing the liquid, then tasting it cautiously.

"Fresh," he confirmed. They still rationed their filled canteens just in case the water ran dry, but it was a steady source of hydration for now.

As they ventured further along the tunnel, a sharp metallic scent hung in the air, thick and clinging to Evelyne's senses like a warning. Strangely, none of the shifters had said a word about it—only Alaric had mentioned it, which was odd, given the shifters' heightened sense of smell. Finally, unable to shake the unease, she turned to Heidara, hoping for confirmation.

"Please tell me you smell that."

Heidara frowned. "I do. It's the stench of dark magic."

"It's so strong. How does it not bother you?"

"It does, but Kaldrek thinks it means we're getting closer. Trust me, I'm doing my best not to vomit."

A shiver crawled down Evelyne's spine. Kaldrek must have been communicating with his pack mind to mind.

"Closer to what?"

"To her. To Vaelora's magic. We've caught traces of it on the Noskari before, but never this strong. Kaldrek also warned us to stay alert. He's been sensing shadows, but says they feel... different."

"And he's the only one who can sense her magic?" Evelyne asked.

"As far as we know, yes. And thank the gods he's our alpha."

When they finally stopped for the night, the pack lit small fires along the walls of rough stone and twisted roots. The space was tight but not unbearable. But it had only been a day, and Evelyne was already weary of the darkness. The wolves could see without issue in their shifted forms, but as humans, they needed the firelight to navigate.

A hush fell over the pack as the flames crackled to life, casting flickering light against the stone. What they had assumed were roots turned out to be something else entirely. Thick strands lined the walls and ceiling, red and twisting and pulsing.

Not plant roots, but veins.

"What the hell are those?" Evelyne breathed.

The pack murmured among themselves, some reaching out, running their fingers over the strange growths—

"Don't touch them!" Kaldrek's voice sliced through the air. "We don't know what they are."

The moment his voice rang out, the veins moved. Like living things, they shuddered and slithered, recoiling into the walls, sucking themselves back into the dirt and rock. They vanished in an instant, leaving no trace behind. And the smell disappeared with them.

Evelyne's skin prickled as she turned to Heidara. "The smell is gone."

Heidara's eyes widened. "That's... unsettling."

"What the fuck was that?" Holden called out to Kaldrek, but he stood rigid.

"Stay away from the walls," he ordered. "We stick to the middle."

Which meant less space and less breathing room. Everyone was pressed in closer now, forced to settle around the fire like caged animals.

After assigning scouts to keep watch, Kaldrek approached where Evelyne, Heidara, Holden, and Alaric were gathered. He and Holden would be taking the second watch, and Evelyne couldn't help but wonder if he ever slept. He was a fierce and commanding leader, yet the quiet way he cared for his pack made something stir deep in her chest—a soft, aching pull that felt dangerously close to love.

She wanted him. His touch, his kiss, but they hadn't had a moment alone to talk. What did he think about whatever this was between them, especially with the eyes of the pack always nearby? Still, the little things, like how he reached for her at night and how his body curved protectively around hers, spoke louder than words ever could.

Before she could sink too deep into thought, Kaldrek's arm slipped around her waist, grounding her. She looked up just as he leaned in and softly kissed her lips.

Her heart stuttered.

He'd done it in front of everyone. To the untrained eye, it was nothing more than a tender moment. But to the wolves, it was a declaration. A claim.

She's mine.

The unspoken words echoed through her, curling heat low in her belly, and she almost laughed at how much she loved hearing them, even just in her head. Kaldrek pulled back with a smile, gentle at first but layered with something darker. Something daring. Like he was waiting for someone to challenge it.

Someone did.

"What is going on between you two?" Alaric's tone was laced with frustration and something else.

Evelyne's stomach twisted. *Shit.*

Kaldrek, damn him, only tilted his head with mocking innocence. "Whatever do you mean?"

Alaric's jaw tightened. He wasn't joking. He'd always looked out for her, especially after stepping in to protect her from the man who had crossed a line. But this was different. This was Kaldrek, an alpha. Someone Alaric knew wouldn't hurt her. Yet the tension between them still crackled, heavy and unspoken. Evelyne felt it. She gently rested her hand on Kaldrek's knee, a quiet signal, a plea for him to ease up.

"Alaric," she began, but he cut her off.

"You two are..." He hesitated as if the words physically pained him. "Together?"

She opened her mouth, then shut it. Were they together? She turned to Kaldrek, hoping for an answer.

"Will it be a problem if we are?" Kaldrek asked, his tone threatening.

Alaric's nostrils flared. "She's not even a wolf."

Ouch. Right for the throat. But the truth of it settled like lead in her stomach. She couldn't ever be Kaldrek's wife or his mate, especially once she returned home. This type of relationship was forbidden and wrong.

"And neither are you, last I checked." Kaldrek's smirk was downright cruel.

"What does that have to do with—"

"If you're going to challenge me on the intimate details of my life, perhaps you should think about where your intentions have been lately." Kaldrek's gaze flicked toward Heidara.

Silence.

Alaric flushed red. His gaze snapped back to Evelyne.

"How *intimate*?"

Evelyne swallowed hard, feeling like her father was interrogating her. Her face heated, and her heart slammed against her ribs. Why did she even care what Alaric thought?

She inhaled and lifted her chin. "What I choose to do intimately with a man is not your concern. You and I are no longer betrothed."

"Evelyne!" Alaric shouted, stepping toward her, but Kaldrek was up instantly, a deadly snarl tearing from his throat.

Evelyne threw out a hand to stop him. "Alaric, please."

Alaric let out a bitter laugh. "Do you even realize what they'll say about you, Evelyne? That you've ruined yourself. And for what? For someone who means nothing in our world?"

Her vision burned. Kaldrek wasn't nothing. Not to her. She didn't have the words for what he meant yet, but Alaric's cruelty lit something in her. Before she could think, her fist flew, landing hard against his jaw.

Alaric stumbled back, clutching his face as stunned silence fell. The entire pack turned. Heidara's mouth hung open.

Holden let out a low whistle. "Shit. Little viper does bite."

Kaldrek grinned wickedly. But Evelyne's heart pounded. Gods, what had she done?

She stepped forward, guilt creeping in. "Alaric, I'm so sorry. I don't know why I—"

Alaric threw up a hand, stopping her. He didn't say a word. He just turned and walked off into the tunnel.

The walls seemed to press in around them, the air heavy with awkward tension. Then Heidara cleared her throat. "I'll check on him. But first, you two…" She looked between Evelyne and Kaldrek, wrinkling her nose. "I'm just glad he found out, honestly. That smell rubs off on you. No mating bond needed."

Holden and Kaldrek howled with laughter.

Evelyne groaned.

***

Once the group had settled and the stress faded, Evelyne shifted the conversation. "Are we really not going to talk about the walls being covered in veins that reeked of rot and metal? Or are we all just pretending that didn't happen?"

Holden huffed, running a hand through his hair. "Oh, we're talking about it. We're just avoiding the part where it might come back and try to strangle us in our sleep."

Kaldrek, however, remained calm. He leaned back in a relaxed position, bracing his weight on his arms, completely unbothered.

"Magic like that—tampered magic, forbidden magic—it always gives off a stench," he explained. "It's because it's unnatural. Blood magic especially. It's not meant to be tapped into; when it is, it leaves behind… things."

Evelyne narrowed her eyes. "Things?"

Kaldrek tilted his head slightly. "Growths. Creatures. Corruptions. Whatever's in this tunnel, whatever Vaelora's magic has left behind, it's probably something twisted from what it once was."

"And that doesn't scare you?" Evelyne asked.

His gaze flicked to her, the faintest ghost of a smirk appearing. "Fear doesn't help you survive."

Holden let out a dramatic sigh, pushing himself to his feet. "I don't care if the walls grow teeth as long as we're not facing the Noskari again. I'd take winding bloodroots over those bastards any day."

With that, he turned, muttering something under his breath as he went to check on the elders in the pack, leaving Evelyne and Kaldrek alone.

CHAPTER 43

A long silence settled as Evelyne watched Kaldrek, the firelight dancing across his face. She wet her lips, searching for the right words.

"You kissed me. In front of the pack."

Kaldrek didn't flinch. "Was that okay?"

"It made for a tense conversation," she admitted. "But I liked it." A soft smile formed on her face.

Something dark flickered in his eyes, and his voice dropped low with intent. "Do you want me to do it again?"

She didn't get the chance to answer. His hand moved up, fingers slipping behind her neck, guiding her face toward his with a gentle pull. The angle sent her pulse racing. His lips hovered just above hers, his breath warm against her mouth.

Heat rushed through her as she whispered, "Yes."

And then he kissed her. Deep and thorough.

She didn't care who saw. Didn't care if half the pack was watching. At that moment, all that existed was the feel of his mouth on hers, his fingers tangled in her hair, and the way he surrounded her. Gods, she was in deep. Not just falling for a man, but for a wolf. An alpha. And still, she couldn't bring herself to care. Not one bit.

Later, when the pack slept for the night, she curled into him, her cheek resting against the steady rhythm of his heart. She didn't wake when he slipped away for his watch, never felt his body shift or the chill that crept in to replace the warmth he left behind.

****

A week passed in the tunnel, the days blurring into one another, swallowed by darkness and the cool, stagnant air. The pack was growing restless, their patience fraying with every mile. Wolves were meant to run beneath the open sky, not caged underground with only flickering firelight to remind them of the world above.

The walls pulsed with their eerie web of bloodroot, the veins surfacing in places to wind through the dirt like living arteries. But they never attacked, never wrapped around their throats in the night like Holden had joked.

Evelyne noticed something one night: the bloodroots always receded when the fire was lit. She didn't believe in coincidences, not when it came to dark magic, and she made a mental note of the pattern. Whatever these roots were, they weren't just remnants of blood magic. They were alive, watching and listening.

Determined not to let the relentless travel wear her down, Evelyne rose early each morning, often before the rest of the pack, joining Heidara and a small group for training. Even in the damp, stifling dark of the tunnels, they practiced. Footwork, close combat, knife drills. Dirt and sweat clung to her skin, exhaustion a constant companion, but she didn't let it pull her under. She needed the movement, the sense of purpose. Still, she couldn't help but long for a proper bath and wondered how disheveled she must look.

Kaldrek never seemed to care.

Privacy didn't exist in the tunnels. Only fleeting seconds snatched in the dark. But Kaldrek made use of every single one. A brief kiss when backs were turned. His hand brushing her waist as they passed. A stolen moment by the fire, his lips on hers like a challenge to anyone watching. It left her yearning for more, but for now, she had to be content with these quiet, stolen touches.

Obren and his pack mostly kept to themselves, though the rift between them and the Ironwolf pack had started to ease, if only slightly. Most nights were filled with bickering over trivial things, but there had only been one real fight, and Holden and Ty had broken it up before it turned bloody. Even so, bonds began forming in the dark, fragile alliances born from shared hardship and the will to survive.

During one of these quieter nights, Evelyne learned more about Obren's fallen pack. He sat beside her, sharpening a dagger with slow, methodical strokes, his eyes distant. She didn't press him, but after a long silence, he finally spoke.

"The Noskari came at night," Obren said, his voice low, hollow. "I was... distracted. Spent the evening wrapped up with a beautiful female while my pack was being slaughtered."

He paused, the sharpening of his dagger slowing.

"I ran when I heard the screams. But it was too late." The guilt in his tone was unmistakable, heavier than anything Evelyne had heard from him before. "We weren't ready for them. The elders, our best fighters... They were gone within minutes. Some didn't even get the chance to shift."

Evelyne swallowed hard. "And the others?"

Obren exhaled and leaned his head back. "They're scattered. Dead. Or too broken to keep fighting. I didn't have a plan when I headed south—just hoped I'd find others willing to stand against her." He let out a dry laugh, shaking his head. "Stumbled into Kaldrek's pack by chance. Lucky me, I guess. Even if the bastard gets under my skin."

Evelyne's chest tightened with sympathy. "I'm sorry," she murmured.

Obren gave a half-hearted shrug, his lips quirking into something that wasn't quite a smile. "Now I need revenge."

She understood that all too well. But even as he sat beside her, revealing glimpses of his past, he never fully let the distance between them close. Not after Kaldrek had made it clear where she stood. The tension between them had shifted into something quieter, resembling friendship, but the unspoken boundary still lingered.

Alaric had kept his distance for a day after she struck him, but eventually, he came around to speak with her.

"I was an ass," he said without preamble, standing stiffly as she tied her boots by the fire.

Evelyne sighed. "Yes, you were."

"I shouldn't have said what I did."

She studied him momentarily before standing and wrapping her arms around him. He exhaled heavily, hugging her back, though he was too proud to say more.

"I'm sorry for striking you," she added against his shoulder.

Alaric pulled back, huffing a small laugh. "I think my jaw is bruised. It was a pretty impressive hit." She winced, but he smiled and added, "But I deserved it."

They settled into a comfortable silence, the tension between them finally easing. It would take time, but she knew they'd be all right. After everything, she couldn't really blame him. Their connection had always been a bit rushed and uncertain, tangled in the chaos of their journey. But now, she understood.

As they sat by the fire later that night, Alaric unrolled his map, frowning at the details that shifted across the enchanted parchment. Evelyne leaned over, watching as patches of darkness flickered across certain areas.

"What's that?" she asked, pointing to the blackened sections.

Alaric tapped the map. "This only started showing up once we entered the tunnels. It reacts to the bloodroot and shows up when it's near."

So it was true. The roots weren't natural at all. They were born of dark magic.

"Did you ever watch how it moves?" Alaric went on. "The way the roots shift? They respond to sound and light. And I don't think they're hiding." He looked up, eyes sharp. "I think they're waiting."

Evelyne swallowed hard. "For what?"

Alaric didn't answer. Neither of them wanted to find out.

***

While the pack prepared to rest for the night, Evelyne and Heidara slipped away, wandering a little farther ahead. They moved quietly, stretching their legs and speaking in low voices, hoping to shake off the weight of exhaustion that clung to them.

"I miss the open air," Heidara admitted, sighing. "Running under the stars, feeling the wind. I swear, if I have to stay underground much longer, I'll lose my mind."

Evelyne hummed and smiled. "I love running, too."

Heidara arched a brow. "You?"

She laughed softly. "I used to sneak out just to run. It was... frowned upon, of course. A noble lady isn't supposed to do such *improper* things." She shook her head. "I never fit in that world. There was always this itch, this need, to run."

Heidara studied her with something like approval before grinning. "I think you would have made a fine wolf."

Evelyne smirked, but didn't respond, her thoughts drifting instead to Aurelia. Her sister had always embodied the perfect noblewoman. In many ways, Heidara reminded her of Aurelia: blonde, beautiful, radiant. The comparison stirred an ache in her chest. She missed her family. Missed Seraphine, whose words of wisdom she had so often dismissed. She would give anything to hear them now.

Heidara opened her mouth to speak, but the ground trembled beneath them, and a sharp, metallic scent surged through the air.

Before they could react, the bloodroots erupted faster than ever, lunging from the walls, ceiling, and floor, writhing like starving serpents. The pack froze in stunned horror. Then came a deafening crack, the splintering of stone and roots, and the tunnel buckled.

In one violent moment, the earth collapsed around Evelyne and Heidara, sealing them inside.

Evelyne coughed, pushing herself up. Not hurt, but shaken. Heidara groaned beside her, clutching her head, looking dazed and weak. Kaldrek and Holden's shouts rang through the dust and rubble.

"We're okay!" Evelyne shouted back, heart pounding. "Just get us out!"

But then she saw it.

A jagged hole yawned open in the rock, revealing a deep, shadowy void. And from its depths, something began to crawl.

The creature emerged slowly, dragging itself on all fours with jerky, unnatural movements. Its body was hunched and contorted, and every limb was wrong in shape and rhythm. Blackened skin stretched over its frame like scorched leather, and long, curling claws scraped against the stone with each step. Filthy fangs jutted from its mouth, slick with something dark and wet. Though its body resembled a human's, its face was a twisted mockery—bat-like, with shriveled nostrils and gleaming, soulless eyes. It was hideous and monstrous. It should not have existed.

Its empty black eyes locked onto her.

Evelyne's breath caught in her throat. Her hands flew to the daggers at her belt, muscles tensing as instinct took over.

The creature lunged without warning.

It moved with terrifying speed, its claws outstretched. Evelyne barely managed to dive to the side, the sound of its claws raking against stone shrieking in her ears. The stench of rot and decay choked her, and its putrid breath burned hot against her skin.

But she didn't let herself freeze. Couldn't.

With a sharp inhale, she shifted her weight and sprang forward, dragging one of her daggers across the creature's exposed gut.

A bloodcurdling squeal wrenched from its throat, the sound so high and shrill it made her ears ring.

Heidara, who had been knocked down during the chaos, pushed herself upright. Her legs wobbled beneath her at first, but she steadied. With a snarl, she charged—a warrior to her core. A fighter born of discipline and survival. And together, they faced the nightmare.

The beast twisted with unnatural speed, black blood oozing from the gash in its side. It whirled toward Heidara with eyes wild and feral, then struck with its razor-sharp claws. Heidara ducked beneath the first blow. Another swipe came, and she turned away, her body moving with practiced precision.

Slash. Dodge. Counter. Her blades sliced through the air in a blur of silver and fury. But the creature didn't slow; it was relentless, driven by something sinister and vicious. In a sudden burst of motion, it lunged for Heidara, and before she could react, its fangs sank deep into her neck, drawing a sharp gasp from her lips.

A frantic scream burst from Evelyne's throat, echoing through the tunnel. On the other side of the collapsed wall, voices exploded. Kaldrek, Holden, and the others began shouting and trying to dig through the rubble. But the noise was distant, muffled by Evelyne's fear, as if the world had narrowed to nothing but the chaos before her.

Something inside her snapped. A white-hot rage surged through her, burning away the panic with a terrifying clarity. With a scream, she lunged, dagger gripped tight, and plunged it into the creature's neck—once, twice, again, and again. It convulsed violently, black blood splattering the stone, but still, she didn't stop.

Heidara lay unmoving, and Evelyne couldn't think, couldn't breathe. She just kept striking, blood coating her arms, her hands slick and trembling, until the beast finally crumpled, lifeless at her feet.

She stood over the creature, chest rising and falling, as the world slowly came back into focus. The rush of blood in her ears slipped away, replaced by the urgent sound of her name being called.

"Evelyne!" Kaldrek shouted frantically. "Can you hear me?"

"Yes," she whispered, breathless, then louder, "Yes, but—"

Her heart plummeted as her gaze landed on Heidara's limp body.

No, no, no—

Evelyne tore at her shirt, pressing the fabric hard against Heidara's throat, desperate to stop the bleeding. To keep her here. Wolves healed faster than humans, but even her magic couldn't mend the wound fast enough.

A low snarl echoed through the tunnel.

Evelyne's head snapped up just in time for her to see another demon crawl from the hole in the rock.

"Kaldrek! There's another one!" she shouted, rising to her feet with measured movements, careful not to draw its gaze too soon.

"You have to hold it off, Evelyne!"

She had no other choice. Gripping her daggers, she planted her feet, raised her arms, and focused.

Breathe. Watch. Move fast.

Evelyne braced herself. The creature lunged first, claws slashing through the air, but she was faster. She pivoted to the side and struck, her dagger slicing across its chest in a clean arc. The wound barely slowed it.

"That's it," Kaldrek's voice rang out from behind the rubble. "Keep moving!"

The beast charged again, and Evelyne ducked low, driving her blade toward its ribs. A brutal kick met her stomach and sent her crashing to the ground, the breath ripped from her lungs.

"No, no. Get up," she whispered to herself, wheezing.

"You've got this," Kaldrek called again.

"Remember to breathe. Assess, then react."

She exhaled, and rolled just as claws tore into the dirt where her head had been. She forced herself upright. Then came a hot flash of pain across her cheek as the creature's claw raked her face. She hissed loudly as blood trickled down her skin, but she got back into a defensive stance.

"You're all right. Pain means you're alive," Kaldrek shouted. "Eyes up, Evelyne."

She could just make out the frantic scrape of claws against stone as the wolves slashed through the rubble. Above it all, Kaldrek's voice cut through, cursing and shouting for them to move faster.

The creature paused, its gaze drawn to the blood on her cheek. The moment passed in a blink before it lunged straight at her. Evelyne screamed as she drove her dagger upward, the blade sinking deep into its abdomen. But the force of its body crashed into hers, slamming her to the ground. Her limbs trembled under its weight, every muscle straining as its rancid breath burned against her throat, fangs poised just inches from her skin.

"Don't give it a chance," Kaldrek growled from the other side. "Do not give up!"

Her vision swam, limbs shaking with effort, but his voice anchored her. It pulled her back to every morning on the training grounds, every bruise and blister earned beneath his unyielding guidance. She remembered the sting of failure, the heat of frustration, the helplessness she'd once felt within another man's grasp. She had trained to take that power back. *He* had prepared her for this very moment.

Gritting her teeth, Evelyne drove the blade deeper.

The wall trapping her and Heidara shattered as stone exploded outward, and Kaldrek charged through, a storm of fury made flesh. With a snarl, he seized the creature and tore it off her with his bare hands, rage pouring from him in raw, lethal waves. He didn't shift. He didn't need to.

He tore into the creature with relentless savagery, ripping and breaking its limbs with brutal force. It screamed and writhed beneath him, but he didn't stop. Not even when it stopped fighting, or when its body lay twitching in the dirt. Evelyne had never seen fury like this. This wasn't just anger; it was something darker, a man completely unhinged.

Crouching low, he gripped his dagger and slit the creature's throat before tearing its head clean from its body. Black blood splattered across his face, leaving him looking wild.

Panting, he turned to her. "You're bleeding." His voice shook with urgency as he scanned her from head to toe, desperate to find the source. And that was when she understood: it wasn't just anger that pushed him past the edge. It was fear... for her. Because that thing had laid its hands on her, pinned her, and hurt her. And that was enough to unmake him.

Evelyne reached out and gently touched his face, and he leaned into her palm and let out a long exhale. Her gaze shifted down the tunnel, where Holden knelt with Heidara in his arms, pressing against the wound as she clung to breath.

Alaric burst through the rubble, eyes wide with panic as he looked between Evelyne and Heidara, clearly torn between two people he cared for and unsure who needed him more.

"Holy hells," he breathed. "What do I do?" He looked to Evelyne, who nodded over to Heidara. A silent command to help her friend, and he didn't hesitate.

"Kaldrek, what was that?" Evelyne asked quietly.

His eyes began to warm to dark brown as he searched her face. "I don't know. I've never seen something like that. It must have emerged from the bloodroot veins, or..." He shook his head. "I honestly don't know, but it's nothing natural. I can feel it. Those creatures were derived from blood magic and have probably been living within this tunnel for years. Growing. Feeding off of anything that dares enter this path."

He returned to his alpha stance.

"We need to keep moving. We pack up now. And Holden?" Holden turned to look at Kaldrek, still holding his sister. "Get her to Lorena."

Holden nodded and swiftly took off in search of the healer.

When the tunnel was finally cleared and declared safe, Kaldrek returned to Evelyne's side, lowering himself beside her and pressing his forehead softly to hers. She'd never seen him so shaken.

"I'm fine," she whispered.

His hands framed her face. "I thought I was going to lose you. I tried, but I couldn't get to you fast enough." He pulled her into a fierce kiss. When he finally broke away, his eyes searched hers, full of awe and something deeper.

"You're so strong. Do you even realize that?"

A rush of pride filled her as Kaldrek gathered her into his arms. No one had ever truly believed she could take care of herself. But he was looking at her like he did. Like he knew she could handle anything.

She smiled softly, rested her head against his chest, and murmured, "Thank you."

CHAPTER 44

They moved fast.

Time blurred as Alaric sat strapped into the wooden sled, Evelyne beside him, pulled by the pack in their relentless push forward. At first, it had been embarrassing to be hauled like baggage, but after the attack, after watching those things emerge from the walls, he didn't care. He just wanted to get the hell out of that tunnel.

The cold bit into him more fiercely now, despite summer having begun. Trapped underground, he had lost all sense of time. He never knew how suffocating it would feel, how soul-draining it was to be swallowed by endless dark, entombed in an abandoned trade route infested with creatures born of blood magic. Creatures that wanted to kill them.

Or worse, *consume* them.

He wondered what awaited them at the end of the tunnel. Were they marching toward their deaths? Toward an army of Noskari? What if Cillian wasn't even alive anymore? The thought made his stomach twist. Evelyne had already lost her father, and if she lost her brother too... he wasn't sure how she'd survive it. Yet she pressed on and never complained.

He had never imagined a lady of Caltheris could withstand the wild, let alone go without silk dresses, painted lips, and warm baths. But Evelyne was still here, still fighting, still pushing through. And he found himself drawing strength from her.

Why hadn't *he* turned back yet?

He'd wanted to. So many times. But he couldn't. Not after what he'd seen. Not after watching Lord Duskwood—the closest friend his father had ever had—murdered in cold blood. That alone should have been enough reason to stay and fight, but deep down, he knew the truth. He stayed for Evelyne, even if they weren't, and would likely never be, lovers. She was his friend.

But there was another reason, too, one he had been trying to ignore since she first looked his way.

Heidara.

Alaric caught himself watching her every time she walked by. She wasn't soft or reserved like the noblewomen he'd grown up around. She was fierce, a storm wrapped in grace and grit. And every time her green eyes met his, it stole the breath right out of his chest.

The night he left in a surge of anger after Evelyne struck him, it was Heidara who found him. He hadn't wanted company or conversation, but she didn't press him. She sat beside him silently in the dim light of the torches, tipped her head back, and breathed a long, steady sigh.

"When I was sixteen," she finally said, her voice quiet, "I fell for a wolf from another pack."

Alaric frowned but said nothing, just listened.

"He had just turned eighteen," she continued, "and he was... perfect. Strong. Dark-haired. Probably would have become an alpha one day. He made my heart race just by looking at me." She smiled at the memory, but it was tinged with something sad. "But two days after I spent a night with him..." She paused, eyes dropping to the ground. "He said he'd found his mate and that our... relationship was over. It's rare for a wolf to meet their mate that soon, but he didn't give me the chance to question it. He just left."

Alaric inhaled sharply. "Just like that?"

She nodded. "I had hoped, prayed, that I would feel the bond with him when I came of age, but there wasn't even a chance for that. Not when I was still only sixteen and he was already mated." She exhaled. "A year later, his entire pack disappeared. Gone. No one knows what happened to them."

Alaric watched her carefully. "That's when you moved on?"

Heidara turned to face him, studying him before finally smiling softly. "It's never easy to let go of someone you once loved. But it's the only way you can truly live. And I like to think that one day, I'll find my mate and finally feel whole."

Then it clicked. She wasn't just sharing a memory; she was letting him see her pain so he could make sense of his own.

Because Alaric had loved Evelyne once. Or something very close to it. And watching her with Kaldrek had torn something open inside him. He'd felt responsible for protecting her for so long, especially after everything she'd endured. But Kaldrek... Kaldrek could protect her in ways Alaric never could.

That truth hit him hard, and in that moment, the anger he'd held on to for days dissolved, replaced by something he hadn't anticipated: peace.

He had been wrong. The noble titles, the rules of courtship, and the hierarchy meant nothing now. These people weren't beneath him. They were warriors. They were family.

He exhaled, his voice quiet as he said, "I'm sorry if I offended you."

Heidara's expression softened as she tilted her head. "We come from different worlds, Alaric. I understand that. But in mine, women aren't seen as lesser for choosing to love someone. We're equals. And while I know you meant no harm, Evelyne deserves to hear your apology directly."

A reluctant smile tugged at his lips. "Yeah. I'll think about it."

She grinned. "That's a start."

And gods, that smile. It did something to him; stirred something profound and unruly he hadn't expected.

He swallowed hard. "Thank you."

"For what?"

His gaze dropped to her fingers, lightly tracing idle circles in the dirt. "For being here. For me."

She paused, then reached over, her hand brushing his. "Anytime."

That was when the thought crept in.

He wasn't just grateful for her presence. He wanted her.

The way her touch lingered. The way his body reacted to something as simple as her fingertips grazing his skin. He tried to shake it, to shove it down, but the warmth that flooded his chest and burned low in his abdomen betrayed him.

Alaric shot to his feet, clearing his throat as he shoved the thought away. What the hell was she doing to him?

Heidara raised an amused brow, clearly noticing the change in him. She stood. "We should get some sleep," she said, tossing the words over her shoulder as she turned to walk away.

Alaric didn't respond, couldn't. He watched the sway of her hips, the way her leather clung to every curve, and desire clawed at him.

Fuck.

***

According to the map, they were now only days away from reaching the end of the route, which would lead them just past the northern mountain range and into the frozen lands of Nerathar—Vaelora's domain.

They were likely deep beneath the mountains, the temperature dropping fast, the cold seeping into their bones. The metallic scent that once came and went now hung heavy in the air, a sign they weren't alone. When they stopped to rest, the pack would need to be ready. Another attack felt inevitable, especially if those grotesque bloodroot golems lurked in the shadows. Alaric never wanted to see one again, but there was no escaping them while in the tunnel.

Fortunately, they'd only had one other encounter since the tunnel collapse. They had passed a narrow fissure in the wall, likely caused by the crushing pressure of the mountain above, when one of the dark, bat-like creatures had clawed its way out, all fangs and death and bloodroot rot, but Kaldrek had brought it down in a single ruthless strike.

He kept the scouts on high alert, never letting anyone stray too far in case the tunnels collapsed again. Especially Evelyne. Though Kaldrek respected her strength and let her hold her own in battle, he was fiercely protective of her. And for that, Alaric couldn't fault him.

So they moved. Traveled, ate, slept, kept going, and never stopped for long, always wary of the shadows watching them from the walls.

***

The tunnel's exit loomed ahead like a gaping maw opening into the frigid night. A blast of icy wind swept through, carrying the scent of snow and something darker. Evelyne shivered, but not from the cold.

They had finally reached the brutal northern lands of Nerathar. As they stepped out of the tunnel, the landscape stretched before them, while the jagged peaks of the northern mountains rose behind, their snow-laden slopes plunging into an expanse of dense, skeletal forest. The land was eerily silent, and the sky overhead was a deep, inky black. One of the elders had mentioned it was a full moon tonight, but no one in the pack would be celebrating, especially with the looming threat of blood magic creatures possibly stalking the shadows.

Tonight's moon wasn't just full. It was a blood moon.

Holden had suggested waiting until morning to explore the land ahead, but they couldn't afford to waste another minute. Every second Cillian remained under Vaelora's control brought him closer to becoming something unrecognizable. Maybe he already was, but Evelyne refused to believe that. She had to hold on to hope. Without it, none of this mattered. Steeling herself, she pushed to the front of the pack, determined to hear the next steps.

Kaldrek's eyes scanned the terrain ahead. "Holden, Ty, Obren, come with me," he commanded. "We're going to scout ahead."

"No," Evelyne interrupted, stepping forward, fists clenched. "You are not leaving me behind."

Kaldrek turned to her. "Evelyne, we don't know what's out there. This isn't a debate."

"I don't care," she snapped. "I didn't come all this way to be left behind like I'm helpless. My brother is out there." She jabbed a finger toward the dark line of trees. "He's the only reason I'm here. I have to find him. I'm going with you."

Evelyne watched as Kaldrek let out a slow breath, jaw tight with frustration. This wasn't a battle he'd win. Not with everything she'd endured to get here, not when her entire purpose was finding Cillian. She'd risked too much to be turned away now, and denying her would only drive a wedge between them.

His eyes shifted to Alaric, who stood beside her, arms crossed and just as resolute. "Fine," Kaldrek said at last. "But Heidara stays with Nathan.

The pack still needs someone watching over them. We'll have them move back into the tunnel while we look around."

Evelyne swallowed her surge of triumph as nerves took hold, tightening in her chest while they crossed into Nerathar. The scouting party departed shortly after rallying the pack and finalizing the plan. The remaining Glaciermaw wolves were uneasy, but Obren volunteered to go alone, unwilling to risk more lives. Meanwhile, Heidara discreetly adjusted the loop on Evelyne's dagger belt, securing the flintlock pistol behind her back and beneath her cloak.

The selected group moved carefully through the snow-covered forest, the silence around them unsettling. Towering trees loomed overhead, their bare branches clawing at the black sky. Wind hissed through the trunks, carrying strange, whispering echoes. Evelyne tightened her cloak and focused on the steady crunch of snow beneath their boots, every step drawing them deeper into the unknown.

"Can we take a moment to think this through?" Alaric murmured, unfolding his map. The faint moonlight offered just enough glow to make out the markings as he traced a path with his gloved finger. "If I had to guess, Vaelora's settled somewhere northwest, just past the iced river. It's the only area that makes sense for a stronghold, since it's far enough from open ground and close enough to the forest's edge. There's a pass here"—he pointed—"that could keep us out of sight. It's our best shot at getting close without being seen. But pushing ahead might not be the wisest move at this hour. And since this area seems clear at the moment, I say we wait for daylight to explore the rest."

Kaldrek nodded, his eyes scanning the treeline. "Then we head back, rest, and decide who scouts with us at first light."

Evelyne wanted to object, but Kaldrek's decision was sound. Venturing into unknown lands crawling with blood-seeking demons, without the safety of daylight, would be sheer madness.

They turned and began retracing their steps through the frozen woods. Evelyne walked beside Kaldrek, her shoulder brushing his arm. She spoke softly, careful not to disturb the hush of the forest. "Tell me about your father. You said he was once the alpha?"

Kaldrek's steps faltered slightly before he caught himself. "He was... a good man," he said at last, his voice almost reverent. "He pushed me hard, as any alpha would his heir, but never without reason. He was fierce, the strongest warrior I had ever known. I always thought he—" He cut himself off, shaking his head. "Evelyne, there's something I need to tell—"

Before Kaldrek could finish, a gust of wind tore through the trees, and he stilled.

"What is it?" Evelyne asked.

Kaldrek didn't answer. Instead, his head snapped toward Alaric, who was already scanning the map, brows furrowed. The air turned cold without warning, and with it came a dreadful hush as the forest seemed to freeze in place. Evelyne's pulse quickened as Kaldrek's arm wrapped tightly around her waist, pulling her close. Then she saw it: black mist creeping between the trees, its tendrils slithering and curling like sentient shadows.

No, no, no.

It darted fast and low, moving over the snow with deathly purpose. The mist thickened into dark shapes, solidifying until monstrous figures stepped from the fog.

Noskari. Dozens of them.

Their forms flickered between flesh and smoke, their eyes gleaming like coals, teeth bared in jagged rows that caught the moonlight.

Kaldrek was the first to move. "Run!" he shouted, already shifting as the word tore from his throat. The pack scattered into motion, but the Noskari were faster as they descended like a wave. There was no escape.

Evelyne barely had time to unsheathe her daggers before being thrown to the ground, her body slamming against the snow and dirt. Sharp claws tore at her cloak. Pain exploded across her ribs as something heavy landed on top of her, pinning her down. A gnarled hand fisted in her hair, yanking her head back.

Fury surged through her veins as she twisted the wrist with the most freedom. She had to act. She hadn't come this far to be drained by a Noskari. With a desperate thrash of her left arm to draw its attention, she yanked her right hand free and drove her dagger into its side. The creature recoiled just long enough for her to suck in a deep breath and stumble backward, ribs screaming with pain.

Kaldrek let out a furious roar and launched into the chaos, claws raking through the Noskari. Holden and Ty shifted seconds later, joining the fight with unrelenting force, while Obren tore through the creatures savagely. But for every one they brought down, more surged from the mist. It was endless. And Alaric—where was he?

Her plan to find him shattered the moment a powerful hand closed around her throat and hoisted her off the ground. Evelyne gasped, a cry tearing from her lips as her vision blurred, dark spots dancing across her sight. Through the haze, she caught a glimpse of Kaldrek charging toward her, but a massive blow struck him mid-lunge, hurling him backward. He hit a tree with a sickening crack and crumpled to the ground.

"NO!" she choked out, thrashing, clawing, but the world was spinning, tilting.

The last thing she felt was the cold, and the sensation of being carried, fast, as if by the wind itself. And then—darkness.

Chapter 45

Cold stone. Iron chains. The stench of blood.

Evelyne stirred, her body screaming in protest as consciousness dragged her back into the nightmare. Her arms were wrenched above her head, shackled to a damp cavern wall, her wrists raw and throbbing. A slow, sickening drip echoed in the silence: the steady trickle of water seeping through cracks in the stone.

She forced her eyes open, blinking against the flickering torchlight.

They were all there.

Kaldrek, bloodied and bound in iron, his chest bare, deep gashes streaking across his skin. Holden, Obren, and Ty, shirtless as well, wore only thin cloths tied around their waists—likely thrown on them by their captors after forcing them back into their human forms. Alaric sat slumped forward, barely moving, blood dripping sluggishly from a gash at his temple. A surge of rage and fear crashed through her, mingling with the stabbing ache in her ribs.

Out of the corner of her eye, she caught movement near the entrance of the cavern. A Noskari stood there, its jagged teeth bared in a wicked, unsettling grin. The firelight cast eerie shadows over its gray skin, illuminating the deep, raised scar on its forearm. The mark she had seen before. *The Sigil of the Lost.* Burned into its flesh like a brand, a permanent reminder of Vaelora's twisted claim on those she had turned. Evelyne swallowed hard, forcing herself to keep breathing and stay alert.

Footsteps echoed, and the very air seemed to shift as a woman entered.

She was breathtakingly beautiful, radiating a commanding presence, with not a trace of fear on her face—even surrounded by bloodthirsty creatures. Evelyne knew exactly who she was. The realization hit like ice in her veins, twisting her stomach with a sickening mix of dread and disbelief, every instinct in her body screaming in warning.

Vaelora.

She moved slowly into the chamber, her silver eyes glinting with dark amusement as they swept over each prisoner. Every second of silence pressed like a knife's edge against Evelyne. Yet to her surprise, Vaelora barely looked at her. After all the warnings, all the threats, she had expected to be the focus.

But Vaelora's gaze locked onto Kaldrek instead.

"I'm so glad we can finally meet, Kaldrek," she drawled softly. "And it seems you brought the girl right to me, just as I'd hoped."

Evelyne's blood ran cold.

Kaldrek's snarl tore through the silence, but Vaelora only smiled, tilting her head. "Is that any way to greet me, *son*?"

The word hit like a punch to the chest.

Son?

Evelyne couldn't move. Couldn't breathe. Her heart slammed against her ribs as she looked to Kaldrek, but it was Holden's expression that shattered her. He wasn't surprised. He had known.

Her throat tightened with betrayal, confusion clawing at her thoughts. Had Kaldrek lied to her? Had he led her into Vaelora's hands on purpose? Had she been nothing but a pawn in something far darker than she'd ever imagined?

Alaric stared at Kaldrek in stunned disbelief, his mouth slightly open. Ty and Obren stood frozen, tension radiating off them, their expressions tight with shock. But Kaldrek... He didn't react with anger or denial. He turned to Evelyne, his eyes full of raw guilt. And in that instant, she knew it was true.

She slowly shook her head, collapsing under the weight of heartbreak. Kaldrek looked away, shame etched into every line of his body. Then he lifted his chin and turned to face Vaelora.

"I'm not your son," he rasped.

Vaelora laughed, the sound curling through the chamber like smoke. "Oh, but you are, Kaldrek," she purred. Her eyes swept across the room once more, daring anyone to argue. "You mean to tell me no one's ever noticed the signs? The white fur of your wolf? Its black, silver-rimmed eyes, when all others glow red? Your ability to sense my magic? Surely someone wondered where that gift came from. But this one," she added, her voice almost sweet as she nodded toward Holden, "this handsome one—he knew, didn't he?"

Kaldrek remained still, clearly seething beneath the surface. His silence said more than any words could.

Vaelora's eyes sparkled with glee. "He must be important to you, if you trusted him with such a truth."

The fury radiating from Kaldrek was unmistakable—Evelyne could feel it rolling off him in heavy waves. Or maybe it was her own anger rising, burning hot at the thought that Holden, her friend, had known and, like Kaldrek, said nothing.

Vaelora's gaze shifted back to Evelyne, her smile curdling into something more sinister as she crouched down.

Without warning, she struck. Her hand lashed out, sharp nails slashing across Evelyne's cheek.

"This little bitch just can't help sticking her nose where it doesn't belong, can she?"

Pain seared through Evelyne's face as warm blood filled her mouth. But she didn't cry out. Wouldn't give her that satisfaction.

A feral growl erupted across the dungeon as Kaldrek exploded in a violent thrash against his restraints, his body trembling with the effort to hold back the shift. Wild rage poured off him, but Vaelora only smiled with delight.

"Oh? Did I touch something precious?" She traced a delicate finger along the fresh wound on Evelyne's cheek, smearing the blood. "I guess killing your father wasn't enough of a message, was it, *girl*?"

Evelyne's heart pounded so hard she swore it might shatter. Then her eyes landed on a figure standing just inside the doorway.

Cillian.

He was alive.

Relief surged through her, and a quiet sob slipped past her lips before she could stop it. He was here—but was any part of her brother still in there? Dread yanked at her stomach as she noticed his pale gray complexion and distant eyes.

Vaelora's voice broke through the fog of emotion. "Perhaps my son couldn't bring himself to let you go," she said, turning to Kaldrek. "Tell me, do you love her?"

Evelyne's eyes snapped to Kaldrek, her pulse roaring in her ears. But he didn't answer. He only narrowed his eyes at Vaelora and kept his chin up.

"I guess not as much as your handsome friend here. Because the look on her face tells me you withheld the truth from her." She clicked her tongue and shook her head. "Now now, Kaldrek, lying is never the way to a woman's heart."

Kaldrek clenched his jaw tightly. Evelyne could tell he was fighting back his words and instincts.

Vaelora laughed. "What a lovely family reunion. Though I'm sure my beloved Cillian couldn't care less if I ripped his dear sister's head from her shoulders."

Evelyne felt the blood drain from her features. Vaelora floated over to Cillian and ran a soft, possessive hand along his face. Black, vacant eyes met hers.

"Would you, my love?" Vaelora purred, her voice laced with poison. To Evelyne's horror, she leaned in and pressed a kiss to Cillian's neck.

Just beneath the edge of his tunic, where the fabric gaped, Evelyne caught sight of a sigil burned into his skin. Only a glimpse, but it was enough. That was the moment true fear took hold. What had she done to him?

Vaelora turned to her thralls. "Shall we continue this discussion some-where... cleaner?" Her voice was playful, as if this were all a game. Without waiting for a response, she turned and began her ascent from the dungeon, her movements unhurried. Cillian followed without question, trailing behind her like a puppet on invisible strings. He never once looked toward Evelyne.

CHAPTER 46

The throne room was a cathedral of shadows. Thick mist slithered along the black marble floors, swallowing the light of the torches lining the walls. The air was eerily cold, like the nights when Noskari were nearby, but Vaelora sat atop her obsidian throne as though she were carved from the darkness itself.

She wore a skin-tight black gown, sleeveless, plunging low enough to leave little to the imagination. She was an exquisite creature of death and seduction, and her eyes gleamed with satisfaction as she regarded her prisoners, now forced to their knees before her dais.

Vaelora pointed lazily at Evelyne. "That one looks far too relaxed. Tighten her chains—I want to hear her cry."

"Argh!" Evelyne gasped as the Noskari wrenched her arms back, the iron biting into her skin.

Vaelora's smile curved sharper. "More. Stretch her until she remembers what helplessness feels like."

Evelyne clenched her jaw, her arms screaming with pain as she fought against the agony.

"Enough!" Kaldrek snarled.

Vaelora sighed, the sound edged with false boredom. "Fine, fine. Are you always this stiff?" She gave a careless flick of her hand, a mocking dismissal, before clearing her throat. "Before we make our little introductions, I believe it's time you finally heard my story." Her gaze slid to

Kaldrek, cruel amusement flickering in her eyes. "Since my darling son couldn't be bothered to share even a single detail."

Evelyne's fingers curled into fists. The truth had splintered something deep inside her. Kaldrek was Vaelora's son. The witch who infected her brother's mind and murdered her father was his *mother*. It couldn't be real. Yet she couldn't deny it now. He had always stood apart from the rest of the pack, and it wasn't just because he was an alpha. It was because witch blood ran through his veins.

Kaldrek exhaled sharply, his voice rough. "We all know what you are. But if you want to gloat, just get on with it."

Vaelora's smirk deepened. "Oh, Kaldrek, still so bitter. But you should know by now that I love to take my time. Just as I instructed my Noskari to do when they drained every last drop from your *mother*."

Evelyne remembered what Kaldrek had told her about his parents—about the woman who had raised him, his true mother in every way that mattered. And even if the details blurred now, tangled between truth and secrecy, one thing was sure: he had loved them deeply. And they had been murdered by Vaelora. That kind of loss didn't fade; it festered, and in Kaldrek, it had turned into something fierce and dangerous. A part of her felt a flicker of sympathy for him... but then she remembered the lies, the possibility that he had manipulated her into walking straight into Vaelora's hands.

Still, one look at him now told her more than any words could. His face was tight with rage, his chest heaving, every muscle in his body straining against the chains like he could break them through sheer fury. He was a storm barely held back.

Across from him, Vaelora remained perfectly calm, tapping her fingers against the armrest of her throne, eyes glittering as she leaned forward, watching him unravel. "I think it's time you all understand who I truly am. What I have sacrificed and what has been stolen from me."

She stood, stepping down from the dais, her gown whispering against the floor.

"My sister, Kaya, and I were born beneath a rare alignment of stars. Twins are an anomaly among witches, and together we were powerful enough to rival the gods. Our bond seemed unbreakable, or so I believed."

Evelyne's lips parted, her mind racing to absorb every word. If she could keep Vaelora talking long enough, maybe—just maybe—Cillian would see or hear something familiar. Something that might help him remember who he was. That his sister was right in front of him.

Vaelora let out a wistful sigh. "We were inseparable as children, my sister and I. We chased knowledge together, tested the boundaries of our magic. Then we discovered a forbidden tome that described how to siphon power from the living." Her lips curled into a pleased smile. "We drained so many. Shifters, seers, witches. Their power became ours."

"You killed them," Evelyne said coldly, the accusation sharp.

Vaelora's glance flicked to her. "You say that like it's unnatural. But tell me, is it unnatural for a wolf to kill its prey?" She laughed softly, mockingly. "We became something greater. And for a time, Kaya agreed." Her expression darkened, lips curling with disdain. "Until he came along."

"Who?" Evelyne asked, keeping her tone neutral while her thoughts still raced.

"Darius," Vaelora spat. "A wolf shifter. Powerful, arrogant. Kaya fell in love with him like some naive little girl. He made her weak. And that weakness was her undoing."

"She turned against you," Evelyne said, pushing the conversation for-ward, hoping it would buy more time; enough to figure out how to get Cillian away from Vaelora's grip.

"She betrayed me. Darius filled her head with nonsense and told her blood magic was cruel and wrong. That she could never be my equal if she continued down our path. He poisoned her against me. So I took something from him."

Evelyne swallowed. "You took something?"

"Oh, I did far more than that." Her voice oozed satisfaction as she let the words hang in the air. "I broke him. Twisted his loyalty until it bent to me. It's fascinating how quickly a man folds once the right elixir slips into his wine." She examined her nails with casual elegance. "And then I took what I needed. Lured him to my bed, conceived a child that would be mine and mine alone. Tethered him to me in a way he could never undo."

A heavy silence followed, crashing down like a wave. Evelyne couldn't stop the bile rising in her throat as she turned and locked eyes with Kaldrek. His expression was still, but there was something haunted in the way he held himself.

Alaric exhaled sharply. "You're lying."

Vaelora chuckled. "Am I? Poor Darius could never forgive himself for what he'd done. When Kaya found out, when she tried to kill me for it, she failed to realize I had already completed the blood magic ritual, and I only needed her death to make it permanent."

Evelyne's heart pounded wildly. "You killed your own sister?"

"Yes, but I didn't stop there." Vaelora's smile widened. "Darius real-ized too late what had happened. He fell into despair, and he took his own life after I killed Kaya. It was quite the tragedy."

Kaldrek drew in a quick breath, his first honest reaction since the nightmare of this conversation began.

"And with their blood spilled, I ascended. Blood magic was finally mine."

What kind of monster was this woman? Not only had she drained other magical beings to fuel her power, but she had also drugged her sister's lover to lure him into her bed, to get back at her sister, to conceive a child, and then slaughtered her own twin as a sacrifice to unlock blood magic. How was Kaldrek processing this? How could he endure hearing that *this* was the woman who birthed him, not out of love, but as a tool? A puppet crafted from her bloodline to replace the sister who had betrayed her.

"Twenty-five years ago, I became something more than a witch. I became eternal. And a mother." Her smile faltered for a moment. "Until my child was stolen from me as I lay recovering on the birthing bed. And somehow, none of my servants could tell me who had done it." Her voice took on a chilling edge. "That was the day I began building my army to hunt for my son and destroy those who stole him from me."

She paused, as if savoring the memory.

"Such a shame I wiped out Darius' entire Rimeclaw pack. I was so certain they were the ones who took you," she said, her dark eyes settling on Kaldrek. "As it turns out, the true thieves were the Ironwolf pack—Darius' most trusted allies. I should have seen it, but I'll blame my own hysteria for clouding my judgment."

Her fingers curled tightly around the arms of her throne, knuckles pale.

"We celebrated the night your *parents* died," she said with a chilling smile. "My Noskari and I threw such a lovely party."

Kaldrek spat at her feet, and her expression twisted, not in rage but disappointment.

"A shame the alpha mark chose you, Kaldrek. You and I could have ruled this world together."

Evelyne's chest tightened. What would he have become if the Ironwolf pack hadn't taken him from this witch? Certainly not the alpha beside her now. Not the man she cared for. He would have been something else. Something twisted; something she might have had to destroy.

She couldn't linger on that thought. Evelyne's voice trembled as she pushed forward, needing to shift the conversation. "And what does any of this have to do with my brother? With the prophecy?"

Vaelora grinned. "Ah, the prophecy. A desperate attempt to stop me. But tell me, Lady Evelyne... how does one destroy a prophecy?"

"You can't."

"Precisely." Vaelora exhaled, as if the subject bored her. "A prophecy cannot be destroyed, only diverted. And I knew the witches of Velenshire would have taken precautions to keep it from unfolding. So I waited. I searched for years, looking for any clue as to what—or rather, who—had become the vessel for the prophecy."

Her gaze slid to Cillian.

"Then I found him. The highborn son of Lord Aron Duskwood. An innocent boy, hidden behind nobility and human frailty. A child bound to a prophecy no one understood—not even I. The Great Rite did its job well, erasing the Duskwood name from every mind. But spells like that don't stay hidden forever. Not with the kind of power I wield now. Even this one, buried deep, eventually began to unravel beneath my touch."

Vaelora began to circle him, her voice laced with dark amusement.

"He was just a boy when I first caught his scent. It was faint and fragmented, but still threaded with that bloodline. I couldn't place it then, but I knew something ancient stirred beneath the surface. So I waited. Watched. Let him grow into the brilliance of his mind until he began to uncover the truth on his own. I only had to offer the slightest nudge."

She stopped beside him, fingers brushing along his jaw with unsettling tenderness.

"That's when I knew. All those years of suspicion had finally led me here. To him. The next male heir of the Duskwood bloodline. The soul fated to carry the light that could destroy me. The prophecy forged at the Solwyn Tree by the witches of Hallowell and the Duskwoods—once the most powerful shifter bloodline in the south. And now, my greatest threat."

Her smile deepened, cold and triumphant.

"So I didn't kill him," she whispered. "I made him love me."

Cillian smiled faintly at Vaelora's words, and it twisted something deep in Evelyne's gut.

"A shifter bloodline?" Evelyne whispered under her breath.

Vaelora's eyes shifted to her.

"Oh? He didn't mention that part either?" she asked, feigning surprise as her brows lifted.

"That he could sense the dormant magic in you? Smell it in your blood—just as I did?" Her gaze slid to Kaldrek then, and she clicked her tongue. "Tsk. Honestly, Kaldrek. Did you truly think deceit would serve you well?"

Evelyne turned toward him where they knelt, and the guilt in his expression hollowed something in her. "Tell me," she said, her voice barely holding together.

He met her eyes. "Evelyne—"

"*Tell me.*"

Kaldrek's eyes shut tight, as though the words cut too deep. "You bear the blood of a wolf lineage," he whispered.

Silence slammed into her like a blow. Her lips parted, but no sound came.

"What?" Alaric's voice broke the stillness. "How could you possibly know that?"

"Because I'm descended not just from wolves, but from witches. What Vaelora said... It's true." Kaldrek exhaled slowly and looked to Evelyne. "I sensed it once. Faintly. That day you... slapped me in your tent." A wry smile tugged at the corner of his mouth, then faded.

"I thought I imagined it. Maybe I didn't want to believe it. But as we grew closer—more connected—it became impossible to ignore. The scent was there." Kaldrek swallowed. "That's when I knew. You were one of us. And I think... I think that's why I was so drawn to you, Evelyne. Because something inside me already recognized you, even if I was too much of a coward to face it."

He shook his head.

"I wanted to tell you. Gods, I did. But everything was happening so fast, and there was never the right moment, and I—" His voice faltered, cracking under the weight of the truth. "Fuck." His head dropped, his shoulders tight with regret.

Evelyne's breath came too fast, too shallow. The truth kept coming, each word a blade carving deeper. That day in the tent, when she'd recoiled in humiliation, thinking he had sniffed her like an animal, he'd *known.*

Another secret. Another betrayal. Something inside her began to fracture. Questions burned through her: about the prophecy, her lineage, and everything she thought she knew. But one question roared louder than the rest.

She looked at Vaelora. "You diverted the prophecy. You infected his mind with some type of dark parasitic demon, just to make him love you. Why?"

"As I told you, a prophecy cannot be destroyed. Had I killed him, another heir would have risen in time. But love?" Vaelora tilted her head. "Love is a leash stronger than death. So I made him mine. My equal. My lover."

"But when he dies, won't the prophecy pass to the next heir?" Alaric asked.

"Of course," Vaelora murmured, gliding down the dais like a shadow made flesh. "Which is why it's so wonderfully convenient that my son placed Evelyne right into my hands." Her smile deepened. "Funny. I hadn't considered it until my scouts reported she was still traveling with the wolves, even after I'd sent a very clear warning. I'll admit, for a moment, I feared she might spoil my fun. But then I realized she could be the key to ending the prophecy entirely." Her black eyes glistened as she looked down at Evelyne. "Because you, my dear, will be his sacrifice. Cillian's final offering so that I may awaken the blood magic once more, seize greater power, and grant my beloved an eternal life... by my side."

"You will not touch her, Vaelora," Kaldrek growled.

Evelyne had never felt so utterly powerless, not for her own sake, but for Cillian. Her brother, who was once radiant in every way, was now tainted by shadow and bound to Vaelora by chains. "You're a monster," she hissed.

"Maybe, but at least I'm a powerful one."

"Bitch," Holden muttered under his breath.

Vaelora sighed with theatrical boredom.

"Charming. But if we're done with the name-calling, can someone please explain why Obren Glaciermaw is still playing house with the Ironwolf pack? I thought we were past this little rebellion phase."

The question hung in the air, but Obren quickly responded, his voice teasing. "How could I resist the chance to kneel before the most beautiful witch queen in the entire continent?"

"The wall you build to hide your true emotions is made of glass, Obren. And I can shatter it with ease."

The confidence in his smirk flickered for a moment, and a muscle in his jaw twitched.

Her tone turned almost affectionate. "I bet you wonder where all your missing packmates went that night. Don't you?" She let the silence stretch, savoring it. "If you swear allegiance to me, I might let you see them again. Though there weren't many left to keep after my army finished feeding."

Obren's restraint snapped. His face flushed red with rage, and without hesitation, he spat at her feet. "You fucking demon."

Vaelora laughed and turned away, her gown sweeping across the bloodstained floor. She raised a hand, curling her fingers lazily. "Cillian, my love, come."

Evelyne's brother obeyed, stepping forward with that same vacant stare, his blackened eyes fixed on Vaelora.

Panic rose in her chest like a scream she couldn't release. What was Vaelora going to do to him? Was she going to force him to kill her—make the others watch as he murdered his sister, powerless to stop it? *Please, gods, no—*

Vaelora leaned in, and whispered one lethal word in Cillian's ear. "Kill."

Evelyne's stomach plummeted, her heartbeat thundering in her ears as she followed the line of Vaelora's gesture.

Not at her.

Not at Obren.

Ty.

She had nearly forgotten he was there. He had been so quiet, so still, saying nothing as the chaos unfolded around him. He had watched from the sidelines, likely analyzing every moment, calculating the best move to protect his alpha and his friends.

Cillian's brow furrowed, his breathing growing ragged, sharp teeth—Noskari teeth—elongating from his mouth. Black veins snaked along his neck and arms as he moved forward, step by step, closing in on Ty.

The room exploded in a storm of fury and anguish.

Kaldrek and Holden thrashed against their chains, snarling, teeth bared, rage cracking through the air, but Cillian didn't look at them. His eyes never left Ty.

Ty, Nathan's younger brother. Ty, who had never known cruelty. Ty, whose mate was still waiting for him in the tunnel, trusting he'd return.

He remained silent on his knees, his chin lifted with quiet defiance. He didn't beg. He didn't flinch. He just turned to Kaldrek and said, voice steady, "Tell Nathan to keep our mate safe. And tell Reyna... Tell her she was my everything."

"NO!" Kaldrek wailed.

Evelyne lost control of her voice. "Cillian!" she screamed. "Cillian, stop! Please!"

The throne room blurred, sound warping and stretching, but she could only focus on her brother. The same brother who once braided her hair when she was sad, who had read beside her for hours in the library, who had always been gentle.

She pleaded, desperate for something to reach him.

Time stilled.

And Cillian lunged.

Ty didn't flinch. There was no cry of pain, no gasp. Just the sickening sound of flesh tearing as Cillian's arm plunged straight through his chest. But he didn't stop there. With a horrifying, wet crack, he ripped upward, splitting Ty's body clean in half.

Blood sprayed, flesh peeled, and in a heartbeat, Ty was nothing but ruin.

Evelyne wailed so loudly she thought her throat would shred to pieces. Kaldrek and Holden roared alongside her, their howls ripping through the air like those of wounded animals. Obren and Alaric stared, their faces frozen in pure horror.

Evelyne's vision blurred with tears, her body trembling so violently she thought she might break apart, but then her eyes snapped to Alaric as she caught Cillian turning his way.

Oh gods, please. Not him.

Cillian stepped back to Vaelora's side, obedient and unfeeling, his hands and chest drenched in blood. He didn't even look down at what he had done.

And that was when Evelyne knew her brother was lost entirely.

CHAPTER 47

He was drowning.

A vast, endless pool of cold, black water, thick with the stench of death and blood, dragged him deeper and deeper. It wrapped around him like a second skin, and he no longer struggled against it. There was no fighting it. No escape. So he let go. He let his body drift where the current took him, let the thing inside him, the darkness that was not *him*, command his limbs, speak with his voice, see through his eyes.

But then he heard it.

A voice, as familiar to him as his own heartbeat. A voice that had filled his childhood with laughter, warmth, and love. *Evelyne.* She was calling his name, screaming it.

She was here with Vaelora.

Oh, no.

Cillian thrashed against the suffocating black, kicking hard, clawing up toward the surface. The weight of the demon inside him pressed down with crushing force, trying to pull him back under. But now, he fought. He fought until his mind broke through the darkness, until he could see, could hear.

He saw her. Chained. Bloodied. Weak. But not broken.

Evelyne had always been strong. Even now. Even like this. And she was here... for him.

Something inside him cracked.

Vaelora spoke. He heard her voice, heard her admit to killing his father. The words sliced through his mind, through the splinters of whatever was left of his shattered soul.

His father was dead. Murdered by the woman he had kissed. Touched. *Loved.*

Had any of it been real? Or had it all been a lie, a perfect illusion wrapped in blood and silk?

His vision blurred and his thoughts scattered. Evelyne. Alaric. They were both here, both captured and fighting for him. So he had to fight too.

He reached inward, searching for the real version of himself—the part buried beneath the demon's grip. It was so close, just within reach. But as soon as his fingers brushed it, the darkness struck. It slammed into him, dragged him back under, and swallowed him whole.

No.

Evelyne's scream tore through the abyss. Cillian blinked, but all he saw was black. She was calling his name again—not just a scream this time, but something pleading, laced with pain and fear. What was happening? What had he done? Panic surged, but he couldn't let it rise. He needed control. He needed to reclaim his body. But not yet. The demon couldn't know he was fighting back. Not again.

He stilled himself and waited for the perfect moment. He knew this darkness now; its traps, its whispers, its lies. It had caged him, but he remembered the way out. So he began to climb, with Evelyne's voice guiding him, anchoring him to the light. Past the endless black. Past the choking pull of the demon's hold. He rose through it all. And as his mind pierced the shadows, he saw it.

His soul.

His *real* soul. The one that had been chosen. The one containing the light to purify all of her darkness.

Vaelora knew it. That was why she had twisted him and made him forget, made him love her, so she could own him completely. The illusion cracked the moment he heard Evelyne's voice through the noise. In that instant, he remembered who he was... and what he was meant to do.

His mind, his gift—there was a reason for it. A reason the prophecy had chosen him. He would uncover the truth before anyone else. He would reclaim the power buried deep within his soul and purge the demon she had planted inside him.

But first, he had to pretend. Hide. Let the parasite believe it still had control. Then, when the time was right, he would reach for that small thread of light. And he would take back his soul to end her.

The throne room had descended into chaos by the time Cillian drifted close enough to touch the edges of his soul. Rage and grief pulsed in the air, thick with the scent of blood. The men around him had turned feral, primal, their fury radiating like heat from a fire too long contained. They glared at him with unfiltered hatred, and just beyond their rage, the body he had torn apart lay in two mangled pieces on the cold stone floor.

He had done that.

He had caused this.

He had broken them.

But he couldn't move. Couldn't react, not without alerting the demon still nestled inside him. So he stood silently, letting it control his limbs as he watched and waited. All the while, Vaelora's voice coiled around him like a noose.

"My Cillian has been gifted with such strength," she purred, her satisfaction clinging to every word. "I feed him with my magic every day, pouring more and more into him so that he may grow strong enough to rule by my side. Just look at him. Look how perfect he is."

She turned to face him, black eyes locking onto his, and Cillian shrank behind them, behind her magic, behind the monster she had forged, praying she couldn't see the real him, still buried beneath the surface.

She had done this. Twisted him. Tainted him. Turned him into a killer.

But he would destroy everything she had built.

His gaze flicked to Evelyne. She looked devastated, as though she already mourned him, had already accepted that he was gone. He couldn't blame her.

She had always fought for him. Now, it was his turn.

Vaelora's voice cut through the moment like a dagger. "Now kill her," she whispered. "Kill her, my love."

And the demon moved.

Cillian thrashed within himself, fighting against the suffocating blackness pressing in from all sides. But the demon was fast and didn't falter. And Evelyne looked afraid. The fear in her eyes undid him.

He was so close to clawing his way back to the surface, back to himself. In desperation, he jerked back, a wild gamble, a distraction. If he could bait the demon and keep it focused, maybe he could draw it out.

When the darkness lunged, Cillian shoved against it, dragging it further from his core. His body and hands still moved. He felt them, heavy and foreign. So much stronger than they should have been. So cold.

His fingers wrapped around Evelyne's throat.

Howls filled the air. Somewhere, Alaric was screaming his name. But Cillian couldn't stop his own hands from killing her.

Evelyne didn't struggle. She didn't claw at his arms or plead. She simply looked at him, truly looked, and a single tear slipped down her cheek.

"I'm sorry I couldn't save you," she whispered.

The words struck something deep within him, fracturing what little remained. Everything began to unravel.

The final battle for his soul had begun.

CHAPTER 48

Kaldrek could do nothing but watch as Cillian stalked toward Evelyne, his eyes black with bloodlust. There was a flicker in his expression, a hesitation so brief it might have been imagined, but Kaldrek saw it. Something inside him was still fighting. Cillian hadn't completely vanished beneath the monster Vaelora had created.

Part of Kaldrek still wanted to tear him apart. The image of Ty's body, split in two on the cold stone floor, was burned into his mind. Ty had been more than a friend; he was pack, closer than blood. Kaldrek had felt the alpha bond tear the moment Ty died. Through it, he'd felt the ripple of agony from Nathan and Reyna. The grief threatened to consume him, but there was no time to mourn.

Vaelora had turned her attention to Evelyne. She had given the command. Cillian was going to kill her next.

Kaldrek couldn't let that happen. He had seen what Cillian was capable of, what those hands had done to Ty. He couldn't bear to watch Evelyne meet the same end. He needed Cillian to fight back, to resist the demon that still lived inside him.

Cillian stood over her, unmoving and hollow-eyed. Evelyne was unarmed, broken-hearted, and vulnerable. And part of that was Kaldrek's fault.

She was going to die, and he was powerless to stop it.

He had to shift. It was the only way to break free, to reach her before it was too late. But the Noskari holding him were too strong. Three of them pinned him in place. One had its claws buried in his shoulder, pressing its fangs to his throat as the other two held his chains. They restrained him just enough to keep him from tearing them apart, and to ensure he had to watch.

Evelyne, the woman who had unraveled him from the moment he found her in his camp, bound and defiant, her golden eyes blazing with challenge, was about to die.

It was breaking him.

He had known other lovers, but none like her. None who saw him for who he truly was, none who made him feel so infuriatingly alive. She was his. Even if fate had not bound them as mates, she was his in every way that mattered.

And he had barely been given time to love her.

But he did love her. Deeply and desperately, enough that it had terrified him. And now Vaelora, the twisted creature who had already taken everything from him—his birthright, his pack, the truth of his blood—was about to take Evelyne too. Kaldrek wasn't sure he could survive losing her.

Would she have stayed if he had told her the truth sooner? If he had confessed everything before they left the tunnels, would Evelyne have believed him? Or would she have seen it as a betrayal, a manipulation designed to break her?

It didn't matter now. Not as Cillian's fingers tightened around her throat. Not as Vaelora began to chant, her voice rising in a dark, rhythmic cadence he believed to be the start of the ritual sacrifice.

"I'm sorry I couldn't save you," Evelyne whispered to her brother.

Kaldrek's primal instinct ignited like wildfire.

He twisted toward the Noskari at his throat and lunged without hesitation. His fangs sank deep into flesh, tearing and shredding with savage precision. He wasn't thinking, only reacting, only trying to draw their attention. If Cillian needed to kill someone, let it be him. Let it be *now*.

Chains groaned as Kaldrek pulled against them with furious strength. One of the Noskari stumbled, unprepared for the sudden force. Kaldrek seized the moment, driving forward with a snarl and sinking his fangs into its throat. Hot, dark blood sprayed across his face.

Vaelora's chant faltered, and she hissed. "That's enough, Kaldrek."

But it was already too late.

Cillian's eyes snapped to the noise just as the throne room shifted. Crimson light flooded through the tall, arched windows, spilling like liquid fire across the stone floor. Through the cracks in the night, the moon now hung in the sky like a bleeding eye. The eclipse had reached its peak.

Shadows stretched unnaturally, slithering along the walls as if alive, drawn to the surge of magic thickening the air. The light was like a tear ripped open in the heavens, and for a breathless moment, all eyes turned to the red glow as it pulsed across the room like a living heartbeat.

Then came the sound of breaking bones and twisting flesh. Followed by the shrieking agony of a body reshaping itself.

Cillian was shifting.

His screams ripped through the air as his body contorted in grotesque ways. Kaldrek knew that pain all too well; the first shift was always the worst, bones snapping and reforming, muscles knotting, fire burning beneath the skin. But Evelyne had no idea what was happening to her brother, no frame of reference for the hell he was enduring.

"Cillian!" she cried, panic-stricken. "What is happening to him? What are you doing to him?" Her voice cracked as she turned her fury to Vaelora.

"Holy fuck," Holden whispered beside Kaldrek, realization sinking in.

Alaric's voice was barely audible over the chaos. "Is he shifting?" Disbelief laced his words.

Evelyne was shaking uncontrollably as she watched her brother transform into something monstrous.

A beast.

A wolf, but unlike any Kaldrek had ever seen.

He was massive, towering over them all. His fur was black as a void, yet his eyes were not the crimson red of a pure wolf bloodline, nor the bottomless black of the Noskari. They glowed gold, bright and radiant, as if a star had been sealed inside him.

Vaelora's smile stretched wide as she circled Cillian, her eyes gleaming with a savage hunger. She moved like a queen admiring a weapon she had carefully forged.

"I always hoped you would shift for me one day," she purred, her voice dripping with satisfaction. "Just look at you. So strong. So perfect." Then her tone sharpened. "Now kill her."

Cillian turned toward Evelyne, his lips curling back to reveal his fangs. Saliva dripped from his muzzle as he crouched low, muscles rippling beneath the sleek black fur. His massive frame radiated lethal intent.

Evelyne stumbled back a step, a broken sob escaping her. "Please, Cillian... come back."

One massive paw struck the marble floor, claws screeching against stone. For a breathless, terrifying moment, Kaldrek was certain he would lunge and tear her apart. But Cillian didn't move closer. Instead, the glow in his eyes intensified—so bright Evelyne had to shield her face.

In a swift motion, Cillian tore his eyes from her and fixed them on Vaelora.

A deep growl rose from his throat as he began a slow, deliberate prowl forward. Kaldrek's pulse hammered. He recognized that look—the slight tilt of the head, the piercing intensity in his eyes. This wasn't submission. Cillian was stalking.

Vaelora's smile wavered. "Go on, love," she said. "Kill her. Complete the sacrifice." But Cillian didn't strike. Instead, he began to circle her with deadly patience, each step radiating controlled rage, a predator waiting for the perfect moment.

A flicker of unease crossed Vaelora's face. "I said kill her!" she snapped, her voice rising in desperation.

But Cillian's lips only peeled back further, another low snarl vibrating deep in his chest.

Vaelora clicked her tongue, forcing a mask of disappointment onto her features. "It seems someone has been fighting the dark power from inside. A shame." She lifted her hands, summoning a storm of black magic. "No matter. I can still break you."

The blast she unleashed roared across the throne room, thick and corrosive. Cillian lunged at her, but a shadowy coil struck him midair, slamming him into the ground hard enough to crack the marble beneath him. He grunted, but immediately tried to rise.

Vaelora's magic exploded outward, her rage a living force. Dark mist surged like snapping whips, lashing through the air and seizing everything in its path. Obren was yanked backward and slammed into a pillar with bone-jarring impact. Holden dropped to his knees, his chains pulling so tight they rattled. A wave of inky mist struck Alaric, driving him to the floor as he coughed, choking on the smothering blast.

And Evelyne—

A thick, oily tendril snaked around her neck, lifting her off the ground. Her feet kicked wildly as she clawed at the shadow choking the life from her.

Kaldrek's blood turned to ice. Fury exploded inside him, hot and consuming.

Cillian was pinned under Vaelora's suffocating magic, her darkness chaining him down again and again. His massive body buckled under its weight, shadows binding his limbs, strangling his movements. And still, he fought. He tore at the magic with his claws. He snapped at it with his teeth. Unlike anything Kaldrek had ever witnessed, his strength held firm against her crushing power.

No other could have withstood it.

No one but Cillian.

Kaldrek's gaze snapped to Evelyne. Her struggles were weakening. Her golden eyes fluttered, her body sagging against the noose of shadow.

He ripped against his chains with a roar that shook the rafters. The Noskari restraining him tightened their grips, claws digging into his arms and shoulders. Kaldrek didn't care. He lunged forward, seizing the nearest Noskari with his bare hands. With a violent twist, he tore its head from its body.

Another Noskari struck at him. Kaldrek ducked low and drove his fist upward, shattering its jaw and sending it crashing. He turned on the third, his hands slick with blood, and ripped its throat open in one savage motion.

Chains clattered around him as he broke free.

Kaldrek shifted in a flash, his wolf form surging forward like a battering ram. He tore through the chaos, his only thought to reach Evelyne and Cillian.

Sensing the shift in the battle, Vaelora shrieked with rage. Her hands blazed with raw magic, flinging bolts of shadow at anything that moved. The throne room shook under the onslaught. Stone split, and torches crashed to the floor, sending plumes of smoke into the air.

One blast caught Kaldrek along the ribs, tearing a burning gouge into his side, but he didn't slow. He and Cillian converged on Vaelora, two forces of nature she could no longer control.

Cillian struck first. His jaws clamped around her shoulder, his strength dragging her down like a wolf bringing down an elk. She shrieked, slashing mindlessly at him with tendrils of dark magic, but Cillian held her firm. He did not let go, no matter how she thrashed or what spells she cast.

Vaelora unleashed a torrent of shadows toward Kaldrek, striking him hard enough that he staggered back a step. But he rallied, lunging forward and slashing his claws across her midsection, spilling more of her foul black blood.

Still, she fought.

Still, she screamed.

The blood moon's crimson glow bathed the room, casting everything in the light of prophecy. And Cillian did not falter. He crushed her beneath the weight of his body, his golden eyes blazing with unrelenting fury. Vaelora lashed out, clawing at him with bursts of lethal magic, but he held firm. After all, he was the weapon fate had forged, and nothing she did could change that.

Kaldrek circled behind her, his claws tearing down her exposed back. Flesh split open, and the stench of blood and rot filled the chamber.

"Kaldrek, please! Please stop!" she cried out, desperation cracking her voice. For a split second, he faltered—and that was all she needed. A tendril of dark magic lashed out, slamming him into a shattered pillar. Pain exploded in his side. He looked down to find a fresh gouge carved into him, shadowy and bleeding like a wound from another realm. His vision blurred, but he saw Cillian still fighting relentlessly.

With a thunderous snarl, Cillian drove Vaelora to the floor again, pinning her with his weight. His claws locked her arms, and his jaw closed over her throat. Power surged through him, radiant and searing. His eyes blazed, and as his teeth pierced her flesh, it was as if he were burning the corruption out of her, stripping her soul bare.

Barely conscious, Kaldrek forced himself forward. The Noskari guarding Evelyne were too distracted by their queen's downfall to notice him creeping closer. In one explosive motion, he lunged, his claws slashing one creature's throat while his jaws crushed the other's neck. Evelyne's chains fell. She gasped, coughing against the mist that had wrapped around her throat, then reached for a length of fallen chain.

Vaelora writhed beneath Cillian, her body convulsing as thick, black blood pooled around her, magic leaking from her wounds like smoke. Her wide eyes found Evelyne standing tall, a chain wound tightly in her hands.

Cillian lifted his head just long enough to meet Evelyne's eyes, then sank his teeth into Vaelora's arm, shifting his hold and making space for Evelyne to step in, as if he knew exactly what she needed to do. He returned to his task without hesitation, drawing out the corruption rooted deep in Vaelora's soul, his power burning steadily through her dark magic.

Kaldrek, still reeling and bloodied, watched through a haze of pain as Evelyne approached. His chest ached. Not from the wound, but from what he saw in her: the woman he had come to love, standing transformed. She was no longer the noble girl he'd once teased, but a warrior—and yet, he realized, she'd always been brave.

"If you kill me…" Vaelora rasped quietly. A twisted smile curled on her blood-blackened lips. "Your fight… won't be—" She broke off, choking as thick, gurgling blood filled her throat. "Won't be over…" Her voice trailed off as exhaustion took over.

Evelyne crouched beside Vaelora's contorted form, chain in hand, and leaned close to her ear. There was no fear in her voice. Only strength. Only rage.

"For my brother," she whispered. "And for my father."

She wrapped the chain around Vaelora's throat and pulled it tight.

Steel dug into skin. Bones strained. Evelyne gave the chain another vicious tug before stepping back to reach behind her waist. From a reinforced loop on her dagger strap, she unhooked the short-barreled flintlock. With calm hands, she flipped open the frizzen and loaded the shot with smooth precision. Kaldrek watched her with a mix of awe and pride as she leveled her father's pistol at Vaelora's face.

"Move, Cillian," Evelyne ordered. He didn't rush, draining every last trace of magic before rising and stepping aside.

Vaelora couldn't scream. Could barely breathe. But the panic in her dimming eyes said enough. She looked to Kaldrek, pleading silently with the son she had once tried to claim.

He stared back, cold and unflinching. *Do it, Evelyne. Now.*

"May you rot in hell," Evelyne spat before firing the pistol.

Time fractured with the blast and bone shattered. Vaelora's head snapped back, and what remained of the immortal queen crumpled lifeless to the floor.

CHAPTER 49

Across the throne room, the remaining Noskari faltered for a single breath. Then they turned and fled, slipping into the shadows like ghosts released from their master's fading grip.

Kaldrek's stomach twisted. The Noskari hadn't died with Vaelora. They still moved like smoke, their bodies shifting into mist with ease. Their skin remained gray, as if the dark magic still pulsed within them. Was it possible their power hadn't come solely from Vaelora, but had rooted itself inside the hosts, drawing strength from within to survive? That was a dangerous possibility.

Her final words echoed in his mind: *If you kill me, your fight won't be over.* The memory sent a chill through him, but he forced it aside as the sharp clatter of chains broke the silence. He turned to see Obren, Holden, and Alaric finally free.

Cillian stood over Vaelora's broken body. Blood dripped from his mouth. His chest rose and fell with shallow, uneven breaths. He did not move or speak. He only watched her corpse, as if daring it to stir again.

Kaldrek shifted back into his human form. Bloodied and battered, he stumbled through the ruined throne room toward Evelyne. She was collapsing, and he caught her just in time, pulling her into his arms. She flinched when his hand grazed her ribs, and pain surged through him as well, a sharp reminder of the wound still bleeding at his side.

"You're hurt," Evelyne whispered.

"I'll be all right," he murmured. "It's already starting to heal." He blinked through the dizziness, focusing on the rhythm of her breath as it began to steady.

Vaelora was dead. The witch who had taken everything from them and ruled through cruelty and fear was finally gone. For the first time in Kaldrek's life, the world felt lighter.

But freedom had come at a terrible cost.

The Noskari had disappeared into the shadows, and Cillian still stood near Vaelora's corpse, locked in a silent struggle with whatever remnants of her magic lingered inside him.

Kaldrek knew what had to come next. He had to get Cillian out of the throne room before the shift back fully took hold. The first transformation was always volatile, full of raw emotion, confusion, and instinct tangled into something dangerous. He couldn't risk Evelyne or the others getting caught in the storm that was about to break.

"You need to get out of here, Cillian," Kaldrek shouted. His voice echoed across the broken marble. "Go. Run!"

But Cillian did not respond. His body buckled and fell, shifting back into his human form as he hit the ground. He trembled violently, his muscles seizing as if something inside him was still fighting to survive. His eyes rolled back.

Evelyne jolted upright. "Cillian!" she rasped, trying to crawl toward him.

Kaldrek pulled her back, holding her tightly. He couldn't let her get too close—not when he didn't know what still lingered inside Cillian, or whether the creature that had torn Ty apart might return. She was angry with him, Kaldrek could feel it, but every choice he'd made had been to protect her. Even before his feelings deepened, that instinct had always been there. From the very first moment he saw her, keeping her safe had been his purpose. So he held on.

"Let go of me, Kaldrek!" Evelyne cried, struggling against him.

But he did not let go. He did not care if she hated him for it, so long as she stayed safe.

Cillian stiffened, and a stream of black mist slipped from his open mouth. It curled upward, dissolving into the air like poison. Cillian writhed as the darkness within him fought to take hold, but he shone with a fierce, golden light—burning from the inside out, as if his very soul sought to purge the shadows. His body glowed brighter with each surge, the dark magic seeping from him in tendrils. But the strain was evident. Kaldrek saw it in the way his arms hung limp, his strength slipping away. He could do nothing but bear witness as Cillian unleashed the full force of his light.

"He'll be consumed," Evelyne whispered, as though recalling a line from the prophecy. "To burn too brightly... is to be consumed." Her voice broke into a cry as she turned toward Cillian. "Stop! You're drawing too much power!" She struggled against Kaldrek's grip. "Please, Kaldrek," she begged, tears streaming down her face. "He's going to lose himself!"

But he held her firmly, unwilling to let her near the volatile force spilling from Cillian. They watched as a final surge of blackness erupted from Cillian's chest and his back arched violently off the marble floor. With a shuddering gasp, he collapsed again. But this time, he did not move.

"Cillian!" Evelyne screamed. "Let me go!"

Kaldrek loosened his grip slowly, waiting for any type of movement, but none came. So he let her go.

She was at her brother's side instantly, dropping to the marble and gathering him into her lap, holding him as if she could keep his soul tethered to her through sheer will alone. But his skin was pale, his face slack.

Kaldrek knew deep in his bones that Cillian was gone.

Alaric dropped to his knees beside them, resting a steady hand on Evelyne's back. The sight of another man touching her stirred no possessiveness in Kaldrek. This was not a battle for dominance, nor a fight for her attention. It was a moment of grief, a quiet offering of comfort between two friends bound by sorrow.

Kaldrek moved with quiet hands, tearing a strip of cloth from Vaelora's dress and gently covering Cillian's body before sinking to his knees beside them in silence.

"Evelyne," he said gently, but she did not respond. She cradled Cillian against her chest, pressing desperate kisses to his forehead.

Her voice cracked as she pleaded with him, her words unraveling into broken sobs. "It's me, Cillian. Evelyne. Please come back. Please, please don't leave me."

Every word ripped through Kaldrek's heart. He couldn't stand the sight of her in pain.

"Evelyne, he is gone," Alaric said hoarsely.

"No! No, please, gods, no!" Evelyne sobbed, clinging to Cillian tighter, rocking him back and forth like she could bring him back through sheer love.

Alaric bowed his head, a low, strangled sound escaping him.

The throne room was silent, the air heavy with grief.

Evelyne had fought so hard to find her brother, to save him. And now she held him dead in her arms, another life stolen by Vaelora's cruelty.

Kaldrek's eyes burned with unshed tears. They had won the battle, but it felt hollow.

"Kaldrek!" Obren's voice rang out through the silence. "Look."

Everyone's attention shifted as Obren pointed toward Cillian. Kaldrek followed his gesture, his gaze landing on Cillian's face.

His eyes were open, vacant and unfocused as he stared up at the ceiling. Something sparked behind them, like a flicker of light.

A moment later, his eyes glowed with a vivid, unmistakable gold.

The pale cast of his skin began to lift as a gentle light stirred within him, growing stronger with each steady heartbeat. It spread outward, spilling over the marble floor like warm sunlight breaking through storm clouds. Everyone watched in awe as Cillian's entire form began to glow, as if the darkness inside him had been driven out by the sheer force of the light rising from within.

Cillian blinked. "Evelyne?" His voice was hoarse and confused, but unmistakably his own.

The room exhaled as one. He was alive.

Holden spoke first. "How did you do that?"

Cillian slowly pushed himself upright, his hands trembling slightly, still flickering with golden light. When he spoke again, his voice was steady. "I am a keeper of light. The one chosen to purify the darkness. The one who can cleanse a soul consumed by shadow."

Evelyne stared at him, stunned and disbelieving. "What?"

Cillian swallowed and let out a long breath. "I had to purge myself of her power, in order to be me." His gaze locked onto Evelyne's with fierce intensity. "It's gone, Evelyne." His voice broke as a sob escaped him, his face crumpling under the weight of relief and grief.

Evelyne threw her arms around him, burying her face in his shoulder. "Of course you figured it out," she whispered. "You're the only one who could."

Kaldrek let out a low exhale and felt something inside him finally ease. They had done it. The Noskari might still haunt the world beyond the shattered palace walls, and more battles surely lay ahead, but none of that mattered right now. Right now, he found himself captivated, unable to do anything but admire Evelyne's strength.

He saw the pain in her eyes when she glanced at him, the betrayal and hurt that still lingered, and it cut deeper than any wound. Yet he managed a small, broken smile as he watched her hold her brother tightly, as if her love alone could somehow make him whole again.

Minutes passed before Kaldrek noticed the faint tremble of her hands and the subtle shift in her expression. Then, suddenly, Evelyne jolted. Her arms slipped from around Cillian. Kaldrek's instincts flared as she gasped and fell backward, her body hitting the marble hard. Every muscle in his body went taut as he watched her drop onto all fours, her fingers clawing at the floor.

"Evelyne?" he called cautiously, stepping forward. But she did not seem to hear him.

She clutched her chest, her breaths coming in shallow, rapid gasps. When she lifted her head, Kaldrek's blood turned to ice.

Her golden eyes flickered, a vivid red flashing through the irises.

Crack.

A scream tore through the throne room, raw and agonized, sharp enough to raise the hairs along Kaldrek's arms. The sound of her pain was like claws raking across his heart.

"Move back!" he barked, throwing out an arm as he advanced.

Cillian's face drained of color as he stumbled back, watching in horror as his sister twisted violently on the floor.

"She's shifting," Kaldrek snapped. "Move back!"

Evelyne's body convulsed, her bones snapping and contorting in unnatural ways. Her screams deepened into something primal, something that no longer belonged to the human world, until where she had once knelt, a wolf stood.

A golden-brown coat gleamed under the crimson light of the blood moon. Her muscles were taut, her entire body coiled with wild, unspent energy. Her eyes, bright and burning red, locked onto them all.

A low snarl curled her lips, exposing fangs meant to tear and kill. Kaldrek's pulse thundered in his ears. He could only think one thing.

Breathe, Evelyne. Please, breathe.

She snapped her head toward him, as if she had heard his voice.

He froze. *Can you... hear me?* He sent the thought out tentatively, barely daring to hope.

Kaldrek?

Her soft and frightened voice brushed against his mind, and Kaldrek nearly staggered from the force of his own relief. She could hear him, speak to him, mind to mind.

Yes, it's me, sweetheart. You are all right. I need you to breathe through this.

Her ears twitched, a slight, instinctive movement that told him she was clinging to the thread between them. Fear trembled through her, but something in his voice must have steadied her, anchored her.

I know you are scared, he sent, keeping his tone calm. *I know the transition was agony. But you have to trust me. You need to run it off.*

He could feel her struggle through the bond, her muscles quivering under the strain of instincts she did not yet understand.

You have adrenaline burning through your veins, he explained. *If you stay, it will take over. You have to move. You have to run before the panic hurts someone you love.*

A low growl rumbled in her throat, raw and conflicted, her whole body shuddering as she teetered between fight and flight. Kaldrek's heart hammered in his chest, but he never let the certainty in his mind falter. He would not lose her to fear. Not now. Not ever.

Run, Evelyne. Run.

Run!

With a sudden, explosive movement, she bolted. Her massive form streaked past the ruined throne room doors and disappeared into the night.

Kaldrek stood frozen, staring after her. His chest tightened at the sight of her wild, magnificent figure vanishing beneath the blood-soaked sky.

Then he turned sharply to the others. "Obren—take Alaric and Cillian back to the pack."

Obren hesitated, glancing at the open doors Evelyne had just vanished through.

Kaldrek met his gaze, his tone like iron. "*Go.*"

Obren nodded, grabbing Alaric and helping a weak Cillian to his feet.

Kaldrek turned to Holden, voice dropping. "Take Ty—"

"I know." Holden's voice was firm, edged with grief. His jaw clenched as he moved toward Ty's body. "I'll bring him back to his mate."

A heavy silence settled between them before Kaldrek shifted once more. He would not leave Evelyne to face this alone. Not when every instinct in him screamed to follow her.

Outside, he surged forward, his paws striking the frozen earth in a steady, relentless rhythm, the wind slicing through his fur like a blade. He listened carefully, tracking the surefooted cadence of her movements carving through the stillness of the night. He followed the sound across the barren landscape until finally, he found her.

The breath caught in his chest, stolen by the sight before him.

Even beneath the crimson haze of the blood moon, her golden-brown fur caught the light, glowing with a brilliance that no darkness could touch. Evelyne wove through the skeletal trees with effortless grace, each movement fluid, instinctive, and sure. Like this life, this unrestrained freedom, had always been hers to claim. She did not hesitate. She did not look back. She ran as if she had waited her entire life for this moment. She was breathtaking, a creature born to be wild and untethered, never meant to be bound by silks or the heavy expectations of a courtly life.

An hour passed in quiet pursuit before Kaldrek finally reached out, sending his thoughts gently into the bond between them.

Evelyne. We need to head back to the others.

There was a brief silence, and he wondered if she had heard him. Then, her voice brushed against his mind, warm and soft.

Soon.

***

As he reached the tunnel, the gathered pack turned toward him, relief and exhaustion etched into their faces. Kaldrek shifted back, muscles tightening against the cold, and accepted the blanket one of the pack members rushed to drape over him. His gaze swept the group, landing on Cillian, who sat beside Alaric, both of them battered but alive. Lorena and Heidara crouched beside them, tending to Alaric's wounds, their soft murmurs of comfort filling the tense air.

Heidara spotted Kaldrek and ran toward him, her eyes darting anxiously past him, searching for someone else.

"She's coming," he murmured.

Heidara threw her arms around him, clutching him tightly. "I was so worried," she whispered, her voice thick with concern.

Beyond her, Kaldrek caught sight of Nathan and Reyna, who sat collapsed into each other, overwhelmed by grief. Reyna sobbed against Nathan's shoulder, her body trembling with the rawness of her pain. She had lost her mate, and there was no greater agony for a wolf. It was a wound that never truly healed, a hollowing of the soul that never fully closed. Nathan, his own sorrow etched into the way his arms gripped her, had lost a brother. They clung together, bound by shared loss and the unbearable ache of separation.

Kaldrek wanted to go to them, to offer his strength, but he knew better. Nothing could touch the depth of a bond shattered by death. Not now. Not yet.

He swallowed hard, forcing down the knot tightening in his chest. Vaelora was gone. Cillian was safe. And Evelyne... Evelyne was a wolf.

The realization still rattled him. His mind reeled back to the first days after they captured her, when he had visited daily, searching her golden eyes for any trace of darkness or deception. There had always been something else, something buried just beneath the surface. A scent. Faint, wild, elusive.

He had leaned in closer, trying to catch it and name the animalistic thread coiled around her essence. She had smacked him for it, furious and defiant.

At the time, he had told himself he imagined it. That it could not possibly be real. But the night had stripped away every certainty he had ever known, leaving his world spinning. Still, nothing, not the ambush, not the bloodshed, not even Vaelora's death, had stunned him as profoundly as watching Evelyne shift before his eyes.

As if drawn by the force of his thoughts, she returned. Kaldrek moved without hesitation, grabbing a cloak and stepping toward her as her body prepared to shift back.

Everything inside him went still when her human form reappeared, golden-eyed and wild. The force of her scent slammed into him so hard it nearly buckled his knees. It encircled him, lush and consuming, a heady mix of sweet jasmine, rich sandalwood, and the lingering heat of spiced honey. It filled every part of him, carved into his very bones, and he knew with terrifying clarity that he never wanted to breathe anything else for as long as he lived. Only this. Only her.

Their eyes met, and in that instant, something primal shifted inside him, something inescapable. A magnetic pull yanked him toward her, so strong it stole his breath, wiped away all thought.

The scent. The pull. Every instinct, every part of him roared with one word.

Mate.

CHAPTER 50

The shift had been unlike anything Evelyne had ever experienced. It was agonizing, overwhelming, and yet profoundly real. Pain and fear tangled with something far more potent, a wildness buried deep within her that had finally broken free. Every nerve in her body sparked to life, every sense sharpened beyond anything she had ever known. It was terrifying. It was exhilarating. And for the first time, she felt complete.

This was who she was meant to be. A wolf. A part of something greater than herself.

For twenty-three years, the truth had been hidden, stolen from her bloodline, erased from memory. The Duskwoods, forgotten. But from what pack? What lineage? And how had Kaldrek been able to speak inside her mind?

The thought of him made her want to scream, rage and frustration twisting inside her so violently it felt like they might tear her apart. He had kept too many things from her, things that mattered. She couldn't understand why. That fury had burned hot when she'd first shifted. Part of her had wanted to knock him to the throne room floor and let her wolf tear into him for the pain he had caused.

But then his calm, husky voice had slipped into her mind, and the anger had dulled, replaced for a fleeting moment by something warmer. Comfort. Connection.

She'd planned to unleash her fury the second she returned to the tunnel, but everything changed the moment she shifted back. The instant their eyes met, something surged between them, an electric pull that reached into her bones. His scent enveloped her, a deep, heady blend of smoke, cedar, and spice. It wrapped around her like wildfire, heat racing through her blood and drawing a shiver from her despite the cold. She could have drowned in it, and part of her wanted to.

She stepped toward him, instinct urging her to close the distance, to surrender to whatever bond pulsed between them. Then her gaze landed on Heidara, and reality crashed back in. The truth—the betrayal—hit like a punch to the chest. Kaldrek and Holden had kept something vital from her. Maybe even the entire pack had known, and she couldn't stop the hurt and rage that flared through her again, searing her skin.

Kaldrek must have sensed it. His voice brushed against her thoughts, soft and cautious, like a whisper carried on the wind.

Heidara does not know.

The shock of hearing him inside her head made Evelyne flinch. She would have to get used to this now—to his presence woven into her being, whether she wanted it or not. That conversation was for another day, but perhaps she could push him out.

Before she could react, Heidara stepped forward and pulled her into a fierce embrace. Evelyne barely felt its warmth—only the weight of her cloak slipping from her shoulders.

Kaldrek moved instantly, catching the fabric and wrapping it around her, already acting as though he had the right to protect her. She held the cloak tightly and turned away from him. He understood the gesture and quietly stepped back, but a part of her still ached for his closeness.

"I'm so glad you're all right," Heidara whispered, holding her tighter. Evelyne breathed in her scent, something soft and earthy, like flowers caught on a breeze. It was pleasant, but nothing like his. Kaldrek's scent still clung to the air, the only one strong enough to reach her even from ten feet away.

"Me too," Evelyne murmured, gently pulling away as she scanned the tunnel for Cillian.

"Follow me." Heidara smiled, and Evelyne held tight to her friend's hand.

***

Kaldrek and Obren agreed that the packs needed a night under the open sky, away from the stifling walls of the tunnel. Everyone set to work, pitching camp nearby. Scouts were assigned to first and second watch; even though Vaelora was dead and the threat of the Noskari had lessened, caution still ruled the night. Everyone needed rest, and though magic now coursed through Evelyne's veins, a deep, bone-weary fatigue still clung to her. At least the worst of her wounds had already healed and the pain in her ribs had faded.

Later, once the camp had finally quieted, Evelyne found herself sitting beside her brother, shivering slightly in the northern night air. She had no idea how many hours had passed since she had first stepped out of the tunnel and everything had fallen apart. The sun could be rising any minute, for all she knew, but there was something she needed to say, something that couldn't wait.

Heavy silence stretched between them, weighted by everything they had endured and lost. It was Cillian who broke it first.

"I had no control," he said, his voice hollow with grief. "I tried, Evelyne. I fought until I had nothing left. But I was drowning in her magic. And then..." He faltered. "I gave up."

Evelyne stayed quiet, listening.

"It was easier to let go," Cillian continued, his gaze distant. "Until I heard you." He turned to her then, golden eyes catching the firelight. The earlier glow had faded, replaced now with sorrow, and something gentler beneath it. "Your voice. It broke through the darkness and made me fight again."

Tears burned at the corners of Evelyne's eyes.

"I fought because you fought for me," he whispered.

She reached out and squeezed his hand. "I would never give up on you," she said fiercely. "Never." She swallowed hard. "Even Father... He never gave up. He died fighting to find you."

Cillian's face crumpled, and he clutched her hand tighter. "He died because of me."

"No," Evelyne said, shaking her head.

"He died fighting for you, loving you. That's what matters."

"I don't know how I'll ever forgive myself," Cillian muttered, pressing his palms hard against his eyes. "The things she made me do... The lives I—" His voice cracked, then rose with fury as he pointed toward Reyna and Nathan, who sat silently near their tent. "I killed your friend. The pack's friend. Someone's mate. That was me!"

Evelyne placed a steady hand on his shoulder. "No, Cillian. That wasn't you. It was her, and the monster she forced into you. We don't blame you for Ty's death."

He dropped his gaze, shoulders trembling. Evelyne gently lifted his chin until their eyes met.

"That wasn't you. Do you hear me? You would never hurt someone like that." She waited, watching him closely. When he didn't respond, she pressed again, softer this time. "Cillian... do you hear me?"

After a long pause, he finally nodded and sat upright.

"You look different," he said, sniffing as he managed a crooked smile. "Better different. It suits you."

"Well, thank you," Evelyne replied dryly. "Turns out a few weeks in the wild with bugs, blood, and zero bathhouses really brings out a girl's glow."

Cillian let out a quiet snort.

Evelyne cleared her throat, her voice steady now. "Cillian, that light... What was it?"

"I'm not sure," he admitted. "I've never felt anything like it. But once I understood what it meant, it was as if something awakened inside me. First, I saw this small glowing thread of light, so I reached for it. And the moment I touched it, it surged through me. That's when I knew what I had to do to stop her." He swallowed. "You used Father's pistol to kill her."

"I did," she said, faltering as the memory flickered through her mind like a ghost.

"Good," Cillian said, voice flat. Evelyne gave his hand a quick pat.

A few peaceful moments passed between them, a rare silence that reminded Evelyne how much she cherished her brother's quiet presence. But just as the calm began to settle, a sharp jolt of panic seized her chest. She gasped, eyes going wide. "Aurelia!"

Cillian's eyes snapped to hers. "What?"

"What if she shifted too?" Evelyne whispered.

Cillian paled. "Oh no," he muttered, running a hand through his hair. "She would lose it."

"What if it happened at court? What if she hurt someone?"

The thought of their impeccably perfect sister losing control at a royal event nearly broke her composure, somewhere between amusement and horror.

"We need to get home," Evelyne muttered.

"Agreed."

CHAPTER 51

Evelyne stood close to the fire, the chill of the night air curling around her as she savored a rare moment of solitude. Cillian had long since turned in, tucked away in one of the makeshift tents the packs had assembled, but her thoughts refused to settle. They spun restlessly, too loud for sleep.

Tilting her head back, she gazed at the stars, drawing in a slow, grounding breath, only to freeze.

That scent. Smoky cedar, wild musk. *Him.*

She turned, already knowing who she'd find.

Kaldrek stood a few feet behind her, his expression shadowed in the firelight. "Evelyne," he said cautiously. "I need... Can I talk to you?"

She folded her arms across her chest, spine straightening. "Well, that depends, Alpha. Can I trust that you'll be honest with me?"

He flinched, but did not retreat. "I should have told you. I wanted to. I had chances, and I didn't take them. That's on me."

The anger she had buried roared back to life. "You lied to me," she said, her voice cracking. "You let me find everything out from *her*."

"I know," he rasped. "And I would give anything to undo that."

Her chest rose and fell with uneven breaths. The betrayal ran deep—but deeper still was the ache in her chest, the invisible pull between them that refused to let go. Part of her wanted to turn away, to strike him and leave him in silence. But her eyes lingered on his face, drawn to the raw pain carved into his features… and the vulnerability he was trying so hard to mask.

"I should have known there was a reason you are so different," she said quietly. "You sense magic because you have the blood of a witch. But do you feel it? Can you wield it?"

Kaldrek's throat bobbed, and for a moment, he simply looked at her, as if weighing how much to reveal.

"No," he said finally. "I don't feel anything inside. I can only sense dark magic when it's around. Like a warning before it comes." He reached for her hand, but dropped his quickly. "And I can sense other magical beings, like… like your wolf lineage, though I questioned its truth for a long time."

Evelyne studied him, truly studied him, seeing not just the pain he carried, but the quiet strength that had kept him standing through it all. He bore the heavy, lonely weight of a life built on half-truths and stolen history. But she needed to know more, and found herself wondering when he had learned the truth about his parents. Because the thought of him discovering it alone, carrying that burden in silence, made her chest ache.

"When did you find out about your mother?"

Kaldrek cleared his throat. "My father told me, and only me. He told me the truth about who I am right before he died."

Evelyne said nothing. She needed to let him continue.

"I lost my parents and my trust in the same night," Kaldrek said, a hollow edge to his voice. "And I couldn't hold it all in. I had to tell someone before it broke me. So when Holden noticed the tattoo had transferred to me, I told him. I had to ask him about it. How could the alpha role pass to someone who wasn't truly part of their bloodline?"

His eyes filled with tears, but he smiled through them, a smile touched with pain and pride.

"Holden, the sentimental bastard, just laughed and told me blood means little when the alpha mark speaks. He said, 'We follow the one it chooses. And it chose you.'" Kaldrek let out a soft, breathless laugh at the memory. "So he and I kept it quiet. To protect the pack and to ensure they wouldn't look at me differently... Wouldn't lose faith in me."

Evelyne's heart twisted for him. Damn him. Even after everything, she still loved him. Loved the man he was underneath all the scars, the man who fought so hard to protect those he cared about.

"Why couldn't you just tell me, Kaldrek?" Her voice trembled, caught between heartbreak and frustration. "You knew why I traveled north, and I trusted you. I let you in. Gods, I fell for you so hard I forgot how to breathe without you. And I truly believed you felt the same."

Kaldrek didn't hesitate.

He stepped forward and took her hands gently but firmly in his own, like he couldn't stand another second of distance between them. The scent of him was so intense and consuming that her body instinctively leaned toward him.

"I didn't tell you," he said, voice ragged, "because I was afraid. Afraid that the truth about my mother, about who I am, would terrify you. That once you knew, you'd turn away. And I couldn't bear that."

His hand rose to her chin, lifting her gaze to his. The pain in his eyes was laid bare and raw.

"You mean everything to me, Evelyne. You gave my life purpose again. You made me feel when I thought I would be numb forever. I know I broke your trust. But please, believe this—I love you. Fuck, I love you so much it hurts. I'd burn the world for you. Destroy anything that dares cause you pain... even if that thing is me." His voice cracked, but he pressed on. "I'm sorry. For the secrets, the lies. They ate me alive, every single day. I told myself I was protecting you, but the truth is... I was a coward. I didn't trust you to be strong enough. But you are. You've always been strong."

He leaned in then, achingly close, his lips brushing the air near her neck. She felt the warmth of his breath, the way he inhaled her like a lifeline, and a low sound rumbled in his throat—half groan, half reverence. Like the very scent of her was enough to drive him to his knees.

His lips barely brushed her skin before he pulled away abruptly, realization flickering across his face like a flame extinguished too soon. "I'm sorry," he muttered, dragging a hand through his tousled hair. "I—I wasn't thinking."

Evelyne's voice was softer when she replied. "I feel it too, Kaldrek. That pull between us."

His eyes locked onto hers, searching. "You do?"

She gave a small nod. "Yes," she whispered, her gaze dropping to his lips as he stepped closer once more.

"I think you're my mate," he said.

The breath caught in her throat. She closed her eyes for a moment, steadying herself.

"When did you sense it?"

"At the tunnel," he said, taking a breath. "Right after you shifted back. It hit me all at once—your scent. It nearly knocked me over. All I could think about was how right it felt to be near you."

She didn't respond right away, just stared at him as the truth hung between them. Deep down, she felt the same.

"I think that's why I've always been drawn to you," he continued, his words quicker now, tinged with nervousness. "Maybe it's the bond. Or maybe it's just... you. But if you don't want it, if it's too much, you don't have to accept the bond. You can reject it."

The ache in his voice squeezed something inside her. She should have told him to go to hell. Should have turned away, hurt still raw in her chest. But instead, part of her reached for him. Wanted to ease the doubt shadowing his face. And that part—however small—was winning.

"I'm still furious with you," she whispered, her voice trembling. "So furious I could scream."

His head dipped low in shame, but he did not step back. He stayed, bearing it, letting her anger wash over him.

"But after everything we've survived..." Evelyne looked up at him, really looked at him, her soul aching with everything they had lost and could still have. "All I want right now is for you to hold me. Please just hold—"

He moved before she finished speaking, closing the remaining space between them and gathering her into his arms. He held her as if he would never let go.

She lifted her hand and touched his face, her fingers brushing his jaw. The bond between them hummed, warm and relentless, threading them together with a force neither could resist.

"But you can never lie to me again," she mumbled against his skin.

"Never," he vowed, the word breaking from him like a promise sealed in blood.

When she kissed him, everything else melted away. The world, the grief, the fear... None of it mattered anymore. Only him. Only them.

His lips lit something wild inside her, a fire that spread with reckless abandon through every nerve of her body. Kaldrek moaned against her mouth, his grip on her waist tightening as he hauled her closer, as if he could not bear even the smallest space between them. His hands tangled in her hair, his touch desperate, as though he feared she might slip away.

Minutes—or maybe only seconds—slipped past before Evelyne realized they were moving. Kaldrek had quietly carried her into his tent. When he gently set her down and began filling a washbasin, her heart still thundered, craving the warmth of his touch. But as soon as her hands slipped into the water, a deep breath escaped her and relief flooded in. At last, she could scrub away the dirt and dried blood clinging to her skin. She rinsed her face and ran wet fingers through her hair, letting the final traces of the night's horrors wash down the basin and away.

Once she finished, Evelyne slipped into a loose shirt and pants before crawling beneath the blankets laid across the ground. The exhaustion in her limbs pressed down like stone. But the moment Kaldrek joined her, his body warm against hers, that heaviness gave way to something far stronger. *Need.*

The bond between them thrummed wildly. It was unbearable now, how his body molded to hers and his scent wrapped around her like smoke and spice, grounding her even as it sparked every nerve. She could lose herself in him, and part of her already had.

She felt the unmistakable press of his arousal against her back, the hard, pulsing proof of his desire. Heat bloomed low in her belly, spreading through her like molten gold, igniting every inch of her skin. Slowly, she turned to face him, her eyes locking onto his. The moment their gazes met, she caught the potent, heady scent of his want. It slammed into her like a lightning strike, making her shudder with the force of it.

Feral urgency crashed over her, wiping away the last threads of restraint. With a broken sound, she reached for him, framing his face with both hands and pulling him into another kiss. Their mouths collided with a clash of teeth and tongues, the kiss messy, greedy, utterly perfect.

Kaldrek groaned against her lips, pinning her onto her back, his body a solid wall of heat pressing her into the blankets.

He buried his face in the curve of her neck, breathing her in like she was the only thing anchoring him to this world. He needed her. And she needed him just as fiercely.

Evelyne threaded her fingers through his hair, tugging just hard enough to make him lift his head and meet her gaze. The yearning she saw in his eyes sent a deep shiver through her, but it still wasn't enough. His hand trailed up her shirt and cupped her breast as he licked and nipped just below her ear, and a small, breathy moan escaped her mouth.

She needed more. She needed *all* of him.

"Kaldrek," Evelyne panted. He stilled above her, frozen, as if he barely dared to breathe. "I want it," she whispered, voice trembling. "You. The bond. Everything."

Yes, he had lied, but he had done it out of fear, not malice. He had been terrified she might leave him, and she may have done the same in his place. It had been selfish, but not cruel. She had become stronger, but also wiser, more willing to see beyond the surface of things. And what they shared was undeniably and fiercely real.

This was not some petty secret whispered in a court full of masks and manipulation. This had been a shield, meant to protect her. He had not derailed her path to finding her brother. He had helped her stay on it. Without Kaldrek and his pack, she would have never made it this far. And now, as everything settled around her, one truth rang louder than the rest: she wanted this bond. She wanted him.

To hell with society. To hell with nobility. She was a wolf, and he was home.

For a heartbeat, he did not move. Then the tension in his face fractured, and a slow, devastating smile spread across his lips. A look of pure happiness and love, as if he had waited his entire life for this moment and never truly believed it would come.

He looked at her like she was the only thing in the world that mattered. And as she watched the light break through the quiet fear he had buried for so long, she knew. He was exactly what she needed.

"Make me yours in every way, Kaldrek. Claim me."

His hands trembled against her skin. "Are you sure?" His voice came out hoarse and restrained. Because he knew exactly what her offer meant. A claiming was permanent. Irrevocable. It would bind them, soul to soul. She would belong to him, and he to her.

Evelyne met his gaze, then slowly tilted her head, exposing her throat in silent invitation.

"I love you," Kaldrek breathed, the words cracking through him like a prayer spoken for the first time.

"I love you too," Evelyne whispered, just as Kaldrek peeled away her shirt and pressed a kiss to the curve of her neck.

A low growl vibrated from deep within his chest, sending a shiver down her spine. His breath fanned hot over her throat as he lingered there, savoring the moment, as if committing it to memory. Then his fangs sank deep into her flesh.

White-hot pleasure tore through her, stealing her breath. Evelyne gasped, bracing for pain, but there was none. Only a rush of ecstasy that seared through her veins and set her soul aflame. She felt everything: the fierce love behind his touch, the trembling desperation in the way he clung to her, and the unbreakable bond snapping tight between them.

Kaldrek shuddered as he tasted her. When he finally lifted his head, his mouth was stained crimson, his pupils blown wide, dark with overwhelming need.

"*Fuck*. You taste like everything I've ever needed," he rasped. The aching want in his voice sent a jolt through her body and she arched into him, needing him closer, needing more.

Kaldrek shifted, rising onto his knees, and began to strip away the last of her clothing with careful hands. His eyes raked over her bare skin, taking her in as if she were something sacred. And Evelyne, lying bare beneath him, didn't feel exposed. She felt cherished. Beautiful.

He leaned down, trailing slow, burning kisses along her throat, her chest, pausing to take her breast into his mouth. His tongue flicked over the sensitive peak, drawing a gasp from her as a slow heat curled low in her belly, building with every lingering caress.

When he pulled back, he undid the laces of his pants with steady hands. Evelyne propped herself on her elbows, watching him stand and shed the last of his clothing.

Her mouth went dry.

Kaldrek was all power and strength, sculpted muscle wrapped in sun-kissed skin. When her eyes drifted lower, she swallowed hard, a flush of want sliding through her.

Yes. She wanted this.

He climbed back over her, covering her body with his own, his eyes locked onto hers the entire time. She reached for him, her fingers brushing along the heat of his rigid length, and he instinctively pressed into her touch. The subtle movement unleashed another surge of longing that rippled through her body.

Guiding her onto her back again, Kaldrek captured her mouth in a kiss so deep it made her dizzy, his hands spreading her thighs with a growing, reckless need. Evelyne gasped when he pressed against her, the feel of him overwhelming, making her ache in places she never knew could feel so empty.

"Please," she whispered desperately.

Kaldrek moved with a gentleness that broke her heart, one hand cradling her face, the other steadying her hip.

He entered her in one slow thrust.

Though he was careful to give her time to adjust, the stretch of him was intense, and Evelyne cried out, her nails clutching at his back. Kaldrek froze, his forehead pressing against hers, like he was breathing through the desperate instinct to move. Once comfortable, she lifted her hips in silent invitation, and he met her with a kiss that stole her breath.

"You're all right," he murmured against her lips. "I've got you."

She nodded, trembling, and he began to move inside her—slow at first, reverent, as if he were worshiping every part of her. The pleasure built steadily, her body molding to his, the bond between them humming louder and stronger. Each thrust sent a ripple of heat through her until her hands clutched at him, pulling him deeper, closer.

He groaned low in his throat, the sound vibrating through her, and then he flipped her, pulling her atop him. He gripped her hips firmly, guiding her movements and staring up at her body. She braced her palms against his chest, feeling the strength beneath her fingers as he drew her down with ravenous intensity. Her nails bit into his skin as a moan escaped her lips, lost to the rising tide of pleasure.

"You're mine, Evelyne," he murmured without breaking rhythm. "And I want the whole fucking world to know I'm yours."

Understanding flooded her. Evelyne tilted his head back and sank her fangs into the strong curve of his throat, claiming him as he had claimed her.

The instant her teeth pierced his skin, Kaldrek *broke*.

A roar tore from his throat, ragged, as if the bond seared through every wall he had ever built. His hands clamped down on her hips, dragging her hard against him as he drove into her with wild need. He moved without restraint now, their bond fully awakened, instinct taking over. Every thrust sent pleasure shattering through her, the movement punishing and beautiful all at once.

"Kaldrek," she gasped, lost in the overwhelming tide of him. A warning she was close.

"Say it again," he rasped with pure lust.

"Kaldrek," she cried, digging her fingers further into his chest.

The pleasure coiled inside her, impossibly tight, until it finally snapped. Evelyne shattered with a moan that echoed through the tent, her body trembling violently as she came apart around him.

Kaldrek followed with a broken curse, his body stiffening, his arms crushing her against him as he poured himself into her, sealing the bond entirely.

They collapsed together, tangled, panting, shaking from its force. Evelyne lay sprawled across his chest, feeling the wild thunder of his heart beneath her cheek. His arms stayed locked around her, his fingers stroking her hair with a tenderness that made her eyes sting.

They were bound now. In blood. In body. In soul. And for the first time in her life, Evelyne knew what it meant to belong completely.

Kaldrek pressed a gentle kiss to the top of her head, breathing in the scent of her hair. "You are everything," he murmured against her. "So perfect. I can hardly believe you're mine."

"And I'm yours," she whispered, smiling against his chest.

He let out a low hum that seemed to settle through him, his breathing slowing until the steady rise and fall of his chest lulled her toward sleep. Wrapped in his warmth, Evelyne's eyes fluttered closed.

Tomorrow, they would begin the long journey back to Caltheris to confront the fractured pieces of the life she had left behind. Evelyne would have to face her mother and sister with painful truths in hand. And Seraphine—gods, how she had missed her. She couldn't allow the Noskari's corruption to reach her family. The thought of losing them to that darkness turned her stomach. She had to protect them. And she would return Cillian home, not as the shattered young man who was stolen from them, but as the wolf he was always meant to become.

Beyond that, the real war loomed.

The Noskari still lingered in the shadows, waiting and watching. Evelyne felt it deep in her bones; their hunger for blood and power had not ended with Vaelora's death. More lives would be at risk. More battles would be fought.

They would need to find the others. The forgotten wolves, the scattered packs, the warriors still willing to stand and fight, because the real battle for their world was just beginning. And while she was grateful to have Obren and his pack by their side, she still needed to learn his true intentions. Now that vengeance had been served, what was it he truly wanted? She would speak to him—but not tonight.

Tonight, she would rest. Tonight, she would lie curled beside her mate, wrapped in his strength, knowing she would not face the coming darkness alone.

CHAPTER 52

The days after Vaelora's downfall passed in a strange, almost dream-like haze.

Alaric had never seen Cillian smile like he did now: freer, lighter, though still carrying the weight of what he had endured. Evelyne and Kaldrek had found their way to each other, their bond a steady, unspoken thing that seemed to anchor the entire group. It should have felt like a happy ending. In many ways, it did.

Even his own life had begun to shift toward something brighter. Each day, Heidara grew closer to him, her smiles softer, her touch lingering a little longer. Alaric dreamed of things he'd never thought he could have: quiet evenings beneath the stars, laughter shared over simple things, a future.

Their journey home had begun by land. No one trusted the tunnels anymore. The Noskari had disappeared, scattered like ash on the wind, but fear still laced every shadow. And everyone knew they would return.

Kaldrek and Obren often spoke of the work ahead, like finding the scattered packs and rallying what strength remained in the northeastern lands. Their journey home would be neither easy nor swift. Yet each dawn, no matter how bitter the frost, they pushed on with their training. The fight ahead demanded discipline and strength, and Alaric welcomed the routine.

He welcomed anything that could drown out the voice.

At first, he had thought it was exhaustion. A trick of the mind after so many sleepless nights. But the voice wasn't fading. It was growing louder and bolder.

It was his voice, but twisted, colder, crueler. It whispered things he did not want to hear. Things that burrowed into his thoughts when he wasn't paying attention.

They are not your friends.

You are nothing to them.

You will be abandoned again. Forgotten.

Sometimes he could ignore it. Pretend it wasn't there. But tonight, sitting by the fire with the others, pretending to laugh at something Heidara said, pretending to be normal, he truly felt it.

His hand twitched without him willing it. His body shifted slightly, leaning in, then pulling back, small movements that were not his own. He tried to still himself, to command his limbs, but it was like shouting into a void.

Someone else was listening now.

A cold sweat broke out across his skin. Panic clawed up his spine. He needed to tell someone. Kaldrek. Evelyne. Anyone. He needed to—

But it was already too late. He felt the moment it happened.

The door inside him slammed shut. The darkness didn't rush in with violence. It moved like a tide, slow and suffocating, pulling him under. His mind screamed, fought, but his body sat still, smiling and nodding at a joke he hadn't heard.

He was no longer the one in control. And no one around the fire noticed a thing.

Alaric screamed in his mind, but the darkness only laughed, dragging him further down. He should have said something. Should have asked for help. Should have told them what was happening—how the blast of inky mist Vaelora hurled at him had buried itself deep inside. How the coughing hadn't driven it out, not all of it. But now... it was too late.

He was already gone.

To be continued...

The story is far from over. Stay tuned for **Book Two of The Solwyn Duology:** ***A Sunwoven Ascent.***

Acknowledgments

First and foremost, I want to thank my biggest support system: my husband, Neil. Thank you for walking beside me through every step of this deeply vulnerable journey. You never judged my messy drafts, only offered encouragement and thoughtful critique. Thank you for sitting next to me each night while I typed away, for being my constant cheerleader, and for always believing in me even when I doubted myself. I truly couldn't have done this without you.

To my closest friends (you know who you are) and family, thank you for your enthusiasm, your kind words, and your unwavering support. I was hesitant to share my goal of publishing a book, not because I didn't believe in the story, but because I care deeply about the opinions of those I love most. But not once did anyone question my ability or passion. Even if this story isn't their cup of tea, I know they'll continue cheering me on, and that means everything.

To my incredible beta readers—Rhea Wright, Rachel Linso, Maja Brickey, Jasmine B., Mindy Woolf, and of course, my husband—thank you for your time, your discretion, and your honest feedback. Your insight helped shape this story into what it is today, and I can't thank you enough for standing by me.

My deepest thanks to The Nerd Fam for their incredible partnership in coordinating and distributing ARCs, and for sponsoring and scheduling the upcoming book tour. To my amazing ARC team—thank you for taking the time to read and share *A Bloodveiled Descent* before its release. Your early support helped bring this story into the world with more strength and heart than I could have imagined.

To my hairstylist and friend, Dusty McEvoy, for taking my first ever author photo. To my cover designer Kelly G., thank you for bringing the themes of my book to life in the most breathtaking way. I couldn't have imagined a more perfect cover. Thank you, Claire B., for combing through every line and helping me refine my writing with such care and precision. And to Carter Norman P., thank you for creating the map that helped breathe life into this world.

To my parents, Kimberly and Kraig Young, thank you for always focusing on the best parts of me and offering unconditional love. To my sister, Marissa Berry, thank you for your protection and constant encouragement.

To my mother-in-law, Diane Opet, and father-in-law, Neil Opet, for bringing so much positivity throughout this journey. And to my sister-in-law, Caitlin Opet—thank you for promising to read my book, even though reading isn't your thing.

Finally, to my three beautiful children, Noah, Desmond, and Elsie, you are my greatest motivation and the reason I dared to chase this dream at all.

Thank you, all of you, from the bottom of my heart. And to my readers—thank you for letting my story find a home with you.

ABOUT THE AUTHOR

Haley M. Opet is a fantasy romance author from Northeastern Pennsylvania. She is a proud mother of three children, who remain her greatest joy and inspiration, as well as five beloved fur babies. Since the age of sixteen, she has shared her life with her high school sweetheart, now her husband, who continues to be the love of her life.

By day, Haley works full-time in the field of Health Information Management. By night, she can often be found immersed in fantasy romance novels—the very genre she now writes. What began as a simple desire to put thoughts to paper soon grew into vivid characters and a world too alive to keep to herself. Recognizing that other readers share her love for the genre, she decided to publish her debut novel and invite others along on the journey.

Haley believes that stories are a place to escape, a chance to wander into realms of magical creatures, fierce heroines, and unforgettable romance. Readers can follow her journey and learn more about upcoming books by joining her newsletter at **www.haleymopet.com**.

www.ingramcontent.com/pod-product-compliance
Lightning Source LLC
Chambersburg PA
CBHW052338110726
47901CB00005B/1270